Royal Temptation:
Becoming His Queen

REBECCA WINTERS

SUSANNA CARR

OLIVIA GATES

MILLS & BOON

First Published in Great Britain 2023
by Mills & Boon, an imprint of HarperCollins*Publishers* Ltd,
1 London Bridge Street, London, SE1 9GF

www.harpercollins.co.uk

HarperCollins*Publishers*
Macken House, 39/40 Mayor Street Upper,
Dublin 1, D01 C9W8, Ireland

ISBN: 978-0-263-31847-0

MIX
Paper | Supporting
responsible forestry
FSC™ C007454

This book is produced from independently certified FSC™ paper
to ensure responsible forest management.

For more information visit: www.harpercollins.co.uk/green

Printed and Bound in Spain using 100% Renewable electricity at
CPI Black Print, Barcelona

BECOMING THE PRINCE'S WIFE

REBECCA WINTERS

To my four wonderful, outstanding children: Bill, John, Dominique and Max.

They've had to put up with a mother whose mind is constantly dreaming up new fairytales like the one I've just written.

Their unqualified love and constant support has been the greatest blessing in my life.

CHAPTER ONE

As Carolena Baretti stepped out of the limousine, she could see her best friend, Abby, climbing the stairs of the royal jet. At the top she turned. "Oh, good! You're here!" she called to her, but was struggling to keep her baby from squirming out of her arms.

At eight months of age, little black-haired Prince Maximilliano, the image of his father, Crown Prince Vincenzo Di Laurentis of Arancia, was becoming big Max, fascinated by sights and sounds. Since he was teething, Carolena had brought him various colored toys in the shape of donuts to bite on. She'd give them to him after they'd boarded the jet for the flight to Gemelli.

The steward brought Carolena's suitcase on board while she entered the creamy interior of the jet. The baby's carryall was strapped to one of the luxury leather chairs along the side. Max fought at leaving his mother's arms, but she finally prevailed in getting him fastened down.

Carolena pulled a blue donut from the sack in her large straw purse. "Maybe this will help." She leaned over the baby and handed it to him. "What do you think, sweetheart?"

Max grabbed for it immediately and put it in his mouth to test it, causing both women to laugh. Abby gave her a hug. "Thank you for the gift. Any distraction is a blessing! The only time he doesn't move is when he's asleep."

Carolena chuckled.

"So you won't get too bored, I brought a movie for you to watch while we fly down. Remember I told you how much I loved the French actor Louis Jourdan when I was growing up?"

"He was in *Gigi,* right?"

"Yes, well, I found a movie of his in my mother's collection. You know me and my love for old films. This one is called *Bird of Paradise.* Since we'll be passing Mount Etna, I think you'll love it."

"I've never heard of that movie, but thank you for being so thoughtful. I'm sure I'll enjoy it."

"Carolena—I know this is a hard time for you, but I'm so glad you decided to come. Vincenzo and Valentino need to discuss business on this short trip. It will give you and me some time to do whatever we want while Queen Bianca dotes on her grandson."

"When Max smiles, I see traces of Michelina. That must delight her."

"I know it does. These days it's hard to believe Bianca was ever upset over the pregnancy. She's much warmer to me now."

"Thank heaven for that, Abby."

"You'll never know."

No, Carolena supposed she wouldn't. Not really. Abby Loretto had offered to be a surrogate mother to carry Their Highnesses' baby, but they'd both been through a trial by fire when Michelina was suddenly killed.

Carolena was thrilled for the two of them who, since that time, had fallen deeply in love and weathered the storm before marrying. Now they had a beautiful baby boy to raise and she was glad to have been invited to join them for their brief holiday.

Today was June fourth, a date she'd dreaded every June for the past seven years. It marked the death of her fiancé, Berto, and brought back horrendous guilt. She and Berto had shared a great love, but it had come to a tragic end too soon. All because of Carolena.

She'd been too adventurous for her own good, as her own wonderful, deceased grandmother had always told her. *You go where angels fear to tread without thinking of anyone but yourself. It's probably because you lost your parents too soon and I've failed you. One day there'll be a price to pay for being so headstrong.*

Tears stung her eyelids. How true were those words.

Berto's death had brought about a permanent change in Carolena. Outside of her professional work as an attorney, she never wanted to be responsible for another human life again. Though she'd dated a lot of men, her relationships were of short duration and superficial. After seven years, her pattern of noncommitment had become her way of life. No one depended on her. Her actions could affect no one or hurt anyone. That was the way she liked it.

Dear sweet Abby had known the date was coming up. Out of the goodness of her heart she'd insisted Carolena come with them on this trip so she wouldn't brood. Carolena loved her blonde friend for so many reasons, especially her thoughtfulness because she knew this time was always difficult for her.

As she strapped herself in, several bodyguards entered the body of the jet followed by black-haired Vincenzo. He stopped to give his wife and son a kiss before hugging Carolena. "It's good to see you. Gemelli is a beautiful country. You're going to love it."

"I'm sure I will. Thank you for inviting me, Vincenzo."

"Our pleasure, believe me. If you're ready, then we'll take off. I told Valentino we'd be there midafternoon."

Once he'd fastened himself in and turned to Abby with an eagerness Carolena could see and feel, the jet taxied to the runway. When it took off into a blue sky, it left the Principality of Arancia behind, a country nestled along the Riviera between France and Italy.

Before heading south, she could see the coastal waters of the Mediterranean receding, but it was obvious Abby and Vincenzo only had eyes for each other. Theirs was a true love story. Watching them was painful. There were moments like now when twenty-seven-year-old Carolena felt old before her time.

Thank goodness she had a movie to watch that she hadn't seen before. The minute it started she blinked at the sight of how young Louis Jourdan was. The story turned out to be about a Frenchman who traveled to Polynesia and fell in love with a native girl.

Carolena found herself riveted when the volcano erupts on the island and the native girl has to be sacrificed to appease the gods by jumping into it. The credits said the film had been made on location in Hawaii and used the Kilauea volcano for the scenes.

As the royal jet started to make its descent to Gemelli, she saw smoke coming out of Mount Etna, one of Italy's volcanoes. After watching this film, the thought of it erupting made her shiver.

The helicopter flew away from the new hot fumarole in the western pit of the Bocca Nuova of Mount Etna. The fumarole was a hole that let out gas and steam. After the scientific team had observed an increased bluish degassing from a vent in the saddle, they sent back video and seismic records before heading to the National Center of Geophysics and Volcanology lab in Catania on the eastern coast of Sicily

En route to the lab the three men heard deep-seated explosions coming from inside the northeast crater, but there was no cause for public alarm in terms of evacuation alerts.

Once the center's helicopter touched ground, Crown Prince Valentino waved off his two colleagues and hurried to the royal helicopter for the short flight to Gemelli in the Ionian Sea. Their team had gotten back late, but they'd needed to do an in-depth study before transmitting vital data and photos.

Valentino's brother-in-law, Crown Prince Vincenzo Di Laurentis, along with his new wife, Abby, and son, Max, would already have been at the palace several hours. They'd come for a visit from Arancia and would be staying a few days. Valentino was eager to see them.

He and Vincenzo, distant cousins, had done shipping business together for many years but had grown closer with Vincenzo's first marriage to Michelina, who'd been Valentino's only sister. Her death February before last had left a hole in his heart. He'd always been very attached to his sibling and they'd confided in each other.

With his younger brother Vitale, nicknamed Vito, away in the military, Valentino had needed an outlet since her death. Lately, after a long day's work, he'd spent time quietly partying with a few good friends and his most recent girlfriend, while his mother, Bianca, the ruling Queen of Gemelli, occupied herself with their country's business.

As for tonight, he was looking forward to seeing Vincenzo as his helicopter ferried him to the grounds, where it landed at the rear of the sixteenth-century baroque palace. He jumped out and hurried past the gardens and tennis courts, taking a shortcut near the swimming pool to reach his apartment in the east wing.

But suddenly he saw something out of the corner of his eye that stopped him dead in his tracks. Standing on the end of the diving board ready to dive was a gorgeous, voluptuous woman in a knockout, fashionable one-piece purple swimsuit with a plunging neckline.

It was just a moment before she disappeared under the water, but long enough for him to forget the fiery fumarole on Mount Etna and follow those long legs to the end of the pool. When she emerged at the deep end with a sable-colored braid over one shoulder, he hunkered down to meet her. With eyes as sparkling green as lime zest, and a mouth with a passionate flare, she was even more breathtaking up close.

"Oh— Your Highness! I didn't think anyone was here!"

He couldn't have met her before or he would have remembered, because she would be impossible to forget. There was no ring on her finger. "You have me at a disadvantage, *signorina.*"

She hugged her body close to the edge of the tiled pool. He got the impression she was trying to prevent him from getting the full view of her. That small show of modesty intrigued him.

"I'm Carolena Baretti, Abby Loretto's friend."

This woman was Abby's best friend? He'd heard Abby mention her, but Vincenzo had never said anything. Valentino knew his brother-in-law wasn't blind... Though they hadn't told him they were bringing someone else with them, he didn't mind. Not at all.

"How long have you been here?"

"We flew in at two o'clock. Right now the queen is playing with Max while Abby and Valentino take a nap." A nap, was it? He smiled inwardly. "So I decided to come out here for a swim. The air is like velvet."

He agreed. "My work took longer than I thought, making it impossible for me to be here when you arrived. I've planned a supper for us in the private dining room tonight. Shall we say half an hour? One of the staff will show you the way."

"That's very gracious of you, but I don't want to intrude on your time with them. I had a light meal before I came out to swim and I'll just go on enjoying myself here."

He got the sense she meant it. The fact that she wasn't being coy like so many females he'd met in his life aroused his interest. "You're their friend, so it goes without saying you're invited." His lips broke into a smile. "And even if you weren't with them, I *like* an intrusion as pleasant as this one. I insist you join us."

"Thank you," she said quietly, but he had an idea she was debating whether or not to accept his invitation, mystifying him further. "Before you go, may I say how sorry I am about the loss of Princess Michelina. I can see the resemblance to your sister in you and the baby. I know it's been devastating for your family, especially the queen. But if anyone can instill some joy into all of you, it's your adorable nephew, Max."

The surprises just kept coming. Valentino was taken aback. The fact that she'd been in Abby's confidence for a number of years had lent a sincere ring to this woman's remarks, already putting them on a more intimate footing. "I've been eager to see him again. He's probably grown a foot since last time."

An engaging smile appeared. "Maybe not quite another foot yet, but considering he's Prince Vincenzo's son, I would imagine he'll be tall one day."

"That wouldn't surprise me. *A presto,* Signorina Baretti."

Carolena watched *his* tall physique stride to the patio and disappear inside a set of glass doors. Long after he'd left, she was still trying to catch her breath. When she'd broken the surface of the water at the other end of the rectangular pool, she'd recognized the striking thirty-two-year-old crown prince right away.

Her knowledge of him came from newspapers and television that covered the funeral of his sister, Princess Michelina. He'd ridden in the black-and-gold carriage with his brother and their mother, Queen Bianca, the three of them grave and in deep grief.

In a recent poll he'd been touted the world's most sought-after royal bachelor. Most of the tabloids revealed he went through women like water. She could believe it. Just now his eyes had mirrored his masculine admiration of her. Everywhere they roved, she'd felt heat trail over her skin. By that invisible process called osmosis, his charm and sophistication had managed to seep into her body.

But even up close no camera could catch the startling midnight blue of his dark-lashed eyes. The dying rays of the evening sun gilded the tips of his medium cut dark blond hair and brought out his hard-boned facial features, reminiscent of his Sicilian ancestry. He was a fabulous-looking man.

Right then he'd been wearing jeans that molded his powerful thighs, and a white shirt with the sleeves shoved up to the elbows to reveal hard-muscled forearms. No sign of a uniform this evening.

Whatever kind of work he did, he'd gotten dirty. She wondered where he'd been. There were black marks on his clothes and arms, even on his face, bronzed from being outdoors. If anything, the signs of the working man intensified his potent male charisma. He wasn't just a handsome prince without substance.

Carolena was stunned by her reaction to him. There'd been many different types of men who'd come into her life because of her work as an attorney; businessmen, manufacturers, technology wizards, mining engineers, entrepreneurs. But she had to admit she'd never had this kind of visceral response to a man on a first meeting, not even with Berto, who'd been her childhood friend before they'd fallen in love.

The prince had said half an hour. Carolena hadn't intended to join the three of them this evening, but since he'd used the word *insist,* she decided she'd better go so as not to offend him. Unfortunately it was growing late. She needed to hurry inside and get ready, but she wouldn't have time to wash her hair.

She climbed out of the pool and retraced her steps to the other wing of the palace. After a quick shower, she unbraided her hair and swept it back with an amber comb. Once she'd applied her makeup, she donned a small leopard-print wrap dress with ruched elbow-length sleeves. The tiny amber stones of her chandelier earrings matched the ones in her small gold chain necklace. On her feet she wore designer wedges in brown and amber.

The law firm in Arancia where she worked demanded their attorneys wear designer clothes since they dealt with an upper-class clientele. Abby had worked there with her until her fifth month of pregnancy when she'd been forced to quit. After being employed there twenty months and paid a generous salary, Carolena had accumulated a wonderful wardrobe and didn't need to worry she wouldn't have something appropriate to wear to this evening's dinner.

A knock at the door meant a maid was ready to take her to the dining room. But when she opened it, she received another shock to discover the prince at the threshold wearing a silky charcoal-brown sport shirt and beige trousers.

He must not have trusted her to come on her own. She didn't know whether to be flattered or worried she'd made some kind of faux pas when she'd declined his invitation at first. Their eyes traveled over each other. A shower had gotten rid of the black marks. He smelled wonderful, no doubt from the soap he used. Her heart did a tiny thump before she got hold of herself.

"Your Highness— This is the second time you've surprised me this evening."

He flashed her a white smile. "Unexpected surprises make life more interesting, don't you think?"

"I do actually, depending on the kind."

"This was the kind I couldn't resist."

Obviously she *had* irritated him. Still, she couldn't believe he'd come to fetch her. "I'm honored to be personally escorted by none other than the prince himself."

"That wasn't so hard to say, was it?" His question brought a smile to her lips. "Since I'm hungry, I thought I'd accompany you to the dining room myself to hurry things up, and I must admit I'm glad you're ready."

"Then let's not waste any more time."

"Vincenzo and Abby are already there, but they didn't even notice me when I passed by the doors. I've heard of a honeymoon lasting a week or two, even longer. But eight months?"

Carolena chuckled. "I know what you mean. While we were flying out, they were so caught up in each other, I don't think they said more than two words to me."

"Love should be like that, but it's rare."

"I know," she murmured. Vincenzo and Michelina hadn't enjoyed a marriage like that. It was no news to Carolena or Valentino, so they left the subject alone.

She followed him down several corridors lined with tapestries and paintings to a set of doors guarded by a staff member. They opened onto the grounds. "We'll cut across here past the gardens to the other wing of the palace. It's faster."

There was nothing stiff or arrogant about Prince Valentino. He had the rare gift of being able to put her at ease and make her feel comfortable.

She looked around her. "The gardens are glorious. You have grown a fabulous collection of palms and exotic plants. Everything thrives here. And I've never seen baroque architecture this flamboyant."

He nodded. "My brother, Vito, and I have always called it the Putti Palace because of all the winged boy cherubs supporting the dozens of balconies. To my mother's chagrin, we used to draw mustaches on them. For our penance, we had to wash them off."

Laughter rippled out of her. "I'm afraid to tell Abby what you said for fear she'll have nightmares over Max getting into mischief."

"Except that won't be for a while yet." His dark blue

eyes danced. No doubt this prince had been a handful to his parents. Somehow the thought made him even more approachable.

"With all these wrought-iron balustrades and rustication, the palace really is beautiful."

"Along with the two-toned lava masonry, the place is definitely unique," he commented before ushering her through another pair of doors, where a staff member was on duty. Their arms brushed in the process, sending little trickles of delight through her body. Her reaction was ridiculous. It had to be because she'd never been this close to a prince before. Except for Vincenzo, of course, but he didn't count. Not in the same way.

They walked down one more hall to the entrance of the dining room where Abby and Vincenzo sat at the candlelit table with their heads together talking quietly and kissing. Gilt-framed rococo mirrors made the room seem larger, projecting their image.

Valentino cleared his throat. "Should we come back?" He'd already helped Carolena to be seated. The teasing sound in his voice amused her, but his question caused the other two to break apart. While Abby's face flushed, Vincenzo got to his feet and came around to give Valentino a hug.

"It's good to see you."

"Likewise. I'm sorry I took so long. It's my fault for leaving work late today, but it couldn't be helped."

"No one understands that better than I do. We took the liberty of bringing Carolena with us. Allow me to introduce you."

Valentino shot her a penetrating glance. "We already met at the swimming pool."

Carolena felt feverish as she and Abby exchanged a silent glance before he walked around to hug her friend. Then he took his place next to Carolena, who still hadn't recovered from her initial reaction to his masculine appeal.

In a moment, dinner was served, starting with deep-fried risotto croquettes stuffed with pistachio pesto called arancini because they were the shape and size of an orange. Pasta with clams followed called spaghetti alle vongole. Then came the main course of crab and an aubergine side dish. Valentino told them the white wine came from their own palace vineyard.

"The food is out of this world, but I'll have to pass on the cannoli dessert," Carolena exclaimed a little while later. "If I lived here very long I'd look like one of those fat Sicilian rock partridges unable to move around."

Both men burst into laughter before Valentino devoured his dessert.

Carolena looked at Abby. "What did I say?"

Vincenzo grinned. "You and my wife have the same thought processes. She was afraid pregnancy would make her look like a beached whale."

"We women have our fears," Abby defended.

"We certainly do!"

Valentino darted Carolena another glance. "In that purple swimsuit you were wearing earlier, I can guarantee you'll never have that problem."

She'd walked into that one and felt the blood rush to her cheeks. That suit was a frivolous purchase she wouldn't have worn around other people, but since she'd been alone… Or so she'd thought. "I hope you're right, Your Highness."

His eyes smiled. "Call me Val."

Val? Who in the world called him that?

He must have been able to read her mind because his next comment answered her question. "My brother and I didn't like our long names, so we gave ourselves nicknames. He's Vito and I'm Val."

"V and V," she said playfully. "I'm surprised you didn't have to wash your initials off some of those putti."

Another burst of rich laughter escaped his throat. When it subsided, he explained their little joke to Vincenzo and Abby.

Carolena smiled at Abby. "I'd caution you never to tell that story to Max, or when he's more grown up he might take it into his head to copy his uncles."

"Fortunately we don't have putti," Vincenzo quipped.

"True," Abby chimed in, "but we do have busts that can be knocked over by a soccer ball."

Amidst the laughter, a maid appeared in the doorway. "Forgive the intrusion, Your Highness, but the queen says it seems the young prince has started to cry and is running a temperature."

In an instant both parents jumped to their feet bringing an end to the frivolity.

Wanting to say something to assure them, Carolena said, "He's probably caught a little cold."

Abby nodded. "I'm sure you're right, but he's still not as used to the queen yet and is in a strange place. I'll go to him." She put a hand on Vincenzo's arm. "You stay here and enjoy your visit, darling."

At this point, Valentino stood up. "We'll have all day tomorrow. Right now your boy needs both of you."

"Thank you," they murmured. Abby came around to give Carolena a hug. "See you in the morning."

"Of course. If you need me for anything, just phone me."

"I will."

When they disappeared out the doors, Carolena got to her feet. "I'll say good-night, too. Thank you for a wonderful dinner, Your Highness."

He frowned. "The name's Val. I want to hear you say it."

She took a deep breath. "Thank you…Val."

"That's better." His gaze swept over her. "Where's the fire?"

"I'm tired." Carolena said the first thing that came into her head. "I was up early to finish some work at the firm before the limo arrived to drive me to the airport. Bed sounds good to me."

"Then I'll walk you back."

"That won't be necessary."

He cocked his dark blond head. "Do I frighten you?"

Your appeal frightens me. "If anything, I'm afraid of disturbing your routine."

"I don't have one tonight. Forget I'm the prince."

It wasn't the prince part that worried her. He'd made her aware of him as a man. This hadn't happened since she'd fallen in love with Berto and it was very disturbing to her.

"To be honest, when you showed up at the swimming pool earlier, you looked tired after a hard day's work. Since it's late, I'm sure you'd like a good sleep before you spend the day with Vincenzo tomorrow."

"I'm not too tired to see you back to your room safely."

"Your Highness?" The same maid came to the entrance once more. "The queen would like to see you in her apartment."

"I'll go to her. Thank you."

He cupped Carolena's elbow to walk her out of the dining room. She didn't want him touching her. The contact made her senses come alive. When they passed the guard and reached the grounds, she eased away from him.

"After getting to know Vincenzo, I realize how busy you are and the huge amount of calls on your time. Your mother is waiting for you."

"I always say good-night to my mother before retiring. If our dinner had lasted a longer time, she would have had a longer wait."

There was no talking him out of letting her get back to her room by herself. "What kind of work were you doing today?" She had to admit to a deep curiosity.

He grinned. "I always come home looking dirty and need to wash off the grime."

She shook her head. "I didn't say that."

"You didn't have to. Volcanoes are a dirty business."

Carolena came to a standstill before lifting her head to look at him. "You were up on Mount Etna?"

"That's right."

His answer perplexed her. "Why?"

"I'm a volcanologist with the National Center of Geophysics and Volcanology lab in Catania."

"You're kidding—" After that movie she'd watched on the plane, she couldn't believe what he'd just told her.

One corner of his compelling mouth lifted. "Even a prince can't afford to be an empty suit. Etna has been my backyard since I was born. From the first moment I saw it smoking, I knew I had to go up there and get a good look. Once that happened, I was hooked."

With his adventurous spirit, she wasn't surprised but knew there was a lot more to his decision than that. "I confess it would be fantastic to see it up close the way you do. Have you been to other volcanoes?"

"Many of them."

"You lucky man! On the way down here I watched a Hollywood movie with Louis Jourdan about a volcano erupting in Polynesia."

"You must mean *Bird of Paradise*."

"Yes. It was really something. Your line of work has to be very dangerous."

For a second she thought she saw a flicker of some emotion in his eyes, but it passed. "Not so much nowadays. The main goal is to learn how to predict trouble so that timely warnings can be issued for cautioning and evacuating people in the area. We've devised many safe ways to spy on active volcanoes over the decades."

"How did your parents feel about you becoming a volcanologist?"

A smile broke the corner of his mouth, as if her question had amused him. "When I explained the reasons for my interest, they approved."

That was too pat an answer. He sounded as if he wanted to get off the subject, but she couldn't let it go. "What argument did you give them?"

His brows lifted. "Did you think I needed one?"

She took a quick breath. "If they were anything like my grandmother, who was the soul of caution, then yes!"

He stopped outside the entrance to her wing of the palace. Moonlight bathed his striking male features, making them stand out like those of the Roman-god statues supporting the fountain in the distance. His sudden serious demeanor gave her more insight into his complex personality.

"A king's first allegiance is to the welfare of his people. I explained to my parents that when Etna erupts again, and she will, I don't want to see a repeat of what happened in 1669."

Carolena was transfixed. "What *did* happen?"

"That eruption turned into a disaster that killed over twenty-nine thousand people."

She shuddered, remembering the film. "I can't even imagine it."

He wore a grim expression. "Though it couldn't happen today, considering the sophisticated warning systems in place, people still need to be educated about the necessity of listening and heeding those warnings of evacuation."

"In the film, there'd been no warning."

"Certainly not a hundred years ago. That's been my

greatest concern. Gemelli has a population of two hundred thousand, so it can't absorb everyone fleeing the mainland around Catania, but I want us to be prepared as much as possible."

"How do you get your people prepared?"

"I've been working with our government to do mock drills to accommodate refugees from the mainland, should a disaster occur. Every ship, boat, barge, fishing boat would have to be available, not to mention housing and food and airlifts to other islands."

"That would be an enormous undertaking."

"You're right. For protection against volcanic ash and toxic gas, I've ordered every family outfitted with lightweight, disposable, filtering face-piece mask/respirators. This year's sightings have convinced me I've only scratched the surface of what's needed to be done to feel at all ready."

"Your country is very fortunate to have you for the watchman."

"The watchman? That makes me sound like an old sage."

"You're hardly old yet," she quipped.

"I'm glad you noticed." His remark caused her heart to thud for no good reason.

"I'm very impressed over what you do."

"It's only part of what I do."

"Oh, I know what a prince does." She half laughed. "Abby once read me Vincenzo's itinerary for the day and I almost passed out. But she never told me about *your* scientific background."

"It isn't something I talk about."

"Well, I think it's fascinating! You're like an astronaut or a test pilot, but the general population doesn't know what you go through or how you put your life on the line."

"That's a big exaggeration."

"Not at all," she argued. "It's almost as if you're leading a double life. What a mystery you are!"

She wouldn't have put it past Abby to have chosen that particular film because she knew about Valentino's profession and figured Carolena would get a kick out of it once she learned about his secret profession.

After a low chuckle, he opened the doors so they could walk down the hallway and around the corner to her room. She opened her door. Though she was dying to ask him a lot more questions about his work in volcanology, she didn't want him to think she expected his company any longer. She was also aware the queen was waiting for him.

"It's been a lovely evening. Thank you for everything."

His eyes gleamed in the semidarkness. "What else do you do besides give unsuspecting males a heart attack while you're diving?"

Heat scorched her cheeks. "I thought I was alone."

"Because I was late getting back, I cut through that part of the grounds and happened to see you. It looks like I'm going to have to do it more often."

He was a huge flirt. The tabloids hadn't been wrong about him. "I won't be here long enough to get caught again. I have a law practice waiting for me back in Arancia."

He studied her for a moment. "I heard you're in the same firm with Abby."

"We were until her marriage. Now she's a full-time mother to your nephew."

A heart-stopping smile appeared. "It must be tough on your male colleagues working around so much beauty and brains."

"They're all married."

"That makes it so much worse."

She laughed. "You're outrageous."

"Then we understand each other. Tomorrow we'll be eating breakfast on the terrace off the morning room. I'll send a maid for you at eight-thirty. *Buona notte,* Carolena."

"Buona notte."

"Val," he said again.

"Val," she whispered before shutting the door. She lay against it, surprised he was so insistent on her using his nickname, surprised he'd made such an impact on her.

After their delicious meal, she wasn't ready for bed yet. Once she'd slipped on her small garden-print capri pajamas, she set up her laptop on the table and started to look up Mount Etna. The amount of information she found staggered her. There were dozens of videos and video clips she watched until after one in the morning.

But by the time she'd seen a video about six volcanologists killed on the Galeras volcano in the Colombian Andes in 1993, she turned off her computer. The scientists had been standing on the ground when it began to heave and then there was a deafening roar. The volcano exploded, throwing boulders and ash miles high and they'd lost their lives.

The idea of that happening to the prince made her ill. She knew he took precautions, but as he'd pointed out, there was always a certain amount of risk. The desire to see a vent up close would be hard to resist. That's what he did in his work. He crept up close to view the activity and send back information. But there might come a day when he'd be caught. She couldn't bear the thought of it, but she admired him terribly.

The playboy prince who'd had dozens of girlfriends didn't mesh with the volcanologist whose name was Val. She didn't want to care about either image of the sensational-looking flesh-and-blood man. When Carolena finally pulled the covers over her, she fell asleep wishing she'd never met him. He was too intriguing for words.

At seven-thirty the next morning her cell phone rang, causing her to wonder if it was the prince. She got a fluttery feeling in her chest as she raised up on one elbow to reach for it. To her surprise it was Abby and she clicked on. "Abby? Are you all right? How's Max?"

"He's still running a temperature and fussing. I think he's cutting another tooth. The reason I'm calling is because I'm going to miss breakfast with you and stay in the apartment with him. It will give Vincenzo and Valentino time to get some work done this morning."

"Understood. I'm so sorry Max is sick."

"It'll pass, but under the circumstances, why don't you order breakfast in your room or out by the pool. I'll get in touch with you later in the day. If you want a limo, just dial zero and ask for one to drive you into town, and do a little shopping or something."

"Don't worry about me. I'll love relaxing by the pool. This is heaven after the hectic schedule at the law firm."

"Okay, then. Talk to you soon."

This was a good turn of events. The less she saw of Valentino, the better.

CHAPTER TWO

By TEN-THIRTY A.M., Valentino could see that Vincenzo wasn't able to concentrate. "Let's call it a day. I can see you want to be with Abby and Max. When I've finished with some other business, we'll meet for dinner."

Vincenzo nodded. "Sorry, Valentino."

"You can't help this. Family has to come first." He walked his brother-in-law out of his suite where they'd had breakfast while they talked. When they'd said goodbye, he closed the door, realizing he had a free day on his hands if he wanted it.

In truth, he'd never wanted anything more and walked over to the house phone to call Carolena Baretti's room, but there was no answer. He buzzed his assistant. "Paolo? Did Signorina Baretti go into town?"

"No. She had breakfast at the pool and is still there."

"I see. Thank you."

Within minutes he'd changed into trunks and made his way to the pool with a beach towel and his phone. He spotted her sitting alone reading a book under the shade of the table's umbrella. She'd put her hair in a braid and was wearing a lacy cover-up, but he could see a spring-green bikini beneath it.

"I guess it was too much to hope you were wearing that purple swimsuit I found you in last evening."

She looked up. Maybe it was a trick of light, but he thought she looked nervous to see him. Why?

Carolena put her book down. "You've finished your work with Vincenzo already?"

He tossed the towel on one of the other chairs. "Between you and me, I think he wanted to take a nap with his wife."

A smile appeared. "They deserve some vacation time away from deadlines."

"Amen. We'll do more work tomorrow when Max is feeling better. Come swim with me."

She shook her head. "I've already been in."

"There's no law that says you can't swim again, is there?" He put his phone on the table.

"No. Please—just forget I'm here."

"I'm afraid that would be impossible," he said over his shoulder before plunging in at the deep end to do some laps. When he eventually lifted his head, he was shocked to discover she'd left the patio and was walking back to her wing of the palace on those long shapely legs.

Nothing like this had ever happened to him before. Propelled into action, he grabbed his things and caught up to her as she was entering the door of her apartment. Valentino stood in the aperture so she couldn't close it on him.

"Did you go away because I'd disturbed you with

my presence? Or was it because you have an aversion to me, *signorina?*"

Color swept into her cheeks. "Neither one."

His adrenaline surged. "Why didn't you tell me you preferred to be alone?"

"I'm just a guest. You're the prince doing your own thing. This is your home. But I had no intention of offending you by leaving the pool."

He frowned. "Yesterday I asked if you were afraid of me. You said no, but I think you are and I want to know why. It's true that though I've been betrothed to Princess Alexandra for years, I've had a love life of sorts. In that way I'm no different than Vincenzo before he married Michelina. But I've the feeling Abby has painted me as such a bad boy to you, you're half terrified to be alone with me."

"Nothing of the sort, Your Highness!" She'd backed away from him. "Don't ever blame her for anything. She thinks the world of you!"

That sounded heartfelt. "Then invite me in so we can talk without the staff hearing every word of our conversation."

She bit her lip before standing aside so he could enter. "I'll get you a dry towel so you can sit down." He closed the door and watched her race through the suite. She soon came hurrying back with a towel and folded it on one of the chairs placed around the coffee table.

"Thank you," he said as she took a seat at the end of the couch.

He sat down with his hands clasped between his legs and stared at her. "What's wrong with you? Though

I've told you I find you attractive, it doesn't mean I'm ready to pounce on you." She averted her eyes. "Don't tell me you don't know what I'm talking about."

"I wasn't going to, and I didn't mean to be rude. You have to believe me."

She sounded sincere enough, but Valentino wasn't about to let her off the hook. "What else am I to think? Last night I thought we were enjoying each other's company while we talked, but today you act like a frightened schoolgirl. Has some man attacked you before? Is that the reason you like to be alone and ran the minute I dived into the water?"

Her head lifted. "No! You don't understand."

"Since you're a special guest, help me so I don't feel like some pariah."

"Forgive me if I made you feel that way." Her green orbs pleaded with him. "This has to do with me, not you."

"Are you this way on principle with every man you meet? Or am I the only one to receive that honor?"

She stood up. "I—I'm going through a difficult time right now." Her voice faltered. "It's something I really can't talk about. Could we start over again, as if this never happened?"

Much as he'd like to explore her problem further, he decided to let it rest for now. "That all depends." On impulse he said, "Do you like to ride horses?"

"I love it. I used to ride all the time on my grandparents' farm."

Good. "Then I'll have lunch sent to your room, and I'll collect you in an hour. We'll ride around the grounds. It's someplace safe and close to Abby, who's hoping you're having a good time. But if you're afraid of what happened to my sister while she was riding, we could play tennis."

"I'm not afraid, but to go riding must be a painful reminder to you."

"I've worked my way through it. Accidents can happen anytime. To worry about it unnecessarily takes away from the quality of life. Don't you think?"

Her eyes suddenly glistened. "Yes," she whispered with such deep emotion he was more curious than ever to know what was going on inside her, and found himself wanting to comfort her. Instead he had to tear himself away.

"I'll be back in an hour." Reaching for his towel and phone, he left the apartment and hurried through the palace to his suite. Maybe by the end of their ride today, he'd have answers…

Carolena stood in the living room surprised and touched by his decency. He'd thought she'd been assaulted by a man and wanted to show her she didn't need to be afraid of him while he entertained her. No doubt he felt an obligation to her with Vincenzo and Abby indisposed.

He was sensitive, too. How many men would have worried she might be afraid to ride after what had happened to his sister? She'd gotten killed out riding, but he didn't let that stop him from living his normal life. His concern for Carolena's feelings increased her admiration for him.

So far she'd been a perfectly horrid guest, while he

was going out of his way to make this trip eventful for her when he didn't have to. This wasn't the behavior of a playboy. The crown prince was proving to be the perfect host, increasing her guilt for having offended him.

Within the hour he came for her in a limo and they drove to the stables across the vast estate. Once he'd picked the right mare for her, they headed out to enjoy the scenery. In time, he led them through a heavily wooded area to a lake. They dismounted and walked down to the water's edge.

"What a beautiful setting."

"We open it to the public on certain days of the month."

"Abby used to tell me she felt like a princess in a fairy tale growing up on the palace grounds in Arancia. If I lived here, I'd feel exactly the same way. You and your siblings must have spent hours here when you were young." On impulse she asked, "Were they interested in volcanology, too?"

His eyes swerved to hers. She had the feeling she'd surprised him by her question. "Quite the opposite."

That sounded cryptic. "What's the real reason you developed such a keen interest? It isn't just because Etna is there."

"It's a long story." There was that nuance of sadness in his voice again.

"We've got the rest of the afternoon." She sank onto her knees in the lush grass facing the water where an abundance of waterfowl bobbed around. "Humor me. Last night I was up until one o'clock looking at video clips of Etna and other volcanoes. They were incredible. I really want to know what drove you to become so interested."

He got down on the grass next to her. "My father had a sibling, my uncle Stefano. He was the elder son and the crown prince, but he never wanted to be king. He fought with my grandfather who was then King of Gemelli.

"Uncle Stefano hated the idea of being betrothed and having to marry a woman picked out for him. Our country has never had a sovereign who wasn't married by the time he ascended the throne. It's the law. But Stefano didn't ever want to be king and left home at eighteen to travel the world. I knew he had various girlfriends, so he didn't lead a celibate life, but he never married.

"In time, volcanoes fascinated him and he decided he wanted to study them. To appease my grandparents, he came home occasionally to touch base. I was young and loved him because he was so intelligent and a wonderful teacher. He used to take me up on Etna.

"The day came when I decided I wanted to follow in his footsteps and announced I was going to attend the university to become a geologist. My parents could see my mind was made up.

"While I was at school, the family got word he'd been killed on the Galeras volcano in the Colombian Andes."

"Valentino—" she gasped. "I read about it on the website last night. One of the people killed was your uncle?"

Pain marred his striking male features. "He got too close. The ash and gas overpowered him and he died."

She shuddered. "That's horrible. I should have thought

it would have put you off wanting anything more to do with your studies."

"You might think it, but I loved what I was doing. Statistics prove that on average only one volcanologist dies on the job each year or so."

"That's one too many!"

"For our family it was traumatic because of the consequences that followed. His body was shipped home for the funeral. A few weeks later my grandfather suffered a fatal heart attack, no doubt from the shock. His death meant my father took over as king with my mother at his side.

"While we were still grieving, they called me into their bedroom and told me they were all right with my desire to be a volcanologist. But they prayed I wouldn't disappoint them the way my uncle had disappointed my grandfather. They said my uncle Stefano had disgraced the family by not taking up his royal duties and marrying.

"I was torn apart because I'd loved him and knew he'd suffered because he'd turned his back on his royal heritage. But when I heard my parents' sorrow, I promised I would fulfill my princely obligation to the crown and marry when the time was right. They wouldn't have to worry about me. Michelina and I made a pact that we'd always do our duty."

"You mean that if she'd wanted to marry someone else other than Vincenzo, she would still have done her duty."

He nodded. "I asked her about that, knowing Vincenzo didn't love her in the way she loved him. She said it didn't matter. She was committed and was hoping he'd fall in love with her one day."

"Did you resent him for not being able to love your sister?"

"How could I do that when I don't love Alexandra? When I saw how hard he tried to make Michelina happy by agreeing to go through the surrogacy process, my affection for him grew. He was willing to do anything to make their marriage better. Vincenzo is one of the finest men I've ever known. When he ended up marrying Abby, I was happy for him."

"You're a remarkable person. So was your sister."

"I loved her. She could have told our parents she refused to enter into a loveless marriage, but she didn't. Uncle Stefano's death had affected all of us, including our brother, Vito. One day after his military service is over, he, too, will have to marry royalty because he's second in line to the throne."

"The public has no idea of the anguish that goes on behind locked royal doors."

"We're just people who've been born to a strange destiny. I didn't want to disappoint my parents or be haunted with regrets like my uncle. Fortunately, Mother is still capable of ruling, and my time to fulfill my obligation hasn't come yet."

"But it will one day."

"Yes."

"It's hard to comprehend a life like yours. May I be blunt and ask you if you have a girlfriend right now?"

"I've been seeing someone in town."

She had to suppress a moan. *Did you hear that, Carolena?* "And she's all right with the situation?"

"Probably not, but from the beginning she's known we couldn't possibly have a future. In case you're wondering, I haven't slept with her."

Carolena shook her head. "You don't owe me any explanation."

"Nevertheless, I can see the next question in your eyes and so I'll answer it. Contrary to what the media says about me, there have been only a few women with whom I've had an intimate relationship, but they live outside the country."

"Yet knowing you are betrothed has never stopped any of them from wanting to spend time with you?"

"No. The women I've known haven't been looking for permanency, either." He smiled. "We're like those ships passing in the night."

It sounded awful. Yet, since Berto, she hadn't been looking for permanency, either, and could relate more than he knew.

"I've warned my latest girlfriend our relationship could end at any time. You're within your rights to condemn me, Carolena."

"I could never condemn you," she whispered, too consumed by guilt over how she'd accidentally brought out Berto's death to find fault with anyone. "You've had every right to live your life like any ordinary man. But like your uncle, it must have been brutal for you to have grown up knowing your bride was already chosen for you."

"I've tried not to think about it."

Her mind reeled from the revelations. "Does your betrothed know and understand?"

"I'm quite sure Princess Alexandra has had relationships, too. It's possible she's involved with someone she cares about right now. Her parents' expectations for her haven't spared her anguish, either."

"No," she murmured, but it was hard to understand. How could any man measure up to Valentino? If Princess Alexandra was like his sister, she'd been in love with Valentino for years. "Does she support your work as a volcanologist?"

"I haven't asked her."

"Why not?"

"Up to now we've been living our own lives apart as much as possible."

"But this is an integral part of your life!"

He sat up, chewing on the end of a blade of grass. "Our two families have spent occasional time together over the years. But the last time my brother was home on leave and went to Cyprus with me and my mother, he told me that Alexandra admitted she never liked the idea that I was a volcanologist."

"And that doesn't worry you?"

He studied her for a long moment. "It's an issue we'll have to deal with one day after we're married."

"By then it will be too late to work things out between you," she cried. "How often do you fly to Catania?"

"Four times a week."

"She's not going to like that, not if she hates the idea of it."

He gave her a compassionate smile. "Our marriage won't be taking place for a long time, so I choose not to worry about it."

"I don't see how you can stand it."

"You learn to stand it when you've been born into a royal family. Why fate put me in line for the throne instead of you, for example, I don't know."

"You mean a woman can rule?"

"If there are no other males. Under those circumstances, she must marry another royal so she can reign. But my grandparents didn't have a daughter. Uncle Stefano should have been king, but he rebelled, so it fell to my father to rule."

Tears trickled down her cheeks. "How sad for your uncle."

"A double sadness, because though he'd abdicated in order to choose his own life, he was burdened with the pain of disappointing his parents."

"There's been so much pain for all of you. And now your own sister and father have passed on."

He nodded. "It's life."

"But it's so much to handle." Her voice trembled. Carolena wanted to comfort him but realized no one could erase all that sadness. She wiped the moisture off her cheeks. "You didn't have to tell me anything. I feel honored that you did."

His gaze roved over her. "Your flattering interest in what I do prompted me to talk about something I've kept to myself for a long time. It felt good to talk about it. Why don't you try it out on me by telling me what's bothering you."

Her eyes closed tightly for a moment. "Let's just say someone that I loved died and it was my fault. Unlike you, I can't seem to move on from the past."

"Maybe you haven't had enough time to grieve."

Carolena could tell him seven years had been more than enough time to grieve. At this point, grief wasn't her problem. Guilt was the culprit. But all she said to him was, "Maybe."

"It might be therapeutic to confide in someone. Even me."

His sincerity warmed her heart, but confiding in him would be the worst thing she could do. To remain objective around him, she needed to keep some barriers between them. "You have enough problems."

"None right this minute."

He stared hard at her. "Was his death intentional?"

"No."

"I didn't think it was. Have you gone for counseling?"

"No. It wouldn't help."

"You don't know that."

"Yes, I do." In a panic, she started to get up. He helped her the rest of the way. "Thank you for being willing to listen." It was time to change the subject. "Your uncle would be so happy to see how he guided you on your particular path, and more especially on how you're putting that knowledge to exceptional use. If I'd had such an uncle, I would have made him take me with him, too. What you do can be dangerous, but it *is* thrilling."

"You're right about that," he said, still eyeing her

speculatively. "Shall we head out? By the time we reach the palace, hopefully Vincenzo will have good news for us about Max and we can all eat dinner together."

"I hope so."

They mounted their horses and took a different route to the stable. A limo was waiting to take them back to her wing of the palace. When they arrived, she opened the car door before he could. "You don't need to see me inside. Thank you for a wonderful day."

He studied her through veiled eyes. "It was my pleasure. I'll call you when I've spoken with Vincenzo."

She nodded before getting out of the limo. After hurrying inside, she took a quick shower, applied her makeup and arranged her hair in a loose knot on top of her head. For the first time in years her thoughts hadn't been on Berto. They'd been full of the prince, who'd brought her alive from the moment he'd appeared at the side of the pool.

No matter that he had a girlfriend at the moment, it was hard to breathe every time Carolena thought of the way he'd looked at her. She could understand why any woman lucky enough to catch his eye would be willing to stay in a relationship as long as possible to be with him. There was no one like him.

Needing to do something with all this energy he'd generated through no fault of his own, she got dressed, deciding to wear a short-sleeved crocheted lace top in the same egg shell color as her linen pants. The outfit was light and airy. She toned it with beige ankle-strap crisscross espadrilles.

While she was waiting for a phone call, she heard

a knock on the door and wondered if it might be the prince. With a pounding heart she reached for her straw bag and opened it, but it was the maid, and Carolena was furious at herself for being disappointed.

"*Signorina?* His Highness has asked me to accompany you to dinner. He's waiting on the terrace."

What about Abby and Vincenzo? "Thank you for coming to get me."

No shortcuts through the grounds this time, but it gave Carolena the opportunity to see more of the ornate palace. By the time she arrived at the terrace, Vincenzo had already joined the prince, but there was no sign of Abby or Max. The two men stood together chatting quietly.

She had the impression this terrace was a recent addition. It was a masterpiece of black-and-white marble checkerboard flooring, Moorish elements and cream-colored lattice furniture in Italian provincial. A collection of exotic trees and flowering plants gave the impression they were in a garden.

Valentino's dark blue gaze saw her first. He broke from Vincenzo and moved toward her wearing jeans and a sand-colored polo shirt. "*Buonasera,* Carolena. You look beautiful."

Don't say that. "Thank you."

His quick smile was a killer. "I hope you're hungry. I told the kitchen to prepare chicken the way Abby tells me you like it."

"You're very kind." Too kind. She flashed him a smile as he helped her get seated. Valentino had no equal as a host. She decided he had no equal, period.

Vincenzo walked over and kissed her cheek before sitting down at the round table opposite her. A sumptuous-looking meal had been laid out for them. A maid came out on the terrace just then and told Valentino his mother wanted to speak to him when he had a minute. He nodded before she left.

"Where's Abby, Vincenzo?"

"Max fussed all day and is still feverish, so we're taking turns."

"The poor little thing. Do you think it's serious?"

"We don't know. Our doctor said it could be a virus, but Max isn't holding down his food. That has me worried."

"I don't blame you. Is there something I can do to help?"

"Yes," Valentino inserted. "If Max is still sick tomorrow, you can keep me company, since Vincenzo will be tied up taking care of his family."

He actually sounded happy about it, but the news filled Carolena with consternation. She'd been with him too much already and her attraction to him was growing. She flicked him a glance. "You don't have to worry about entertaining me. I brought my laptop and always have work to do."

"Not while you're here." Valentino's underlying tone of authority quieted any more of her excuses. "No doubt you and Abby had intended to visit some of the shops and museums in Gemelli while on holiday, but I can think of something more exciting for tomorrow *if* you're up to it."

Vincenzo shot her a glance she couldn't decipher. "Be careful."

She chuckled. "Is that a warning?"

After finishing his coffee, a glimmer of a smile appeared. "On my first business visit here years ago, Valentino dangled the same option in front of me."

"What happened?"

He studied her for a moment. "That's for you to find out."

"Now you've made me nervous."

"Maybe you should be." She couldn't tell if Vincenzo's cryptic response was made in jest or not.

"You've frightened her," Valentino muttered. Again, Carolena was confused by the more serious undertone of their conversation.

"Then I'm sorry and I apologize." Vincenzo put down his napkin and got to his feet. "Enjoy your evening. We'll talk again in the morning. Please don't get up."

"Kiss that baby for me and give Abby my love."

"I will."

She'd never seen Vincenzo so preoccupied. Being a new father wasn't easy, but she sensed something else was on his mind, as well.

"What went on just now?" she asked as soon as he left the terrace.

Valentino had been watching her through narrowed eyes. "I'm afraid he thinks my idea of a good time could backfire." Carolena believed there was more to it than that, but she let it go for now.

"You mean it might be one of those surprises that's the wrong kind for me?"

"Possibly."

"Well, if you don't tell me pretty soon, I might expire on the spot from curiosity."

She thought he'd laugh, but for once he didn't. "I'd like to take you sailing to Taormina. It's an island Goethe called 'a part of paradise.' The medieval streets have tiny passages with secrets I can guarantee you'll love."

"It sounds wonderful, but that wasn't the place you had in mind when you were talking with Vincenzo."

"I've had time to think the better of it."

A rare flare of temper brought blood to her cheeks. "Vincenzo is Abby's husband, not mine."

"And he enjoys her confidence."

"In other words, he's trying to protect me from something he thinks wouldn't be good for me."

"Maybe."

Carolena's grandmother used to try to protect her the same way. But if she got into it with the prince, she'd be acting like the willful child her grandparent used to accuse her of being. Averting her eyes, she forced herself to calm down and said, "It's possible Max will be better, but in case he isn't, I'd love a chance to go sailing. It's very kind of you."

She heard his sharp intake of breath. "Now you're patronizing me."

"What do you expect me to do? Have a tantrum?" The question was out of her mouth before she could stop it. She was mortified to realize she was out of control. Something had gotten into her. She didn't feel at all herself.

"At least it would be better than your pretense to mollify me," came the benign response.

What? "If you weren't the prince—"

"I asked you to forget my title."

"That's kind of hard to do."

"Why don't you finish what you were about to say. If I weren't the prince…"

"Bene." She sucked in her breath. "If neither of you were princes, I'd tell you I've been taking care of myself for twenty-seven years and don't need a couple of guys I hardly know to decide what's best for me. If that sounds ungracious, I didn't mean for it to offend you, but you did ask."

A look of satisfaction entered his eyes. "I was hoping you would say that. How would you like to fly up on Etna with me in a helicopter? We'll put down in one spot and I'll show you some sights no visitor gets to see otherwise."

Gulp. She clung to the edge of the table from sheer unadulterated excitement. Valentino intended to show her that ten-thousand-foot volcano up close? After seeing that movie, what person in the world wouldn't want the opportunity? She couldn't understand why Vincenzo thought it might not be a good experience for her.

"You love your work so much you'd go up there on your day off?"

"You can ask that after what I revealed to you today? Didn't you tell me you thought it sounded thrilling?"

"Yes." She stood up and gazed into those intelligent,

dark blue eyes. Ignoring the warning flags telling her to be prudent, she said, "I'd absolutely love it."

A stillness surrounded them. "Never let it be said I didn't give you an out."

"I don't want one, even if Vincenzo thought I did."

A tiny nerve throbbed at the side of his hard jaw. "If Max is still sick in the morning, we'll leave around eight-thirty. You'll need to wear jeans and a T-shirt if you brought one. If not, you can wear one of mine."

"I have one."

"Good, but you can't go in sandals."

"I brought my walking boots."

"Perfect."

"I'll see you in the morning then."

As she started to leave, he said, "Don't go yet."

Valentino—I can't spend any more time with you tonight. I just can't! "Your mother is waiting for you and I have things to do. I know the way back to my room."

"Carolena?"

With a pounding heart, she paused at the entrance. "Yes?"

"I enjoyed today more than you know."

Oh, but I do, her heart cried.

"The horseback ride was wonderful. Thank you again." In the next breath she took off for the other wing of the palace. Her efforts to stay away from him weren't working. To see where he spent his time and share it with him was too great a temptation to turn down, but she recognized that the thing she'd prayed would never happen was happening!

She was starting to care about him, way too much.

Forget the guilt over Berto's death that had prevented her from getting close to another man. Her feelings were way too strong for Valentino. Already she was terrified at the thought of handling another loss when she had to fly back to Arancia with Abby and Vincenzo.

But if she said she wasn't feeling well now and begged off going with him tomorrow, he'd never believe her. Though she knew she was walking into emotional danger by getting more involved, she didn't have the strength to say no to him. *Help.*

CHAPTER THREE

LETTING CAROLENA GO when it was the last thing he wanted, Valentino walked through the palace to his mother's suite. The second he entered her sitting room he was met with the news he'd been dreading all his adult life.

While he'd been riding horses with Carolena, his mother had worked out the details of his coming marriage to Princess Alexandra of Cyprus. Both royal families had wanted a June wedding, but he'd asked for more time, hoping for another year of freedom. Unfortunately they'd forced him to settle on August tenth and now there was no possibility of him changing his mind.

Tonight his mother had pinned him down, gaining his promise there'd be no more women. By giving his word, it was as good as writing it in cement.

Ages ago he and Michelina had talked about their arranged marriages. Valentino had intended to be true to Alexandra once their marriage date was set, but he'd told Michelina he planned to live a full life with other women until his time came.

She, on the other hand, never did have the same problem because she'd fallen in love with Vincenzo long before they were married and would never have been unfaithful to him. Vincenzo was a good man who'd kept his marriage vows despite the fact that he didn't feel the same way about her. Valentino admired him more than any man he knew for being the best husband he could under the circumstances.

But after seeing Abby and Vincenzo together while they'd been here, he longed for that kind of love. A huge change had come over Vincenzo once he and Abby had fallen for each other. He was no longer the same man. Valentino could see the passion that leaped between them. Last night he'd witnessed it and knew such a deep envy, he could hardly bear it.

After eight months of marriage their love had grown stronger and deeper. Everyone could see it, his mother most of all. Both she and Valentino had suffered for Michelina. She'd had the misfortune of loving Vincenzo who couldn't love her back in the same way. It would have been better if she hadn't fallen for him, but he couldn't handle thinking about that right now.

The only thing to do where Alexandra was concerned was try to get pregnant soon and build a family the way his own parents had done. Even if the most important element was missing, children would fill a big hole. That's what Michelina had tried to do by going ahead with the surrogacy procedure.

Unfortunately, he hadn't counted on the existence of Carolena Baretti. Her unexpected arrival in Gemelli had knocked him sideways for reasons he hadn't been able to identify yet. Instead of imagining his future life, his thoughts kept running to the gorgeous brunette who was a guest in the other wing of the palace.

Something had happened to him since he'd come upon Abby's friend in the swimming pool that first evening. He'd promised his mother no more women and he'd meant it. But like a lodestone he'd once found on an ancient volcano crater attracting his tools, her unique personality and stunning physical traits had drawn him in.

He'd met many beautiful women in his life, but never one like her. For one thing, she hadn't thrown herself at him. Quite the opposite. That in itself was so rare he found himself attracted on several levels.

Because she was Abby's best friend, she was already in the untouchable category, even if he hadn't promised his mother. Yet this evening, the last thing he'd wanted to do was say good-night to her.

They'd shared a lot today. Intimate things. Her concern for him, the tears she'd shed for his uncle, touched him on a profound level. He'd never met a woman so completely genuine. To his chagrin she made him feel close to her. To his further disgust, he couldn't think beyond having breakfast with her in the morning.

With his blood effectively chilled now that the conversation with his mother was over, he excused himself and called for his car to come around to his private entrance. He told his driver to head for Tancredi's Restaurant on the east end of the island, a twenty-minute drive.

Once on his way, he phoned his best friend from his university days to alert him he was coming. Matteo owned the place since his father had died. He would be partying in the bar with a few of their mutual friends now that there were no more customers.

After the limo turned down the alley behind the restaurant, Matteo emerged from the backdoor and climbed inside.

"Ehi, Valentino—"

"Sorry I'm late, but tonight certain things were unavoidable."

"Non c'è problema! It's still early for us. Come on. We've been waiting for you."

"I'm afraid I can't."

"Ooh. Adriana's not going to like hearing that."

"She's the reason I asked you to come out to the limo. Can I depend on you to put it to her gently that I won't be seeing her again?"

He frowned. "Why not?"

They stared at each other before Matteo let out an epithet. "Does this mean you're finally getting married?" He knew the union had been arranged years ago.

Valentino grimaced. "Afraid so." Once he'd gone to his mother's apartment, she'd forced him to come to a final decision after talking with his betrothed's parents. "They're insisting on an August wedding and coronation. The president of the parliament will announce our formal engagement next week."

He realized it was long past time to end his brief, shallow relationship with Adriana. For her best interest he should have done it a month ago. Instinct told him she would be a willing mistress after his marriage, but Valentino didn't feel that way about her or any woman. In any case, he would never go down that path.

Matteo's features hardened. "I can't believe this day has finally come. It's like a bad dream."

A groan escaped Valentino's throat. "But one I'm committed to. I've told you before, but I'll say it again. You've been a great friend, Matteo. I'll never forget."

"Are you saying goodbye to me, too?" he asked quietly.

His friend's question hurt him. "How can you even ask me that?"

"I don't know." Matteo drove his fist into his other palm. "I knew one day there was going to be a wedding and coronation and I know of your loyalty. Now everything's going to change."

"Not my friendship with you."

"I hope not. It's meant everything to me."

"My father told me a king has no friends, but I'm not the king yet. Even when I am, you'll always be my friend. I'll call you soon." He clapped him on the shoulder before Matteo got out of the limo. Once he'd disappeared inside the restaurant, Valentino told his driver to head back to the palace. But his mood was black.

After a sleepless night he learned that Max wasn't any better, so he followed through on his plans to pick up Carolena at her apartment. He found her outside her door waiting for him. The sight of her in jeans and a T-shirt caused another adrenaline rush.

Her eyes lifted to his. "Is there anything else you can think of I might need before we leave?"

He'd already taken inventory of her gorgeous figure and still hadn't recovered. "We'll be flying to the center in my helicopter. Whatever is missing we will find there."

"Then I'm ready." Carolena shut the suite and followed him down the hallway and out the doors. They crossed the grounds to the pad where his helicopter was waiting. "I hope this isn't a dream and I'm going to wake up in a few minutes. To see where you spend your time kept me awake all night."

Nothing could have pleased Valentino more than to know she was an adventurous woman who'd taken an interest in his research. But he knew in his gut her interest in him went deeper than that. "Perhaps now you'll understand that after a day's work on the volcano, I have trouble getting to sleep, too."

Besides his family and bodyguards, plus close friends like Matteo, he rarely shared his love for his work with anyone outside of his colleagues at the center. For his own protection, the women he'd had relationships with knew nothing about his life.

He'd called ahead to one of the center's pilots who would be taking them up. The helicopter was waiting for them when they touched down.

"Dante Serrano, meet Signorina Carolena Baretti from Arancia. She's the best friend of my brother-in-law's wife. They're staying at the palace with me for a few days. I thought she might like to see Etna at closer range."

The pilot's eyes flared in male admiration and surprise before he shook Carolena's hand and welcomed her aboard. This was a first for Valentino, let alone for Dante, who'd never known Valentino to fly a female with him unless she happened to be a geologist doing work.

He helped her into the seat behind the pilot, then took the copilot's seat. While the rotors whined, he turned to her. "Your first volcano experience should be from the air."

"I'm so excited to be seeing this up close, I can hardly stand it." Her enthusiasm was contagious. "Why does it constantly smoke?"

"That's because it's continually being reshaped by seismic activity. There are four distinct craters at the summit and more than three hundred vents on the flanks. Some are small holes, others are large craters. You'll see things that are invisible or look completely different from the surface."

"You're so right!" she cried after they took off. Once they left Catania, they passed over the fertile hillsides and lush pines. "The vistas are breathtaking, Val. With the Mediterranean for a background, these snow-topped mountains are fabulous. I didn't expect to see so much green and blue."

Her reaction, on top of her beautiful face, made it impossible for Valentino to look anywhere else. "It's a universe all its own."

'I can't believe what I'm seeing."

The landscape changed as they flew higher and higher. "We're coming up on some black lava deserts. Take a good look. Mount Etna is spitting lava more violently than it has in years, baffling us. Not only is it unpredictable, the volcano is raging, erupting in rapid succession."

He loved her awestruck squeals of delight. "I suppose you've walked across those deserts."

"I've climbed all over this volcano with Uncle Stefano."

"No wonder you love your work so much! I would, too!"

"The range of ash fall is much wider than usual. That's why I always come home dirty."

"Now I understand. Come to think of it, you did look like you'd been putting out a fire."

Dante shared a grin with Valentino. "Signorina Barctti," He spoke over his shoulder. "Even in ancient times, the locals marveled at the forces capable of shooting fountains of lava into the sky. In Greek and Roman mythology, the volcano is represented by a limping blacksmith swinging his hammer as sparks fly.

"Legend has it that the natural philosopher Empedocles jumped into the crater two thousand five hundred years ago. What he found there remained his secret because he never returned. All that remained of him were his iron shoes, which the mountain later spat out."

"That's a wonderful story, if not frightening."

All three of them laughed.

"The really fascinating part is coming up. We're headed for the Bove Valley, Etna's huge caldera. You're going to get a bird's-eye view of the eastern slope." They flew on with Dante giving her the full treatment of the famous volcano that produced more stunned cries from Carolena.

"How big is it?"

"Seven kilometers from east to west, six kilometers from north to south."

She was glued to the window, mesmerized. Valentino knew how she felt. He signaled Dante to fly them to Bocca Nuova.

"When we set down on the side of the pit, you'll see a new fumarole in the saddle between the old and new southeast crater. I want you to stay by me. This is where I was working the other day. You won't need a gas mask at this distance, but you can understand why I want every citizen of Gemelli to be equipped with one."

"After seeing this and hearing about your uncle Stefano, I understand your concern, believe me."

Before long, he helped her out and they walked fifty yards to a vantage point. "This is a place no one is allowed except our teams. The organized tours of the thousands of people who came to Etna are much farther below."

Soon they saw the vent releasing the same bluish gas and ash he'd recorded the other day.

"This fumarole was formed by that long fissure you can see."

While they stood there gazing, the noise of explosions coming from deep within the volcano shook the ground. When she cried out, he automatically put his arm around her shoulders and pulled her tight against his side. He liked the feel of her womanly body this close.

"Don't be alarmed," he murmured into her fragrant hair. "We're safe or I wouldn't have brought you up here."

She clung to him. "I know that, but I have to tell you a secret. I never felt insignificant until now." Those were his very thoughts the first time he'd come up on Etna. After a long silence, she lifted her eyes to him. In them he saw a longing for him that she couldn't hide when she said, "It's awesome and mind blowing all at the same time."

Those dazzling, dark-fringed green eyes blew him away, but not for the reasons she'd been alluding to. He was terrified over the feelings he'd developed for her. "You've taken the words right out of my mouth."

The desire to kiss her was so powerful, it took all the self-control he possessed not to crush her against him. He was in serious trouble and knew it.

Fighting his desire, he said, "I think you've seen enough for today. We've been gone a long time and need to eat. Another day and I'll take you on a hike through some lava fields and tunnels you'll find captivating." *Almost as captivating as I'm finding you.*

"I doubt I'll ever be in Gemelli again, but if I am, I'll certainly take you up on your offer. Thank you for a day I'll never *ever* forget." He felt her tremulous voice shake his insides.

"Nor will I." The fact that she was off-limits had no meaning to him right now.

On their way back to the center, he checked his phone messages. One from Vincenzo and two from his mother. He checked Vincenzo's first.

I'm just giving you a heads-up. Max isn't doing well, so we're flying back to Arancia at nine in the morning Sorry about this, but the doctor thinks he may have gas-

*troenteritis and wants to check him out at the hospital.
Give me a call when you're available.*

Valentino's lips thinned. He was sorry about the
baby, but it meant Carolena would be leaving in the
morning.

The queen's first message told him she was upset
they were going to have to leave with her grandson.
She was crazy about Max and her reaction was understandable. Her second message had to do with wedding
preparations. Since he couldn't do anything about either situation at the moment, he decided to concentrate
on Carolena, who would be slipping away from his life
much sooner than he'd anticipated.

Once they touched down at the center and had
thanked Dante for the wonderful trip, they climbed on
board Valentino's helicopter. But instead of flying back
to the palace where his mother expected him to join her
the second he got back, he instructed his pilot to land
on the royal yacht anchored in the bay. They could have
dinner on board away from the public eye.

Carolena was a very special VIP and the crew would
think nothing of his entertaining the close friend of his
new sister-in-law who was here with the prince of Arancia visiting the queen.

He called ahead to arrange for their meal to be served
on deck. After they arrived on board and freshened
up, they sat down to dinner accompanied by soft rock
music as the sun disappeared below the horizon. Both
of them had developed an appetite. Valentino loved it
that she ate with enjoyment.

"Try the Insolia wine. It has a slightly nutty flavor

with a finish that is a combination of sweet fruit and sour citrus. I think it goes well with swordfish."

"It definitely does, and the steak is out of this world, Val. Everything here in Gemelli is out of this world."

From the deck they could see Etna smoking in the far distance. She kept looking at it. "To think I flew over that volcano today and saw a fumarole up close." Her gaze swerved to his. "Nothing I'll ever do in life will match the wonder of this day, and it's all because of you."

He sipped his wine. "So the surprise didn't turn out to be so bad, after all."

"You know it didn't." Her voice throbbed, revealing her emotion. "I can't think why Vincenzo warned me against it. Unless—"

When she didn't finish, he said, "Unless what?"

"Maybe watching Michelina when she had her riding accident has made him more cautious than usual over the people he loves and cares about. Last night I could tell how worried he was about Max."

Valentino hadn't thought of that, but he couldn't rule it out as a possibility, though he didn't think it was Vincenzo's major concern. Now that they were talking about it, his conversation at dinner with Vincenzo in front of her came back to haunt him.

He'd been warning Valentino, but maybe not about the volcano. Unfortunately, Vincenzo had always been a quick study. Possibly he'd picked up on Valentino's interest in Carolena. Whatever had gone on in Vincenzo's mind, now was the time to tell her about the change in their plans to fly back to Arancia.

"I checked my voice mail on the way to the yacht. You can listen." He pulled his cell phone from his pocket and let her hear Vincenzo's message.

In an instant everything changed, as he knew it would. "The poor darling. It's a good thing we're going home in the morning. I'm sure Max will be all right, but after no sleep, all three of them have to be absolutely miserable."

Make that an even four.

The idea of Carolena leaving Gemelli filled him with a sense of loss he'd never experienced before. The deaths of his father and sister were different. It didn't matter that he'd only known her twenty-four hours. To never be with her again was anathema to him.

He could have predicted what she'd say next. "We'd better get back to the palace. I need to pack."

"Let's have our dessert first. You have to try *cassata alla sicilana*." Anything to prolong their time together.

"Isn't that a form of cheesecake?"

"Cake like you've never tasted anywhere else."

An impish smile broke one corner of her voluptuous mouth. "Something tells me you're a man who loves his sweets."

"Why do you think that?"

"I don't know. Maybe it's because of the way you embrace life to the fullest and enjoy its richness while at the same time reverencing it. When the gods handed out gifts, you received more than your fair share."

He frowned. "What do you mean?"

"There aren't many men who could measure up to

you. Your sister used to sing your praises to Abby, who said she worshipped you."

"The feeling was mutual, believe me."

"According to Abby, Michelina admitted that the only man who came close to you was Prince Vincenzo. That's high praise indeed. Luckily for your country, you're going to be in charge one day."

One day? That day was almost upon him!

For the wedding date to have been fixed at the same time he'd met Signorina Baretti, the pit in Valentino's stomach had already grown into a caldera bigger than the one he'd shown her today.

He'd spun out every bit of time with her he could squeeze and had no legitimate choice but to take her back to the palace.

"It's getting late. I'm sure Vincenzo will want to talk to you tonight."

Valentino shook his head. "With the baby sick, that won't be happening." In truth, he wasn't up to conversation with Vincenzo or his mother. For the first time in his life he had the wicked instinct to do what he wanted and kidnap this woman who'd beguiled him.

"I have a better idea. It's been a long day. We'll stay on the yacht and fly you back on time in the morning. I'll instruct the maid to pack your things. As for tonight, anything you need we have on board."

Carolena's breath caught. "What about your girlfriend? Won't she be expecting you?"

His dark blue eyes narrowed on her face. "Not when I'm entertaining family and friends. As for the other question you don't dare ask, I've never brought a woman on board the yacht or taken one up on the volcano."

He'd been so frank and honest with her today, she believed him now. His admission shook her to her core. "If I didn't know better, I would think you were propositioning me," she teased to cover her chaotic emotions. There she went again. Saying something she shouldn't have allowed to escape her lips.

His jaw hardened. "I'm a man before being a prince and I *am* propositioning you, but I can see I've shocked you as much as myself."

She could swear that was truth she'd heard come out of him. Carolena was Abby's friend, yet that hadn't stopped him, and obviously that fact wasn't stopping her. It was as if they were both caught in a snare of such intense attraction, they knew no boundaries.

"Do you want to know something else?" he murmured. "I can see in those glorious green eyes of yours that you'd like to stay on board with me tonight. True desire is something you can't hide. We've both felt it since we met, so there's no use denying it."

"I'm not," she confessed in a tremulous voice. Carolena could feel her defenses crumbling and started to tremble. Never had she been around a man who'd made her feel so completely alive.

"My kingdom for an honest woman, and here you are."

"Only you and Vincenzo could say such a thing and get away with it."

Her humor didn't seem to touch him. "Tell me about

the man who died. You *were* speaking about a man. Are you still terribly in love with him?"

His question reached the core of her being. "I'll always love him," she answered honestly.

He reached across the table and grasped her hand. "How long has he been gone?"

She couldn't lie to him. "Seven years."

After a moment of quiet, he said, "That's a long time to be in love with a memory. How did he die?"

"It doesn't matter. I don't want to talk about it."

Those all-seeing eyes of his gazed through to her soul. "Yet somehow you still feel responsible for his death?"

"Yes."

"Has it prevented you from getting close to another man?"

"I've been with other men since he died, if that's what you mean."

"Carolena—tell me the truth. Is there one man who's vitally important to you now?"

Yes. But he's not in Arancia.

"No one man more than another," she dissembled.

She heard his sharp intake of breath. "Then do you dare stay with me the way you dared to get close to Etna's furnace today? I'm curious to see how brave a woman you really are."

His thumb massaged her palm, sending warmth through her sensitized body until her toes curled. "You already know the answer to that."

"Dance with me, *bellissima*," he begged in a husky

whisper. "I don't give a damn that the crew can see us. You've entranced me and I need to feel you in my arms."

It was what she wanted, too. When she'd heard Vincenzo say that they were leaving in the morning, she'd wanted to cry out in protest that she'd only gotten here. She hadn't had enough time with Valentino. *Not nearly enough.*

He got up from the table and drew her into his arms. She went into them eagerly, aching for this since the time he'd put his arm around her up on the volcano. It felt as if their bodies were meant for each other. She slid her arms around his neck until there was no air between them. They clung out of need in the balmy night air that enveloped them like velvet.

His hands roved over her back and hips as they got a new sense of each other only touch could satisfy. They slow danced until she lost track of time. To hold and be held by this amazing man was a kind of heaven.

She knew he was unattainable. Abby had told her he'd been betrothed to Princess Alexandra in his teens, just like Vincenzo's betrothal to Princess Michelina. One day Valentino would have to marry. He'd explained all that yesterday.

Carolena understood that. It didn't bother her since she shunned the idea of commitment that would lead to her own marriage. Marriage meant being responsible for another person's happiness. She couldn't handle that, but selfishly she did desire this one night with Valentino before she flew back to Arancia and never saw him again.

Tonight he'd made her thankful she'd been born a

woman. Knowing he wanted her as much as she wanted him brought indescribable joy. One night with him would have to be enough, except that he still hadn't kissed her yet and she was dying for it. When he suddenly stopped moving, she moaned in disappointment.

His hands squeezed her upper arms. "The steward will show you downstairs to your cabin," he whispered before pulling the phone from his pocket. "I'll join you shortly."

Carolena was so far gone she'd forgotten about the prying eyes of the crew, but Valentino was used to the whole world watching him and did what was necessary to keep gossip to a minimum. Without words she eased away from him and walked over to the table for her purse before following the steward across the deck to the stairs.

The luxury yacht was a marvel, but Carolena was too filled with desire for Valentino to notice much of anything. Once she reached the cabin and the steward left, she took a quick shower and slipped into one of the white toweling bathrobes hanging on a hook. The dressing room provided every cosmetic and convenience a man or woman could need.

She sat in front of the mirror and brushed her hair. *Entranced* was the right word. Though she knew she'd remain single all her life, she felt as if this was her wedding night while she waited for him to come. The second he entered the room he would hear the fierce pounding of her heart.

Soon she heard his rap on the door. "Come in," she called quietly. He walked in and shut the door behind him, still dressed in the clothes he'd worn during their trip.

Without saying anything, he reached for her hand and drew her over to the bed where he sat down and pulled her between his legs. His gaze glowed like hot blue embers. Everywhere it touched, she was set on fire. Her ears picked up the ragged sound of his breathing.

"You look like a bride."

But, of course, she wasn't a bride, and she sensed something was wrong. She could feel it. "Is that good or bad?"

He ran his hands up and down her arms beneath the loose sleeves of her robe as if even his fingers were hungry for her. "Carolena—" There was an unmistakable plea for understanding in his tone.

"Yes?" Whatever was coming, she knew she wasn't going to like it.

"I talked frankly with you yesterday about my personal life. But what you couldn't know was that last night after you went back to your room, I met with my mother." His chest rose and fell visibly. "While you and I were out riding, my wedding date to Princess Alexandra was finally set in stone. We're being married on August tenth, the day of my coronation."

Carolena stood stock-still while the news sank in. That was only two months from now…

"Though I made the promise to my mother that I'd be faithful to Alexandra from here on out, I really made it to myself and have already gotten word to my latest girlfriend that it's over for good."

She could hardly credit what she was hearing.

"But little did I know I was already being tested by none other than Abby's best friend."

A small cry escaped her throat. "I shouldn't have come, but Abby kept insisting." She shivered. "This is all my fault, Val."

"There you go again, taking on blame for something that's no one's fault. If we were to follow that line of thinking, shall I blame myself for inviting Vincenzo to come on this trip? Shall we blame him for bringing his wife and her best friend?"

His logic made Carolena feel like a fool. "Of course not."

"At least you admit that much. In my whole life I've never wanted a woman more than I've wanted you, since the moment we met at the swimming pool. But it's more than that now. Much more."

"I know. I feel it, too." But she remained dry eyed and smiled at him. "The gods are jealous of you. They're waiting for you to make a mistake. Didn't you know that?"

He squeezed her hands gently. "When I dared you to stay with me tonight, I crossed a line I swore I would never do."

"I believe you. But the fact is, it takes two, Val. I didn't know your wedding date had been set, of course. Yet even knowing you were betrothed, I crossed it, too, because I've never known desire like this before, either. I've never had an affair before."

"*Carolena...*"

He said her name with such longing, she couldn't stand it. "Let's not make this situation any more impossible. Go back to the palace tonight knowing you've passed your test."

"And leave you like this?" he cried urgently, pulling her closer to him. "You don't really mean that!"

"Yes. I do. You have Vincenzo to think about, and a mother who's waiting for your return. Your wedding's going to take place soon. You need to concentrate on Alexandra now."

But she knew he wasn't listening. He got to his feet, cupping her face in his hands. "I don't want to leave you." He sounded as if he was in agony. "Say the word and I won't."

Abby could hear her grandmother's voice. *You go where angels fear to tread without worrying about anyone else but yourself.*

Not this time, *nonnina.*

"Thank you for your honesty. It's one of your most sterling qualities. You truly are the honorable man your sister idolized. But I have enough sins on my conscience without helping you add one to yours."

His brows formed a bar above his eyes. "You told me you caused the death of the man you loved, but you also said it wasn't intentional."

She averted her eyes. "It wasn't."

"Then no sin has been committed."

"Not if we part now. I don't want you going through life despising yourself for breaking the rule you've set. Believe it or not, I *want* you to go, Val," she told him. "After the promise you made to your parents when your uncle died, I couldn't handle it otherwise."

"Handle what? You're still holding back on me. Tell me what it is."

"It's no longer of any importance."

"Carolena—"

He was willing to break his vow for her because he wanted her that much. Just knowing that helped her to stay strong. But he didn't realize all this had to do with her self-preservation.

"Val, if it's all right with you, I'd like to remain on board until tomorrow morning and then fly back to the palace. But please know that when I leave Gemelli, I'll take home the memory of a man who for a moment out of time made me feel immortal. I'll treasure the memory of you all my life."

She pulled away from him and walked over to the door to open it. *"Addio,* sweet prince."

CHAPTER FOUR

THE MOMENT VALENTINO walked into the palace at eleven that night, he texted Vincenzo, who was still up. They met in Valentino's suite.

"How did your day go?" his brother-in-law asked after he'd walked into the sitting room.

Valentino was still on fire for the woman who'd looked like a vision when he'd walked into her cabin.

"After we left Etna, I thought Carolena would like dinner on the yacht where there's a wonderful view of the island. She's staying there overnight. My pilot will fly her back in the morning. You should have seen her when we got out of the helicopter and walked over to view one of the fumaroles. She was one person who really appreciated the experience."

"Michelina would never step foot on Etna and was always afraid for you. Sorry about this morning. I guess I thought it might frighten Carolena."

Valentino had forgotten about his sister's fear. It showed how totally concentrated he'd been on Carolena. "If she was, she hid it well. Now I want to hear about Max. How is he?"

"For the moment both he and Abby are asleep. It'll be a relief to get him home. After the doctor tells us what's wrong and we can relax, I'd like it if you could arrange to fly to Arancia so we can talk business."

He nodded. "I'm as anxious as you to get started on the idea we've discussed. I'll clear my calendar." It would mean seeing Carolena again. He was going to get the truth out of her one way or another.

"Abby thinks Carolena would be a good person to consult over the legalities of the plans we have in mind. Did I mention her expertise is patent law? It's exactly what we need."

She was a patent attorney? Valentino's heart leaped to think he didn't need to find an excuse to see her again when he had a legitimate reason to be with her before long. On his way to the palace, he'd come close to telling the pilot he'd changed his mind and wanted to go back to the yacht.

"Valentino? Did you hear what I said?"

"Sorry. The news about her work in patent law took me by surprise. Abby and Carolena are both intelligent women. With them being such close friends and attorneys, it will be a pleasure to have them consult with us. I've worried about finding someone we could really trust."

"Amen to that. We don't want anyone else to get wind of this until it's a fait accompli," Vincenzo muttered. "Abby asked me to thank you for taking such good care of Carolena today."

If he only knew how dangerously close Valentino had come to making love to her. Once that happened, there'd be no going back because he knew in his gut he'd want her over and over again. That would jeopardize both their lives and put them in a different kind of hell.

"It's always a rush to go up on Etna with someone who finds it as fascinating as I do."

"She really liked it?"

"I wish I had a recording while we were in the air."

Vincenzo smiled. "That'll make Abby happy. She brought Carolena along because seven years ago yesterday her fiancé was killed days before she became a bride. Apparently this date in June is always hard for her. They were very much in love."

Fiancé?

Valentino's gut twisted in deepest turmoil when he remembered telling her she looked like a bride. More than ever he was determined to find out what kind of guilt she'd been carrying around all this time.

"Abby says she dates one man after another, but it's only once or twice, never really getting to know anyone well. She believes she's depressed and is pretty worried about her. Abby was hoping this trip would help her get out of herself. Sounds like your day on the volcano may have done just that."

The revelations coming one after the other hit Valentino like a volcanic bomb during an eruption.

"I hope so."

"I'd better get back to our suite. It'll be my turn to walk the floor with Max when he wakes up again. My poor wife is worn out."

"From the looks of it, so are you." He patted Vincenzo on the shoulder before walking him to the door.

"I'll have breakfast sent to your suite at eight. Carolena will be waiting for you on the helicopter."

"Thanks for everything, Valentino."

"The queen says this will pass. She ought to know after raising me and my siblings. See you in the morning."

After his brother-in-law left, Valentino raced out of the palace to the swimming pool. He did laps until he was so exhausted he figured he might be able to sleep for what was left of the rest of the night. But that turned out to be a joke. There were certain fires you couldn't put out.

The next morning when he walked out to the landing pad with Vincenzo and his family, Carolena was still strapped in her seat. One of his security men put the luggage from her room on board as he climbed in.

Other than a smile and another thank-you for the tour of the volcano, she displayed no evidence of having missed Valentino or passing a tormented night. They were both accomplished actors playing roles with such expertise they might even have deceived each other. Except for the slight break he heard in her voice that caused his heart to skip several beats.

Four days later Carolena had just finished taking a deposition in her office and had said goodbye to her client when her new secretary, Tomaso, told her Abby was on the line. She hoped it was good news about the baby and picked up.

"Abby? How are you? How's Max?"

"He's doing great. The gastroenteritis is finally gone."

"Thank heaven!"

"I feel so terrible about what happened on our trip."

"Why do you say that? I was sorry for you, of course, but I had a wonderful time!"

"You're always such a good sport. I know it made Valentino's day for someone to be excited about his work."

"He's an incredible man, Abby." Carolena tried to keep the tremor out of her voice.

"He was impressed with you, too. That's one of the reasons I'm calling. He flew into Arancia this morning so he and Vincenzo can talk business."

She almost had heart failure. It was a good thing she was sitting down. Valentino was here?

"Since you're a patent law attorney, both men want you to meet with them. They need your legal counsel along with mine."

Her pulse raced off the chart. "Why?" She'd thought she'd never see him again and had been in such a depression, she'd decided that if she didn't get over it, she would have to go for professional help.

"They're putting together a monumental idea to benefit both our countries. I'll tell you all about it when you get here. Can you come to the palace after work? The four of us will talk and have dinner together."

Carolena jumped up from her leather chair. No, no, no. She didn't dare put herself into a position like that again. Legitimate or not, Valentino had to know how hard this was going to be for her. She didn't have his self-control.

If for any reason she happened to end up alone with him tonight, she might beg him to let her spend the night because she couldn't help herself. How wicked would that be? She'd spend the rest of her life mourning another loss because there could never be another time with him. This was one time Carolena couldn't do what Abby was asking.

"I'm afraid I can't."

"Why not?"

"I have a date for the symphony."

"Then cancel it. I just found out this morning that Valentino is rushed for time. Did I tell you his wedding and coronation are coming up in August?"

She bit her lip. "No. I don't believe you mentioned it."

"He'd hoped to get this business settled before flying back to Gemelli tomorrow."

Here today, gone tomorrow? She couldn't bear it. This request had put her in an untenable position. What to do so she wouldn't offend her friend? After racking her brain, she came up with one solution that might work. It would *have* to work since Carolena didn't dare make a wrong move now.

She gripped the phone tighter. "I have an idea that won't waste Valentino's time. Would it be possible if you three came to the office this afternoon?" Neutral ground rather than the palace was the only way for her to stay out of temptation's way.

"I'm afraid not. It would require too much security for the two of them to meet anywhere else. The security risk is higher than usual with Valentino's coronation coming up soon. How would it be if you cleared your slate for this afternoon and came to the palace? Say two o'clock?"

By now Carolena was trembling.

"We'll talk and eat out by the pool. If you leave the palace by six-thirty, you'll be in time for your date."

Carolena panicked. "I'd have to juggle some appointments." That was another lie. "I don't know if Signor Faustino will let me. I'm working on a big case."

"Bigger than the one for the princes of two countries?" Abby teased.

Her friend had put her on the royal spot. The writing was on the wall. "I—I'll arrange it." Her voice faltered.

"Perfect. The limo will pick you up at the office at one forty-five. Come right out to the terrace by the pool after you arrive."

"All right," she whispered before hanging up.

In an hour and a half Carolena would be seeing Valentino again. Already she had this suffocating feeling in her chest. It was a good thing she had another client to take up her time before the limo came for her. When she left the office she'd tell Tomaso she was going out for a business lunch with a client, which was only the truth.

Luckily she'd worn her sleeveless black designer shift dress with the crew neck and black belt to work. She'd matched the outfit with black heels. There was no need to do anything about her hair. All she had to do was touch up her makeup. When she showed up at the palace, it would carry out the lie that she'd be going to the symphony later.

Valentino had just finished some laps in the pool when he saw Carolena walk past the garden toward them in a stunning, formfitting black dress. Only a woman with her figure could wear it. Abby had told him she was going to the symphony later with a man.

She'd parted her hair in the middle above her forehead and had swept a small braid from each side around to the back, leaving her dark hair long. Two-tiered silvery earrings dangled between the strands. He did a somersault off the wall of the pool to smother his gasp.

If he'd hoped that she wouldn't look as good to him after four days, he could forget that! The trick would be to keep his eyes off her while they tried to do business. While Abby laid out their lunch beneath the overhang, Vincenzo sat at one of the tables working on his laptop. Both of them wore beach robes over their swimsuits. Max was down for a nap in the nursery.

She headed for Abby. A low whistle came out of Vincenzo and he got up to greet her. "I've never seen you looking lovelier, Carolena."

"Thank you," she said as the two women hugged.

Valentino climbed out of the shallow end of the pool and threw on a beach cover-up. "We're grateful you could come this afternoon."

Carolena shot him a brief glance. "It's very nice to see you again, Val. Signor Faustino was thrilled when he found out where I was going. Needless to say, he considers it the coup of the century that I've been summoned to help the princes of Gemelli and Arancia with a legal problem."

Abby was all smiles. "Knowing him, he'll probably make you senior partner at their next meeting."

"Don't wish that on me!" That sounded final.

Valentino moved closer. "You mean, it isn't your dream?"

"Definitely not." She seemed so composed, but it was deceiving, because he saw a nerve throbbing frantically at the base of her throat where he longed to kiss her.

He smiled. "Our conversation on the deck of the yacht was cut short and didn't give us time to cover your dreams before I had to leave."

Being out of the sun, she couldn't blame it for the rose blush that crept into her face. "As I recall, we were discussing *your* dreams for Gemelli, Val."

Touché. But his unrealized personal dream that had lain dormant deep in his soul since his cognizance of life was another matter altogether.

"In truth, I hope to make enough money from the law practice that one day in the future I can buy back my grandparents' small farm and work it." Her green eyes clouded for a moment. "I'm a farmer's daughter at heart."

"I understand your parents are not alive."

"No, nor are my grandparents. Their farm was sold. There have been Barettis in Arancia for almost a hundred years. I'm the only Baretti left and want to keep up the tradition by buying the place back."

Had her fiancé been a farmer, too? Valentino knew a moment of jealousy that she'd loved someone else enough to create such a powerful emotion in her.

"I had no idea," he murmured, "but since it's in your blood, that makes you doubly valuable for the task at hand." His mind was teeming with new ideas to keep her close to him.

"Abby said you and Vincenzo were planning something monumental for both your countries. I confess I'm intrigued."

"Hey, you two," Abby called to them. "Come and help yourselves to lunch first, then we'll get down to business."

He followed Carolena to the serving table. After they'd filled their plates, they sat down at one of the round tables where the maid poured them iced tea. Once they'd started eating, he said, "Vincenzo? Why don't you lay the groundwork for the women and we'll go from there."

"Our two countries have a growing problem because of the way they are situated on coastal waters. We all know the land around the Mediterranean is one of the most coveted terrains on earth. Over the years, our prime properties of orange and lemon groves that have sustained our economies for centuries have been shrinking due to man's progress. Our farmers are being inundated with huge sums of money to sell their land so it can be developed for commercial tourism."

"I know that's true," Carolena commented. "My grandfather was approached many times to sell, but he wouldn't do it."

Vincenzo nodded. "He's the type of traditional farmer fighting a battle to hold on to his heritage. Farmers are losing their workers, who want to go to the city. In the process, we're losing a vital and precious resource that has caused Valentino and me to lose sleep. Something has to be done to stop the trend and rebuild the greatness of what we've always stood for. We've come up with an idea to help our farmers by giving them a new incentive. You tell them, Valentino."

Carolena's gaze swerved to him. He could tell Vincenzo had grabbed the women's attention.

"We need to compete with other countries to increase our exports to fill the needs of a growing world market and build our economies here at home. The lemons of Arancia are highly valued because of their low acidity and delicate flavor.

"Likewise the blood oranges of Gemelli are sought after for their red flesh and deep red juice. The juice is exceptionally healthy, being rich in antioxidants. What we're proposing is to patent our fruit in a joint venture so we can grow an enviable exporting business.

"With a unique logo and marketing strategy, we can put our citrus fruits front and center in the world market. When the buyer sees it, they'll know they're getting authentic fruit from our regions alone and clamor for it."

"That's a wonderful idea," Carolena exclaimed. "You would need to be filed as a Consortium for the Promotion of the Arancian Lemon and the Gemellian Blood Orange. The IGP logo will be the official acknowledgment that the lemons and oranges were grown in your territories according to the traditional rules."

Vincenzo leaned forward. "That's exactly what we're striving for. With the right marketing techniques, the citrus business should start to flourish again. We'll come up with a name for the logo."

"That's easy," Abby volunteered. "AG. Two tiny letters stamped on each fruit. You'll have to make a video that could be distributed to every country where you want to introduce your brand."

Bless you, Abby. She was reading Valentino's mind. He needed more time alone with Carolena to talk about their lives. Abby had just given him the perfect excuse. He exchanged glances with Vincenzo before he looked at Carolena.

"The right video would sell the idea quickly, but we need a spokesperson doing the video to put it across. You'd be the perfect person for several reasons, Carolena."

"Oh, no." He saw the fear in her eyes and knew exactly what put it there, but he couldn't help himself. What he felt for Carolena was stronger than anything he'd ever known.

"You have the looks and education to sell our idea," Valentino persisted. "We'll start in Gemelli with you traveling around to some of the orange groves. With a farming background that dates back close to a century, you'll be the perfect person to talk to the owners."

Valentino could tell by the way Vincenzo smiled at Carolena that he loved the idea. His friend said, "After you've finished there, we'll have you do the same thing here in Arancia with our lemon farmers. We'll put the video on television in both countries. People will say, 'That's the beautiful Signorina Baretti advertising the AG logo.' You'll be famous."

She shook her head. "I don't want to be famous."

"You get used to it," Valentino quipped. "While you're in Gemelli, you'll stay at the palace and have full security when you travel around with the film crew.

I'll clear my calendar while you're there so I can be on hand. The sooner we get started, the better. How long will it take you to put your affairs in order and fly down?"

"But—"

"It'll be fun," Abby spoke up with enthusiasm. "I can't think of another person who could do this."

"Naturally you'll be compensated, Carolena," Vincenzo added. "After coming to the aid of our two countries, you'll make enough money to buy back your grandparents' farm, if that's what you want."

She got up from the chair on the pretense of getting herself another helping of food. "You're all very flattering and generous, but I need time to think about it."

Valentino stared up at her. "Do that while you're at the symphony tonight with your date, and we'll contact you in the morning for your answer." He could swear she didn't really have plans. She proved it when she looked away from him.

Forcing himself to calm down, he checked his watch. "Since we have several hours before you have to leave in the limo, I suggest we get to work on a script. Perhaps the video could start with you showing us your old farm. It will capture everyone's interest immediately. We'll shoot that segment later."

"It's a beautiful place!" Abby cried. "You'll do it, right?" she pleaded with her friend. "You've worked nonstop since law school. It's time you had some fun along with your work. Your boss, Signor Faustino, will get down on his knees to you."

Vincenzo joined in. "I'll have you flown down on the jet."

Valentino found himself holding his breath.

You go where angels fear to tread, Carolena.

The words pummeled her as the royal jet started its descent to Gemelli's airport. As she saw the smoke of Etna out of the window, memories of that glorious day and evening with Valentino clutched at her heart.

She'd be seeing him in a few minutes. If this offer to do the video had been Valentino's wish alone, she would have turned him down. But the excitement and pleading coming from both Abby and Vincenzo two days ago had caused her to cave. Deep down she knew a great deal was riding on this project for their two countries.

After another sleepless night because of Valentino, she'd phoned Abby the next morning to tell her she'd do it. But her friend had no idea of her fatal attraction to him.

It *was* fatal and Valentino knew it. But he was bound by a code of honor and so was she. If she worked hard, the taping could be done in a couple of days and she could go back to Arancia for good.

One of Valentino's staff greeted the plane and walked her to her old room, where she was once again installed. He lowered her suitcase to the parquet floor. "In forty-five minutes His Highness will be outside in the limo waiting to take you for a tour of some orange groves. In the meantime, a lunch tray has been provided for you."

"Thank you."

After quickly getting settled, she ate and changed

into jeans and a blouson, the kind of outfit she used to wear on her grandparents' farm. Earlier that morning she'd put her hair in a braid to keep it out of her way. On her feet she wore sensible walking boots. Inside her tote bag she carried a copy of the script, which she'd read over many times.

Before walking out the door, she reached for it and for her grandmother's broad-brimmed straw hat she'd always worn to keep out the sun. Armed with what she'd need, she left the room for the limo waiting out at the side entrance of the palace.

When she walked through the doors, Valentino broke away from the driver he'd been talking to and helped her into the limo. The sun shone from a blue sky. It was an incredible summer day. Once inside, he shut the door and sat across from her wearing a navy polo shirt and jeans. He looked and smelled too marvelous for words.

Within a minute they left the palace grounds and headed for the outskirts of the city. "I've been living for you to arrive," he confessed in his deep voice. "How was the symphony?"

His unexpected question threw her. "Wonderful."

"That's interesting. I found out it wasn't playing that night, nor did you go to dinner with your boyfriend. In case you were wondering, the limo driver informed Vincenzo you told him to take you back to your apartment. Why manufacture an excuse?"

Heat rushed to her face. "I'm sure you know the reason."

"You mean that you were afraid you might end up alone with me that evening?"

"I thought it could be a possibility and decided to err on the side of caution."

"Once I overheard Vincenzo tell Abby about your fictional evening out, you don't know how close I came to showing up at your apartment that night."

This wasn't going to work. The longing for him made her physically weak. "Does your mother know you flew me up on Etna?" she blurted.

"She has her spies. It's part of the game. That's why I didn't attack you on the deck of the yacht."

"But we danced for a long time."

He leaned forward. "Dancing is one thing, but the steward would have told her I didn't spend the night with you. In fact, I wasn't in your room more than a few minutes."

"She's no one's fool, Val."

"What can I say?" He flashed her a brief smile. "She's my mother. When she thought you'd gone out of my life by flying back to Arancia with Abby and Vincenzo, no doubt she was relieved. But now that you're here again so soon, she knows my interest in you goes deeper than mere physical attraction."

"With your marriage looming on the horizon, she has every right to be upset."

"That's a mother's prerogative. For that, I apologize."

Valentino's life truly wasn't his own. Every move he made was monitored. Only now was she beginning to appreciate how difficult it must have been for him growing up, but she couldn't worry about that right now. She had a job to do. The sooner she got to it, the sooner she could fly back to Arancia. *Away from him*

The surrounding countryside basked under a heavenly sun. They came to the first grove where the trees were planted in rows, making up football-pitch-length orchards. She watched men and women in blue overalls go from tree to tree, quickly working their way up and down ladders to fill plastic crates with the brightly colored produce. It brought back memories from her past.

The limo pulled to a stop. "We'll get out and walk from here."

He opened the door to help her. With a shaky hand she reached for her hat. The moment she climbed out, the citrus smell from the many hectares of orange groves filled her senses.

Valentino's dark blue eyes played over her face and figure with a hunger that brought the blood to her cheeks. When she put the hat on her head, he felt the rim of it. "I like that touch of authenticity."

"It was my grandmother's. I thought I'd wear it to bring me luck." Maybe it would help her to keep her wits. But already she was suffering from euphoria she shouldn't be feeling. It was because they were together again. For a while, happiness drove away her fears as they began walking toward the *masseria,* the typical farmhouse in the area.

"As you can see, the groves here have a unique microclimate provided by the brooding volcano of Etna. Warm days and cool nights allow us to produce what we feel are the best blood oranges in the world."

"You ought to be the one on the video, Val. I can hear your love of this island in your voice."

"Yet anyone will tell you a beautiful woman is much more exciting to look at."

Not from her vantage point. Valentino was drop-dead gorgeous. Abby had said as much about Michelina's older brother before Carolena had ever even seen a picture of him.

Several of the security men went on ahead to bring the grove owner to her and Valentino. The man and his son were delighted to be interviewed and would have talked for hours. No problem for them to be part of the video.

After saying goodbye, they drove on to the next orange grove, then the next, stopping for a midafternoon lunch brought from the palace kitchen. Six stops later they'd reached the eastern end of the island. Already it was evening. They'd been so busy, she hadn't realized how much time had passed.

Carolena gave him a covert glance. "There wasn't one farmer who didn't want to be a part of your plan to keep people on the farms and grow more profits."

He sat back in the seat looking relaxed, with his arms stretched out on either side of him. "You charmed everyone. Being a farmer's daughter and granddaughter got them to open right up and express their concerns. I marveled at the way you were able to answer their questions and give them the vision of what we're trying to do."

"I had a script. You didn't. Give yourself the credit you deserve, Val. They fell over themselves with joy to think their prince cares enough about the farmers to honor them with a personal visit. Securing their future secures the entire country and they know it."

"I believe Vincenzo and I are onto something, Carolena, and you're going to be the person who puts this marketing strategy over. After a hard day's work, this calls for a relaxing dinner. I've told the driver to take us to a restaurant here on the water where we can be private and enjoy ourselves. I called ahead to place our order."

This was the part she was worried about. "I think we should go back to the palace."

"You're worrying about my mother, but since she's been worrying about me since I turned sixteen, it's nothing new. I hope you're hungry. We're going to a spot where the *tunnacchiu 'nfurnatu* is out of this world. The tuna will have been caught within the last hour."

It was impossible to have a serious talk with Valentino right now. After they'd eaten, then she'd speak her mind.

The limo pulled down a narrow alley that led to the back entrance of the restaurant he'd been talking about. Valentino got out first and reached for her hand. He squeezed it and didn't let go as he led them to a door one of the security men opened for them.

Cupping her elbow, he walked her down a hallway to another door that opened on to a small terrace with round candlelit tables for two overlooking the water. But they were the only occupants. She shouldn't have come to this romantic place with him, but what could she do?

The air felt like velvet, bringing back memories of their night on the yacht. A profusion of yellow-and-orange bougainvillea provided an overhang Carolena found utterly enchanting.

He helped her to be seated, then caressed her shoulders. She gasped as his touch sent a white-hot message through her. "I've been wanting to feel you all day." Between the heat from his body, plus the twinkling lights on the water from the other boats, she sensed the fire building inside her.

"Benvenuto, Valentino!" An unfamiliar male voice broke the silence, surprising Carolena.

Valentino seemed reluctant to remove his hands. "Matteo Tancredi, meet my sister-in-law's best friend, Carolena Baretti. Carolena, Matteo is one of my best friends and the owner of this establishment."

"How do you do, *signor.*" She extended her hand, hoping his friend with the broad smile and overly long brown hair didn't notice the blush on her face.

"I'm doing very well now that Valentino is here. He told me he was coming with the new star of a video that is going to make Gemelli famous."

She shook her head. "Hardly, but we're all hoping this venture will be a success."

"Anything Valentino puts his mind to is certain to produce excellent results." She heard a nuance of deeper emotion in his response. Still staring at her, he said, "I'll bring some white wine that is perfect with the fish. Anything you want, just ask."

"Thank you."

The two men exchanged a private glance before Matteo disappeared from the terrace. Valentino sat down opposite her. A slight breeze caused the candle to flicker, drawing her attention to his striking features. She averted her eyes to stop making a feast of him.

"Where did you meet Matteo?"

"At the college in Catania."

"Is he married?"

"Not yet. He was studying geology when his father took ill and died. The family needed Matteo to keep this place running, so he had to leave school."

"Wasn't there anyone else to help?"

"His mother and his siblings, but his father always relied on Matteo and didn't like the idea of him going to college."

"Matteo's the eldest?"

"Yes."

"Like the way your father relied on you rather than your younger brother?"

He stared at her through shuttered eyes. "Yes, when you put it that way."

"I can see why. After watching you as you talked with the farmers today, I think you should be the one featured on the film, Val. You're a natural leader."

Before she could hear his response, Matteo brought them their dinner and poured the wine. "Enjoy your meal."

"I'm sure it's going to taste as good as it smells. I think I'm in heaven already," she told him.

"Put it in writing that you were in heaven after eating the meal, and I'll frame it to hang on the wall with the testimonials of other celebrities who've eaten here. But none of them will be as famous as you."

Gentle laughter fell from her lips. "Except for the prince, who is in a category by himself."

"Agreed."

"What category is that?" Valentino asked after Matteo had left them alone.

"Isn't it obvious?" She started eating, then drank some wine.

He picked at his food, which wasn't at all like him. "For one night can't you forget who I am?" Suddenly his mood had turned darker and she felt his tension.

Over the glass, she said, "No more than you can. We all have a destiny. I saw you in action today and am so impressed with your knowledge and caring, I can't put it into words. All I know is that you should be the one featured on the video, not me.

"There's an intelligence in you that would convince anyone of anything. First thing tomorrow, I'm flying back to Arancia while you get this video done on your own. Then your mother will have no more reason to be worried."

His brows furrowed in displeasure. "Much as she would like you to be gone, you can't do that."

"Why not?"

"Because you're under contract to Vincenzo and me." As if she could forget. "The economic future of our two countries is resting on our new plan of which you are now an integral part."

She fought for breath. "But once I've finished the other video session in Arancia, then my work will be done. Just so you understand, I'm leaving Gemelli tomorrow after the filming and won't be seeing you again."

"Which presents a problem for me since I never want you out of my sight. Not *ever*," he added in a husky whisper.

She couldn't stop her trembling. "Please don't say things like that to me. A relationship outside a royal engagement or marriage could only be a tawdry, scandalous affair, so why are you talking like this?"

"Because I'm obsessed with you," he claimed with primitive force. "If it's not love, then it's better than love. I've never been in love, but whatever this feeling is, it's not going away. In fact, it's getting worse, much worse. I'm already a changed man. Believe me, this is an entirely new experience for me."

Incredulous, she shook her head. "We hardly know each other."

"How long did it take you to fall in love with your fiancé?"

She let out a small cry. "How did you find out I had a fiancé?"

"Who else but Abby."

"I wish she hadn't said anything."

"You still haven't answered my question."

"Berto and I were friends on neighboring farms before we fell in love. It's not the same thing at all."

"Obviously not. At the swimming pool last week you and I experienced a phenomenon as strong as a pyroclastic eruption. It not only shook the ground beneath us *before* we were up on the volcano, it shook my entire world so much I don't know myself anymore."

"Please don't say that!" She half moaned the words in panic.

"Because you know it's true?" he retorted. "Even if you weren't the perfect person to do this video for us, I would have found another means to be with you. I've given you all the honesty in me. Now I want all your honesty back. Did you agree to do this video because you wanted to help and felt it was your duty because of your friendship with Abby? Or are you here because you couldn't stay away from me?"

She buried her face in her hands. "Don't ask me that."

"I have to. You and I met. It's a fact of life. Your answer is of vital importance to me because I don't want to make a mistake."

"What mistake? What on earth do you mean?"

"We'll discuss it on the way back to the palace. Would you care for dessert?"

"I—I couldn't." Her voice faltered.

"That makes two of us."

When Matteo appeared, they both thanked him for the delicious food. He followed them out to the limo where they said their goodbyes.

Once inside, Valentino sat across from her as they left the restaurant and headed back to the city. He leaned forward. "Tell me about your fiancé. How did he die?"

She swallowed hard. "I'd rather not get into it."

"We're going to have to." He wasn't about to let this go until he had answers.

"Th-there was an accident."

"Were you with him when it happened?"

Tears scalded her eyelids. "Yes."

"Is it still so painful you can't talk about it?"

"Yes."

"Because you made it happen."

"Yes," she whispered.

"In what way?"

Just remembering that awful day caused her lungs to freeze. "I was helping him with his farm chores and told him I would drive the almond harvester while he sat up by the yellow contraption. You know, the kind that opens into a big upside-down umbrella to catch all the almonds at once?"

"I do. More almonds can be harvested with fewer helpers."

She nodded. "He said for me to stay back at the house, but I insisted on driving because I wanted to help him. I'd driven our family's tractor and knew what to do. We'd get the work done a lot faster. Berto finally agreed. As we were crossing over a narrow bridge, I got too close to the wall and the tractor tipped. Though I jumped out in time, he was thrown into the stream below.

"The umbrella was so heavy, it trapped his face in six inches of water. He couldn't breathe—I couldn't get to him or move it and had to run for help. By the time his family came, it was too late. He'd…drowned."

In the next second Valentino joined her on the seat and pulled her into his arms.

"I'm so sorry, Carolena."

"It was my fault, Val. I killed him." She couldn't stop sobbing.

He rocked her for a long time. "Of course you didn't. It was an accident."

"But I shouldn't have insisted on driving him."

"Couldn't he have told you no?"

She finally lifted her head. Only then did he realize she'd soaked his polo shirt. "I made it too difficult for him. My grandmother told me I could be an impossible child at times."

Valentino chuckled and hugged her against his side. "It was a tragic accident, but never forget he wanted you with him because he loved you. Do you truly believe he would have expected you to go on suffering over it for years and years?"

"No," she whispered, "not when you put it that way."

"It's the only way to put it." His arms tightened around her. "Abby told me he was the great love of your life."

No. Abby was wrong. Berto had been her *first* love. Until his death she'd thought he'd be her only love. But the *great* love of her life, the one man forbidden to her, was holding her right now. She needed to keep that truth from him.

"As I told you before, I'll always love Berto. Forgive me for having broken down like that."

CHAPTER FIVE

VALENTINO KISSED HER hair. "I'm glad you did. Now there
are no more secrets between us." Before Carolena could
stop him, he rained kisses all the way to her mouth,
dying for his first taste of her. She turned her head away,
but he chased her around until he found the voluptuous
mouth he'd been aching for.

At first she resisted, but he increased the pressure
until her lips opened, as if she couldn't help herself.
He felt the ground shake beneath him as she began to
respond with a growing passion he'd known was there
once she allowed herself to let go.

Because they were outside the entrance and would
need to go in shortly, he couldn't do more than feast on
her luscious mouth. His lips roved over each feature,
her eyelids, the satin skin of her throat, then came back
to that mouth, giving him a kind of pleasure he'd never
known before.

They kept finding new ways to satisfy their burning
longing for each other until he didn't know if it was his
moan or hers resounding in the limo. *"Carolena—"* he
cried in a husky voice. "I want you so badly I'm in pain."

"So am I." She pulled as far away from him as she could. "But this can't go on. It should never have happened. Have you told Vincenzo about me?"

"No."

"I'm thankful for that. After being on the yacht with you, I suppose this was inevitable. Maybe it's just as well we've gotten this out of our system now."

He buried his face in her neck. "I have news for you, *bellissima*. You don't get this kind of fire out of your system. It burns hotter and hotter without cessation. Now that I know how you feel about me, we need to have a serious talk about whether I get married or not."

Her body started to tremble. *"What did you say?"*

"You heard me. I made a vow to myself and my mother there'd be no more women, and I meant it. So what just happened between us means an earthshaking development has taken place we have to dea—"

"Your Highness?" a voice spoke over the mic, interrupting him. "We've arrived."

Carolena let out a gasp. "I can't get out yet. I can't let the staff see me like this—"

He smiled. "There's no way to hide the fact that you've been thoroughly kissed. How can I help?"

"Hand me my bag so I can at least put on some lipstick."

"You have a becoming rash, all my fault."

She groaned. "I can feel it. I'll have to put on some powder."

"Your bag and your hat, *signorina*. Anything else?"

"Don't come near me again."

"I'm accompanying you to your apartment. Are you ready?"

"No." She sounded frantic. "You get out first. I'll follow in a minute."

"Take your time. We're not in a hurry." He pressed another hot kiss to her swollen lips before exiting the limo a man reborn. This had to be the way the captive slave felt emerging from his prison as Michelangelo chipped away the marble to free him.

In a minute she emerged and hurried inside the palace. Valentino trailed in her wake. He followed her into her apartment and shut the door. But he rested against it and folded his arms.

"Now we can talk about us in total privacy."

She whirled around to face him. "There *is* no us, Val. If you were a mere man engaged to a woman you didn't love, you could always break your engagement in order to be with a person you truly care about. In fact, it would be the moral thing to do for both your sakes."

"I hear a but," he interjected. "You were about to say that since I'm a prince, I can't break an engagement because it would be immoral. Is that what you're saying?"

A gasp escaped her lips. "A royal engagement following a royal betrothal between two families who've been involved for years is hardly the same thing."

"Royal or not, an engagement is an engagement. It's a time to make certain that the impending marriage will bring fulfillment. My sister hoped with all her heart the marriage to Vincenzo would bring about that magic because she loved him, but he wasn't in love with her and it never happened."

"I know. We've been over this before," Carolena said in a quiet voice. "But you made a vow to yourself and your family after your uncle Stefano's death. I agreed to come to Gemelli in order to help you and Vincenzo. I—I rationalized to myself that our intense attraction couldn't go anywhere. Not with your wedding dawning.

"But now for you to be willing to break your engagement to be with me is absolutely terrifying. You've helped me to get over my guilt for Berto's death, but I refuse to be responsible for your breakup with Princess Alexandra. You made a promise —".

"That's true. I promised to fulfill my royal duty. But that doesn't mean I have to marry Alexandra. After what you and I shared a few minutes ago, I need more time. Day after tomorrow parliament convenes. You and I have forty-eight hours before my wedding is officially announced to the media. *Or not.*"

If he was saying what she thought he was saying…

"You're scaring me, Val!"

"That's good. On the yacht you had the power to keep me from your bed, which you ultimately did. Your decision stopped us from taking the next step. But tonight everything changed.

"Whatever your answer is now, it will have eternal consequences for both of us because you know we're on fire for each other in every sense of the word. Otherwise you would never have met with me and Vincenzo to discuss our project in the first place. Admit it."

She couldn't take any more. "You're putting an enormous burden on me—"

"Now you know how *I* feel."

"I can't give you an answer. You're going to be king in seven weeks!"

"That's the whole point of this conversation. There'll be no coronation without a marriage. I'll need your answer by tomorrow night after the taping here is finished. Once parliament opens its session the next morning and the date for my wedding is announced, it will be too late for us."

Carolena was in agony. "That's not fair!"

His features hardened. "Since when was love ever fair? I thought you found that out when your fiancé died. I learned it when my sister died before she could hold her own baby."

Tears ran down her cheeks once more. "I can't think right now."

"By tomorrow evening you're going to have to! Until then we'll set this aside and concentrate on our mission to put Gemelli and Arancia on the world map agriculturally."

"How can we possibly do that? You've done a lot more than proposition me. I can hardly take it in."

"That's why I'm giving you all night to think about it. I want a relationship with you, Carolena. I'm willing to break my long-standing engagement to Princess Alexandra in order to be with you. In the end she'll thank me for it. Gemelli doesn't need a king yet."

"You can't mean it!"

"Had I not told you of my engagement, we would have spent that night on the yacht together. But the fact that I *did* tell you proved how important you were to me. I realized I wanted much more from you than one night of passion beneath the stars. Sleeping together to slake our desire could never be the same thing as having a full relationship."

His logic made so much sense she was in utter turmoil.

"However, there is one thing I need to know up front. If your love for Berto is too all consuming and he's the one standing in the way of letting me into your life, just tell me the truth right now. If the answer is yes, then I swear that once this video is made, I'll see you off on the jet tomorrow night and our paths will never cross again."

She knew Valentino meant what he said with every fiber of his being. He'd been so honest with her, it hurt. If she told him anything less she'd be a hypocrite.

"I would never have wanted to sleep with you if I hadn't already put Berto away in my heart."

"That's what I thought," he murmured in satisfaction.

"But when you speak of a relationship, we're talking long-distance. With you up on the volcano while I'm in court in a different country... How long could it last before you're forced to give me up and find a royal bride in order to be king? Your mother would despise me. Abby would never approve, nor would Vincenzo. The pressure would build until I couldn't stand the shame of it."

His eyes became slits. "Do you love me? That's all I want to know."

Carolena loved him, all right. But when he ended it—and he'd be the one to do it—she'd want to die. "Love isn't everything, Val."

"That's not what I wanted to hear, Carolena."

"I thought you gave me until tomorrow evening for my answer."

"I made you a promise and I'll keep it. Now it's getting late. I'll say good-night here and see you at eight in the morning in this very spot. *Buona notte,* Carolena."

Valentino was headed for his suite in the palace when his brother came out of the shadows at the top of the stairs wearing jeans and a sport shirt instead of his uniform. "Vito? What are you doing here? I didn't know you were coming!"

They gave each other a hug. "I've been waiting for you."

Together they entered his apartment. "I take it you've been with mother."

"*Sí.* She phoned me last week and asked me to come ASAP." Valentino had a strong hunch why she'd sent for her second son. "I arranged for my furlough early and got here this afternoon."

"It's good to see you." They sat down in the chairs placed around the coffee table. "How long will you be here?"

"Long enough for me to find out why our mother is so worried about you. Why don't you tell me about the woman you took up on the volcano last week before you spent part of the night dancing with her on the yacht. And all this happening *after* you'd set the date for your marriage to Alexandra."

Valentino couldn't stay seated and got out of the chair. "Do you want a beer?"

"Sure."

He went in the kitchen and pulled two bottles out of the fridge. After they'd both taken a few swallows, Vito said, "I'm waiting."

"I'm aware of that. My problem is finding a way to tell you something that's going to shock the daylights out of you."

With a teasing smile, Vito sat back in the chair and put his feet up on the coffee table. "You mean that at the midnight hour, you suddenly came upon the woman of your dreams."

Valentino couldn't laugh about this. "It was evening, actually. I'd just come from the helicopter. Carolena was in the swimming pool ready to take a dive."

"Aphrodite in the flesh."

"Better. Much better." The vision of her in that bathing suit never left him. He finished off the rest of his beer and put the empty bottle on the table.

"Abby's best friend, I understand. Did I hear mother right? She's helping you and Vincenzo with a marketing video?"

He took a deep breath. "Correct." Valentino explained the project to his brother.

"I'm impressed with your idea, but you still haven't answered my question." Vito sat forward. "What is this woman to you? If word gets back to Alexandra about your dining and dancing with her on the yacht, you could hurt her a great deal."

Valentino stared hard at his brother, surprised at the extent of the caring he heard in his voice. "For the first time in my life I'm in love, Vito."

"You?"

He nodded solemnly. "I mean irrevocably in love."

The news robbed his brother of speech.

"I can't marry Alexandra. There'll be no wedding or coronation in August, no announcement to Parliament."

Color left Vito's face before he put his bottle down and got to his feet. He was visibly shaken by the news.

"Until I met Carolena, I deluded myself into thinking Alexandra and I could make our marriage work by having children. Now I realize our wedding will only doom us both to a life of sheer unhappiness. I don't love her and she doesn't love me the way Michelina loved Vincenzo.

"Despite what our parents wanted and planned for, *I* don't want that kind of marriage for either of us. Tomorrow evening I'm planning to fly to Cyprus and break our engagement. The news will set her free. Hopefully she'll find a man she can really love, even if it causes a convulsion within our families."

Somehow he expected to see and hear outrage from his brother, but Vito did neither. He simply eyed him with an enigmatic expression. "You won't have to fly there. Mother has invited her here for dinner tomorrow evening."

His brows lifted. "That doesn't surprise me. Under the circumstances, I'm glad she'll be here. After I see Carolena off on her flight back to Arancia, I'll be able to concentrate on Alexandra."

"What are you planning to do with Carolena? You can't marry her, and Mother doesn't want to rule any longer."

Valentino cocked his head. "I'm not the only son.

You're second in line. All you'd have to do is resign your commission in the military and get married to Princess Regina. Mother would step down so you could rule. As long as one of us is willing, she'll be happy."

"Be serious," he snapped. "I'm not in love with Regina."

His quick-fire response led Valentino to believe his brother was in love with someone else. "Who is she, Vito?"

"What do you mean?"

"The woman you *do* love." His brother averted his eyes, telling Valentino he'd been right about him.

"Falling in love has totally changed you, Val."

"It has awakened me to what's really important. Carolena makes me feel truly alive for the first time in my life!"

Vito shook his head in disbelief "When am I going to meet her?"

"The next time I can arrange it."

"When will you tell Mother you're breaking your engagement?"

"After I've talked to Alexandra and we've spoken to her parents. Will you meet the princes at the plane for me? Carolena and I will be finishing up the filming about that time You'd be doing me a huge favor."

His brother blinked like someone in a state of shock. "If that's what you want." When he reached the door to leave, he glanced around. "Val? Once you've broken with Alexandra, you can't go back."

"I never wanted the marriage and have been putting it off for years. She hasn't pushed for it, either. We're both aware it was the dream of both sets of parents. I've always liked her. She's a lovely, charming woman who deserves to be loved by the right man. But I'm not that man."

After a silence, "I believe you," he said with puzzling soberness.

"A domani, Vito."

The film crew followed behind the limo as they came to the last orange grove. Carolena looked at the script one more time as the car pulled to a stop, but the words swam before her eyes. The hourglass was emptying. Once this segment of the taping was over, Valentino expected an answer from her.

Though he hadn't spoken of it all day, the tension had been building until she felt at the breaking point. She couldn't blame the hot sun for her body temperature. Since last night she'd been feverish and it was growing worse.

After reaching for her grandmother's sun hat, she got out of the limo and started walking down a row of orange trees where the photographer had set up this scene with the owner of the farm and his wife.

Her braid swung with every step in her walking boots. She felt Valentino's eyes following her. He watched as one of the crew touched up her makeup one more time before putting the hat on her head at just the right angle. She'd worn jeans and a khaki blouse with pockets. Casual yet professional.

Once ready, the filming began. Toward the end of the final segment, she held up a fresh orange to the camera. "Eating or drinking, the blood orange with the AG stamp brings the world its benefits from nature's hallowed spot found nowhere else on earth." She let go with a full-bodied smile. "*Salute* from divine Gemelli."

Valentino's intense gaze locked onto hers. *"Salute,"* he murmured after the tape stopped rolling and they started walking toward the limo. "The part you added at the end wasn't in the script."

Her heart thudded unmercifully. "Do you want to redo it?"

"Anything but. I've always considered Gemelli to be 'nature's hallowed spot.' You could have been reading my mind."

"It's hard not to. As I've told you before, you show a rare reverence for the island and its people."

As he opened the limo door for her, the rays of the late-afternoon sun glinted in his dark blond hair. "Your performance today was even more superb than I had hoped for. If this video doesn't put our message across, then nothing else possibly could. I'm indebted to you, Carolena. When Vincenzo sees the tape, he'll be elated and anxious for the filming to start in the lemon groves of Arancia."

"Thank you." She looked away from him and got in the limo, taking pains not to brush against him. Once he climbed inside and sat down opposite her, she said, "If we're through here, I need to get back to the palace."

"All in good time. We need dinner first. Matteo has not only lent us his boat, he has prepared a picnic for us to eat on board. We'll talk and eat while I drive us back." Despite having dinner plans that night, Val decided spending time with Carolena on her last night was too important to miss. He would make arrangements to see Princess Alexandra at the palace afterward.

Carolena had this fluttery feeling in her chest all the way to the shore, where they got out and walked along the dock to a small cruiser tied up outside the restaurant. There would be no crew spying on them here. His security people would be watching them from other boats so they could be strictly alone.

Throughout the night Carolena had gone back and forth fighting the battle waging inside her. By morning she knew what her answer would be. But right now she was scared to death because he had a power over her that made her mindless and witless.

While Valentino helped her on board and handed her a life jacket to put on, Matteo appeared and greeted them. The two men chatted for a minute before Val's friend untied the ropes and gave them a push off. Carolena sat on a bench while Valentino stood at the wheel in cargo pants and a pale green sport shirt.

After they idled out beyond the buoys, he headed into open calm water. Having grown up on an island, he handled the boat with the same expertise he exhibited in anything he did.

She saw a dozen sailboats and a ferry in the far distance. High summer in the Mediterranean brought the tourists in droves. Closer to them she glimpsed a few small fishing boats. Most likely they were manned by Valentino's security people.

When they'd traveled a few miles, he turned to her.

"If you'll open that cooler, I'll stop the engine while we eat."

Carolena did his bidding. "Your friend has made us a fabulous meal!" Sandwiches, salad, fruit and drinks. Everything they needed had been provided. Because of nerves, she hadn't been hungrier earlier, but now she was starving. By the way his food disappeared, Valentino was famished, too.

When they couldn't eat another bite, she cleaned things up and closed the lid. "Please tell Matteo the food was wonderful!" She planned to send him a letter and thank him.

Valentino took his seat at the wheel, but he didn't start the engine or acknowledge what she'd said. "Before we get back, I want an answer. Do I call off the engagement so you and I can be together without hurting anyone else? I haven't touched you on purpose because once I do, I won't be able to stop."

The blood pounded in her ears. She jumped to her feet and clung to the side of the boat. The sun had dropped below the horizon, yet it was still light enough to see the smoke from Etna. Everywhere she looked, the very air she breathed reminded her of Valentino. He'd changed her life and she would never be the same again.

But her fear of being responsible for someone else wasn't the only thing preventing her being able to answer him the way he wanted. Already she recognized that if she got too close to him, the loss she would feel when she had to give him up would be unbearable. To be intimate with him would mean letting him into her heart. She couldn't risk that kind of pain when their affair ended. An affair was all there could ever be for them.

If she left Gemelli first thing in the morning and never saw him again, she'd never forget him, but she'd convinced herself that by not making love with him, she could go on living.

"It's apparent the answer is no."

His voice sounded wooden, devoid of life. It cut her to the quick because she knew that by her silence she'd just written her own death sentence.

Slowly she turned around to face him. His features looked chiseled in the semidarkness. "I saw the light in every farmer's eyes when they talked with you. They were seeing their future king. Putting off your wedding and coronation to be with me won't change your ultimate destiny.

"But you were right about us. What we felt at the pool was like a pyroclastic eruption. They don't come along very often. I read that there are about five hundred active volcanoes on earth, and fifteen hundred over the last ten thousand years. That's not very many when you consider the span of time and the size of our planet. You and I experienced a rare phenomenon and it was wonderful while it lasted, but thank heaven it blew itself out before we were consumed by its fire. No one has been hurt."

"No one?" The grating question fell from the white line of his lips. She watched his chest rise and fall visibly before he made a move to start the engine.

In agony, Carolena turned and clung to the side of

the boat until he pulled into a dock on palatial property some time later.

A few of his staff were there to tie it up. After she removed her life jacket, Valentino helped her off the boat and walked her across the grounds to her apartment. By the time they reached her door, her heart was stuck in her throat, making her feel faint.

"I'm indebted to you for your service, Carolena. Tomorrow my assistant will accompany you to the helicopter at seven-thirty. He'll bring your grandmother's hat with him. Your jet will leave at eight-fifteen from the airport."

Talk about pain...

"Thank you for everything." She could hardly get the words out.

His hooded blue eyes traveled over her, but he didn't touch her. *"Buon viaggio, bellissima."*

When he strode away on those long, powerful legs, she wanted to run after him and tell him she'd do anything to be with him for as long as time allowed them. But it was already too late. He'd disappeared around a corner and could be anywhere in the palace by now.

You had your chance, Carolena. Now it's gone forever.

CHAPTER SIX

"ABBY?"

"Carolena—thank heaven you called! Where are you?"

"I'm back at the office."

"You're kidding—"

"No." Carolena frowned in puzzlement.

"I thought you'd be in Gemelli longer."

"There was no need. I finished up the video taping last evening. I'm pleased to say it went very well. This morning I left the country at eight-fifteen. When the jet landed in Arancia, I took a taxi to my apartment and changed clothes before coming to the firm. It's amazing how much work can pile up in a—"

"Carolena—" Abby interrupted her, which wasn't like her.

She blinked. "What's wrong?"

"You don't know?" Her friend sounded anxious.

"Know what?" She got a strange feeling in the pit of her stomach.

"Vincenzo's source from Gemelli told him that the queen opened parliament this morning without Valentino being there and no announcement was made about his forthcoming marriage. Parliament only convenes four times a year for a week, so the opportunity has been missed."

Carolena came close to dropping her cell phone.

"When you were with him, did he tell you anything? Do you have any idea what has happened?"

"None at all." It was the truth. Carolena could say that with a clear conscience. "When the taping was over last evening, we returned to the palace with the camera crew and I went straight to bed once I got back to my apartment."

She had no clue where Valentino had gone or what he'd done after he'd disappeared down the hall. But if he had been in as much turmoil as Carolena... She started to feel sick inside. "This morning I had breakfast in my room, then his assistant took me to the helicopter at seven-thirty and wished me a good flight. I know nothing."

"It's so strange. Vincenzo has tried to get through to him on his cell phone, but he's not taking calls. Something is wrong."

"Maybe he decided to announce it at the closing."

"I said the same thing to my husband, but he explained it didn't work that way. Any important news affecting the country is fed to the media early on the first day for dissemination."

"Maybe Valentino and the princess decided to postpone their wedding for reasons no one knows about. From what I've seen of him, he's a very private person."

"You're right, but over the last year he and Vincenzo

have grown close. My husband is worried about him. Frankly, so am I."

That made three of them.

Carolena gripped the phone tighter. She'd told Valentino a relationship with him wouldn't work, so if he'd decided to call off the wedding, then he did it for reasons that had nothing to do with her. She refused to feel guilty about it, but she'd grown weak as a kitten and was glad she was sitting down.

"I'm sure he'll get back to Vincenzo as soon as he can. Do you think it's possible there was some kind of emergency that required his presence at the volcanology lab in Catania?"

"I hadn't even thought of that. I'll ask Vincenzo what he thinks."

For all Carolena knew, Val had returned the boat to Matteo where he could confide in his friend in private before parliament opened. But like Vincenzo, she was getting more anxious by the minute.

"Did I tell you Valentino had a copy made of the video? His assistant brought it to me. I've got it right here and will courier it to the palace so you and Vincenzo can see what you think."

"I have a better idea. Come to the palace when you're through with work. We'll have a light supper and watch it. Maybe by then Vincenzo will have heard from him. I take it you haven't seen the video yet."

"No, and I have to tell you I'm nervous."

"Nonsense. I'll send the limo for you at five o'clock. Max will be excited to see you."

"That little darling. I can't wait to hold him." The

baby would be the distraction she needed. But until quitting time, she had a stack of files to work through.

"*Ciao,* Abby."

Three hours later Abby greeted her at the door of their living room, carrying Max in her arms. His blue sunsuit with a dolphin on the front looked adorable on him. "If you'll take the video, I'll tend him for a while." Then, to the little boy, "You remember me, don't you?"

She kissed one cheek then the other, back and forth until he was laughing without taking a breath. "Oh, you precious little thing. I can tell you're all better."

In a few minutes Vincenzo joined them. The second Max saw him, he lunged for his daddy. Their son was hilarious as he tried to climb on everything and clutched at anything he could get his hands on.

After they ate dinner in the dining room, Abby put the baby to bed and then they went back to the living room to watch the video. The whole time her hosts praised the film, Carolena's thoughts were on Valentino, who'd been standing next to the cameraman watching her.

Where was he right now? Enough time had gone by for her anxiety level to be off the charts.

When the film was over, Vincenzo got to his feet and smiled at her. "It's outstanding from every aspect, but *you* made it come alive, Carolena."

"It's true!" Abby chimed in.

"Thank you. I enjoyed doing it. The farmers were so thrilled to meet Valentino in person and listen to his ideas, it was really something to watch."

"Tomorrow we'll drive to the lemon groves to set up appointments."

Abby hugged her. "You were fabulous, Carolena! That hat of your grandmother's was perfect on you. I'm sorry she's not alive to see you wearing it."

Carolena would have responded, but Vincenzo's cell phone rang, putting a stop to their conversation. He checked the caller ID, then glanced at them. "It's Valentino. I'll take it in the bedroom." With those words Carolena's heart fluttered like a hummingbird's wings.

Abby let out a relieved sigh. "Finally we'll learn what's going on. If he hadn't called, I was afraid my husband would end up pacing the floor all night. He worries about Queen Bianca, who's had her heart set on this marriage. She really likes Alexandra."

Every time Abby said something, it was like another painful jab of a needle, reminding Carolena of the grave mistake she could have made if she'd said yes to Valentino. Last night had been excruciating. Several times she'd let down her resolve and had been tempted to reach for the phone. The palace operator would put her call through to Valentino. And then what? She shivered. Beg him to come to her room so they could talk?

When she thought she couldn't stand the suspense a second longer, Vincenzo walked into the living room. For want of a better word, he looked stunned. Abby jumped up from the couch and ran over to him. "What's happened, darling?"

He put his arm around her shoulders. "He and Alexandra have called off their marriage."

Valentino had actually done it?

"Oh, no—" Abby cried softly.

"Valentino has spoken with the queen and Alexandra's parents. It's final. He told me he doesn't want to be married unless it's to a woman he's in love with." Carolena felt Vincenzo's searching gaze on her, causing her knees to go weak. Had Valentino confided in him about her?

"Michelina always worried about him," Abby whispered.

Vincenzo looked at his wife. "Evidently, Alexandra feels the same way, so in that regard they're both in better shape than their parents, who've wanted this match for years. He says that after sixteen years of being betrothed, he feels like he's been let out of prison. I'm one person who can relate to everything he said."

Abby hugged him tightly.

"But there's a big problem. Bianca doesn't want to continue ruling, so it will be up to parliament if they'll allow Valentino to become king without a wife. It's never been done, so I doubt it will happen."

"Where's Valentino now?"

"Since Vito is home on leave from the military and wants to spend time with their mother, Valentino is planning to fly here in the morning and finish up our project with Carolena."

The news was too much. Carolena sank into the nearest chair while she tried to take it all in.

"I told him we watched the video and have a few ideas. Apparently he's seen it several times, too, and has some suggestions of his own. We'll ask the nurse to tend Max so the four of us can make a day of it."

By now Carolena's stomach was in such upheaval, she was afraid she was going to be sick. "In that case, I need to leave and study the script we wrote for the filming here before I go to bed. Thanks for dinner. I'll see you tomorrow."

Abby walked her to the door. "I'll phone you in the morning to let you know what time the limo will come for you. It all depends on Valentino." She stared at Carolena. "He's fortunate that Alexandra wasn't in love with him. If Michelina hadn't loved Vincenzo so much, he—"

"I know," Carolena broke in. "But their two situations weren't the same and your husband is an honorable man." What had happened to Valentino's promise to not fail his parents like his uncle Stefano had done?

Abby's eyes misted over. "So is Valentino. Rather than put himself and Alexandra through purgatory, he had the courage to go with his heart. I admire him for that. The volcanologist in him must be responsible for going where others fear to tread. With that quality he'll make an extraordinary king one day when the time is right."

But he wouldn't, not if he followed in his uncle's footsteps.

With those words, Carolena felt her grandmother's warning settle on her like the ash from Mount Etna.

"See you tomorrow, Abby." They hugged.

"There's a limo waiting for you at the front entrance, but before you go, I have to tell you I've never seen you looking more beautiful than you did in that video. There was an aura about you the camera captured, as if you were filled with happiness. Do you know you literally glowed? The sadness you've carried for years seems to have vanished."

It was truth time. "If you're talking about Berto, then you're right. The trip to Gemelli has helped me put the past into perspective. I thank you for that. *Buona notte,* dear friend."

Valentino's jet landed at the Arancia airport the next morning at 7:00 a.m. He told the limo driver waiting for him to drive straight to Carolena's condo building.

At quarter to eight they pulled around the back. He'd arrived here fifteen minutes early on purpose and would get inside through the freight entrance. Abby had told her they'd come for her at 8:00 a.m., but Valentino told Abby he'd pick up Carolena on the way from the airport to save time. They could all meet at the first lemon grove on the outskirts of Arancia at nine.

One of his security people went ahead to show him the way. Though she planned to be outside waiting, he wanted the element of surprise on his side by showing up at her door ahead of time.

The knowledge that he was free to be with her set off an adrenaline rush like nothing he'd ever known. He rounded the corner on the second floor and rapped on the door. A few seconds later he heard her voice. "Who's there?"

Valentino sucked in his breath. "Open the door and find out."

After a silence, *"Your Highness?"* It came out more like a squeak.

"No. My name is Val."

Another silence. "It *is* you."

The shock in her voice made him smile. "I'm glad you remembered."

"Of course I remembered!" she snapped. That sounded like the woman he'd first met. "You shouldn't have come to my condo."

"Why not? Circumstances have changed."

"They haven't where I'm concerned." Her voice shook.

"That's too bad because the pyroclastic eruption you thought had blown itself out was merely a hiccup compared to what's happening now."

"I can't do this."

"Neither of us has a choice."

"Don't say that—"

"Are you going to let me in, or do I have to beg?"

"I—I'm not ready yet," she stammered.

"I've seen you in a bathrobe before." The sight of her had taken his breath.

"Not this time!"

The door opened, revealing a fully dressed woman in a peasant-style white blouse and jeans. Her long sable hair, freshly shampooed, framed a beautiful face filled with color. With those green eyes, she was a glorious sight anytime. "Please come in. I need to braid my hair, but it will only take me a minute." She darted away.

He shut the door. "I'd rather you left it long for me," he called after her before moving through the small entrance hall to her living room. It had a cozy, comfortable feel with furnishings that must have belonged to her family. Lots of color in the fabric. Through the French doors he glimpsed a book-lined study with a desk and computer.

"I'm afraid it will get too messy."

Valentino had expected that response and wandered around the room. There was a statue on an end table that caught his eye. On close examination it turned out to be a reproduction of Rodin's *The Secret*. The sculpture of two white marble hands embracing could have described both the evocative and emotive nature of his experience with Carolena.

He found it fascinating she would have chosen this particular piece. There was an intimacy about it that spoke to the male in him. She was a woman of fire. He'd sensed it from the beginning and wanted to feel it surround him.

Next, he saw some photographs of her with a man in his early twenties, their arms around each other. This had to be Berto. They looked happy. The loss would have been horrendous in the beginning.

On one of the walls was a large framed photograph of a farmhouse. No doubt it was the one she wanted to buy back one day. His gaze dropped to the table below it, where he was able to look at her pictures comprising several generations.

"I'm ready."

He picked up one of them. "Your parents?" He showed the photo to her.

"Yes."

"There's a strong resemblance to your mother. She was beautiful."

"I agree," she said in a thick-toned voice.

"What happened to them?"

Her eyes filmed over. "Mother could never have another child after me and died of cervical cancer. A few years later my father got an infection that turned septic and he passed away, so my grandparents took over raising me. Later on, my grandfather died of pneumonia. He worked so hard, he just wore out. Then it was just my grandmother and me."

He put the picture down and slid his hands to her shoulders. "You've had too much tragedy in your young life."

Her eyes, a solemn green, lifted to his. "So have you. Grandparents, an uncle, a sister and a father gone, plus a kingdom that needs you and will drain everything out of you…"

Valentino kissed her moist eyelids. "You're a survivor, Carolena, with many gifts. I can't tell you how much I admire you."

"Thank you. The feeling is mutual, but you already know that." She'd confined her hair in a braid, which brought out the classic mold of her features.

"I came early so we could talk before we meet Vincenzo and Abby."

He could feel her tension as she shook her head and eased away from him. "Even though you've broken your engagement to Princess Alexandra, which is a good thing considering you don't love her, what you've done changes nothing for me. I don't want an affair with you,

Val. That's all it would be until you have to marry. After your uncle's death, you made that promise to yourself and your parents, remember?"

"Of course." He put his hands on his hips. "But I want to know about you. What do *you* want?"

The grandfather clock chimed on the quarter past. "It's getting late." She walked to the entrance hall.

Valentino followed her. "I asked you a question."

She reached for her straw bag on the credenza. "I want to finish this taping and get back to my law practice."

He planted himself in front of the door so she couldn't open it. "Forget I'm a prince."

Her jaw hardened. "That's the third time you've said that to me."

"What would you want if I weren't a prince? Humor me, Carolena."

He heard her take a struggling breath. "The guarantee of joy in an everlasting marriage with no losses, no pain."

That was her past grief talking. "As your life has already proved to you, there is no such guarantee."

Her eyes narrowed on him. "You *did* ask."

"Then let me add that you have to grab at happiness where you find it and pray to hold on to it for as long as possible."

"We can't. You're a prince, which excludes us from taking what we want. Even if you weren't a prince, I wouldn't grab at it."

His face looked like thunder. "Why not?"

"It—it's not important."

"The hell it isn't."

"Val—we need to get going or Abby and Vincenzo will start to worry."

"The limo is out in the back, but this conversation isn't over yet." He turned and opened the door. After their stops at the various farms, they would have all night tonight and tomorrow night to be together, not to mention the rest of their lives. "I brought your hat with me, by the way."

"Thank you. I would hate to have lost it."

He escorted her out to the limo. With the picture of the marble statue still fresh in his mind, he reached for her hand when they climbed into the car. He held on to it even though he sat across from her. The pulse at her wrist was throbbing.

"Was the Rodin statue a gift from Berto?"

"No. I found it in a little shop near the Chapelle Matisse in Vence, France, with my grandmother. I was just a teenager and we'd gone to France for the weekend. She didn't care for the sculpture, but I loved it and bought it with my spending money. I don't quite know why I was so taken with it."

"I found it extraordinary myself. It reminded me of us. Two would-be lovers with a secret. With only their hands, Rodin's genius brought out their passion." He pressed a kiss to the palm of hers before letting it go.

"I don't like secrets."

"Nor I, but you're being secretive right now."

"Now isn't the time for serious conversation."

"There'll be time later. Vincenzo has planned our itinerary. The farmer at the first grove speaks Mentonasc, so Abby is going to be our translator. She won't want to be in the video, but when we start taping tomorrow, Vincenzo and I are depending on you to get her in it. A blonde and a brunette, both beauties, will provide invaluable appeal."

"You're terrible," she said, but he heard her chuckle. Some genuine emotion at last.

"Matteo told me about the special bottle of Limoncello you express mailed to him from Arancia to thank him for the picnic. The man was very touched, especially by your signature on the label with the five stars next to it."

"You have a wonderful friend in him."

"He has put it up on the shelf behind the counter where all the customers will see it. When your video is famous, he will brag about it. Before we got off the phone he asked me to thank you."

"That was very nice of him." Before long they arrived at the first lemon grove. "It looks like we've arrived."

"Saved by the bell," he murmured.

Praying the others wouldn't look too closely at her, Carolena got out of the limo. It was a good thing the filming wouldn't be until tomorrow. If she'd had to deal with the crew's makeup man, he would know she felt ill after making her exit speech to Valentino.

To her relief, Abby was already talking to the farmer and his two sons. Being fluent in four languages made her a tremendous asset anytime, but Carolena could tell this farming family was impressed that Prince Vincenzo's wife could speak Mentonasc.

He introduced everyone. She could tell the family was almost overcome in the presence of two princes, but Abby had a way of making them feel comfortable while she put her points across. Before long, the four of them left to move on to the next grove. Carolena would have stayed with Abby, but Valentino cupped her elbow and guided her to their limo.

"We all need our privacy," he murmured against her ear after they got back in the car. He acted as though they'd never had that earlier conversation. Even though he sat across from her, being this close to him caused her to be a nervous wreck. His half smile made him so appealing, it was sinful.

"It's a good thing I'll be along tomorrow, too. The younger men couldn't take their eyes off of you. I'm going to have to guard you like a hawk."

In spite of how difficult it was to be alone with him, she said, "You're very good on a woman's ego."

"Then you can imagine the condition my ego is in to be the man in your life. In feudal times they'd have fought me for you, but they'd have ended up dying at the end of a sword."

"Stop—"

He leaned forward, mesmerizing her with those dark blue eyes. "I *am* the man in your life. The only man."

A shudder passed through her body. "I won't let you be in my life, and I can't be the woman in yours. When the taping is over, we won't be seeing each other again."

"Then you haven't read your contract carefully."

Her pulse raced in alarm. "I didn't sign a contract."

"You did better than that. You gave me and Vincenzo

your word. That's as good as an oath. Implicit in the contract is your agreement to deliver the videos and fly-ers with the AG logo to the fruit distributors around the country. We'll go together. It'll take at least a week. For-tunately my brother will be around to help my mother."

Aghast, she cried, "I can't be gone from the firm that long."

"Vincenzo already cleared it with Signor Faustino. Day after tomorrow we'll fly back to Gemelli to begin our tour. By then the tapes and flyers will be ready. I haven't had a vacation in two years and am looking forward to it."

She could see there was no stopping Valentino. Fear and exhilaration swept over her in alternating waves. "What about your work at the geophysics center?"

"I'm long overdue the time off. You're stuck with me. For security's sake, we'll sleep on the yacht at night and ferry across to the island by helicopter during the day. Don't worry. I won't come near you, not after you made your thoughts clear to me."

"You promise?"

He sat back. "I promise not to do anything you don't want me to do. It'll be all business until this is over."

"Thank you." She knew he would keep his promise. The only problem was keeping the promise to herself to keep distance between them.

"Our last stop tomorrow will be the Baretti farm. Judging from the photograph in your living room, the house has a lot of character."

"I loved it, but I don't want us to bother the new owners."

"We won't. You let us know when to stop and the cameraman will take some long shots while you talk about life on the farm growing up. When the film is spliced, we'll start the video with your visit. Will it be hard to see it again?"

Her heartbeat sped up. "I don't know."

"We don't have to do that segment if you decide against it."

"No. I'd like to do it as a tribute to my family." Emotion had clogged her throat.

"I'm glad you said that because I long to see the place where you grew up. I want to learn all about you. The first tree you fell out of, your first bee sting."

Valentino was so wonderful she could feel herself falling deeper and deeper under his spell. "I know about the putti but have yet to learn which staircase at the palace was your first slide. No doubt you spent hours in the Hall of Arms. A boy's paradise."

"Vito and I had our favorite suits of armor, but we put so many dents in them, they're hardly recognizable."

"I can't imagine anything so fun. My friends and I fought our wars in the tops of the trees throwing fruit at each other. The trouble we got into would fill a book. My grandmother would tell you I was the ringleader. And you were right. I did fall out of a tree several times."

His low chuckle warmed her all the way through and set the tone for the day. She had to admit it was heaven to be with him like this. Carolena needed to cherish every moment because the time they spent together would be coming to an end too soon.

Eight hours later when she was alone back at her condo, she called Abby's cell phone, desperate to talk about what was happening to her.

"Carolena?"

"Sorry to bother you." She took a deep breath. "Are you free?"

"Yes. The baby's asleep and I'm in the bedroom getting ready for bed. Vincenzo and Valentino are in the study talking business. Everything went so well today, they're both elated and will probably be up for another couple of hours. What's wrong?"

She bit her lip. "I'm in trouble."

"I *knew* it."

"What do you mean?"

"You and Valentino. Vincenzo and I watched you two that first night while we were having dinner when he couldn't take his eyes off you. You're in love."

No—

"My husband was certain of it when Valentino took you up on Mount Etna. You're the reason he called off his wedding."

"Don't say that, Abby! We haven't fallen in love. He's just infatuated. You know... forbidden fruit. It'll pass."

"He's enjoyed a lot of forbidden fruit over the years, but he never ended it with Alexandra until he met you."

"That's because he was with me the night his mother insisted on setting the wedding date. When confronted with the reality, it made him realize he can't marry a woman he doesn't love. *That* I understand. But it wasn't because of me. All I did was serve as the catalyst."

"Are you only infatuated, too?"

"What woman wouldn't be?" she cried in self-defense. "Unfortunately he's the first man since Berto to attract me, but I'll get over it."

After a pause. "Have you—"

"No!" she defended.

"Carolena, I was only going to ask if you two had talked over your feelings in any depth."

"Sorry I snapped. We've talked a little, but I'm afraid of getting too familiar with him." She'd come so close to making love with him.

"I've been there and know what you're going through. Let's face it. No woman could resist Valentino except a strong woman like you. He's temptation itself. So was Vincenzo. You'll never know how hard it was to stay away from him."

"Yes, I do. I lived through that entire experience with you. But my case is different. Please try to understand what I'm saying. Everything came together to lay the groundwork for the perfect storm because that's all it is. A perfect storm."

"Then what's the problem?"

"He wants me to fly down to Gemelli the day after tomorrow and spend a week distributing all the marketing materials with him. I—I can't do it, Abby."

"If you're not in love with him, then why can't you go? He has employed you to do a job for him."

"How can you of all people ask me that? Don't you remember after the baby was born? Your father hid you and was ready to fly you back to the States to get you away permanently from Vincenzo so there'd be no hint of scandal."

"But Vincenzo found me and proposed."

"Exactly. Your situation was unique from day one. Vincenzo was married to a princess before he married you. You carried his baby and the king made an exception in your case because he could see his son was in love with you. It's not the same thing at all with Valentino and me. He only *thinks* he's in love."

"So he's already gone so far as to tell you how you feels?"

She swallowed hard. "Like I said, I'm a new face, but certainly not the last one. Be honest, Abby. Though he never loved Alexandra, he'll have to find another royal to marry. In the meantime, if people see me with him, they'll link me with his broken betrothal and there really will be a scandal. I don't want to be known as the secret girlfriend who caused all the trouble."

Her statue of *The Secret* had taken on a whole new meaning since morning. She'd never look at it again without remembering the way he'd kissed her in the limo.

"What trouble? No one knows about you."

"No one except the entire palace staff, his best friend on the island, his colleagues at the volcanology institute in Catania *and* his mother. By the time we've traveled all around the island, the whole country will have seen us together. The queen doesn't want me back in Gemelli."

"Valentino loves her, but he makes his own decisions. If he wants you there, she can't stop him except to bring pressure to bear on you."

"What should I do?"

"I'm the last person to ask for advice."

"Do it anyway. I trust your judgment."

"Well, if I were in your shoes, I believe I'd give myself the week to honor my commitment to him. In that amount of time you'll either lose interest in each other or not. No one can predict the future, but while you're still under contract, do your part. Maybe it will help if you treat him like the brother you and I always wished we'd had."

A brother...

CHAPTER SEVEN

"VAL? SINCE WE'RE already on the eastern side of the island, why don't we stop for dinner at Matteo's restaurant before we fly back to the yacht." She wanted people around them and thought the suggestion pleased him.

"I'll call ahead and see what can be arranged."

Matteo looked happy to see them, but the place was busy and they could only chat for a moment with him. After another delicious dinner, she hurried out to the limo with Valentino, anxious to leave. They headed for the heliport on the eastern end of the island. Within a few minutes they were flying back to the yacht.

In three days they'd covered a lot of territory. He'd stuck to business while they'd dispensed the videos and flyers. When they were in the limo, he sat across from her and there was no touching beyond his helping her in and out of the car.

Each night she'd pleaded fatigue to keep her distance from him. To her surprise, he'd told her he, too, was tired and didn't try to detain her before she went to her cabin. Instead, he'd thanked her for a wonderful job and wished her a good night's sleep. She was a fool to wish that he wasn't quite so happy to see her go to bed.

The queen's spies would find no fault in him. His behavior abated Carolena's fears that the time they·were forced to spend together on this project would make her too uncomfortable. In truth, she discovered she was having fun doing business with him. He knew so much about the economics that ran his country, she marveled. With others or alone, they had fascinating conversations that covered everything including the political climate.

Valentino remained silent until they'd climbed out of the helicopter. "We need to talk. Let's do it in the lounge before you go to bed."

She walked across the deck with him. When they entered it, she sat down on one of the leather chairs surrounding a small table.

"Would you like a drink?"

"Nothing for me, thank you."

He stood near her, eyeing her with a sober expression. "What were you and Matteo talking about while I took that phone call from Vito?"

Carolena had known he'd ask that question. "He… wanted to know if you'd broken your engagement. I told him yes."

"What else did he say?"

She couldn't handle this inquisition any longer. "Nothing for you to worry about. He's not only a good friend to you, he's incredibly discreet." She looked away to avoid his piercing gaze. "He reminds me of Abby in the sense that I'd trust her with my life."

Valentino studied her until she felt like squirming.

"Do you feel the same about me? Would you trust me with your life?"

The question threw her. She got up from the chair. "I'm surprised you would ask that when you consider I went up on the volcano with you. I'll say good-night now." It was time to go to bed.

"I'd still like a more in-depth answer." The retort came back with enviable calm. "Tell me what you meant earlier when you said you wouldn't grab at happiness even if I weren't a prince?"

"Do I really have to spell it out for you?"

"I'm afraid you do." His voice grated.

She eyed him soberly. "I don't want to be in love again and then lose that person. I've been through it once and can't bear the thought of it. Call me a coward, but it's the way I'm made.

"Whatever you do with the rest of your life, I don't want to be a part of it. As I told you on the yacht the night I thought I would be sleeping with you, I'll never forget how you made me feel, but that's a happy memory I can live with and pull out on a rainy day.

"To have an affair now is something else again. I couldn't do it with you or any man because it would mean giving up part of myself. And when the affair was over, I wouldn't be able to stand the pain of loss because I know myself too well."

He rubbed the back of his neck. "Thank you for your answer. It's all making sense now. Just so you know, I'll be flying to the palace early in the morning."

She was afraid to ask him why, in case he felt she was prying.

"You can sleep in, though I don't know another female who needed her beauty sleep less than you. The steward will serve you breakfast whenever you want it."

"Thank you."

"After I return at ten, we'll do our tour of the south end of the island."

His comment relieved her of the worry that he wouldn't be gone long. Already she missed him, which was perfectly ridiculous.

"After work we'll take the cruiser to a nearby deserted island where we'll swim and watch the wildlife. It's a place where we ought to be able to see some nesting turtles. If it were fall we'd see the flamingos that migrate there on their way to and from Africa. You should see it before you fly back to Arancia."

"I can't wait."

"Neither can I. You'll love it. *A domani.*"

Valentino knocked on Vito's bedroom door early the next morning. His brother was quick to open it wearing a robe. He needed a shave and looked as if he hadn't had any sleep. "What was so urgent I needed to fly here this early?"

Dark shadows below Vito's eyes testified that his younger brother was in pain. "Thanks for getting here so fast. Come on in."

He'd never seen Vito this torn up, not even after Michelina's death. "I take it this isn't about Mother. What's wrong?" He moved inside and followed him into the living room.

Vito spun around, his face full of too many lines for

a thirty-year-old. "I have a confession to make. After you hear me out, I'll understand if you tell me to get the hell out of your life."

Valentino's brows furrowed. "I'd never do that."

"Oh, yes, you would. You will." He laughed angrily. "But I can't keep this to myself any longer." His dark brown eyes filled with tears. "Do you want to know the real reason I went into the military five years ago?"

"I thought it was because you wanted to, and because our father said you were free to do what you wanted."

He shook his dark head. Vito resembled their mother. "What I wanted was Alexandra."

A gasp came out of Valentino. Those words shook him to the foundations.

"I fell in love with her. I don't know how it happened. It just did."

Valentino knew exactly how it happened. He knew it line and verse.

"All the years you were betrothed, you were hardly ever around, and when you were, it was only for a day. Whereas I spent a lot of time with her. One night things got out of control and I told her how I felt about her. We went riding and she told me she was in love with me, too. We ended up spending the weekend together knowing we could never be together again."

"Vito—"

"You were betrothed to her, and the parents had another woman picked out for me, so I left to join the military with the intention of making it my career for as long as possible. I was a coward and couldn't face you, but I should have."

Pure unadulterated joy seized Valentino. He didn't need to hear another word. It suddenly made sense when he remembered his brother occasionally telling him things about Alexandra that surprised Valentino. It explained the huge relief he saw in Alexandra's eyes when he'd called off the marriage. But what he'd thought was relief was joy.

In the next breath he gave his brother the biggest bear hug of his life, lifting him off the ground. "You're more in love with her than ever, right?"

Vito staggered backward with a look of disbelief in his eyes. "Yes, but how come you're acting like this? You have every right to despise me."

He shook his head. "Nothing could be further from the truth. If anything, I've been the despicable one for not ending it with Alexandra years ago. I knew something earthshaking had happened to make you go away. I was afraid I'd offended you in some way. Now that you've told me, I'm so incredibly happy for you and Alexandra, you could have no idea.

"Don't waste another moment, Vito. All this time you two have been in pain... Give up your commission and marry her. Grab at your happiness! Mother loves her, and her parents want to join our two families together. When they find out you're going to be king instead of me, they'll be overjoyed."

"I don't want to be king."

"Yes, you do. You told me years ago. The point is, *I* don't. I never wanted it."

"But—"

"But nothing," Valentino silenced him. "Mother is

perfectly healthy. Maybe she's going to have to rule for a lot longer than she'd planned."

His brother rubbed the back of his neck in confusion. "What's going on with you? Do I even know you?"

He grinned. "We're brothers, and I've got my own confession to make, but you'll have to hear it later. In the meantime, don't worry about me. And don't tell Mother I've been to the palace this morning. I'll be back in a few days." He headed for the door and turned to him. "When I see you again, I'd better hear that you and Alexandra have made your wedding plans or there *will* be hell to pay."

Valentino flew out the door and raced across the grounds to the helicopter. The knowledge that Vito and Alexandra had been lovers had transformed him, removing every trace of pain and guilt.

"Carolena?"

She peered around the deck chair where she'd been reading a magazine in her sunglasses. "Hi!"

This morning she'd put her vibrant hair back in a chignon and was wearing pleated beige pants with a peach-colored top her figure did wonders for. Between her sensational looks and brilliant mind, she was his total fantasy come to life.

"If you're ready, we'll get business out of the way, then come back and take off for the island." He'd told one of the crew to pack the cruiser with everything they'd need if they wanted to spend the night there.

Throughout the rest of the day they'd gotten things down to a routine and touched base with the many heads of fruit consortiums in the district. The plan to market the island's blood oranges under the AG logo had already reached the ears of many of them with rave results.

Valentino had demands for more of the videos made in Gemelli than he'd anticipated. He gave orders to step up production of the flyers, too. Two more days and he and Carolena would have covered the whole country. By this time next year he'd know if their efforts had helped increase their exports around the world and produced financial gains.

As he'd told Carolena, there were no guarantees in life. This plan of his and Vincenzo's to help their countries' economies was only one of many. It was far too early to predict the outcome, but since she'd come into his life, he had this feeling something remarkable was going to happen.

With their marketing work done, Valentino drove the cruiser under a late-afternoon sun along a string of tiny deserted islands with rocky coastlines.

Carolena had been waiting for this all day. "What's that wonderful smell in the breeze?"

"Rosemary and thyme. It grows wild here among the sand dunes and beaches. Vito and I spent a lot of our teenage years exploring this area. In the fall this place is covered with pink flamingos, herons and storks. We used to camp out here to watch them and take movies."

"I envy you having a brother to go on adventures with. No one's childhood is idyllic, but I think yours must have come close."

"We tried to forget that we were princes put into

a special kind of gilded cage. However, I would have liked your freedom."

"But it wouldn't have exposed you to the world you're going to rule one day. Someone has to do it."

He lifted one eyebrow. "That's one way of looking at it. Ten years ago we worked on our father to get legislation passed in parliament to declare this a natural preserve so the tourists wouldn't ruin it. Since that time, our Gemellian bird-watching society has seen continual growth of the different species, and I've had this place virtually to myself."

She laughed. "Seriously, that has to be very gratifying to you." His dedication to the country's welfare continued to astound Carolena. "This is paradise, Val. The sand is so white!"

He nodded. "It feels like the most refined granulated sugar under your feet. We'll pull in to that lagoon, one of my favorite spots."

The water was as blue as the sky. They were alone. It was as if they were the only people left on earth. After he cut the engine, she darted below to put on her flowered one-piece swimsuit. It was backless, but the front fastened up around the neck like a choker, providing the modesty she needed to be around Val.

When she came back up on deck, she discovered he'd already changed into black trunks. The hard-muscled physique of his bronzed body took her breath. His gaze scrutinized her so thoroughly, he ignited a new fire that traveled through hers.

"Not that the suit you're wearing isn't delectable, but what happened to that gorgeous purple concoction you were wearing when we first met? I've been living to see you in it again."

A gentle laugh broke from her. "You mean that piece of nothing?" she teased. "I've never owned anything indecent before. When I saw it in the shop before I flew down here with Abby, I decided to be daring and buy it. I was a fool to think I'd be alone."

"The sight of you almost in it put an exclamation point on the end of my grueling workday."

She blushed. "*Almost* being the operative word. You're a terrible man to remind me."

"You're a terrible woman to deprive me of seeing you in it again."

Carolena had been trying to treat him like a brother, but that was a joke with the heat building between them. She needed to cool off and there was only one way to do it. She walked to the end of the cruiser and without hesitation jumped into the water.

"Oh—" she cried when she emerged. "This feels like a bathtub! Heaven!"

"Isn't it?"

She squealed again because he'd come right up next to her. They swam around the boat, diving and bobbing like porpoises for at least half an hour. "I've never had so much fun in my life!"

He smiled at her with a pirate's grin that sent a thrill through her. "I'll race you to shore, but I'll give you a head start."

"You're on!" She struck out for the beach, putting everything into it. But when she would have been able to stand, he grabbed hold of her ankles and she landed in the sand. Laughter burst out of her. "That wasn't fair!"

He'd come up beside her and turned her over. "I know," he whispered against her lips. "But as you've found out, I play by a different set of rules. Right now I'm going to kiss the daylights out of you."

"No, Val—" she cried, but the second she felt his hungry mouth cover hers, she couldn't hold off any longer. This time they weren't in the back of the limo while the driver was waiting for them to get out.

There was nothing to impede their full pleasure as they wrapped their arms around each other. Slowly they began giving and taking one kiss after another, relishing the taste and feel of each other. While their legs entwined, the warm water lapped around them in a silky wet blanket.

"You're so beautiful I could eat you alive. I'm in love with you, *adorata*. I've never said it to another woman in my life, so don't tell me it isn't love."

She looked into his eyes blazing with blue fire. "I wasn't going to," she cried in a tremulous whisper before their mouths met in another explosion of desire. Carried away by her feelings, she quit fighting her reservations for the moment and gave in to her longings. She embraced him with almost primitive need, unaware of twilight turning into night.

"I'm in love with you, too, Val," she confessed when he allowed her to draw breath. "I've been denying it to myself, but it's no use. Like I told you on the yacht that first night, you make me feel immortal. Only a man who had hold of my heart could make me thankful I've been born a woman."

He buried his face in her throat. "You bring out feelings in me I didn't know were there. I need you with me, Carolena. Not just for an hour or a day." He kissed her again, long and deep, while they moved and breathed as one flesh.

"I feel the same way," she whispered at last, kissing his jaw where she could feel the beginnings of a beard. No man had ever been as gorgeous.

"Another time we'll come out here in the middle of the night to watch the turtle fledglings hatch and make their trek to the water. Tonight I want to spend all the time we have on the cruiser with you. It's getting cooler. Come on before you catch a chill."

He got up first and pulled her against him. Dizzy from the sensations he'd aroused, she clung to him, not wanting to be separated from him for an instant, but they had to swim back to the boat. Valentino grasped her hand and drew her into the water. "Ready?"

"Yes."

Together they swam side by side until they reached the back of the cruiser. He levered himself in first so he could help her aboard. "You take a shower while I get the cruiser ready for bed. We'll eat in the galley. But I need this first." He planted another passionate kiss on her mouth, exploring her back with his hands before she hurried across the deck and down the steps.

She'd packed a bag with the essentials she'd need. After carrying it into the shower, she turned on the water and undid her hair. It felt marvelous to wash out the sand and have a good scrub. Aware Valentino would want a shower, too, she didn't linger.

Once she'd wrapped her hair in a towel and had dried herself, she pulled out her toweling robe. But when she started to put it on, it was like déjà vu and stopped her cold. What was she doing?

Yes she'd broken down and admitted that she loved him, but nothing else had changed. Though he'd spoken of his love and need to be with her all the time, he was still a prince with responsibilities and commitments she could never be a part of.

Abby had suggested she treat Valentino like a brother in order to make it through the rest of the week, but that tactic had been a total and utter failure. Carolena was painfully, desperately in love with him.

If they made love tonight, her entire world would change. She'd be a slave to her need for him and act like all the poor lovesick wretches throughout time who'd made themselves available to the king when he called for them.

It was sick and wrong! No matter how much she loved Valentino, she couldn't do that to herself. Carolena couldn't imagine anything worse than living each minute of her life waiting for him to reach out to her when he had the time. Once he married and had children, that really would be the end for her.

If she couldn't have him all to herself, she didn't want any part of him. There was no way to make it work. None. She'd rather be single for the rest of her life.

On the yacht that first night she'd told him he'd passed his test and could leave her cabin with a clear conscience. Now it was time for her to pass her test and go away forever.

She quickly put on clean underwear and a new pair of lightweight sweats with short sleeves. The robe she buried in the bottom of the bag. After removing the towel, she brushed her hair back and fastened it at the nape with an elastic.

After putting her bag outside the door, she headed straight into the galley and opened the fridge to get the food set out for them. When she'd put everything on the table, she called to him. A minute later he showed up in a striped robe. He'd just come out of the shower and his dark blond hair was still damp. Talk about looking good enough to eat!

She flashed him a smile. "Is everything fine topside?"

"We're set for the night." His eyes took in her sweats. Carolena knew her friendly air didn't fool him, but he went along with her. "I like your sleepwear. Reminds me of Vito's military fatigues."

"This is as close as I ever hope to get to war," she quipped. "Why don't you sit down and eat this delicious food someone has prepared for us." He did her bidding. She poured coffee for them. "How is your brother, by the way? Will he be in Gemelli long before he has to go back on duty?"

"I don't know." His vague answer wasn't very reassuring. "He wants to meet you when we get back to the palace."

She bit into a plum. "I'm afraid that won't be possible."

Lines marred his handsome features. "Why would you say something like that? He's my only sibling still alive. Naturally I want him to meet you and get to know you."

"Under normal circumstances there's nothing I'd like more, but nothing about you and me is normal."

His head reared back. "What are you trying to tell me now?"

Carolena eyed him with a frank gaze. "I've already admitted that I'm in love with you, but I've come to my senses since we came back on board and I don't intend to sleep with you tonight or any other night. I want a clean break from you after I've finished out my contract, so there's no need to be involved with any members of your family."

He got that authoritative look. It was something that came over him even if he wasn't aware of it. "There isn't going to be a break."

"So speaks the prince. But this commoner has another destiny. Don't ask me again to forget that you're royalty. It would be pointless. Do you honestly believe I could stand to be your lover in your secret life and watch you play out your public life with a royal wife and children? Other foolish women have done it for centuries, but not me."

Valentino tucked into his pasta salad, seemingly not in the least bothered by anything she'd said.

"Did you hear me?"

"Loud and clear." He kept on eating.

Her anger was kindled. "Stop acting like a husband who's tired of listening to his nag of a wife. Have you ever considered why she nags him?"

"The usual reasons. I had parents, too, remember."

"You're impossible!"

Quiet reigned until he'd finished his coffee. After he put down the mug, he looked at her with those intelligent dark blue eyes. "How would *you* like to be my wife? I already know you have a temper, so I'm not shaking in my boots."

Her lungs froze. "That was a cruel thing to say to me."

His sinuous smile stung her. "Cruel? I just proposed marriage to you and that's the answer you give me?"

Carolena shook her head. "Stop teasing me, Val. Why are you being like this? I thought I knew you, but it's obvious I don't. The only time I see you serious is when you're wearing your princely mantle."

He sat back in the chair. "For the first time in my life, I've taken it off."

She started to get nervous. "Just because you broke your engagement, it doesn't mean you've changed into someone else."

"Oh, but I have!"

"Now you're scaring me again."

"Good. I like it when you're thrown off base. First, let me tell you about my talk with Vito this morning."

Carolena blinked. "That's where you were?"

"He sent me an urgent message telling me he needed to see me as soon as possible. Otherwise I would never have left you."

This had to do with their mother. Guilt attacked her. "Is your mother ill?" she asked.

"No. Last week I told Vito I was breaking my engagement to Alexandra. Since I had business with you,

I asked him to meet the princess's plane when she flew in to Gemelli."

"She came to the palace?"

"That's right. What I didn't know until this morning was that Vito and Alexandra were lovers before he went into the military."

The blood hammered in her ears.

"He signed up intending to make a career of it in order to stay away from her permanently. Neither my parents nor I knew why."

"Those poor things," she whispered.

Valentino nodded. "But after hearing that I'd broken our engagement, he found the courage to face me this morning. To my surprise, I learned she was on the verge of breaking it off with me, but Vito wanted to be the one to tell me. That was why she was so happy that I got there first."

Carolena could hardly take it in. "You mean, they've been in love all these years?"

"Yes. It's the forever kind."

She was dumbstruck.

"When I left Vito, I told him there'd better be a marriage between the two of them soon or he'd have to answer to me. Mother will have no choice but to see him crowned king. The promise that one of her sons will reign makes everything all right. He'll rule instead of me. No one will have to be disappointed, after all."

By now Carolena's whole body was shaking. "Are you saying you'd give up your dream in order to marry me?"

"It was never my dream. My parents thrust the idea upon me as soon as I was old enough to understand."

Dying inside, she got to her feet. "Does your mother know any of this?"

"Maybe by now, which brings me to what I have to say to you. I meant what I said earlier tonight. I want you with me all the time, day and night. Forever." He cocked his head. "Did you mean what you said the other day at your condo when I asked you what *you* wanted?"

Hot tears stung her eyelids. "Yes. But we both concluded it wasn't possible."

"Not both—" He leaned forward and grasped her hand. "I told you that true love had to be grabbed and enjoyed for the time given every mortal. When I asked you to fly up on Etna with me even though you knew there was a risk, you went with me because you couldn't bear to miss the experience."

"That was a helicopter ride. Not a marriage. There can't be one between you and me. You're supposed to be the King!"

"Am I not supposed to have any say in the matter, *bellissima?*"

"Val… You're not thinking clearly."

"I'm a free man, Carolena, and have never known my path better than I do now. When Michelina passed away, Vincenzo was free to marry Abby and he did so in the face of every argument. Lo and behold he's still the prince.

"Whether the government makes him king after his father dies, no one can say. As for me, I'll still be a prince when I marry you. The only difference is, I'll work for Vito after he's crowned."

"You mean *if* he's crowned. Your mother will forbid it."

"You don't know Vito. He wanted Alexandra enough to go after her. It looks like he's got the stuff to make a remarkable king. Once Mother realizes their marriage will save her relationship with Alexandra's parents, she'll come around."

"Does Vito want to be king?"

"I don't think he's given it much thought since everyone thought I'd be the one to assume the throne. But when we were younger and I told him I wanted to be a full-time volcanologist, he said it was too bad I hadn't been born the second son so I could do exactly what I wanted.

"When I asked him what he wanted, he said it might be fun to be king and bring our country into the age of enlightenment. Then he laughed, but I knew he wasn't kidding."

"Oh, Val…"

"Interesting, isn't it? At times, Michelina made the odd remark that he should have been born first. She and I were close and she worried for me always having to do my duty. I worried about her, too. She was too much under the thumb of our parents who wanted her marriage to Vincenzo no matter what."

"If people could hear you talk, they'd never want to trade places with you." She had a tragic look on her beautiful face. "As for your poor mother…"

"She's had to endure a lot of sorrow and disappointment and I'm sorry for that. Naturally I love her very much, but she doesn't rule my life even if she is the queen. I'm not a martyr, Carolena. It turns out Vito isn't, either. To have to marry another royal is archaic to both of us, but in his case he happened to fall in love with one."

"Your mother will think you've both lost your minds."

"At first, maybe. But just because she was pressured into marriage with my father doesn't mean Vito or I have to follow suit. The times have changed and she's being forced to accept the modern age whether she likes it or not. Michelina went through a surrogate to have a baby with Vincenzo. That prepared the ground and has made her less rigid because she loves her grandson."

"But you're her firstborn. She's pinned her hopes on you."

"Haven't I gotten through to you yet? Her hopes aren't mine. When I decided to get my geology degree, she knew I was going to go my own way even if I ended up ruling. After she finds out that Vito wanted to be betrothed to Alexandra years ago instead of me, she's going to see that you can't orchestrate your children's lives without serious repercussions."

"I'm too bewildered by all this. I—I don't know what to say."

"I want you for my wife. All you have to say is yes."

She sank back down in her chair. "No, that isn't all."

"Then talk to me. We've got the whole night. Ask me anything you want."

"Val—it isn't that simple."

"Why not?"

"I—I don't know if I want to be married."

"Because there are no guarantees? We've already had this conversation."

"But that was when we were talking hypothetically."

"Whereas now this is for real?"

She lowered her head. "Yes. For one thing, I don't think I'd make a good wife."

"I've never been a husband. We'll learn together."

"Where would we live?"

"Shall we buy your family's farm and live there?"

Carolena's head flew back. "I would never expect you to move to a different country and do that—your work for the institute is far too important!"

Valentino was trying to read between the lines, but she made it difficult. "I can tell the thought of living at the palace holds little appeal. We'll get our own place."

Her body moved restlessly. "You'd hate it. After a while you'd want to move back."

"There's nothing I'd love more after a hard day's work than to come home to my own house and my own bride. Would you like us to buy a farm here? Or would you prefer working for a law firm in Gemelli?"

She looked tortured. "I don't know." She got up from the chair again. "I can't answer those questions. You haven't even talked to your mother yet. It would be pointless to discuss all this when she doesn't know anything that's gone on with you."

"When we get back to the palace day after tomorrow, we'll go to her and tell her our plans."

"But we don't have any plans!"

He got to his feet. "We love each other and don't want to be separated. That forms the foundation of our plans. Come to bed with me and we'll work out the logistics of when and where we want to be married, how many children we want to have. Do we want a dog?"

"I'm not going to sleep with you."

"Yes, you are. There's only one bed on the cruiser, but if you ask me not to make love to you, I won't."

After a minute, she said, "You go on ahead. I'll be there once I've cleaned up the kitchen."

"I'll help. This will get me into practice for when we're married."

They made short work of it.

"I'll just get ready for bed," Carolena said.

"You do that while I turn out the lights."

She hurried out of the galley. He could tell she was frightened. Valentino was, too, but his fears were different. If he couldn't get her to marry him, then his life really wouldn't have any meaning.

Once he'd locked the door at the bottom of the stairs, he made a trip to the bathroom to brush his teeth. The cabin was cloaked in darkness when he joined her in bed still wearing his robe. She'd turned on her side away from his part of the bed. He got in and stretched out on his back.

"Val?"

"Yes?"

"Berto and I never spent a night together alone."

His thoughts reeled. "Not even after you were engaged?"

"No. Our families were old-fashioned."

He sat up in bed. "Are you telling me you two never made love?"

"It was because we didn't want to lie to the priest who'd asked us to wait."

"So you've never been intimate with a man."

"No. After he was killed, I kept asking myself what we'd been waiting for. I know now that a lot of my grief had to do with my sense of feeling cheated. I was so sure another man would never come along and I'd never know fulfillment. It made me angry. I was angry for a long time."

He squeezed her shoulder. "Carolena…"

"Once I started dating, I went through guy after guy the way the tabloids say you've gone through women. But after knowing you for the last week, it all had to have been made up because you don't have that kind of time."

A smile broke the corners of his mouth.

"The fact is, I don't have your experience, but that part doesn't bother me. I just wanted you to know the truth about me. I have no idea if I'd be a satisfying lover or not."

She was so sweet, it touched his heart. "That could work both ways."

"No, it couldn't. When you were kissing me out in the lagoon, I thought I might die on the spot from too much ecstasy." That made two of them. "I'm frightened by your power over me."

His brows knit together. "Why frightened?"

"Because I'm afraid it's all going to be taken away from me."

She'd had too many losses.

"Don't you know I have the same fear? I lost hope

of ever finding a woman I could love body and soul. Yet the moment I was resigned to my fate, I discovered this exquisite creature standing on the diving board of my swimming pool. You've changed my life, Carolena Baretti."

He rolled her into his arms and held her against his body. "I want to be your husband."

She sobbed quietly against his shoulder. "I need more time before I can tell you yes or no. I have too many issues welling up inside of me.

"When I get back to Arancia, I'm going to make an appointment with a professional. I hope someone can help me sort all this out. I should have gone to counseling after Berto died, but I was too wild with pain to even think about it. Instead, I started law school and poured all my energy into my studies."

"How did you end up becoming an attorney?"

"My grandmother insisted I go to college. She said I needed to do something else besides farming in case I had to take care of myself one day. For an old-fashioned woman, she was actually very forward thinking.

"While I was at school studying business, we met with some professors for career day. One of them encouraged me to try for the law entrance exam. I thought why not. When I succeeded in making a high score, the rest was history. Eventually I met Abby and for some reason we just clicked. The poor thing had to listen while I poured out my heart about Berto, but school did help me."

He had to clear the lump in his throat. "Work's a great panacea."

"Yes, but in my case it made me put off dealing with the things that were really wrong with me. Meeting you has brought it all to the surface. I don't want to burden you with my problems, Val. I can't be with you right now. You have to understand that if I can't come to you having worked things out, then it's no good talking about marriage. Please tell me you understand that."

She was breaking his heart. Abby had told him she'd been in a depression for a long time. Carolena reminded him of Matteo, who had certain issues that wouldn't allow him to marry yet.

He clutched her tighter, terrified he was going to lose her. "I do," he whispered into her hair. *I do.* "Go to sleep now and don't worry about anything."

"Please don't say anything to your mother about me. Please," she begged.

"I promise I won't."

"You always keep your promises. I love you, Val. You have no idea how much. But I can't promise you how long it's going to take me before I can give you an answer."

CHAPTER EIGHT

FOUR DAYS LATER the receptionist at the hospital showed Carolena into the doctor's office in Arancia for her appointment.

"*Buongiorno,* Signorina Baretti." The silver-haired psychologist got to his feet and shook her hand before asking her to sit down.

"Thank you for letting me in to see you on such short notice, Dr. Greco. Abby has spoken so highly of you, I was hoping you could fit me in."

"I'm happy to do it. Why don't you tell me what's on your mind."

"I should have come to someone like you years ago."

"Let's not worry about that. You're here now. Give me a little background."

He made a few notes as she started to speak. Pretty soon it all came gushing out and tears rolled down her cheeks. "I'm sorry."

"It's all right. Take your time."

He handed her some tissues, which she used. Finally she got hold of herself. "I don't know what more to tell you."

"I don't need to hear any more. What I've gleaned from everything you've told me is that you have two problems. The biggest one is an overriding expectation of the prince. Because he isn't meeting that expectation, it's preventing you from taking the next step in your life with him."

"Expectation?" That surprised her. She thought she was going to hear that she was losing her mind.

"I find you've dealt amazingly well with everything that's gone on in your past life. But you've got a big problem to overcome, and unless you face it head-on, you'll remain conflicted and depressed."

It was hard to swallow. "What is it?"

"You've just found out the prince wants to marry you. But it means that for your sake he plans to give up his right to sit on the throne one day as king and you don't like that because you've never imagined he could do such a thing. It hasn't been your perception. To some degree it has shocked and maybe even disappointed you, like glitter that comes off a shiny pair of shoes."

Whoa.

"When you were telling me about all the farmers you met who held him in such high esteem, your eyes shone with a bright light. I watched your eyes light up again when you told me how he's preparing the country in case of an eruption on Mount Etna. Your admiration for him has taken a hit to learn he's willing to be an ordinary man in order to be your husband."

"But his whole life has been a preparation for being king."

"Let me put this another way. Think of a knight

going into battle. In his armor astride his horse, he looks splendid and triumphant. But when he takes it off, you see a mere man.

"Your prince is a man first. What you need to do is focus on that."

She kneaded her hands. "Valentino's always telling me to forget he's a prince."

"That's right. The man has to be true to himself. If he had nothing to bring you but himself, would you take him?"

"Yes—" she cried. "He's so wonderful you can't imagine. But what if he marries me and then wishes he hadn't and wants to be king?"

"How old did you say he was?"

"Thirty-two."

"And he called off his wedding to a princess he doesn't love?"

"Yes."

"Then I'd say the man is more than old enough to know his own mind."

"It's just that he already makes a marvelous ruler."

"I thought you said his mother is the ruler."

"Well, she is."

"And he's not the king, so what you're telling me is that he's still marvelous just being a man, right?"

His logic was beginning to make all kinds of sense. "Yes."

"Your other problem is guilt that could be solved by a simple conversation with the queen."

Carolena gulped. "I don't think I could."

"You're going to have to because you're afraid she'll

never forgive you if you marry her son, thus depriving him of his birthright."

Dr. Greco figured all that out in one session? "What if she won't?"

"She might not, but you're not marrying her, and the prince isn't letting her feelings stand in the way of what he wants. It would be nice to have her approval, of course, but not necessary. There's no harm in approaching her and baring your soul to her. She'll either say yes or no, but by confronting her, you'll get rid of that guilt weighing you down."

Valentino had promised he wouldn't talk to his mother about her yet…

"My advice to you is to go home and let this percolate. When you've worked it all out, let me know."

It was scary how fast he'd untangled her fears so she could understand herself. The doctor was brilliant. She jumped to her feet, knowing what she had to do. "I will, Doctor. Thank you. Thank you so very much."

Valentino hunkered down next to Razzi. Both wore gas masks. "Those strombolian explosions are building in intensity."

"You're not kidding. Something big is going on."

He and Razzi had been camped up there for three days taking readings, getting any activity on film. His work kept him from losing his mind. He had no idea how long it would be before he heard from Carolena.

Valentino wasn't surprised to see that a new lava flow had started from the saddle area between the two Southeast Crater cones.

"Look, Razzi. More vents have opened up on the northeast side of the cone."

"There's the lava fountain. It's getting ready to blow."

He gazed in wonder as a tall ash plume shot skyward. Though it was morning, it felt like midnight. Suddenly there were powerful, continuous explosions. The loud detonations that had continued throughout the night and morning sent tremors through the earth.

"We're too close!" The ground was getting too unstable to stand up. "More lava fountains have started. This is it. Come on, Razzi. We need to move back to the other camp farther down."

They recognized the danger and worked as a team as they gathered their equipment and started their retreat. He'd witnessed nature at work many times, but never from this close a vantage point.

The continual shaking made it more difficult to move as fast as they needed to. Halfway to the other camp a deafening explosion reached his ears before he was thrust against the ground so hard the impact knocked off his gas mask.

Everything had gone dark. He struggled to find it and put it back on. In frustration he cried to Razzi, but the poisonous fumes filled his lungs. For the first time since coming up on Etna, Valentino had the presentiment that he might not make it off the volcano alive.

His last thought was for Carolena, whose fear of another loss might have come to pass.

Once Carolena had taken a taxi back to her condo, she made a reservation to fly to Gemelli later in the day.

This was one time she didn't want to burden Abby with her problems.

Officially, Carolena was still out of the office for another week, so she didn't need to make a stop there to talk to Signor Faustino. All she needed to do was pack another bag and take care of some bills before she called for a taxi to drive her to the airport.

The necessity of making all her own arrangements caused her to see how spoiled she'd become after having the royal jets at her disposal. It seemed strange to be taking a commercial jet and traveling in a taxi rather than a limo. Everything took longer. She was tired when she arrived in Gemelli at five-thirty that evening and checked herself into a hotel.

Because she hadn't seen or heard from Valentino for the past four days, she was practically jumping out of her skin with excitement at the thought of being with him again. Her first order of business was to phone the palace. She wanted to surprise him.

After introducing herself to the operator, she asked to speak to Valentino, but was told he was unavailable. The news crushed her. Attempting to recover, she asked if she could speak to Vito Cavelli. Through his brother she could learn Valentino's whereabouts, and possibly he would help her to meet with the queen.

Before long she heard a male voice come on the line.

"Signorina Baretti? It's really you?"

"Yes, Your Highness."

"Please call me Vito. You're the famous video star."

"I don't know about famous."

"You are to me. Mother and I have seen the video. It's superb."

"Thank you. I was just going to say that if anyone is renowned, it's you for drawing all those interesting mustaches on the putti around the outside of the palace."

He broke into rich laughter that reminded her so much of Val, she joined in. "Are you calling from Arancia?"

She gripped her phone tighter. "No. I just flew in to Gemelli and am staying at the Regency Hotel."

"*Grazie a Dio* you're here," he said under his breath. His sudden change of mood alarmed her.

"What's wrong?"

"I was hoping you could tell me. Four days ago Valentino left for Catania, but I haven't talked to him since. I've left message after message."

That meant he was working on Etna.

"*Signorina?* Does my brother know you're here?"

"Not yet. I wanted to come to the palace and surprise him."

"Do you have his private cell phone number?"

"Yes. As soon as we hang up, I'll call him."

"Once you've reached him, will you ask him to return my call? I have something important to tell him."

Her brows furrowed. It wasn't like Valentino to remain out of reach. He was too responsible a person to do that. "Vito?"

"*Sì?*"

"There's a favor I'd like to ask of you."

"Name it."

"Would it be possible for me to talk to your mother

either tonight or in the morning? It's of extreme importance to me."

"I'm afraid she's not in the country, but she should be back tomorrow afternoon and then we'll arrange for you to meet with her."

More disappointment. "Thank you. Is she by any chance in Arancia?" Maybe she was visiting Vincenzo and Abby. Carolena should have called her friend, after all.

"No. She flew to Cyprus and left me in charge. I guess Valentino told you about me and Alexandra. The families are together now, discussing our plans to marry. We're thinking in four weeks."

It really was going to happen. "I'm very happy for you, Vito. I mean that sincerely."

"Thank you. I wish I could say the same for my brother."

"What do you mean?"

"It's my impression you're the only person who knows what's going on with him. He's not answering anyone's calls. This is a first for him. Our mother is worried sick about him."

Her eyes closed tightly. Carolena was the one responsible for him shutting down. She took a fortifying breath. "Now that I'm back, I'll try to reach him. Once I've contacted him, I'll tell him to get in touch with you immediately."

"I'd appreciate that. Good luck."

Fear clutched at her heart. Vito knew his brother better than anyone. To wish her luck meant she was going to need it. What if Valentino couldn't call anyone? What if he was in trouble? Her body broke out in a cold sweat.

"Good night, Vito."

"Buona notte, signorina."

As soon as she hung up, she phoned Valentino's number. Forget surprising him, all she got was to leave a message. In a shaky voice she told him she was back in Gemelli, that she loved him and that she was dying to see him. Please call her back.

Crushed because she couldn't talk to him, she got information for Tancredi's Restaurant so she could talk to Matteo. Maybe he'd spoken with Valentino. To her chagrin she learned it was his night off. If she'd like to leave a message… Carolena said no and hung up. The only thing to do was go looking for Valentino.

Again she rang for information and called the airport to schedule a commuter flight for seven in the morning to Catania airport. From there she'd take a taxi to the center where she'd been before. Someone would know how to reach Valentino if he still hadn't returned her call.

She went to bed and set her alarm, but she slept poorly. Valentino still hadn't called her back. At five in the morning she awakened and dressed in jeans and a T-shirt. After putting on her boots, she fastened her hair back in a chignon and left to get some food in the restaurant. Before taking a taxi to the airport, she knew she'd better eat first.

Everywhere she went was crowded with tourists. The commuter flight was packed and she had a long wait at the Catania airport before she could get a taxi to drive her to the institute.

Once she arrived, she hurried inside and approached the mid-twenties-looking man at the reception desk.

He eyed her with male appreciation. "May I help you, *signorina?*"

"I need to get in touch with Valentino Cellini."

The man smiled. "And you are…?"

"Carolena Baretti. I'm an attorney from Arancia who's been working with His Highness on a special project. I have to see him right away."

"I'm afraid that's not possible."

She refused to be put off. "Why not?"

"He's out in the field."

"Then can you get a message to him?"

"You can leave one here. When it's possible for him, he'll retrieve it."

This was getting her nowhere. "Would it be possible to speak to one of the pilots for the center? His name is Dante Serrano. He was the one who recently flew me up on Etna with the prince."

The fact she knew that much seemed to capture his attention. "I'll see if I can locate him." He made a call. After a minute he hung up. "Signor Serrano will be coming on duty within a few minutes."

"In that case, I'll wait for him in the lounge. Will you page me when he gets here?"

"Of course."

"Thank you."

Carolena hadn't been seated long when the attractive pilot walked over to her. She jumped up to greet him, but his expression was so solemn she knew something was wrong.

"Good morning, Dante. I was hoping to talk to you. I haven't been able to reach Valentino."

"No one's been able to reach him or his partner, Razzi. They were camped near a new eruption. The base camp received word that they were on their way back to it, but they lost contact."

"You mean th—"

"I mean, no one has been able to reach them yet."

"Then it must be bad," she cried in agony and grabbed his arms. "I can't lose him, Dante. I can't!"

"Let's not talk about that right now," he tried to placate her. "Half a dozen choppers have already taken off to search for them. This is my day off, but I was called in to help. Valentino's the best of the best, you know."

"I *do* know!" Carolena cried. "My life won't be worth living without him! I'm going with you!"

"No, no. It's too dangerous."

"I *have* to go with you. It's a matter of life and death to me. I love him. We're going to be married."

His eyes rounded before he exhaled a labored breath. "All right. You can come, but you'll do everything I say."

"I promise."

She followed him through the center and out the rear doors to the helipad. They ran to the helicopter. Once she'd climbed inside and strapped herself in the back, he found a gas mask for her. "When I tell you to do it, I want you to put this on."

"I will."

Another pilot joined them. Dante made a quick introduction, then started the engine. The rotors whined. Within seconds they lifted off.

At first, the smoking top of Etna didn't look any different to her. But before long the air was filled with ash. Afraid to disturb Dante's concentration, she didn't dare ask him questions. After ten minutes, the sky grew darker.

As the helicopter dipped, she saw the giant spectacular ash plume coming from a crater filling up with lava. She gasped in terror to think Valentino was down there somewhere.

"Put on your gas mask, *signorina*. We're going to land at the base camp."

She was all thumbs, but finally managed to do it after following his instructions. When they touched ground, Carolena thought there might be thirty geologists in the area wearing gas masks, but visibility was difficult.

"I want you to stay in the chopper until I tell you otherwise." By now he and the copilot had put on their masks.

"I will, but please find him."

"Say a prayer," he murmured. She bowed her head and did exactly that. To lose him now would kill her.

The two men disappeared. In a minute she heard the whine of rotors from another chopper. It set down farther away. People ran to it. She watched in agony as she saw a body being unloaded from it. Valentino's?

Forgetting Dante's advice, she climbed out of the chopper and started running. The victim was being transported on a stretcher to one of several tents that had been set up. She followed and worked her way inside the entrance, but there were too many people around to see anything.

The copilot who'd been on the chopper stood nearby. She grabbed at his arm.

He looked at her. "You weren't supposed to leave the chopper."

"I don't care. Is it Valentino?"

"I don't know yet, but I'll find out."

She held her breath until he came back. "It's Valentino's partner, Razzi."

"Is he…"

"Alive," he answered. "Just dazed from a fall."

"Where's Valentino?"

"The other chopper is bringing him in."

"So they found him!"

"Yes."

Her heart started to beat again. "Thank you for telling me that much." She hurried outside, praying for the other chopper to come.

The next minute felt like an eternity until she heard the sound of another helicopter coming in to land. She hurried over to the area, getting as close as she was allowed until it touched ground.

Carolena watched the door open, but there was no sign of Valentino. She was close to fainting, when Dante pulled her aside. Through his mask he said, "Valentino's head struck some volcanic rock. When they transported him out, he was unconscious but alive."

"Thank heaven." She sobbed quietly against him as they walked toward Dante's chopper.

"You can say that again. He's already been flown to the hospital. I'll fly you there now. Before long you'll be able to visit him."

"Thank you for bringing me up here. I'm indebted to you."

"He's lucky you love him enough to face danger yourself. Not every woman or man has that kind of courage."

She didn't know she had any until she'd been put to the test. It was only because of Valentino. He was her life!

"Razzi said they were eyewitnesses to an explosion that could have gotten them killed. I've heard that the footage they captured on film is the best that's ever been recorded at the institute. The guys are heroes."

They were. "So are you, Dante."

"Yeah?" He smiled.

"Yeah."

Carolena's thoughts drifted back to her conversation with Dr. Greco. He'd said it best. *And he's not the king, so what you're telling me is that he's still marvelous just being a man, right?*

"Your Highness?"

Valentino was lying in bed with his head raised watching television when a nurse came in. He'd been told he had a concussion and would have to stay in the hospital overnight for observation. Much as he wanted to get out of there, every time he tried to sit up, his head swam.

"Yes?"

"Do you feel up to a visitor?"

There was only one person he wanted to see. If she ever came to a decision and it was the wrong one, he wished his body had been left on the side of the volcano.

"Who is it?"

"This person wanted it to be a surprise."

It was probably Vito, who would have been contacted hours ago. He'd want to see Valentino for himself before he told their mother her firstborn was alive and well. But in case it wasn't his brother, Valentino's mind ran through a possible list of friends and colleagues. If it were Vincenzo, he would have just walked in.

"Shall I tell this person you're still indisposed?"

While he was trying to make up his mind, he heard a noise in the doorway and looked up to see Carolena come rushing in the room. "Val, darling—" she blurted in tears and flew toward him.

At the sight of her in a T-shirt and jeans she filled out to perfection, an attack of adrenaline had him trying to get out of bed. But she reached him before he could untangle his legs from the sheet and try to sit up. She pressed against him, wetting his hideous hospital gown with her tears.

"Thank heaven you're alive! If I'd lost you, I would have wanted to die."

He wrapped his arms around her, pulling her up on the bed halfway on top of him. "I'm tougher than that. How did you know I was in here?"

Moisture spilled from her fabulous green eyes. "I flew down to Gemelli last evening. When you didn't answer my call and Vito couldn't get through to you, either. I flew to Catania this morning and took a taxi to the institute."

Valentino was in shock. "You were there this morning?"

"Yes! I had to see you, but then Dante told me you were up on the volcano and there'd been no contact from you since the latest eruption, so I flew up there with him to the base camp."

His blood ran cold. "He took you up there?"

"He wouldn't have, but when I told him you and I were getting married and I couldn't live without you, he took pity on me and let me go with him to look for you."

It was too much to digest. His heart started to act up. "You're going to marry me?"

"As soon as we can." She lifted her hand to tenderly touch his head. "You're my man and I want everyone to know it." In the next breath she covered his mouth with her own. The energy she put into her kiss was a revelation.

"Adorata—" He could believe he'd died on Etna and had just awakened in heaven.

She pressed him back against the pillow and sobbed quietly until the tears subsided. His Carolena was back where she belonged.

"Did you know your mother is in Cyprus seeing about the plans for Vito's wedding to Alexandra? While they have their big day after all they've been through, wouldn't it be thrilling if we had our own private wedding with Vincenzo and Abby for witnesses as soon as possible? I'd love it if we could say our vows in the chapel at the palace.

"And while we're gone on a honeymoon, Vincenzo and Abby could stay at the palace with your mother so she could spend time with Michelina's little boy. I want everyone to be happy. The two of us most of all. What do you think?"

Tears smarted his eyes. She really understood what Valentino was all about. He shaped her face with his hands. "First, I think I want to know what has caused this dramatic change in you."

"A very wise doctor helped me get to the core of what was ailing me. He said I had a fixation on your royal person, which was true. He told me I was disappointed you were willing to forgo being king in order to marry me.

"But my disappointment really covered my guilt over your decision and it made me afraid. Then he asked me if I couldn't love the ordinary man instead of the prince. He said something about looking at you without your crown and battle armor. That question straightened me out in a big hurry and I couldn't get back down here fast enough to tell you."

"Battle armor?" Would wonders never cease? He kissed her lips once more. "Remind me to send the doctor a big bonus check for services rendered."

"I already wrote him one." She ran kisses along his jawline. "You've got a beard, but I like to see you scruffy."

"Maybe I'll let it grow out."

"Whatever you want. Oh—there's just one more thing. The doctor says my guilt will be cured after I've talked to your mother. Even though she'll never forgive me for ruining her dreams for you, I have to confront her."

"We'll do it together tonight."

"But you'll still be in here. The doctor won't release you until tomorrow. We'll talk to her then."

"In that case, come closer and give me your mouth again."

She looked toward the door. "Isn't this illegal? What if someone catches us?"

"Do we care? This is my private room."

"Darling," she whispered, hugging him to her. He was all she ever wanted. "What happened on the volcano? I have to know."

He let out a sigh and rehearsed what went on after the first lava fountain appeared. "When I saw that plume shoot into the atmosphere, I knew we needed to run for our lives."

She gripped him harder. "Were you terrified?"

"Not then. The sight was glorious."

"I saw it from a distance. I don't think there's anything in nature to compare to it."

"There isn't." He rubbed his hands over her back. "Do you remember when you were up there with me the first time and the ground shook?"

Carolena shivered. "I'll never forget."

"Well, try to imagine it so strong, neither Razzi nor I could stand up. That's when it started getting exciting. But the moment came when the force threw me forward. I hit the ground and lost hold of the things I was carrying. Then my gas mask came off."

"Val—"

"That's when I got scared because I couldn't find it in the darkness."

At this point she wrapped her arms around his neck and wept against his chest. "Dante says you're a hero for getting close enough to record the data. I adore you."

His breath caught. "You mean, you're not going to tell me I have to give up my profession?"

She lifted her head. "Are you kidding? Nothing could be more exciting than what you do. I plan to go up with you a lot. When we have children, you can introduce them to the mountain. We'll get the whole family in on the act."

A week later, Carolena sat in front of the same mirror in the same cabin on the yacht brushing her hair. She'd just showered and put on the white toweling robe hanging on the hook in the bathroom.

But there were differences from the first time she'd come down to this room. The first time she'd been on board, the yacht was stationary. Now it was moving. But the gentle waters of the Ionian carried it along like so much fluff. Their destination was the Adriatic. Valentino had mentioned Montenegro as one of their stops. To Carolena, it was all like part of a dream.

Only two hours ago the priest had performed the marriage ceremony in the chapel in front of loved ones and Valentino's best friend, Matteo. On her ring finger flashed an emerald set in white gold. She was now Signora Valentino Agostino Cellini, and she was nervous.

How strange for her to have been so fearless before marriage when she'd thought they were going to make love the first time. Now she really was a bride and her heart thudded with sickening intensity at the thought of it.

A rap on the door caused her to get up jerkily from the dressing table chair. When she turned, she saw that Valentino had slipped into the room wearing a navy robe. He moved toward her, so sinfully handsome her mouth went dry.

"I can tell something's wrong, *bellissima*. I know you missed your parents and grandparents at our wedding. I'd like to think they were looking on and happy. Let me be your family from now on."

It was a touching thing for him to say. She sucked in her breath. "You are. You're my whole life."

His eyes caressed her. "I thought you'd enjoy recreating our first night on board, but maybe you would have preferred someplace else."

"Never. This is the perfect place."

"As long as you mean it."

"Of course I do."

She didn't know what his intentions were until he picked her up in his arms. "Then welcome to my life, *sposa mia*."

He lowered his mouth to hers and drank deeply as he carried her through the hall to the master suite. After he followed her down on the bed, he rolled her on top of him. "Never was there a more beautiful bride. I realize we've only known each other a short time, yet it seems like I've been waiting for you a lifetime. Love me, Carolena. I need you," he cried with such yearning, she was shaken by a vulnerability he rarely showed.

No longer nervous, her instincts took over and she began loving him. The rapture he created took her to a place she'd never been before. Throughout the night they gave each other pleasure she didn't know was possible.

"Don't ever stop loving me," she begged when morning came around. If they slept at all, she didn't remember. "I didn't know it could be like this, that I could feel like this." She laid against him, studying the curve of his mouth, the lines of his strong features. "I love you, Val. I love you till it hurts. But it's a wonderful kind of hurt."

"I know." He ran his hands through her hair. "Pleasure-pain is ecstasy. We have the rest of our lives to indulge in it to our heart's content." He gave her an almost savage kiss. "To think what we might have missed—"

"I don't want to think about it. Not ever. You set me on fire the first time you looked at me. Not everyone loves the way we do. It's overpowering."

"That's the way it should be when it's right."

She kissed his jaw. "Do you know who looked happy last night?"

"My mother."

Carolena raised up on her elbow. "You saw it, too?"

"She'd never admit it, but deep down she's glad her sons have found true love, something that was denied her."

Her eyes teared up. "After meeting you, I knew she'd always been a great mother, but the accepting way she has handled our news has made me admire her more than you could ever know. I'm growing to love her, Val.

I want to get close to her. She's missing her daughter and I'm missing my grandmother."

He hugged her tighter. "Do you have any idea how much it means for me to hear you say that?"

"It's so wonderful belonging to a family again. To belong to you."

"*You're* so wonderful I can't keep the secret Vincenzo wanted to tell you himself. When he springs it on you, promise me you'll pretend you knew nothing about it."

"They're going to have a baby."

His dark blue eyes danced. "If they are, I don't know about it yet. This particular secret concerns you."

"What do you mean?"

"Instead of handing you a check for invaluable services rendered to both our countries, he approached the latest owner of your grandparents' farm. After some investigation, he learned they're willing to sell it to you, but there's no hurry."

"*Val—* Are you serious?"

He rolled her over on her back and smiled down at her. "I thought that would make you happy. We'll use it as our second home when we fly to Arancia for visits."

"Our children will play in the lemon grove with Abby and Vincenzo's children."

"Yes. And when we get back from our honeymoon, we'll decide where we want to live."

She cradled his handsome face in her hands, loving him to distraction. "It's already been decided by Vito, but it's his secret. You have to promise not to tell him I told you."

His brows quirked. "My brother?"

"Yes. He said he's willing to be king so long as you're close by to help him. To quote him, 'The two Vs stick together.' He's already started a renovation of the unoccupied north wing of the palace where he says you two used to play pirates.

"I found out it has a lookout where you can see Etna clearly. It's the perfect spot for all your scientific equipment. He said the wing will be permanently closed off from the rest of the palace so it will be our own house with our own private entrance."

Her husband looked stunned. "You're okay with that?"

"I love the idea of being close to family. Think how much fun it would be for his children and ours, and they'll have a grandmother close by who will dote on them."

The most beautiful smile imaginable broke out on his face. "Are you trying to tell me you want a baby?"

"Don't you? After last night, maybe we're already pregnant."

"To make certain, I think we'll stay on a permanent honeymoon."

She kissed him until they were breathless. "You were right about the fire, darling. It keeps burning hotter and hotter. Love me again and never stop."

"As if I could…"

* * * * *

PRINCE HAFIZ'S
ONLY VICE

SUSANNA CARR

To Sarah Stubbs, with thanks for her guidance
and encouragement.

CHAPTER ONE

HER LOVER'S PICTURE was on the front page of every paper in the small newsstand.

Lacey adjusted the dark sunglasses that concealed her bright blue eyes and squinted at the newspaper on display. Although the headline was in Arabic, the print was big and bold. She could tell that something important had happened. Something that could explain the jubilant attitude that shimmered in the marketplace. No doubt Prince Hafiz had made his countrymen proud again.

She wondered what he had done this time as she requested the daily English paper in halting Arabic. Did he add a fortune to the royal coffers? Convince another industry to make the Sultanate of Rudaynah their headquarters? Win an award?

She decided it would be best to wait until she got home before she read the paper. Lacey took another glance at the pictures of Hafiz that covered the stall. His expression was solemn, but it didn't stop the secret thrill sweeping across her heated skin. It was unnerving that Hafiz could elicit that kind of response through a photograph.

The photo was an official head shot the palace systematically offered to the press, but while the image was familiar, it always grabbed the reader's notice. No one could look away from Prince Hafiz's mysterious dark eyes and harsh mouth. He was devastatingly handsome from his luxuriant black hair to his sharp bone structure. Women watched him from afar, too awed of his masculine beauty.

Or perhaps they sensed his raw power beneath his sophisticated manners. Lacey had instantly recognized the sexual hunger lurking below his ruthless restraint. His primitive aura was a silent warning that most women heeded. But for Lacey, it drew her closer.

She had found Hafiz's relentless self-discipline fascinating. It had also been a challenge. From the moment they had met, she had been tempted to strip him from his exquisitely tailored pinstripe suit and discover his most sensual secrets.

Just the thought of him made her impatient to get back home. She needed to return before Hafiz got there. His workload would crush a lesser man, but he still managed to visit Lacey at nightfall.

The blazing sun began to dip in the desert sky, and she didn't want to contemplate how Hafiz would respond if she weren't home.

He never asked what she did during the day, Lacey thought with a frown. At first his lack of interest had bothered her. Did he think time stood still for her until he appeared?

There were moments when she wanted to share her plans and ideas, even discuss her day, but she had always held back. She wasn't ready to reveal the work she had done. Not yet. Lacey wanted to show Hafiz what she was capable of. How she could contribute.

She wanted to show that she was ready to make his sultanate her permanent home.

It hadn't been easy. There were days, weeks, when she had been homesick. Lonely and bored. She had missed her wide circle of friends and colorful night-life, and she craved the basic comforts.

It was aggravating that the newspaper hadn't been delivered today at her penthouse, but that wasn't surprising. After living in the small Arabian country for almost six months, Lacey still hadn't gotten used to sporadic service, frequent power outages and laborers arriving at work anywhere from three hours to three days late.

Her connection to the outside world was just as erratic. The communication services were usually down, like today. When they were running, the content was heavily censored.

Definitely not the lifestyle she had enjoyed in St. Louis. Not that she was complaining, Lacey hurriedly assured herself. She was willing to forego many comforts and conveniences for the one thing she couldn't get back in the States: Hafiz.

Lacey shivered with anticipation and handed the coins to the newspaper boy. She practiced her Arabic and felt a sense of accomplishment when the young man understood her. Lacey shyly tugged at the bright orange scarf wrapped around her head and tucked in a wayward strand of hair.

Maybe she was ready to show Hafiz what she had learned over the past few months. She wasn't fluent and didn't know everything about the culture, but she was getting impatient. It was time to meet his family and friends.

Lacey bit her lip as she imagined making that demand. The idea made her uncomfortable. She had been stalling. Not because his family was royal but because she was worried she would push too soon.

Lacey didn't want to give an ultimatum. The last time she'd taken a stand she had lost everything. She wasn't ready to lose Hafiz. Unlike her parents, who had no problems walking away from her in pursuit of their dreams, Hafiz hadn't been able to bear leaving her and had brought her to his home. Well, not his home, but his home country.

As much as she wanted to be part of Hafiz's life and share her life with him, she needed to be patient. She had to trust that Hafiz knew what he was doing. Lacey sighed deeply. She wasn't used to allowing another to take charge.

But she was in a country that followed different codes of conduct. She was also in love with a prince, and she didn't know much about royal life. Her presence in Hafiz's world required delicacy.

Lacey was amazed that Hafiz could even breathe among all the rules and regulations. But not once did he complain. His strong shoulders never sagged from the burden. The man was driven to attack every challenge and reach a goal he never discussed, but Lacey guessed that world domination was just the beginning. His obligations were never far from his mind. That is, until he was in bed with her. Then the world stopped as they fulfilled every fantasy their bodies craved and every wish their hearts desired.

Pleasure nestled low in her stomach, beneath the stifling black gabardine caftan. Lacey stuffed the English newspaper into her plastic shopping bag that contained the crimson desert flowers. She hoped the article offered good news, although she couldn't imagine the press saying anything less than flattering.

She hurried off the curb, and the blowing horn of a filthy truck had her jumping back to the sidewalk. Reddish clouds billowed from the dirt road and settled into a fine layer on her soft black boots.

She waved her hand in front of her face, blinking away the grit. Lacey wrinkled her nose at the tart smell of animals, car fumes and rotting sewage. She knew the small country just recently came into wealth, but if this was a decade of progress, she was grateful she hadn't seen the unenlightened country.

A memory flickered of Hafiz talking about his country when they had first met. He'd spoken with love and pride about the rich heritage and romance of the desert. Hafiz had described the tribal music and the exotic spices lingering in the starry nights. When he'd told the story of how the sultanate had been named after the first sultana, Lacey had thought Rudaynah had to be a romantic paradise.

Never trust a man's idea of romance, Lacey decided as she determinedly stepped into traffic. The high-pitched ring of bicycle bells shrieked in her ears as she zigzagged her way across the street. She dodged a bored donkey pulling a cart of pungent waste matter. A bus whipped past, her plastic bag swatting against one of the male passengers hanging outside the overcrowded and rusted vehicle.

Lacey hurried to her apartment in earnest. Shadows grew longer and darker as the sun dipped precariously closer to the horizon. She nodded a greeting to the armed guards at the gates of the condominium complex. The men, all in olive green uniforms and sporting bushy mustaches, waved her in without a pause in their conversation.

She scurried across the bare courtyard, pausing only as a big insect with a vicious-sounding buzz flew in front of her. Gritting her teeth as she shuddered with revulsion, Lacey turned the corner to access the private elevator that would lead her straight to the penthouse apartment.

She halted when she saw a man waiting for the elevator. Lacey barely had time to gasp as her mind snatched a flurry of disjointed images. A white flowing robe. A golden chord over the white *kaffiyeh* that covered his hair. She didn't need to see the man's face to sense the impenetrable wall of arrogant masculinity. Of power and privilege. There was only one man who enjoyed a life with no limitations or impossibilities.

"Hafiz?" she whispered.

Prince Hafiz ibn Yusuf Qadi whirled around. "Lacey?" He moved forward and stared at her. He slowly blinked and frowned. His sexy and glamorous mistress was wearing a shapeless caftan and a hideous scarf. There wasn't a hint of makeup on her pale face, but she was still a stunning beauty.

"What are you doing down here?" Prince Hafiz plucked off her sunglasses. He needed to see her eyes. He could always tell what she was thinking and feeling when he met her bright blue gaze.

After he snatched the glasses, Hafiz pushed down the head scarf and was rewarded with a cascade of copper-red curls. His fingers flexed. He wanted to touch her hair. Fan it out and allow the last rays of the sun to catch the fiery color. Sink his fingers into the soft weight as he kissed her hard.

Instead, he slowly, reluctantly, let his hand fall to his side. He gripped her sunglasses until the tips of his fingers whitened. He could not touch her. Not here, not in public. One graze, one brush of skin, and he wouldn't stop.

It didn't help that Lacey wanted to greet him with a kiss. The sight of her closed eyes and parted lips whirled him back to the first time he'd seen her. That fateful night he had entered the luxury hotel near the St. Louis waterfront.

The lobby had bustled with activity and there was a piano bar to the side. The deceptively languorous music had caught his attention, but it was her singing that had made him turn around. Soft and clear like the voice of a well-bred lady, but so rich and velvety that it sparked his wicked imagination.

And when he had seen her, his heart had slammed against his ribs. Lacey was an intriguing mix of contrasts. She had looked like an innocent girl, but her voice held a wealth of experience. Her red hair had flowed past her shoulders like a veil, touching the simple blue evening gown. It should have been a modest dress that covered her from her slender neck to her delicate ankles, yet it had lovingly clung to every curve.

Hafiz had known she was trouble, but that hadn't stopped him from walking toward the piano as she'd coaxed a longing note from the ivory keys.

She hadn't seen his approach as she closed her eyes and raised her flushed face to the sky, swept away from the music. And he had allowed her to take him with her.

Hafiz forced himself to the present and away from the untroubled past. His gaze drifted to the voluminous black gown veiling her body from his eyes. For some reason, that irked him. "What are you wearing?"

She opened her eyes and frowned before she placed her hands on her hips. The movement gave him some indication of where the soft swells and curves were underneath her outfit. "I could ask the same about you," she said as her wide eyes roamed over his appearance. "I have never seen you like this. It's straight out of *Lawrence of Arabia.*"

Lacey's voice was deep and husky as the desire shone in her eyes. When she looked at him like that... His skin flushed and pulled tight. How did this woman make him this hot, this fast, without even touching him?

His body hardened, and he gulped in the hot desert air. He could take Lacey against this hidden corner and capture her cries of ecstasy with his mouth within minutes. All he needed was... Hafiz shook his head slightly. What was he thinking? The last thing he needed was for the sultan to discover he had a mistress living in the shadow of the palace.

"This is a *dishdasha,"* he explained gruffly as he tried to contain the lust that heated his blood. "I wear it for royal functions. Now explain what you are doing outside alone."

She held up her plastic bag and lightly jostled the contents. "I went shopping."

"Shopping," he repeated dully.

"Yes, I wear this whenever I leave the apartment." She glided her hand down the black gabardine with the flair of a game show model demonstrating a prize.

"I know Rudaynah only asks tourists to dress modestly, but I don't know if I fall in that category. I'm not quite a tourist, but I'm not quite a resident, am I? I didn't want to take any chances."

Hafiz barely heard the question. *Whenever she left?* She had done this more than once? Routinely? What did she do? Where did she go? And with whom?

It wouldn't be with a man. He knew he could trust Lacey. She had fallen in love with him that first night and saw no reason to deny it.

But he didn't like the possibility that she had a life apart from him. He was the center of her world, and he didn't want that to end. "Whenever you leave?" he asked as his eyebrows dipped into a ferocious frown. "How often do you go out?"

"You don't need to worry about me." Lacey's smile dropped. "Or are you worried that one of your friends or relatives will meet me?"

Hafiz heard the edge in her tone and felt her impatience. He surrendered to the need to touch her and delve his hands into her hair. He needed to feel the connection that sizzled between them.

Hafiz spanned his fingers along the base of her head and tilted her face up. "I thought you spend your days playing your music," he murmured distractedly.

"And dreaming about you?"

"Of course," he said with a slanted smile.

Her smooth brow wrinkled as she considered what he said. "I can think of you while I'm shopping. I'm talented that way."

"No." His sharp tone stanched any argument. "No more excursions. You don't know the language or the country."

"How else am I going to learn if I don't get out and—"

"You have servants who can shop for you. Yes, yes." He held his hand up as she tried to interrupt. "You've already told me. You're not comfortable with the idea of someone waiting on you. But they are here to take care of you."

"You can't hide me inside all the time," she insisted as she pressed her hand against his chest. His heart thudded from her touch. "I'm not Rapunzel."

"I know," he said resignedly. She often mentioned that European fairy tale. She once told him the basic story line, but someday he needed to read it in case there was more he should know.

Lacey leaned against the wall and sighed. Hafiz flattened his hands next to her head, her sunglasses dangling from his loose grasp. He stared at her mouth, his lips stinging with the need to kiss her.

But this was as close as he would allow himself. If he leaned into her softness, he wouldn't leave.

The tip of her tongue swept along her bottom lip. "Hafiz, we're outside," she reminded him, her voice hitching with scandalized excitement. "You shouldn't be this close."

He knew it, but it didn't stop him. She was his one and only vice, and he was willingly addicted. He had already risked everything to be with her. Each day he made the choice to risk everything for her. But now the choice was taken away from him, and it was all coming to an end.

He bent his head and stopped abruptly. He should pull away. Hafiz remained still as he stared at Lacey's mouth. Their ragged breathing sounded loud to his ears. One kiss could bring him peace or could set him on fire. One kiss would lead to another.

As if he were in a trance, Hafiz grazed his fingertips against her brow. He caressed her cheek, wishing it were his mouth on her. Hafiz swallowed hard as he remembered how her skin tasted.

He shouldn't be with her. No, it was more than that. He shouldn't *want* to be with her. Lacey Maxwell was forbidden.

Wanting Lacey went against everything he had been taught. He should only find honorable and chaste women from his sultanate attractive. Yet the only woman he noticed was Lacey.

She was bold and beautiful. Instead of hiding her curves, she flaunted her body. She showed no shame in her desire for him. And instead of trying to tame him, Lacey encouraged the wild streak inside him that he had tried so hard to suffocate.

The sound of his heartbeat pounded in his ears as he stroked Lacey's jaw. She tilted her head, exposing her slender throat. He wanted to sweep his fingers along the elegant column and dip his hand beneath the caftan. He wanted to hear her shallow breaths turn into groans and whispers.

But that would be reckless. Hafiz dragged his thumb against her lips. He traced the shape of her mouth over and over until her lips clung to his skin.

Lacey turned her face away. Hafiz gripped her chin and held her still. With a growl of surrender, he bent down to claim her mouth with his.

"Hafiz," she whispered fiercely. "We will be seen."

That warning could form ice in his sizzling veins

like no other. His chest rose and fell as he reined in runaway needs. With great reluctance, he drew away.

"We should leave before one of the neighbors spots me," Lacey said shakily as she pulled the scarf over her head.

Disappointment scored his chest as she tucked her glorious hair away. "I don't like seeing you covered up like this." He never thought about how he would feel seeing his woman veiled, but it felt intrinsically wrong to conceal Lacey's captivating beauty and character.

"Believe me, I don't like wearing it." She reached for her sunglasses. "It's like an oven, but it makes me invisible and that's all that matters."

He flashed a disbelieving look. "Lacey, you could never be invisible."

Her smile was dazzling as she blushed with pleasure. It was as if he had given her the ultimate compliment.

"Take off your scarf," he insisted in a rough whisper. "No one will see. Everyone will be at prayer." Hafiz wondered why he resented the scarf and sunglasses so much that he was willing to risk the chance of discovery. He reached for her arm and pulled her close.

"Don't be too sure. Most people acted like they were ready to celebrate tonight. I don't know why—" The plastic bag fell from her wrist. She bent down to retrieve the contents, and he followed her descent. Her sharp cry startled him.

"Lacey?" He looked down at the cracked cement floor and didn't understand what was wrong when he saw the dark red flowers resting unblemished on the floor. He almost missed the English newspaper with his picture on the front page. The bold head-line grabbed him by the throat and hurtled him into despair.

Prince Hafiz to Marry

CHAPTER TWO

LACEY STARED AT the engagement announcement. Her mind refused to comprehend the words. "Marry?" she whispered. Her wild gaze flew to Hafiz's harsh face. "You're getting married?"

She waited in agony as he rose to his full height. He looked very tall and intimidating. Almost like a stranger.

Lacey didn't realize she was holding her breath until he answered. "Yes."

The single word sent her universe into a spiral. "I don't…I don't…" She stared at the headline again, but the pain was too raw, too intense. She hurriedly stuffed the newspaper and flowers back into the bag.

Her hands shook as the rage and something close to fear swirled inside her. Fear of losing everything. Pure anger at the thought of Hafiz with another woman. The fury threatened to overpower her. She wanted to scream at the injustice and claw at something. Stake her claim. Hafiz belonged to her.

"You have been with another woman." She couldn't believe it. "All this time, you were with someone else."

Hafiz's eyes narrowed at the accusation. "No. You

have been the only woman in my life since I met you in St. Louis a year ago."

She was the only woman, and yet he was going to marry another? Lacey fumbled with her sunglasses and tossed them in the bag. "Then how are you...I don't understand."

He braced his feet a shoulders' width apart and clasped his hands behind his back, preparing for battle. "I met the bride today and she agreed."

Lacey's mouth gaped open. "You just met her?" She snatched the flicker of hope and held on tight. "So, it's an arranged marriage."

Hafiz let out a bark of humorless laughter. "Of course."

"Then, what's the problem?" She moved slowly as she stood. Her arms and legs felt limp and shaky. She lurched as she stepped on the hem of her insufferable caftan. "Say that you won't get married."

He looked away. "I can't." Regret tinged his voice.

Lacey wanted to stamp her foot and demand a better answer, but she knew she wouldn't get it. Not with his shuttered expression and the regal tilt of his stubborn chin. "It's not like you're the crown prince," she argued, "although I don't understand that since you're the oldest son. But this means you have more freedom."

Hafiz's eyes closed wearily for a brief moment. "For the last time, the sultan chooses the next in line for the throne. My father chose my brother. And, no, I don't have any freedom in this matter, even though I will never rule. In my case, I have less."

She didn't want to hear that. Thick emotions already clogged her aching throat. "You should never have agreed to marry this woman," she said as her voice wobbled.

He turned his attention back to her. "I gave my consent," he said gently. "I can't take it back."

What about the promises he made to her? The ones he made first. The ones about how they would be together. Didn't those promises matter? Didn't *she* matter?

"Why did you agree in the first place?" She held the plastic bag to her chest. She would rather hold on to something solid and strong like Hafiz until the emotional storm passed, which would still leave her feeling battered and stinging with pain, but he would prevent her from breaking. "You should have refused."

"I couldn't this time." Hafiz winced the moment he revealed too much. He pressed his lips into a straight line.

Lacey stared at him with open suspicion. "This time?" she echoed. "How long have you been looking for a wife?"

"Could we not discuss this here?" he bit out tersely. "Let's go back to the apartment." He guided her to the elevator, keeping a firm hand on her arm as she still weaved from the unpleasant shock. He pressed the call button, and she watched as if her life depended on it, but her brain couldn't register the simple, everyday action.

"Marry," she repeated and shook her head. "I don't believe this. Why didn't you tell me?"

"I am telling you." He kept his eyes on the descending lighted floor numbers.

"Now. After everything is settled." She couldn't be bothered to hide the accusation in her voice.

He spared a glance at her. "Not quite, but it is official as of this morning. I wanted to tell you before you found out from another source."

That explained the missing newspapers. "How considerate." She felt his start of surprise from her bitter sarcasm, but she didn't care. Hafiz was getting married. To someone else. The knowledge stabbed at her heart. It was a wonder she didn't break from the piercing force. "When is the wedding taking place?"

"After Eid." His answer was almost swallowed by the clank and thump of the arriving elevator.

Eid. That holiday came after the month of Ramadan, if she recalled correctly. She remembered something being mentioned in the paper about that coming soon. "Three months?" she made a guess.

He held the sliding metal doors open for her. "More or less."

Lacey walked into the elevator compartment, her head spinning. Three months. She only had three months with Hafiz.

What was she thinking? She had no more time left. Oh, God. She wasn't strong enough to handle this. She was going to shatter from the pain. Hafiz was an engaged man. Off-limits. And she never had any warning.

Her mouth suddenly felt dry as she instinctively pressed the burgeoning wails and sobs into silence until they were ready to burst from her skin. "You should have told me you were looking for a wife."

"I wasn't. I have no interest in getting married. I held it off for as long as possible."

Lacey reeled back in shock. Hafiz had no interest in marriage? *At all?* Not even to her? If that was the case, then what had the past six months been about?

"My parents were looking for a wife for me," he clarified sternly.

"But you knew they were," she argued. "You knew this was going to happen."

Hafiz said nothing and pressed the top floor button several times as the elevator doors slowly shut.

Winning that point of the argument was a hollow victory. "How long have they been looking?" A part of her wanted to know, the other part wanted to deny that any of this was happening.

He stood silently, his jaw tightly clenched. A muscle twitched in his cheek. Lacey thought for a moment he didn't hear her and was about to repeat the question when he finally answered. "A couple of years."

"A...couple of *years*?" She couldn't possibly have heard that correctly. Lacey folded her arms across her chest. "From the time that you knew me, from the very first time you *propositioned* me, you were also on the marriage market? And not once did you find the chance to tell me?"

Why would he? Lacey thought bitterly. He hadn't considered her to be in the running. She was just a bit of fun on the side. A temporary distraction. Oh, she was a fool.

"Marriage negotiations are delicate and complex," he explained as impatience roughened his words. "It could have taken even longer to find a suitable match."

Suitable. She sneered at the term. It was a code word for the right bloodline and the right upbringing from the right family. Not a blue-eyed American who was also an unemployed nightclub musician.

Oh, and suitable meant someone who was pure and virginal. She mustn't forget that.

The injustice of it all flared to new heights. "Not once did you tell me, and yet I dropped my entire life to be with you." Her voice raised another octave. "I moved to the far-off corners of the earth, to this hell—"

"The Sultanate of Rudaynah is not hell." His low growl was similar to that of a wild cat ready to pounce.

"—And exist solely for you and your pleasure! And you don't have the decency to tell me that you're getting married?" Her eyes narrowed into a withering glare.

He gestured with his hands. "Calm down."

"Calm down?" She thought now was as good a time as any to rant. She was ready to punctuate her tantrum by throwing her shopping bag at his sinfully gorgeous face. "Calm down! No, I will not calm down. The man I love, the man I sacrificed everything for is throwing it all away right back into my face," she hissed, her cheeks hot with fury. "Believe me, this is not a time to calm down."

Hafiz was suddenly in front of her. He made a grab for her, but she raised her hands, warding him off. Lacey fought the urge to burrow her head into his shoulder and weep.

"I am not throwing you away, damn it. How could I?" he asked as his bronze eyes silently pleaded for understanding. "You are the best thing that has ever happened to me."

Lacey looked away and tilted her head against the corner. She needed something to lean against anyway as her knees were incapable of supporting her. A buzzing filled her head. She took short, even breaths of the stifling air and blinked back the dark spots.

As the elevator made its slow, rocky ascent, Lacey realized that Hafiz must be equally unnerved by the turn of the events. He had cursed. Another first for the day. Hafiz never, ever cursed. But then, he always controlled the situation and his environment with the same iron will he used over his temper.

Over himself, really. The man never drank alcohol or gambled. He did not live in excess. His sculpted muscles were that of an athlete in training. He barely slept, too busy working to improve the living conditions of Rudaynah. When he wasn't fulfilling his royal and patriotic duties, he met every family obligation. Even marry his parent's choice.

The only time he went wild, the only time he allowed his control to slip, was when they were in bed. Lacey winced, and the first scalding teardrop fell.

Tears streamed out of her eyes and burned jagged lines down her hot cheeks. Why had she thought Hafiz was considering a future with her? Not once did he mention the possibility of happily-ever-after. Never did the word "marriage" ever cross his lips.

But the dream had been harbored deep in her heart, secretly growing. It had been incredibly naïve and wrong to think all she had to do was be patient. She thought that if she came here and slowly entered the culture, she would eventually stand publicly by Hafiz's side as his wife.

Only that dream died the moment Hafiz pledged himself to another. She gasped as the words plunged into her heart. The surrounding blackness she had been fighting back swiftly invaded her mind.

Pledged to another...

The buzzing grew louder and almost masked Hafiz's shout of alarm.

"Lacey!" Hafiz caught her as she slid down the wall. He plucked off her scarf, and her head lolled to one side. He supported her head with his shoulder and noted that her unnaturally pale face was sticky with sweat. He patted her clammy cheek with his hand. "Lacey," he repeated, trying to rouse her.

Her eyelashes fluttered. "So hot."

He gathered her in his arms. The ill-fitting black gown bunched around her slender figure. "I'll take care of you," he promised, holding her tighter. And he would, he vowed to himself, until his last breath. No matter what she thought, he would never cast her aside.

The elevator finally stopped on the penthouse floor. He searched her features, vaguely aware how her curly long hair hung defiantly like a copper flag and her bare legs dangled from the crook of his elbow, exposing her ivory skin for the world to see. If they were caught in this compromising embrace, so be it. Lacey's safety and comfort were always top priority, but now it was more essential than his next heartbeat, Hafiz decided as he stepped out of the elevator and onto the open-air hallway to the apartment.

The sun was setting. Dark reds and rich purples washed the sky as evening prayers were sung from a nearby loudspeaker. Hafiz kept his eyes out for any potential trouble, but he saw no one strolling the grounds or outside the condominiums across the courtyard. But from the domestic sounds emitting from the neighbors' homes on the other floors, the situation could change in an instant.

Carrying Lacey to her front door at a brisk pace, Hafiz noted he wasn't even breathing hard from lifting her. She weighed barely anything. He glanced down at her face and the fragility struck him like a fist.

Not for the first time did he wonder if moving Lacey to Rudaynah had been the best decision for her. Life in hiding had taken its toll. Why hadn't he seen that before? Or did he not want to see it?

Lacey stirred as if she was acutely aware of his perusal. "I'm fine," she murmured and tentatively ran her tongue over her parched lips.

"No, you're not." He leaned heavily against the doorbell and waited at the iron grille door until the American servant wearing a loose T-shirt and cargo pants came to the door.

"Your Highness! What happened?" Glenn asked as he unlocked the door bolts with economical movements. His craggy face showed no alarm, but his watchful eyes were alert. His body, lean from many years of military training, vibrated with readiness to act on the first command from his employer.

"It's all right. She fainted from the heat." Hafiz kicked off his sandals at the door and moved past the older man. "I'll get her into the shower. Have your wife prepare something very cold and sweet for her to drink."

"I'm sorry, Your Highness." Glenn raked his hand over his bristly gray hair. "She said—"

"It's all right," he repeated, calling over his shoulder as he made way to the master bedroom. "Lacey has always had a problem following directions."

"I'm not dead, you know," Lacey said with her eyes closed. "I can hear every word."

"Good, because I do not want you venturing outside again without Glenn," Hafiz said as he stepped into the large room where he spent many hours exploring Lacey's body and revealing the darkest recesses of his heart. This time the sumptuous silks and oversized pillows didn't stir his hot blood. He wanted to tuck Lacey between the colorful sheets and not let her out of bed until she regained her vibrancy. "He is your bodyguard and—"

"He is to play the role of my next of kin if any questions are asked because single women are not allowed to travel alone in this country," Lacey ended in a monotone. She let out a slow, stuttering sigh that seemed to originate from somewhere deep inside her. "I know."

"Then, don't let it happen again." He pushed the bathroom door open with his bare foot. Slapping the light switch outside the door with the palm of his hand, he entered the windowless room now flooding with light.

"It won't."

The determination in her voice made him hesitate. He cautiously watched her face as he set her down gently, sliding her feminine curves along his length. For once her expression showed nothing. Her eyes veiled her feelings. Usually her eyes would darken with righteous indignation, glow with rapturous delight and twinkle with every emotion in between. The sudden change in her behavior troubled him.

He wanted to hold her close until he could read her thoughts, but Lacey had other ideas as she moved away from him. "Can you stand on your own?" he asked.

"Yes." She took another step back and shucked off her cloth boots. The movements lacked her usual energy.

He kept one hand outstretched in case he had to catch her as he started the shower full blast. Hafiz turned his attention on Lacey and quickly divested her of her black caftan.

"Lacey!" His startled hoarse cry echoed in the small room. The sight of her barely-there peach lingerie was a shocking contrast against the conservative cloth. Hafiz's body reacted immediately. The heavy black material dropped from his fists and flopped on the wet floor.

"What?" She inspected her arms and legs. "What's wrong?"

He cleared his throat, wishing he could also clear the sharp arousal tightening his body. "You're supposed to wear several layers of clothes under the caftan." He unhooked the front closure of her bra, his knuckles grazing her breast. He saw the tremor in his hands. He was acting like a callow youth.

"Are you kidding?" She skimmed the high-cut panties down her legs and kicked them aside. "I would boil alive."

His gaze traveled as the peach satin landed on the black fabric. The searing image branded in his mind. The way he would look at women in the shapeless caftan was forever changed. He swallowed roughly as he controlled his baser instinct. "What if you had gotten caught?"

"No one would have found out. You are the only person who has shown enough nerve to get that close." She arched her eyebrow in disapproval.

And he was going to keep it that way. "Here, get under the water." He pulled her to the showerhead.

"Oh! Ow!" Lacey squealed in dismay as the icy cold spray hit her body. She jumped back and rubbed her hands over her arms. "This is so cold."

"You'll get used to it in just a minute," he replied as he always did to her comments on the lack of heated water. The familiarity calmed him while her beaded nipples made his brain sluggish.

"You can leave now," she said through chattering teeth. She looked away from him and tested the temperature by dipping her foot in the cold water.

He leaned against the door and folded his arms across his chest. "I don't want you passing out in the shower."

"I won't. Now go before your royal gown gets soaked." She shooed him away with her hands.

She had a point. The bathroom, already hot as a sauna, was in the traditional Rudaynahi design, with the exception of a European commode. The concrete floor had a drain and was also to be used as the shower floor. Since there was no plastic curtain or glass shower door, the water was already spraying every inch of the bathroom.

"If you're sure," Hafiz said and flashed a wicked smile. "But I can just as easily take it off."

She glared back at him. "I'm sure."

His smile turned wry at her ungracious rejection.

He shouldn't have made the offer. He knew that but went for it anyway. "I'll be outside," Hafiz said. Lacey didn't respond as she stuck her head fully under the spray.

He stepped out of the bathroom and almost collided with the housekeeper who carried a small tray into the bedroom. The tall frosty glass of juice rattled against a plate of figs and dates.

"How is she doing?" Annette asked as she set the tray on the bedside table. "Do we need to call a doctor?"

"No, she's not sick." The uncertain look of the older woman irritated him. If he truly felt Lacey needed medical care, he would call the American doctor who'd already discovered that cashing in favors from a prince was worth more than any currency in a country that relied heavily on the bartering system.

The physician was brilliant and up to date on medicine. Hafiz had seen that firsthand when Lacey arrived in the country and had drunk water that had not been purified. That week had been torture, and Hafiz was insistent that she was given the best care, no matter what. Hafiz would never place secrecy above Lacey's well-being, and it stung to have someone silently questioning his priorities.

"She's overheated," he explained, keeping the defensiveness out of his voice. "The shower is already doing wonders."

"We threw away the newspapers like you requested, but we never thought Lacey would leave to get one." The woman twisted the pleat of her yellow sundress with nervous hands and slid a worried glance at the closed bathroom door.

"It's no one's fault," he said. No one's but his own. He should have prepared Lacey for the possibility of his wedding, but he'd held on to the hope that his intended bride would have declined the offer. "Please, find something light for her to wear."

"Of course." The housekeeper gratefully accepted the task and opened the doors to the armoire, revealing gossamer-thin cotton in every color of the rainbow.

Hafiz walked into the simply appointed drawing room and tried to recapture the peace he always felt whenever he stepped into this home. Decorated with an eclectic mix of wood tables carved in the severe Rudaynahi style and chunky upholstered sofas from the Western world, Lacey had managed to add her upbeat personality with tribal throw rugs and colorful paintings from local artisans.

The apartment was more than a home. It was a haven. It was the only place he felt both passion and peace. The only place in the world he experienced unconditional love.

Hafiz walked slowly to the grand piano that sat in the middle of the room and under the carefully positioned spotlight. It had been incredibly difficult shipping the instrument into the country. Flying in a piano tuner every couple of months was no easy feat, but seeing Lacey's joy and listening to her soulful music made it all worthwhile.

He fingered the sheet music scattered on the polished black wood. The woman had the talent to become a successful recording artist. Hafiz had told her enough times, but she always shook her head in disagreement. Music was a big part of her, but she didn't want to be consumed with the ladder of success like her parents, who were still striving for their big break. She didn't have the desire.

But she stored up all her passion for him. Did that make him feel less guilty in whisking her to his country? The edges of the sheet music crinkled under his fingertips. Because she had no interest in pursuing a career? Because she didn't have family ties?

Hafiz pondered the question as he walked to the doors leading to the balcony that overlooked the Persian Gulf. He admitted that it made it easier to ask her to drop everything and follow him. To stay in the apartment and wait for him. Not once had she complained or shown resentment until today.

And she had every right. He had risked everything for more time with Lacey. The relationship they had was forbidden. And now, as of today, it was impossible.

Only Hafiz didn't allow that word in his vocabulary, and he wasn't willing to let the idea invade his life with Lacey.

"What are you still doing here?" Lacey asked at the doorway on the other side of the long room.

Hafiz turned around. Lacey's wet hair was slicked back into a copper waterfall. She had changed into a pink cotton caftan that clung to her damp skin. Gold threads were woven into the fabric and sparkled like stars.

"Are you feeling better?" he asked, silently watching the housekeeper duck into the kitchen.

"Much. You're free to go." She walked toward the front door.

"Lacey, we need to talk."

"No kidding, but I don't want to right now." She

gripped the thick door handle. "You have had years to think about this. I have had less than an hour."

"Lacey—" He crossed the room and stood in front of her, prepared to take the brunt of her anger and soak up her tears.

"I want you to go." She flung open the door.

Hafiz's shoulders flexed with tension. Every instinct told him to stay, but he knew what she said made sense. It was strange to have her as the calm one and he filled with impetuous emotions. He didn't like the role reversal.

Hafiz agreed with a sharp nod. "I will be here tomorrow after work." He leaned down to brush her cheek with a gentle kiss.

She turned her head abruptly. "Don't." Her eyes focused on the hallway outside the iron grille.

His heart stopped. Lacey had never rejected his touch. "What are you saying?" he asked in a low voice as his lungs shriveled, unable to take in the next breath.

The muscles in her throat jerked. "You shouldn't touch me." The words were a mere whisper. "The moment you became engaged, the moment you chose another woman, we no longer exist."

Hafiz grasped her chin between his thumb and forefinger. "You don't mean that," he said, staring at her intensely. As if he could change her mind through his sheer willpower.

"Yes, I do."

He swallowed down the rising fear. "Obviously, you are still suffering from your collapse." The tip of his thumb caressed the angry line of her bottom lip.

Lacey yanked away from his touch. "I'm thinking quite clearly. You made your choice." She took a step back behind the door, shielding herself from him. "And this is mine."

"You are going to regret those words. You can't send me away." He stepped toward her, ready to prove it.

Lacey's glare was so cold it could have frozen the desert air seeping into the apartment. "Do you want me to cause a scene in front of this complex to get you to leave?"

Her threat surprised Hafiz. That wasn't like her. She knew his weak spots but had always protected him. Now she was so angry, she was becoming a dangerous woman.

Would she try to hurt him because he was getting married? No, not Lacey. She was loyal to him…but when she thought she didn't have any competition. How could he convince her that this marriage was in name only?

He decided to change his strategy. "I will return," he said, shoving his feet into his sandals. The expensive leather threatened to snap under his angry motions. "And you will be here waiting for me."

Defiance flared in her blue eyes. "Don't tell me what to do. You have no right."

"You still belong to me, Lacey," he announced as he left. "Nothing and no one will change that."

CHAPTER THREE

THE WHITE ROBES slapped angrily against Hafiz's legs as he stormed into his office. He would rather be anywhere else but here. Although the palace's murky shadows descending on the spartan rooms were good companions to his dark mood this evening.

"Your Highness." His private secretary clumsily hung up the phone. The withered old man bowed low, his fragile bones creaking. "His Majesty wishes to speak to you."

Hafiz set his jaw as dread seeped inside him. The day couldn't get any worse. The sultan didn't command appointments from his eldest offspring unless there was or would be an unpleasant event.

"When did he make this request?"

"Ten minutes ago, Your Highness," the elderly man answered, his focus on the threadbare Persian rug. "I called your cell phone and left several messages."

Of course. He had turned off his phone so he wouldn't bend to the overwhelming need to call Lacey. His show of confidence that she would follow his orders was going to cost him in more ways than one. Hafiz wanted to roar with frustration, but he needed to stay calm and focused for the sultan.

Hafiz turned and checked his appearance in the gilt-edged mirror. He didn't see anything Sultan Yusuf would find offensive, but the ruler didn't need to hunt long for something to disapprove about his son. Unable to delay the inevitable, Hafiz set his shoulders back and strode to the palace offices.

When he entered the sultan's suite, Hafiz stood respectfully at the double doors and waited to be announced. As one of the secretaries hurried to the massive wooden desk to convey the message to the sultan, Hafiz grew aware of the sideway glances and growing tension. He coldly met the employees' stares one by one until the gazes skittered down in belated respect.

Sultan Yusuf dismissed his secretaries with the flick of his hand. The men hurried past Hafiz and through the doors. Their expressions of grateful relief concerned him.

The sultan continued to sit behind his desk and read a note on thick white paper. He took his time to deign to acknowledge his son's presence. "Hafiz," Sultan Yusuf finally said.

Hafiz approached the sultan. "Your Majesty." Hafiz gave the briefest deferential nod as defiance flowed through his veins.

The sultan tossed the paper on to his desk. "Be seated."

The lack of mind games made Hafiz suspicious, which it was probably supposed to achieve. Hafiz sat down on the chair across from the desk. Tradition dictated that he should keep his head down and his gaze averted. He was never good at tradition.

The sultan leaned back in his chair, steepled his fingers, and studied Hafiz. Not even a whisper of affection crossed his lined face. "You are very fortunate that the Abdullah daughter agreed to the marriage."

Fortune had nothing to do with it. It didn't matter who his bride was. He was marrying this woman for two reasons. It was his royal duty and it was another step toward redemption.

"This girl knows about your—" the king's fingers splayed apart "—misspent youth, as does her family."

Hafiz clenched his teeth and willed his hands to stay straight on his knees. He would not respond. He would not allow his father to spike his temper.

"They will use that knowledge to their advantage as the wedding preparations draw closer. The dowry is not nearly worthy enough for a prince. We're fortunate they didn't demand a bridal price."

Hafiz still said nothing. His teeth felt as if they would splinter. His fingers itched to curl and dig into his knees.

"Have you anything to say, Hafiz?"

He did, but most of it wasn't wise to say aloud. "I regret that my past mistakes still cost our family." And his regret was as honest as it was strong. Nothing could erase the suffering he'd caused Rudaynah. The simple truth destroyed him, and his life's mission was to prevent any future suffering from his hand.

"As do I." Sultan Yusuf sighed heavily. "The reason I'm telling you this is that I expect many maneuvers from the Abdullah family." He smacked his lips with distaste as he mentioned his future in-laws. "Any male relative could trick you. Talk you down the dowry. Say you made a promise or agreement when there was none."

Annoyance welled up inside Hafiz's chest. From

years of practice, his expression didn't show his feelings. Hafiz negotiated multi-million-dollar deals, brokered delicate international agreements and increased the wealth of this country ten times over. But his family didn't respect his accomplishments. They only remembered his mistakes.

"You will have no interaction with the Abdullah family," the sultan commanded. "All inquiries must be directed to my office. Do you understand, Hafiz?"

"Yes, Your Majesty." He didn't have a problem following that order. If that was the purpose of the meeting, Hafiz wondered why the sultan didn't dictate a memo so he didn't have to speak to his son.

"After all," the ruler continued, "your mother and I cannot afford another scandal from you."

Hafiz closed his eyes as the pain washed over him. He should have seen that coming.

"This marriage must happen." The sultan tapped an authoritative finger on the desk. The thud echoed loudly in Hafiz's head. "If the engagement is broken, it will shame this family."

Shaming the family was his sole specialty. The statement was left unspoken, but Hafiz could hear it plainly in his father's manner. It wasn't anything his conscience hadn't shouted for more years than he cared to remember.

"You've already lost your right to the throne because of your poor choices," Sultan Yusuf said with brutal frankness. "If you harm this agreement, I will make certain you lose everything you hold dear."

Did his father think he would try to sabotage the wedding agreement? Hafiz was stunned at the possibility. Hadn't his actions proven he would sacrifice his personal wants for the good of the country?

"But, if you do not cause any delay or scandal—" he paused and sliced a knowing look "—I will give you the one thing you desire."

Hafiz flinched. His mind immediately went to Lacey. A white-hot panic blinded him. Did the sultan know about her?

"Marry the bride I choose, and you will resume your rightful place. You will become the heir to the throne once again."

Lacey's fingers dragged against the ivory keys of her piano, but she didn't play a note. She couldn't. The music inside her had been silenced.

Glenn and Annette had retired hours ago, but she couldn't sleep no matter how hard she tried. Her body felt limp and wrung out, and her mind craved for oblivion.

What was it about her? Why was she so easy to discard? First her parents and now Hafiz. She didn't understand it.

Lacey always held on to the belief that she would have bonded with her parents if they had taken her on the road with them. They would have remembered her birthdays and special occasions. They wouldn't have forgotten her all those times or accidentally left her to fend for herself on school vacations. If they hadn't sent her off to live with distant relatives or family friends, she would have some sort of relationship today with her mother and father.

But now she knew her parents didn't get the full blame. There was something wrong with her. It didn't matter how freely and completely she gave her love; she would not get it in return. She was unlovable.

Lacey stood and walked to the balcony doors and peered outside. No lights glowed against the darkness. Outside appeared silent and empty.

If only her mind would quiet down like the town below her. She leaned her head against the glass pane that was now cool from the desert night. The moment Hafiz had left, fragmented thoughts and fears had bombarded her mind. She'd paced her room as unspoken questions whirled through her head. She'd stared numbly at the walls for hours.

No matter how much the housekeeper had tried to tempt her with food, Lacey refused to eat. Her throat, swollen and achy from crying, would surely choke on the smallest morsel. Sustenance meant nothing and she had curled up on Hafiz's side of the bed. There she had muffled her cries in his pillow when one more minute of living without him became unbearable.

Her mind felt as chaotic as the clothes jumbled inside her suitcase. She packed her belongings, which were pathetically few. It was a mocking symbol of the emptiness of her life before she'd met Hafiz and her barren future without him. Only now she had even less, because she was leaving everything behind along with her heart.

Lacey frowned, trying to hold her emotions together. There were too many things she had to do, like finding a new home.

Lacey pressed the heels of her hands against her puffy eyes. The business of breaking up was beyond her. She needed a fresh start. Somewhere that held no memories. A place where Hafiz couldn't find her.

Not that he would follow her across the world. He'd made his choice. And it wasn't her. It was never going to be her.

She didn't want to know anything about the woman who got to share Hafiz's life. The one who would wear his ring, bear his name and carry his children in her womb. Lacey blinked as her eyes stung, but she'd already used up her tears.

Lacey twisted around when she heard the key in the lock. Hope stuttered through her exhausted body as Hafiz entered. He halted when he saw her across the room.

"Hafiz." She instinctively moved toward him like a moth to a flame. "What are you doing here?"

She stared at him, memorizing every detail. He was dressed like a laborer. While the outfit was an unusual choice for a member of the royal family, Hafiz lent a sophisticated elegance to the rough work clothes.

The simple tunic was as black as his short hair. The cotton sluiced down his muscular chest and skimmed past his knees. His jeans strained against his powerful legs as he slid his feet out of scuffed sandals. His high-tech watch was nowhere to be found, but the royal ring gleamed proudly on his hand.

"I wasn't sure you would be here." His hands clenched and unclenched the keys.

Lacey guiltily flashed a look in the direction of the bedroom where her bags were packed and stowed away under the bed. "And you're checking up on me?" she asked as her eyebrows arched with disbelief. "You could have called."

"No. I came here to say goodbye." He set down the key with hypnotic slowness. "Tonight."

She froze as the words pummeled her bruised heart. Tonight? Her chest heaved, and she struggled for her next breath. "Now?"

Hafiz nodded. "I had a meeting with the sultan earlier this evening." He stared at the keys as though he wanted to snatch them back. "If any of my actions prevent the forthcoming marriage, I will lose everything."

"Your father threatened you?" she whispered in horror.

"The sultan warned me," he corrected. "And I can't help but wonder if he knows about you. Maybe not your name or where you live, but that I have someone like you in my life."

Someone like you... The phrase scratched at her. What did it mean? More importantly, what did it mean to Hafiz?

She stood in front of him, and placed her hand on his arm, offering him comfort. Not that he needed it. Hafiz had the strength to stand alone. "You shouldn't be forced to marry someone you don't love."

Her words seemed to startle him. "Lacey," Hafiz said in a groan as he cupped her cheek with his hand. "A royal marriage never has anything to do with love. It has always been that way."

She closed her eyes as she leaned into his hand, knowing it would be the last time he would caress her. She gathered the last of her self-discipline and withdrew from his touch. Energy arced and flared between them.

"I will miss you, Hafiz," she said brokenly as her throat closed up. The tears she thought couldn't happen beaded on her eyelashes.

Hafiz let out a shuddering breath. He swept his fingertip against the corner of her eye, taking her tears with him. The moisture clung to his knuckle, and he rubbed it into his skin with his thumb, silently sharing her agony.

The image took a chink out of her hard-earned resolve. Lacey wrapped her arms around her stomach before she crumbled altogether. "I had so many questions to ask you, and now I can't remember what they were." All except for one that danced on her tongue. "Did you ever love me?"

Silence throbbed in the air.

Lacey blinked at the question that had tumbled from her mouth. *Of all the things to ask,* her mind screamed.

Hafiz went unnaturally still.

"I don't know why I asked." She shrugged as her pain intensified. "Please, don't answer that."

The words were ripped from deep within her. She desperately wanted to know the answer. She never questioned it before, but she had been living in a fantasy.

Lacey had always felt Hafiz loved her. It was in his touch, in his eyes, and in his smile. But he never said the words, even when she chanted her declaration of love in the height of ecstasy.

It was too late to find out. If he didn't love her, she would never recover. If he did love her, then she would never let go. Even if he was married, even if he kept her hidden. And she couldn't let that happen.

Hafiz frowned. "Lacey..."

"Ssh." She silenced him by pressing her fingers against his parted lips. *"Please."*

He covered her hand with his and placed soft kisses

in the heart of her palm. "I don't want you to leave," he said against her skin.

"Then, come away with me!" She impulsively tangled her fingers with his and pulled him away from the door. His torn expression shamed her. She drew back and let go of his hand. "I'm sorry. That was wrong."

He moved swiftly and crushed her against him. "I can't leave Rudaynah," he whispered, his breath ruffling her hair. "And you can't stay. I don't know what I'm going to do without you. I'm only half alive when you are not around."

He didn't want to give her up, but he had the strength to do it when she wanted to ignore the inevitable. Hafiz would flourish without her while she wilted into a slow death. "In time, you'll forget all about me."

He tightened their embrace. "How can you say that?"

"You will," she predicted with a sigh. It happened to her before, and nothing she did would stop it from happening again. "You need to leave." Now, before it became impossible. Before she threw herself at his feet and begged him to stay.

"Yes." He gradually relaxed his hold but didn't let go. "This was already a risk."

She looked up into his face. The scent of the desert night clung to his warm skin. The steady and strong beat of his heart pounded under her hand. The passion he felt for her shone in his eyes. This was how she wanted to remember him. "Goodbye, Hafiz."

He lowered his face and gently brushed his mouth against hers. Like Lacey, he kept his eyes open, needing to commit this last kiss to memory. The unshed tears in her eyes blurred his image. Lacey's lips clung to his. The craving to deepen the kiss radiated between them. She felt his need to carry her away and the struggle to leave her behind.

"I have to go," he murmured against her mouth.

"I know." The world tilted as he withdrew, and his arms dropped away from her. She felt exposed and weak. A single tear spilled down her cheek. "I wish…" She stopped and bit her lip.

"You wish what?" When she didn't answer, he grabbed her upper arms with his large hands. "Tell me," he pleaded, his fingers biting into her flesh.

"No." She shook her head. She had to be strong and ignore her wants. For both of them. "I wish you… happiness."

Hafiz shook her slightly until tendrils of her hair fell in front of her face. "That was not what you were going to say. Don't end this on a lie," he ordered, agony threading his voice. "Don't leave me with a half-spoken wish, so that I will go mad trying to figure out what you wanted to say."

Lacey looked away. She'd ruined the moment, all because she couldn't let him go. "I can't."

"Tell me what you wish," he said against her ear, teasing her willpower with his husky voice full of promise. "I will make it come true if it's in my power."

"I wish we…" She swallowed. Damn her weakness! "I wish we had at least one more night."

She saw the gleam in Hafiz's bronze eyes. Her request unleashed something dark and primitive inside him. He wanted to claim her, possess her so completely that she would never forget him. As if she could.

"I can grant you that wish," he promised as his features sharpened with lust. "Tonight."

"No." Lacey shook her head. They had to stop now. If she went to bed with him tonight, she would do everything in her power to keep him there. "We can't. You are an engaged man. The sultan has warned you—"

"This is my wish, too." He gathered her close and lifted her in his arms before he strode to the bedroom. "Don't deny me one more night."

CHAPTER FOUR

LACEY CLUNG TO Hafiz as they entered her bedroom.
The bedside lamp offered a faint glow in the large
room, casting shadows on the unmade bed. Hafiz
barely broke his stride when he kicked the door shut.

She wasn't sure why he wasn't rushing to the bed.
Lacey felt the urgency pulsating between them. This
was the last time they would be together. They had to
get a lifetime into one night.

The unfairness of it all hit Lacey, and she tried to
push it away. She didn't want to focus on that. She
wasn't going to waste her last moments with Hafiz
on something she couldn't control.

The only thing she could do was make one beautiful and lasting memory. Have something that could
ease the pain when she thought about the love she
lost.

Hafiz stood by the edge of the bed, and Lacey knelt
on the mattress before him. She pressed her hands
against his cheeks and looked deep into his eyes.

She bit the inside of her lip to prevent from speaking when she saw Hafiz's sadness. It wasn't like him
to show it, but the emotion was too strong; he couldn't
contain it. Lacey closed her eyes and rested her head

against his chest. She wanted to ease his pain. Take
it away from him.

She was hurting, too. It hurt knowing that after
tonight she wouldn't see him, and she couldn't touch
him. She wouldn't be allowed anywhere near him.

Her shaky breath echoed in the room.

"Lacey?" Hafiz's voice was tender as he smoothed
his hand against the crown of her head.

She tilted her face up and sought his mouth. She
poured everything she felt into the kiss. She held nothing back. The pain and the anger. The love and the
unfulfilled dreams.

The heat between them wasn't a slow burn. It flared
hot and wild. Lacey sensed the dangerous power behind it, but this time she didn't care. In the past they
danced around it, knowing it could rage out of control.
This time she welcomed it. Encouraged it.

Hafiz bunched her caftan in his fists. She knew it
was a silent warning. He needed to leash his sexual
hunger, or it could become destructive.

She didn't think that was possible. There was nothing left to destroy. She wanted to climb the heights
with Hafiz and disregard the possibility of plunging
into the depths.

Lacey wrenched her mouth away from Hafiz. Her
breath was uneven as her chest rose and fell. She
watched him as she tore off her caftan, revealing that
she wore nothing underneath.

As she tossed her clothes on to the floor, a part of
her warned her to slow down. This was not what she
wanted their last night to be like. She wanted it soft
and romantic. This was primal and elemental. And she
couldn't stop. She didn't *want* to slow down.

Hafiz shucked off his tunic, exposing his muscular chest. She reached out with the intention to trail her hand down his warm, golden skin. Instead she hooked her hand over the low-slung waistband of his jeans and pulled him close. She gasped as the tips of her breasts rubbed against his coarse chest hair.

Hafiz stretched his arms and wrapped his hands around the bedposts. His move surprised her. He didn't gather her close or take over. He was giving the control to her.

It was a rare gift. Hafiz was always in control. She watched him as she boldly cupped his arousal. A muscle bunched in his jaw, but he said nothing. He didn't move as she teased him with her hands. She lowered the zipper and pushed his clothes down his legs

She wasn't gentle as she stroked him. She felt the tension rise inside him and felt the bedposts rattle under his grip. But even a man like Hafiz had his limits. He suddenly growled and grabbed Lacey's arms.

His kiss was hard and possessive. Her heart raced as the anticipation built deep inside her.

Hafiz tore his mouth away, and she tumbled down on to her back. She was sprawled naked before him. The ferocious hunger in his eyes made her shiver as the excitement clawed at her. She needed Hafiz, and she would go mad if she had to wait.

"Now," she demanded. She almost couldn't say the word, her chest aching as her heart pounded against her ribs. She rocked her hips as the desire coiled low in her pelvis.

Hafiz didn't argue. He grabbed the back of her legs and dragged her closer. Her stomach gave a nervous flip when she saw his harsh and intense expression.

After he wrapped her legs around his waist, Hafiz ruthlessly tilted her hips. She felt exposed. Wild and beautiful. Vulnerable and yet powerful.

Her heart stopped as he drove into her. Lacey moaned as she yielded, arching her body to accept him. There was no finesse or sophistication. Her hips bucked to an ancient rhythm as she met his thrusts.

She wanted to hold on to this moment and make it last, but she couldn't tame the white heat that threatened to overpower her. Lacey closed her eyes and allowed the sensations to claim her as she cried out Hafiz's name.

Hours later, they lay together. Lacey's back was tucked against Hafiz's chest. Her long hair, tangled and damp with sweat, was pushed to the side as he placed a soft kiss on her neck. The blanket and sheets were in disarray on the floor, but Lacey didn't feel the need to warm their naked bodies. Hafiz's body heat was all she needed.

Lacey deliberately took an even breath and slowly exhaled. She wasn't going to cry. Not yet. She didn't want Hafiz's last memory of her to include that.

She focused her attention on their joined hands, barely visible in the darkened room. She idly played with his hand, rubbing his palm and stroking the length of his fingers. Hafiz did the same, as if silently memorizing every inch of her hand.

They were so different, Lacey decided. Hafiz's hand was large and strong. Hers was more delicate. Her job as a pianist relied on her hands while Hafiz never used his for physical labor. His skin was golden and hers was ivory.

Her fingers clenched his. She stared at their clasped hands, noticing the soft shine of Hafiz's royal ring. She glanced at the window, her heart aching with knowing, when she saw the light filtering through the gap in the curtains.

The night had ended. Their time was over.

Lacey was reluctant to point it out. If Hafiz wasn't going to comment on it, why should she? After all, they didn't define when night ended. The people of Rudaynah didn't start the day until close to noon.

She knew she was grasping for more time. Lacey bit her lip as she watched Hafiz twist his fingers around hers. She wanted to grab his hands and hold them tight.

She was in danger of never letting him go.

Lacey glanced at the window again. They had not squeezed out every minute of their night together. How long had they spent gazing in each other's eyes, holding each other, not saying a word? But she wouldn't regret those quiet moments. They meant something to her. It made her feel connected to Hafiz.

Lacey swept the tip of her tongue along her bottom lip before she spoke. "It's morning."

Her voice shattered the peaceful silence. She felt the tension in Hafiz's muscles before his fingers gripped hers.

"No, it's not," Hafiz replied in his deep, rumbling voice as his warm breath wafted against her ear.

She frowned and motioned at the window. "It's sunrise."

"I disagree." Hafiz gently turned her so she lay on her back. "The sun is still rising. It isn't morning yet. We still have time."

He wasn't ready to end this, either. Lacey gazed lovingly at his face above hers. She brushed her fingertips along his jaw, the dark stubble rough against her skin.

"I love you, Hafiz."

A dark and bittersweet emotion she couldn't define flashed in his eyes. Hafiz slowly lowered his head and bestowed a gentle kiss on her lips.

She didn't move as he placed another soft kiss on her cheek and yet another on her brow. It was more than saying goodbye. He touched her with reverence.

She closed her eyes, desperate to hide her tears, as Hafiz cupped her face with care. He tipped her head back against the pillows and kissed her again. His mouth barely grazed hers.

Lacey wanted to capture his lips and deepen the kiss. But Hafiz slid his mouth to her chin before leaving a trail of kisses along her throat.

She swallowed hard as Hafiz darted his tongue at the dip of her collarbone before pressing his mouth against the pulse point at the base of her throat. She gasped as he suckled her skin between his sharp teeth and left his mark on her.

He didn't need to brand her. She was already his, and nothing—not time, not distance—would change that.

"Hafiz…" she said in a moan as she reached for him. He stopped her and wrapped his hands around her wrists before lowering her arms on the mattress.

"Shh," he whispered as he settled between her legs. He continued his path and kissed the slope of her breast. Lacey arched her spine as he teased her with his mouth.

Hafiz knew how to touch her, how to draw out the pleasure until it became torment. She hissed between her teeth as he laved his tongue against her tight nipple before drawing it into his hot mouth.

She fought against his hold, wanting to grab the back of his head, needing to hold him against her chest, but Hafiz didn't let go.

As sweat formed on her skin while she trembled with need, Hafiz silently continued his descent down her abdomen. Lust, hot and thick, flooded her pelvis. She rocked her hips insistently as Hafiz licked and nibbled and kissed her.

His path was slow, lazy and thorough. She glanced at the window. The sunlight was getting brighter and stronger.

Hafiz bent his head and pressed his mouth on her sex. Lacey moaned as she bucked against his tongue. He released her wrists to spread her legs wider. Lacey grabbed his head, bunching his short hair in her fists as he pleasured her.

She tried to hold back, wanting to make this last, but her climax was swift and sharp. She cried out as it consumed her. Her hips bucked wildly as she rode the sensations.

Her stomach clenched with anticipation as Hafiz slid his hands under her hips. His touch was urgent. She opened her eyes to see him tower over her. There was a primitive look in his eyes as he knelt between her legs.

She felt the rounded tip of his erection pressing against her. Hafiz entered her fully, and she groaned with deep satisfaction. She watched as he closed his eyes and tipped his head back as he struggled for the last of his control.

Lacey's flesh gripped him hard as she felt her body climbing fast toward another climax. She bucked against Hafiz, and he braced his arms next to her. He recaptured her hands and curled his fingers around hers.

"Hafiz…" she whimpered as he rested his forehead against hers. She went silent as he met her gaze. She allowed him to watch her every emotion and response flicker in her eyes. She hid nothing as she climaxed again, harder and longer.

And when her release triggered his, she didn't look away. Lacey let Hafiz know how much pleasure she received from watching him. She heard his hoarse cry before she closed her eyes, allowing exhaustion to claim her.

Lacey's eyes bolted open. The first thing she heard was the drone of the high-speed ceiling fan. Then she noticed the sheets tucked neatly around her body.

Panic crumbled on top of her. She jackknifed into a sitting position and looked at Hafiz's side of the bed. It was empty.

"No," she whispered. "Noooo." She pushed the sheets away as if he would suddenly appear.

She wildly looked around the room. She knew she'd asked for this night only, but she wished she had asked for more. Much more. Even if she knew it wasn't possible, she would have thrown her pride to the wind and begged for more time.

Lacey stumbled out of bed and grabbed for her

robe. Hafiz's side of the bed was warm. There was a chance that he was still there.

"Hafiz?" she called out with a nervous tremble as she tied the sash of her robe. The silence taunted her. Biting down on her bottom lip, she opened the bedroom door. Hope leached from her bones as she stared into the empty drawing room.

Lacey slammed the door shut and ran to the window, her bare feet slapping against the floor. She ripped the curtains to the side and searched the quiet streets.

Her heart lodged in her throat as she saw the familiar figure walking across the street.

For a brief moment, Lacey thought she was mistaken. The man didn't stride through the streets with regal arrogance. Hafiz walked slowly. Hesitantly. His head was bowed, his shoulder hunched.

She raised her fists, ready to beat at the glass and call for him to turn around.

Instinct stopped her. She knew it was hard for him to walk away. Probably just as difficult as it was to let him leave. She had to be strong. For him, if not for herself.

She pressed her forehead against the window, letting her fingers streak against the glass. "Hafiz..." she cried weakly.

Her eyes widened as she watched him slow to a halt. It was impossible for him to have heard her whimper. Hafiz turned slightly to the side and caught himself before glancing at her window.

Her heart pounded until she thought her ears would burst from the sound. She needed one more look. Just one more so she could carry it with her to ease her loneliness. She needed another look to remember that she was loved once.

But she also didn't want him to turn around. She needed him to be strong. She needed to see his strength and know that he was going to be okay. That he was going to stand alone as he had before he met her.

Lacey pressed her lips together, her breath suspended as Hafiz paused. Tears cascaded down her cheeks as she felt her future clinging to this moment.

Hafiz straightened his shoulders and resolutely turned away. Lacey felt shell-shocked. Her future took a free fall into the dark and desolate abyss.

It was a bittersweet sight for her to see Hafiz stride away. She stared at him, sobbing noisily until he turned the corner. Her gaze didn't move from the empty spot just in case he changed his mind. Her vision blurred and her eyes stung as she kept watch for the possibility that he needed to steal one more glance.

But it wasn't going to happen. He was strong enough for the both of them. The knowledge chipped away at her as she sank against the wall into an untidy heap.

It was over. They were no longer together.

Lacey felt as if she was going to splinter and die. And she had no idea how she was going to prevent falling apart without Hafiz holding her tight and giving a piece of his strength to her.

CHAPTER FIVE

HAFIZ REALIZED HE must have looked quite fierce by the way the office workers cowered when he strode in. *Too bad,* he thought as he cast a cold look at a young businessman who had the misfortune of being in his eyesight. Hafiz didn't feel like altering his expression.

Usually he looked forward to coming into his downtown office in the afternoon once he had met all of his royal duties for the day. It felt good to get out of the palace that was as quiet as a mausoleum. Although it had been built by his ancestors, the historical site—or the people inside it—didn't reflect who he was. The royal viziers were too concerned with protocol and tradition. They didn't like any new idea. Or any idea *he* had.

The royal court seemed to have forgotten that he was brought up to serve and look after the sultanate. His education and experience had been focused on international relations and business. He had so many plans and initiatives to improve the lives of his countrymen, but no one wanted to listen to the prince who had fallen out of favor. That would change once he married the sultan's choice.

He strode to his desk and noted that, unlike his

troubled mind, everything in his office was in order. The modern building, complete with state-of-the-art equipment, usually crackled with energy from dawn to dusk. The sultan and the palace had no say in what went on in these offices. Here Hafiz had the freedom to explore and take risks.

The young men he employed outside of the palace were unquestionably loyal, efficient and brilliant. They were men who were educated outside of Rudaynah, but returned home so they could make a difference. They spoke Arabic and English fluently, usually within the same sentence. They were comfortable in business suits and traditional Rudaynahi robes. Men very much like him, except for a few drops of royal blood and a few years in the world that had stripped away any idealism.

From the corner of his eye, Hafiz saw his executive secretary hurry toward him. One of the office assistants was already at his desk, trying to look invisible while carefully setting down a mug of coffee. The bitter scent was welcoming since he hadn't slept for days. Hafiz walked around his desk, determined to lose himself in his work.

"Good afternoon, Your Highness," the secretary said cautiously as he tugged at his silk tie. The man eyed him like he would a cobra ready to strike. "The changes in your schedule have been entered—"

Hafiz's attention immediately began to fade, which was unlike him. He was known for his focus and attention to detail, but he had been distracted for the past few days. Perhaps he was coming down with something. It had nothing to do with Lacey. He did not wallow in the past. He didn't focus on the things he couldn't change. He had moved on from Lacey.

Lacey. He refused to look at the window, but the pull was too great. Hafiz reluctantly looked outside, his gaze automatically seeking Lacey's penthouse apartment. A few months ago, he had picked the office building specifically for the view. He had found himself staring out of the window throughout the workdays, even though he knew he wouldn't catch a glimpse of Lacey. The knowledge that she was there always brought him peace. Until now.

The buzzing of his cell phone shattered his reverie. His gut twisted with anticipation and dread. Only a few people had this number. He grabbed the phone and looked at the caller ID. Disappointment crashed when he saw it wasn't Lacey. Hafiz dismissed his secretary with the wave of his hand and took the call.

"Your Highness? This is Glenn," Lacey's bodyguard quickly said to identify himself. "I'm sorry to call you, but we've hit a setback. Our exit visas have been delayed."

"Nothing works on time in Rudaynah." Hafiz rubbed his hand over his forehead and gave a short sigh of frustration. A sense of unease trickled down his spine. Was the palace behind this? Did they know about Lacey?

Hafiz discarded that thought. The palace wouldn't be concerned about an American nightclub singer. "Did they say why?"

"No. I bribed the right government officials, sat down and had tea at the chief of police's office, but I'm not getting any information."

Hafiz glanced out the window again. He had to

get Lacey out before her presence could ruin everything he had worked toward. "Ordinarily I would have someone from the palace make a special request with the right official, but that would bring unwanted attention. We will have to wait it out. They should be ready in another day or two."

"Yes, sir."

"Would you please put Lacey on the phone, and I'll explain it to her." He shouldn't talk to Lacey. After all, they had said their goodbyes. He wanted that night to be their last memory, but he also didn't want her to think he had abandoned her when she needed assistance.

There was a beat of silence, and Glenn cleared his throat. "Miss Maxwell is not here, sir."

"What?" Hafiz stared at Lacey's apartment. She had promised that she wouldn't venture out again. "Where is she?"

"She is at the Scimitar having tea with friends."

Hafiz's muscles jerked with surprise. *Friends?* What friends?

His gaze darted across the skyline to the luxurious hotel. The tall building was like a glass and metal spiral reaching out to the sun, reflecting the rays against the dark windows. "I don't understand."

"I apologize, sir. I would have accompanied her, but I was dealing with the exit visas. She had left before I got back."

Lacey had friends? Hafiz felt his frown deepen. Lacey had a world outside of the apartment. A world that didn't include him. He wasn't sure why he was so surprised. Lacey had a large group of friends in St. Louis.

But she never talked about these friends. That was strange. Lacey told him everything. Or he thought she did. Why had she been hiding this information?

"Who are these friends?" Hafiz asked tersely, interrupting Glenn's excuse. If one of them had a male name… Hafiz gritted his teeth and clenched his hand into a fist.

"No need to be concerned, sir," Glenn replied. "These women are above reproach. They are the wives of ambassadors and government ministers."

Hafiz went cold as he remained perfectly still. His ex-mistress was socializing with the most influential and powerful women of Rudaynah? The very mistress he broke up with so he could marry another? Hafiz slowly closed his eyes as the tension wrapped around his chest and squeezed. Glenn was incorrect. He had every reason to worry.

Lacey always thought the tearoom at the Scimitar was an unlikely mix of cultures. She stared at the plate that offered scones and slices of cinnamon date cake. A copper *cezve* for Turkish coffee sat next to an ornate silver teapot. A golden table runner with an intricate geometric design lay on top of the white linen tablecloth.

"You look so different in Western clothes," Inas told Lacey as she nibbled on a fried pastry ball that was dipped in a thick syrup. "I hardly recognized you."

"I feel different," Lacey admitted as she self-consciously tucked her hair behind her ear. She felt undressed wearing a simple green dress with long sleeves and a high neckline. Her makeup was minimal, and her shoes had a low heel. She was covered, but it didn't feel as if it was enough. "It's strange not wearing a caftan."

"Why the sudden change?" Janet, an ambassador's wife, asked as she patted a linen napkin to her bright red lips. Tall, blond and willowy, Janet had lived in the sultanate for years but chose not to wear the native clothes, no matter how warm the weather turned. "We're still in Rudaynah."

"I'm trying to get used to my old clothes," Lacey explained, but it wasn't the whole truth. When she'd first moved here, Lacey had originally chosen to wear the scarves and caftans, believing it was the first step to enter this world. Now she realized it had been a waste of time. "Although I really didn't fit in here."

"Nonsense." Inas flipped her long black braid over her shoulder. "You were one of my hardest-working students. So determined. If you had stayed here a little longer, I'm sure you would have become proficient in Arabic."

"Thank you." She had wanted to surprise Hafiz with her grasp of the language. One of her goals had been to watch his face soften when she declared her love in his native tongue.

"I don't know what our charity is going to do without you," Janet said with a sigh. "We made great strides once you joined. Are you sure you have to leave right away?"

"Yes, we need to move. It's urgent for my…uncle to get to his next work project." Part of her wished she could have left on the first flight out, but she was finding the idea of permanently leaving Hafiz very difficult. "We're just waiting for the exit visas."

"Those are just a formality," Inas insisted. "But if

you're still going to be here this weekend, you must attend my daughter's wedding reception. The marriage contract ceremony is for family only, but the reception is going to be here for all of our friends. Oh, and you should see the dancers we hired for the *zaffa* procession!"

"I would like that." She had heard every detail about the upcoming wedding and wanted to be there to share her friend's special moment. But her moments with Hafiz had come first, and she had reluctantly declined because it would have interfered with her time with him.

What had Hafiz given up to spend time with her? Lacey frowned as the thought whispered into her mind. She shouldn't compare. Hafiz was a busy and important man.

"Most of the royal court will be there because my husband and the groom's father are government ministers. I know you couldn't attend before because your aunt and uncle had a previous engagement, but this will be the last time we see each other. Extend the invitation to them and…" Inas frowned when the quiet buzz of conversation suddenly died. She set down her teacup, her gold bracelets tinkling, as she looked over her shoulder. "What's happening?"

"I'm not sure," Janet murmured as she craned her neck. "Everyone is looking at the door to the lobby."

"Oh, my goodness," Inas whispered and turned to face her friends. Her eyes were wide with delight. "It's the prince."

Lacey flinched at her friend's announcement. Her heartbeat stuttered over the possibility of seeing Hafiz again. "Which one? Which prince?"

"The oldest. Hafiz."

Lacey struggled for her next breath when she saw Hafiz being escorted through the tearoom. He effortlessly commanded attention. It wasn't because the aggressive lines of his dark business suit emphasized his muscular body, or the haughty jut of his chin. It wasn't because he walked like a conqueror or because of his royal status. It was because he exuded a power that indicated that he was a valuable ally or a dangerous opponent. This was someone who could ruin a man's life with the snap of his fingers or steal a woman's heart with a smile.

Hafiz strode past her, never meeting her startled gaze. His face was rigid, as if it had been hewn from stone.

He didn't see her. Lacey's lips parted as she stared after him. How was that possible? She would always capture his gaze the moment she walked into the room.

A thousand petty emotions burst and crawled under her skin. She wouldn't give in to them. She shouldn't care that she was invisible three days after he left her. She expected it. That would have always been her status in public had she stayed with Hafiz.

And she didn't want a life like that, Lacey reminded herself, closing her eyes and drawing the last of her composure. She didn't want to come in second, even if it meant a life without Hafiz. She refused to be on the side. She wouldn't be an afterthought again.

"He's gorgeous," Janet said in a low voice as they watched Hafiz stride out of the tearoom to what she suspected was the private dining areas.

"So is his fiancée," Inas informed them. "I know the Abdullah family."

Lacey winced. She wished she hadn't heard that. She didn't want to know anything about the woman who got to marry Hafiz. It was easier for her that way.

Janet leaned forward. "What is she like?"

"Nabeela is the perfect Rudaynahi woman."

Lacey's muscles locked. Now she had a name to go with the woman. Somehow that made it worse. She didn't want to put a name or a face to the person who got the man she loved.

"She has been groomed for life at the palace. Her parents were hoping she would marry a royal adviser or minister. They never thought the sultan and his wife would choose her to become a princess. She'll make a good wife for Hafiz."

No, she won't. He's mine. The thought savagely swiped at her like a claw. It tore at the thin façade she'd carefully constructed after finding out about Hafiz's wedding, exposing the truth that bled underneath. It punctured the festering pain she tried to ignore.

She knew Hafiz was going to be married, but she didn't allow herself to think past the wedding. She thought of Nabeela as the bride. She'd never thought of them as a couple. As partners. As husband and wife.

Lacey looked down hurriedly, the table weaving and buckling before her eyes. The knowledge made her physically ill. She knew it wasn't a love match, but it didn't stop the bilious green ribbons of jealousy snaking around her heart.

Her poisonous emotions ate away at her until she felt like a brittle, hollowed-out shell. A series of primal responses, each sharper than the previous one, battered her mind, her heart and her pride.

"Well, I heard it's not Nabeela's beauty that made Prince Hafiz accept," Janet said in a sly tone.

Lacey wanted to change the topic immediately. But she was scared to open her mouth, not sure if her secrets or a scream of howling pain would spill out. She stared at her teacup and forced herself to reach for it. She didn't like how her hands trembled.

"Rumor has it that the sultan and the prince made an agreement," Janet whispered fiercely. "If he marries this Nabeela without incident, Hafiz will become the crown prince."

Lacey's breath hitched in her throat. She set the cup down before it snapped in her hands. So that was the reason. It made sense, and she didn't question it.

Lacey sank back in her plush chair and tilted her head up. She stared at the mosaic ceiling made of lapis lazuli as the low murmur of different languages faded into a hum. The clink of fine china blurred into nothing as her thoughts spun wildly.

She always knew Hafiz was ambitious. Driven and determined. A man like Hafiz couldn't give up the chance of the throne. Even if it meant discarding his mistress. Although now she wondered if it had been a difficult decision for him. She couldn't compete with a crown.

She should have seen the signs. After all, she had been in this position before. Her parents had been just as driven, just as single-minded with their dreams to become rich and famous. Once they decided having a child was holding them back, they had abandoned her with a swiftness that still took her breath away.

But this time she hadn't looked for signs because she thought they were in love. She had wanted to believe that this time she wasn't the burden. That she was not only welcomed into Hafiz's life, but that he would move heaven and earth to be with her.

When was she going to learn? She did not inspire that kind of devotion. No one would ever love her like that.

"What about his brother?" Lacey's voice sounded rough to her ears. She pushed her plate away with tense fingers. "I thought he was the crown prince."

"Ashraf?" Janet asked. "Yes, I wonder how he feels about this new development. He's been the heir to the throne for a decade."

"A decade?" Lacey repeated slowly. "How old is he?"

"Just a few years younger than Prince Hafiz," Janet said, glancing at Inas for confirmation. "He became the heir to the throne when Hafiz lost his birthright."

Lacey blinked slowly as a buzzing sound grew in her ears. "Hafiz lost—?" She gripped the edge of the table as her heart fluttered against her rib cage. "I mean,...*Prince* Hafiz? What do you mean by birthright?"

"He was in line to be the next sultan," Janet explained.

Lacey tilted her head sharply. Her arms went lax as she slumped in her chair. She felt as if she was missing a vital piece of information. "He was *supposed* to inherit the throne? When did this happen?"

"How do you not know this?" Inas's eyes widened as she leaned over the table. "I thought we covered this during your history lessons."

Lacey slowly shook her head. "How can a prince be displaced in the line of succession?" She was hesitant to even ask. Did he renounce his right? Did he commit a heinous crime? Neither sounded like something Hafiz would do. "You have to do something really bad, right?"

"I don't have all the details on that, but I can tell you this." Inas gave a cautious glance at the tables surrounding them before she went on. "It had something to do with a woman."

Lacey felt her lungs shrivel up as the bitter taste of despair filled her mouth. Hafiz lost everything over a woman? Numbness invaded her bones, protecting her before she doubled over from the intense pain.

"What woman?" Lacey asked dully. She must have been extraordinary for Hafiz to take such a risk. It didn't make sense. The man would do anything to protect and serve his country. He did not put anyone before his duty. Hafiz did not put *himself* before Rudaynah.

"I heard it was a mistress," Janet said quietly. "A series of mistresses."

Inas shrugged. "One woman is all that it would take to lose the throne."

A mistress. No, *mistresses*. She shouldn't be surprised. Hafiz was incredibly sophisticated and knowledgeable in the bedroom. Yet for some reason she felt as if her role in his life was different from all the other women. That she was somehow special.

Maybe she was special. Maybe… Lacey clenched her hands together under the table. She should stop trying to make her relationship with Hafiz into a fairy tale.

But why had he risked everything again by bringing her to his sultanate? By starting the relationship in the first place? What provoked him to flaunt authority and break the rules again?

Again? There was no indication that he went without a mistress after he lost his right to the throne. Lacey went cold. Was bringing his mistress to the sultanate something he did often? Did he get a new model every year? Lacey slowly closed her eyes. Her jaw trembled as the hot tears stung her eyes.

She needed to figure out what was going on. She wanted to go home, lock herself in her room and curl up in a ball to ward off the anguish that was crashing against her in waves. But first she had to leave the tearoom before she embarrassed herself.

Lacey opened her eyes and kept her head down before anyone saw her distress. "Oh, look at the time!" she said as she barely glanced at her wristwatch. "I didn't realize it was so late."

Her movements felt awkward as she rose from the table and said goodbye to her friends. The flurry of hugs and promises did nothing to calm her. Her heart pumped fast as she struggled with the information about Hafiz's past.

She turned and saw one of the hotel bellmen standing in front of her. His blue uniform was the same color as the mosaic ceiling. "Miss Maxwell? Are you leaving?" the young man asked. "A Mr. Glenn called for you. He says it's urgent."

"Oh!" She clumsily patted her purse and realized she didn't bring her cell phone because it hadn't been charged due to another power outage. "Is there a phone I can use?"

"Please follow me to one of the conference rooms, and you may contact him in private."

"Thank you." She hurried after the bellman, her legs unsteady after the surprise she had received. She felt dizzy, as if her world had been knocked off its axis. Lacey was out of breath by the time she reached the conference room. She managed to give the man a simple nod as he opened the door with a flourish.

She stepped inside the long room and felt the door close behind her. The conference room was intimidating with its heavy furniture and arched ceilings. The thick blue curtains were pulled shut, and the silence was oppressive.

Lacey frowned when she noticed there was no phone on the oversized conference table. She inhaled the familiar scent of sandalwood that never failed to stir a deep craving inside her.

Hafiz.

It was her only warning before her spine was pressed up against the wall.

Strong arms bracketed her head. Hafiz's broad shoulders were encased in an expensive suit jacket. She wanted to cling on to them. She looked up and saw that Hafiz's face loomed above hers.

He was just a kiss away. After convincing herself that she would never be able to touch him, having him so close was overwhelming. She leaned forward as her eyelashes drifted shut.

"What the hell are you up to, Lacey?" Hafiz asked through clenched teeth.

CHAPTER SIX

SHE STIFFENED AND her lashes fluttered. Hafiz's brown eyes shone with cold anger. Lacey's stomach quavered at his ferocious look. It was not the kind of greeting one lover gave to another.

But then, they weren't lovers anymore. Any momentary fantasy she harbored broke like crackling ice. They might have been alone in the room, but they were not together. They were acquaintances. Their past was erased as if it never existed. She needed to remember that.

She rested heavily against the wall as if it was the only thing in the room that seemed to be able to support her. She tilted her chin and looked directly at Hafiz. "Good afternoon to you, too, Your Highness," she replied as tears pushed against the backs of her eyes.

"Lacey," he bit out. "I want an answer."

She pressed her lips together and dug her fingers against her purse. Lacey wished she could turn off her emotions with the same effortlessness as Hafiz. She wished his cool treatment didn't feel like a slap in the face.

She looked away and wrapped her arms around her middle. She couldn't handle the lack of intimacy in his dark eyes. She already missed the aura of shared secrets that cocooned them for a year.

She felt as if she was being tugged into a sandstorm and had nothing to hold on to. She could only rely on herself. It had always been that way. When she first met Hafiz, she thought she wouldn't be so alone in the world. Now she understood that it had been an illusion.

"I was having tea with a couple of my friends," she said, hating how her voice cracked.

"Why is this the first I've heard about these so-called friends?"

"You never asked." Lacey felt the flare of anger. "You never asked about my day or how I was coping living in this country." The anger burned hotter, and she ducked under his arm and walked away. "You just assumed I spent every waking moment in my apartment. Did you think I powered down until you returned?"

"If you wanted to share something, there was nothing and no one holding you back." Hafiz's eyes narrowed as he watched her move to one end of the table. "Why am I hearing about this now?"

She shrugged. Some of it was her fault. She was reacting in the same way as when she had felt her parents' interest slipping. She'd known if she wanted to retain Hafiz's attention, have him keep coming back, she needed to be positive. She had to be entertaining, and put all of the focus on him. If she had been too needy, he would start to distance himself.

"How is someone like you friends with an ambassador's wife? Or the wife of a deputy minister?"

Lacey raised her eyebrow and met his gaze. She

would not show how much those words hurt. "Someone like me?"

"You know what I mean." Hafiz rubbed the back of his neck with impatience. "You don't share the same status or have the same interests."

"So, what you're really asking is how a mistress became friends with respectable women?" she asked in a cool tone.

"Yes." Hafiz crossed his arms. "That's exactly what I'm saying."

The room tilted sickeningly for a moment. Did he know what he was saying? Did he care? She closed her eyes and swallowed. "You do realize that you're the one who made me a mistress."

"And you accepted the offer."

His indifference cut like a knife. A sarcastic rejoinder danced on her tongue like a hot pepper.

"Why are you friends with these women," he asked, "and why did you meet with them today?"

"Do you know why I play the piano?" Lacey asked as she pulled out a chair and sat down at the head of the table.

Hafiz gave her an incredulous look and spread his arms out wide. "What does this have to do with the women you were with?"

"A lot of people think I play piano because I grew up in a musical environment," Lacey continued as if he hadn't spoken. "My parents are musicians, so, therefore, I must have their interests rub off on me."

Hafiz leaned his shoulder against the wall. "Get to the point, Lacey."

"My parents didn't care if I took up a musical instrument or not. I thought that if I learned how to play the piano, and played exceptionally well, I could be part of their lives. They would take me on the road with them and I wouldn't be left behind all the time."

"And?"

The corner of her mouth twitched as she remembered her parents' harsh and immediate rejection to that plan. How her father had declared that one of the benefits of the road trips was taking a break from being parents. "It didn't work. But for some reason, I thought it would work this time."

Hafiz frowned. "This time?"

"When you invited me to live here, I thought we were building toward a future. A life together." She hastily looked away. She was embarrassed by her ignorance, her belief that they would live happily ever after. "And I worked to make this my new home. Inas is very proud of her heritage and she used to be a teacher. She's been my Arabic and history tutor."

"You've been learning Arabic? I've never heard you speak it."

She saw the deep suspicion in his eyes and a dull ache of disappointment spread through her chest. "I wasn't ready to show off my language skills just yet. I'm nowhere near fluent."

His mouth twisted, and she knew he didn't believe her. "And the ambassador's wife?"

"I met Janet at her charity against hunger. We've been working together for the past six months." Her voice trailed off when she noticed that she was following the same pattern and getting the same results.

Both times she had placed all of her energy into another person's interest. Both times she had thought the commitment would pay off. That they would see how she fit seamlessly into their world and welcome her with open arms. At the very least, appreciate her efforts.

It shouldn't be this hard to keep her loved ones in her life. She had to stop giving her all to people who didn't want it. Didn't want her.

"And you just happen to become friends." Hafiz's voice broke through her thoughts. "With the two women who could destroy everything I've worked for if they mention a rumor to one of their powerful friends or husbands."

"Is that what you're worried about?" Lacey began to tap her fingers on the table. "In all our time together, I've never done anything to hurt you. Why would you think I'd do that now?"

"Because you thought I would marry you one day, and instead I'm marrying someone else. You want revenge."

"Wait a minute! Are you saying—" She sat up straight and pressed her hands against her chest. "Do you think I'm trying to—"

He speared her with an icy cold glare. "Hell hath no fury like a woman scorned."

"Scorned woman? You've scorned me? No, you've sacrificed me, but—"

"And you needed to hit me back." He widened his arms as if offering her another shot.

"You think I have the power to hurt you?" she asked through barely parted lips. She realized that she did have that power, temporarily. "That's why you didn't tell me. I never thought you were a coward. And you aren't. You just don't give information unless it's in your interest."

She bit the inside of her lip as he walked to her, his stride reminding her of a stalking panther.

"Explain yourself, Lacey," he said softly with just a bite of warning.

"The agreement between you and the sultan," she said hurriedly. "The one about you becoming the crown prince if you marry his choice of bride."

Surprise flashed in his dark eyes before he placed his fists on his lean hips. "How do you know about that?"

Lacey dipped her head as the last glimmer of hope faded. So it was true. He gave her up for a chance to become the next sultan. "Everyone knows."

"The agreement came after I was engaged," he said stiffly before he turned around. "I don't know why I'm explaining this to you."

You mean, to someone like you, Lacey silently added. "Do you want to be the sultan?"

Hafiz's shoulders grew rigid as he turned around. "Of course. I know I can do the job. For the past ten years, I've worked hard to prove it to others."

"Don't you want to do something different?" she asked.

"Why would I give up this opportunity?"

Why would he, other than to have a life that would include her? It wasn't worth the sacrifice. And he supposedly made the decision to end their relationship *before* the sultan's offer.

"Look at the impact you've made on your own," she pointed out. "Think of what else you could do without the interference of the palace."

"You don't understand, Lacey," he said wearily as

he thrust his fingers in his dark hair. "I was born for this. It's my destiny."

"I know. It's why you push yourself." Her toe tapped a nervous staccato beat before she dove into uncharted territory. "It's not out of ambition, is it? You're looking for redemption."

He tilted his head as if he was scenting danger. As if she was getting too close to his secret. Too close to the truth.

"You lost your birthright ten years ago. That's why your brother was chosen over you. And you've been trying to get it back."

She knew the truth. Shame swept through Hafiz. It burned through his veins, and he instinctively hunched his shoulders to ward it off.

He looked at the floor, unable to meet her eyes, even though she had the right to judge him. "How do you know about that?" he asked hoarsely.

The tapping of her toe halted. The silence vibrated around him. "I wish I had heard it from you."

Hafiz said nothing. He wished he could have denied it, but he'd withstood the disgrace for nearly a decade. It should be no different now.

But it was. He didn't want Lacey to know about his mistakes. About the person he used to be.

Lacey was the first to break the silence. "Why didn't you tell me?"

Because he was a better person when he was with Lacey. He could be the man he wanted to be, the prince he strived to become for his country. She believed he could do the impossible, and he knew he could with her by his side. Had she known about his past, would she still have believed? He knew she wouldn't.

But Lacey knew now. And her opinion meant the most to him. He didn't know how he would stand up against her disillusionment. "It's not something I'm proud of."

"So you hid it from me?" she asked. He heard the anger wobbling in her voice. "You only showed me one side of you? I thought we had been closer than that."

Hafiz pulled open a curtain and let the bright sunlight stream in the dark room. The image of his beloved country didn't soothe the twinge inside him. He was drowning in regret and there was no hope of escape.

He bunched his hands into tight fist, imagining the relief if he punched through the glass. He could hear the shattering window in his mind, but he wouldn't act on the impulse. But, oh, what he wouldn't do to get out of this room…away from Lacey's steady gaze.

"You were just a teenager when you lost your title as crown prince?"

"No, I was an adult. I was twenty-one." Hafiz had a feeling that was the easiest question he would be facing from Lacey.

"Really?" She made a sympathetic cluck with her tongue. "That's harsh. Being twenty-one is all about pushing the limits. Pushing boundaries."

He shook his head. It should have warmed his heart that Lacey automatically defended him, but he knew it wasn't going to last. "It's different for me."

"Because you're a prince? The heir to the throne?"

"Because my country came into a great deal of

wealth when I was eighteen. I was sent to the States to get an education. To learn how to protect and grow the wealth." He took a deep breath and turned to face her. "Instead I spent it."

Her eyes widened as her mouth open and shut. "All of it?" she croaked out.

"No. It doesn't matter how many millions I spent." The amount was branded into his soul for eternity, but the numbers could never convey the suffering of others. "I spent it. I stole it." He still flinched at the stripped-down version of his action. "I stole the money from the people of Rudaynah for my own pleasure. I was the playboy prince the tabloids love to hate."

Lacey stared at him as if he was a stranger to her. It was better than looking at him with the disgust he felt for himself. "That doesn't sound like you at all."

"It was me," he said brutally. "Look it up. The sultan tried to hide the story, but you can find it if you look hard enough. My spending habits had been legendary," he said, humility threading his voice.

"What stopped it?"

"The sultan received reports and called me home. The moment I returned I saw how Rudaynah had yet to see any progress. It humbled me. Shamed me more than any lecture or punishment."

Lacey frowned. "And your punishment for spending the money was losing your right to the throne?"

"No. I was stripped of any responsibility or authority. Of any rights or privileges. I was spared getting lashes because of my royal status. I didn't leave Rudaynah until I could regain my father's trust. And

I still didn't leave the borders until I felt it was necessary."

"But that doesn't explain to me how you lost your birthright."

The punishment he'd received was paltry considering his crime, but the sultan didn't want people to know the whole story. "One of the reports the sultan received had to do with my mistress at the time."

"I see," she said stiffly.

"You don't see." He looked directly in her blue eyes and braced himself. "My mistress became pregnant."

Lacey turned pale, but she regained her composure. "Is it yours?" she asked brusquely.

"I found out too late that she had an abortion," Hafiz said, the bitterness corroding inside him. "I've often wondered if the sultan campaigned for and funded it. Not directly, of course," he added cynically.

"I still don't understand—"

"Don't you get it, Lacey?" he barked out. "I couldn't uphold the expectations placed on me. I proved I wasn't leadership material." The list of his sins bore down on him. "I used the money for my own pleasure. I couldn't make my country proud. I couldn't provide the security of giving a rightful heir to the throne. But most of all, I couldn't protect my unborn child."

"Hafiz," Lacey said grimly as she walked toward him. He braced himself for her to launch into a tirade. For a stinging slap. It wouldn't hurt nearly as much as her disappointment.

She surprised him by placing a gentle hand on his arm. He looked down at her, bemused by the sincerity gleaming in her eyes. "Don't let your mistakes define you. You are a good man."

He drew back. She still believed in him. How could she? Wasn't she listening? "You're biased, but thanks."

"Give me some credit. I wouldn't give up everything familiar for a playboy prince. I certainly wouldn't follow any man to the ends of the earth."

"I believe the term you're looking for is 'this hell'," he reminded her.

Lacey looked chagrined but wouldn't be deterred. "And Rudaynah needs you. The mistake you made will serve you well." She paused, obviously searching for the right words. "You have risen from your past like…a phoenix from the ashes. You're stronger and smarter. You have worked hard all these years to take care of your countrymen."

But he would never regain the trust of the people. His brother kept his distance, as if poor judgment was contagious. His own parents couldn't stand the sight of him.

"I am not the kind of man you're trying to make me out to be." But he wanted to be. He wanted to deserve her admiration.

"You're good for Rudaynah. This sultanate needs you," Lacey insisted and cupped his face with her hand. "If I thought otherwise, I would take you away with me."

Hafiz leaned into her touch just as his cell phone rang. They both jumped as the harsh sound echoed in the cavernous room.

"Don't answer it," Lacey whispered.

"It would be Glenn. He would only call if it was important." He reached for the phone and answered it. "Yes?"

"Our exit visas have been denied," Glenn said.

A coldness settled inside Hafiz as he considered what that could mean. "Did they give a reason?"

"No, but they were acting strange. As if it hasn't happened before. What do you want me to do next, Your Highness?"

"Let me get back to you." Hafiz ended the call and pressed the phone against his chin as he stared out the window. He quickly analyzed the sultan's latest move and what it represented. He didn't like any of the answers.

"Is something wrong?" Lacey asked.

"Your exit visas have been denied," he murmured as he considered his next move.

"I thought the process was just a formality." Lacey gasped, and she clapped her hand over her mouth. "Your father knows about me. He knows I'm your mistress."

"Let's not jump to conclusions. It could be a clerical error." Hafiz wanted to calm Lacey, but he knew his answer wouldn't soothe her.

"This doesn't make sense. Why can't I leave the country? Wouldn't your father give me the red carpet treatment to the first car out of here?"

"Not necessarily," Hafiz replied grimly.

Lacey pressed her lips together. "What's going on?"

"There's a possibility," he said, emphasizing the word, "that the sultan sees your presence as an advantage to him. It would make me the most agreeable groom."

"I don't like the sounds of that," Lacey said. "Am I in trouble? Is he going to use me to get to you?"

"I should have predicted it," Hafiz muttered. "The sultan had done this before."

"When? Ten years ago?" Lacey took a deep breath. "Hafiz, I need to know. What happened to your last mistress? The one who got pregnant?"

CHAPTER SEVEN

HAFIZ LEANED AGAINST the windowpane and closed his
eyes as the guilt swamped him. He never forgot that
time in his life, and he refused to forgive himself. The
actions he took, the mistakes he made were part of him
and had influenced his decisions to this day. And yet,
he tried not to look too closely and inspect his flaws.

"Her name was Elizabeth," he said quietly. "I had
already earned my reputation as the playboy prince
when I met her in Monte Carlo."

"What was she like?" Lacey asked.

"Beautiful. Professional. Ambitious."

Lacey frowned. "You make her sound cold and unfeeling."

What he had shared with Elizabeth had nothing
to do with warmth and affection. "She made her way
through life as a mistress. Our relationship had been
purely physical, and we both wanted it that way."

Because he hadn't been interested in romance or
commitment. He had been too busy partying, gam-
bling and exploring the world outside of Rudaynah
and royal life.

Hafiz forced himself to continue. He knew Lacey
needed to hear this. "We had only been together for a

few months when I found out she was pregnant." Hafiz looked away. "I didn't handle the news well. I wish I could take back that moment and react differently."

"What did you do?" Lacey asked.

He didn't want to give a voice to the memories that haunted him. The moments that had demonstrated what kind of man he had been. Only he hadn't acted like a man.

"I was furious. Scared," he admitted with a sigh. "I knew that a baby was going to change everything. I swore the baby couldn't possibly be mine. I didn't *want* it to be mine."

Lacey rested her hand against his shoulder. "I can't imagine you acting like that, Hafiz."

"It was me. A spoiled and selfish prince who knew his freedom was about to be taken away from him. I accused Elizabeth of being unfaithful. I wasn't going to let her trap me or extort money from me." Hafiz raked his hand through his hair. "I hate the way I treated her."

"That may have been your first reaction, but I'm sure you saw reason once you calmed down."

Hafiz shook his head. Lacey thought too highly of him. He slowly turned around and faced her. "I left Elizabeth," he said, watching the surprise in Lacey's eyes. He hunched his shoulders as the remorse weighed heavily on him. "My father had demanded that I return home, and I used that as a way to hide from my responsibilities."

Lacey stared at him in disbelief. "You wouldn't do that."

"That was the lowest time of my life. I was trying to hide what I had done and conceal the person I was.

Hide everything from the sultan and my countrymen. At times, I tried to hide the truth from myself."

"Impossible."

"It wasn't that hard to do. I wanted to convince myself that Elizabeth was the villain. I believed she tried to trick me and that she got what she deserved for attempting to get her claws into a prince."

"When did you decide she was not the villain?"

"It wasn't just one event. I started seeing how I treated everyone during that time. I should have treated her better. I had cut off all contact. And somehow I had convinced myself that I did the right thing."

"Did you try to find her after that and make it right?"

He nodded. "I wasn't able to travel, but I wasn't going to let it stop me. I was done making excuses. I had one of my representatives track her down." Hafiz took a deep breath. "But I was too late. Elizabeth had gotten an abortion."

The silence permeated the room as Hafiz remembered getting that call. He had shattered from the grief. He had never been the same man after knowing he hadn't protected and provided for his unborn son.

"I was furious at myself," Hafiz said quietly. "If I had shown Elizabeth any concern or any sign that she could depend on me, she wouldn't have taken extreme measures."

"And you think your father was behind that?"

"I'm sure of it. Elizabeth had hinted it to my representative, but I think she was too afraid to speak plainly. She was afraid to cross the sultan, with good reason."

"Should I be afraid?"

"No," Hafiz said. "You can depend on me. I will not abandon you."

Lacey moved closer to him until her hip brushed against his. "I'm sorry. I'm sorry that my presence in your life is causing so many problems." The air around them pulsed with energy, but Hafiz didn't reach out for her. His fingers flexed, but his hands stayed by his side.

"You're not a burden," he said gruffly. Having Lacey in his life had been a gift.

Lacey leaned forward and pressed her forehead against his shoulder. Hafiz tensed and remained where he stood. It was still a risk. If someone walked into this room and saw him alone with Lacey…he didn't want to think about the consequences.

Hafiz cleared his throat and took a step away from her. "I have to go. I know how to fix this."

"What are you going to do?" she called after him as he strode to the door.

He set his mouth into a grim line. "Whatever it takes."

"This wedding reception is one of the most lavish I've seen. I don't know how Inas and her husband paid for it," Janet said a few days later as they slowly made their way through the crowded ballroom to the buffet. "I can't wait to eat."

"Where are the men?" Lacey asked. The ballroom was packed with women. Bright, garish colors swirled around Lacey and her friend Janet as the conversations swelled to an earsplitting decibel. Heavy perfumes of every imaginable flower clashed against one another.

"They are in the ballroom across the hall having

their party," Janet informed her. "The men and women in Rudaynah don't celebrate together. This way the women can literally let their hair down and dance."

Lacey glanced at the stage where the bride sat. It seemed strange to Lacey that the newlywed couple would spend their wedding reception apart. Did it signify what was yet to come? That the marriage meant separate paths, separate lives, for the couple? Was this what all marriages were like in this country?

She studied the group of relatives on the stage surrounding the bride. "I still don't see Inas."

"We'll find her. By the way, I love what you're wearing. I thought you had given up wearing the traditional caftan."

"Thank you." Lacey glanced down at her pale blue caftan. She hadn't been certain about the transparent sleeves or the modest neckline. The skirt flared out gently, and the intricate embroidery design that ran down the front of the caftan matched her slippers. "I wanted one chance to wear it before I leave."

"Did you get your exit visas sorted out?"

"Uh…yes," she lied. "I'll be leaving very soon." As in tonight. But she couldn't let anyone know that.

She glanced at her jeweled watch and winced. The wedding reception had started late, and she should have returned home by now and gathered her things.

"Janet, why don't you go on ahead to the buffet? I have to leave."

"Already?" She shook her head. "You're going to miss the professional dancers and the wedding march. Not to mention the food!"

"I know, but I'm glad I had a chance to be here. I just hope leaving early doesn't offend Inas."

"She'll understand," Janet said as she hugged Lacey goodbye. "You'll probably find her near the door greeting all the guests."

Lacey fought her way through the cluster of women. She couldn't help but wonder if Hafiz's wedding reception would be like this. She pushed the thought aside. She wasn't going to torture herself imagining what Hafiz's wedding to another woman was going to be like.

Lacey saw her friend near the entrance. "Inas!" She waved and hurried to greet the mother of the bride. "Inas, this wedding is beautiful. And your daughter!" She glanced at the woman on stage in the back of the ballroom. The young woman wore an embroidered red gown and veil. Heavy gold jewelry hung from her wrists and throat. "She looks like a princess."

"Lacey, I'm so happy to see you." Inas gave her a kiss on each cheek. "And you wouldn't believe who is here!"

The woman almost squealed. Lacey couldn't imagine who would cause this level of excitement. "Who?"

"Inas?" An older woman's voice wafted over them. Inas's demeanor changed rapidly. Her smile widened, and she trembled with exhilaration. Inas struggled to lower her eyes as she gave a curtsey to the woman. She folded her hands neatly in front of her as she spoke respectfully in Arabic.

Lacey took a step back. Her instincts told her to melt into the crowd and disappear.

"Allow me to introduce you," Inas said as she grasped Lacey's elbow and brought her forward. Lacey stared at the older woman who wore a white scarf over her gray hair and a brocade caftan that concealed her body.

"Your Majesty, this is Lacey Maxwell. I tutored her in Arabic while she was visiting our sultanate. Lacey, this is the Sultana Zafirah of Rudaynah."

And Hafiz's mother. Lacey's knees buckled, and she quickly covered it up with a shaky curtsey.

She glanced at the sultana through her lashes and found the older woman inspecting her like a mangled insect carcass. It took every ounce of willpower for Lacey not to meet the woman's gaze. *This was probably why Hafiz didn't want you to meet his family.*

Lacey covertly looked at the exit and wondered how she was going to extract herself from this situation. Her mind went blank as panic congealed in her throat. "I understand one of your sons will be married soon," Lacey said in what she hoped was a respectful tone. "Congratulations."

The sultana stiffened, and Lacey wondered if she had broken some protocol. "Thank you," Sultana Zafirah said with a sniff.

Lacey hesitated, uncertain how to proceed. "I'm sure Miss Abdullah will be a worthy addition to your family."

The sultana gave a careless shrug. "More worthy than my son."

A startled gasp quickly evaporated in Lacey's throat as indignation mushroomed inside her chest. How dare the sultana say that about Hafiz? Lacey was stunned that the woman would say it to a stranger. There was no telling what was said in private.

Lacey looked away and fought back her words. Didn't Sultana Zafirah see how much her son worked and sacrificed to correct his mistakes? Didn't she care that he strove to become worthy, all the while knowing he would never reach his goal? Or was the sultana unwilling to recognize what her son has already achieved?

Tears smarted Lacey's eyes as hope shriveled up inside her. Why did Hafiz want to be with his family instead of her? The idea alone was like a knife sliding between her ribs before it gave a vicious twist. Was this what he really wanted?

How could she leave Hafiz here to face this alone? But deep down, she knew she wasn't an ally. She was a liability. She was going to leave so Hafiz could become the man he wanted to be. She wanted Rudaynah to benefit from his ideas and leadership, and she wanted the people to recognize his worth and abilities.

On a purely selfish level, she wanted her sacrifice to mean something. She wanted it be worth the pain, if that was possible.

The ballroom suddenly plunged into darkness. The initial squeals from the crowd turned into groans of people who were used to power outages. Lacey blinked wildly as the darkness shrouded her. She could already feel the difference in temperature as the air conditioner silenced.

"Nothing to worry about, Miss Maxwell." Sultana Zafirah said. The royal entourage bumped Lacey as they quickly surrounded the sultana. "The generator will turn on soon."

"Yes, Your Majesty."

The emergency lights gradually came on, casting an eerie green over the wedding guests. Just as everyone cheered, the lights blinked and flared before shutting off.

"No, no, no." Inas said. "This cannot happen at my daughter's wedding."

"I'll go see if there are any lights on in the hotel," Lacey offered. Sensing she only had a few minutes before the lights and power returned, she slowly retreated.

Using the flurry of activity to her advantage, Lacey turned around and made her way to the exit. Her hands brushed against the heavy metal door. She wrenched the handle, opening the door a crack, and found the hallway was just as dark as the ballroom. The moment she passed the threshold, she breathed a sigh of relief.

As much as she wanted to celebrate her friend's special moment, she found the business of marriage in Rudaynah too depressing. It wasn't a union of two hearts as much as it was a business alliance. The combining of two families and two properties.

The lights came back on, and she heard the murmurs of delight from the ballroom. Lacey hurried down the steps to the main lobby when she saw a familiar figure in a gray pinstripe suit waiting at the bottom of the stairs.

"Where have you been?" Hafiz asked, glancing at his wristwatch. "We were supposed to meet at your apartment."

"Hafiz?" She remembered that the sultana and the most influential people in the country were in the next room. He was placing himself at risk. "You can't be here. It's too dangerous. Your—"

"I'm fully aware of it," Hafiz said as he fell into

step with her. "If you want to get to Abu Dhabi tonight, we must leave now."

"I'm sorry I'm late. I'm never late."

Hafiz set his mouth in a grim line. "My limousine
is waiting right outside the entrance. Once we leave,
then we will discuss what you were doing with my
mother."

Lacey stiffened as she heard the accusation in his
tone. How did he find out about that? She didn't have
to see Hafiz's face to know he was angry. But why
was he blaming her?

"I didn't know the sultana was going to make an
appearance. How would I?"

Hafiz muttered something succinct as he ushered
her out the hotel. Guilt slammed through her. She
didn't want to be a hindrance. She hated being the
cause of his troubles.

Lacey paused. She wasn't a hindrance. She wasn't a
liability. The only thing she was guilty of was loving a
man who didn't think she was good enough to marry.

CHAPTER EIGHT

HAFIZ KEPT HIS anger in check as he got into the waiting limousine. Tonight he had to send away the one person who mattered the most to him. He wanted to rage against the world, destroy everything around him and allow the fury to consume him. Instead he closed the car door with deliberate care.

The car jerked into full speed. He barely glanced at Lacey sitting regally on the other side of the back seat. He didn't trust himself to speak or look at her.

What was it about this woman? Did she trigger a self-destructive tendency in him? Why had he been willing to risk everything for Lacey? What made him lower his guard when they had been in danger of discovery? Why couldn't he have fallen for someone who would make his life easier?

"I have nothing to say." Lacey stared straight ahead. "I did nothing wrong."

He sliced his hand in the air. "Yes, you did," he replied in a low growl. In the past Lacey's hurt would have destroyed him until he did everything in his power to make her happy, but at the moment he wished she would see the world through his eyes.

"I don't have to explain myself," Lacey continued.

"My friend introduced me to your mother. She thought I was worthy enough to meet the sultana. Why don't you?"

"Does your friend know everything about you?" The words were dragged from his mouth. "Is she aware that you are the prince's mistress?"

"Of course not." Lacey said and rolled her eyes.

He speared a hard look at Lacey. She had spent half a year in his country but still didn't have a basic understanding how the Sultanate of Rudaynah worked. He risked everything to help her tonight. It would be scandalous if he were found alone with a woman. If it were discovered that she was his mistress, the results would be cataclysmic.

"I'm sorry if my meeting the sultana made you uncomfortable," she said angrily.

Was she? Had she not suggested a few days ago how he was better off without that title? Lacey had to be furious that her dream life ended abruptly while he was offered the one thing he had relentlessly worked toward. It wouldn't take much to crush his chances, but Hafiz didn't want to believe Lacey could be that diabolical.

"No, you're not. You want me to be uncomfortable and worry. You're enjoying it." Hafiz grabbed a hold of the door as the limousine took a sharp, fast turn. "I want to know the whole truth. How long have you known my mother?"

"I just met her," Lacey insisted. "It's not like we had an in-depth conversation."

Hafiz shook his head. Her eyes shone with innocence, and yet he didn't trust that the meeting was happenstance. She could have arranged to meet the sultana and dropped a few bombshells. He didn't want to think of how many times those blue eyes possibly duped him in the past.

"I swear, I didn't tell her anything."

And yet, despite careful planning of keeping his family and private life separate, his mother managed to meet his mistress. "This is not happening," he muttered. Being introduced to a mistress or concubine was considered a deep offense to the sultana. If the truth came out, he would pay the penalty for it. "You planned this, didn't you?"

"Planned what? An introduction with your mother?" Lacey asked listlessly, as if the fight had evaporated from her. She looked out the window at the dusty city streets whizzing past them.

"You hinted at it when you first arrived here. How you wanted to meet my family. Then it turned into a bold request and finally a demand."

Lacey rubbed her hands over her face and gave a deep sigh. "That was before I understood our relationship was completely forbidden. That I was somehow beneath you and not good enough to meet your family."

Beneath him? Where did she get that idea? "I told you that it was complicated."

"But you didn't tell me that it was impossible." She returned her attention to the window as if she couldn't bear to look at him. "I should have known something was up when you didn't introduce me to your friends. I was so naïve."

"I have nothing to apologize for."

She shook her head. "You brought me over here

under false pretenses. I thought we were going to live together."

Hafiz's mouth dropped open in surprise. "I never made that offer. Us, together in the palace?" He shuddered at the thought. "We would have been cast out in seconds."

"Obviously you and I had different ideas about being together. I didn't think you would hide my existence from your family."

"And when you realized that meeting them wasn't going to happen, you decided to take matters into your own hands."

"Like my introduction to your mother? What would be the point?" She turned to face him. "What do you think I did? Just walk up to her and say, 'Hi, I'm Lacey. I'm Hafiz's mistress and I hope to continue even after he's married?' Do you really think I'm capable of that?"

He stared at her with disbelieving horror as something close to panic clenched his stomach. "You would if you thought it would help."

"Help?" She watched him with growing suspicion. "Help what?"

"To stop me from getting married." She would eventually realize that he wasn't going to stop it. He accepted that his future wasn't going to be happy or loving. He had known that for the past decade.

"For the last time," she said, her voice rising, "I was not trying to wreck your wedding. I am going against every instinct I have by not fighting for you." She tilted her head back and rested it against the seat. "Is that what makes you so suspicious? You gave me up and thought I would fight for you. For us. Because I immediately backed off, I must be up to something?"

"You think I gave you up easily? That there was no thought involved, no hesitation? I had put off my marriage for as long as possible so I could be with you."

"You put off your marriage so you could get a better deal," Lacey said through clenched teeth. "Like getting another shot at becoming the crown prince. Then you couldn't get rid of me fast enough."

"Lacey, I am not your parents. Try not to compare me with them. I didn't discard you to pursue my life's ambition."

Lacey's eyes narrowed into slits. "Don't bring my parents into this."

"You think I'm abandoning you out of ambition just like your parents. You act as if my life is going to overflow with happiness and abundance once you're out of my life. Do you think your parents had a better life without you?"

"Yes!" she bit out.

Hafiz drew his head back and stared at her. "You're wrong, Lacey. They missed out on so much."

"No, you are wrong. I held them back from what they really wanted in life. Once I was gone, they pursued their passion. They are happier than they've ever been."

Did she think he wouldn't look back at their time together? That he wouldn't feel the regret of letting her go? "Why do you act like I'm giving you up for something better? I am entering a marriage with a stranger," he reminded her.

"You made a choice, Hafiz. And it wasn't me. It was never going to be me."

A thought suddenly occurred to him. *She had been waiting for this to happen.* "You're not fighting for me because deep down you knew I was going to have to make a choice one day. And you knew it wasn't going to be in your favor."

"I'm not fighting for you because I know we have run our course." She gave a sharp intake of breath and tossed her hands in the air. "I should have just kept our relationship to a one-night stand and be done with you."

"Excuse me?" Anger flashed hot and swift inside him. What he and Lacey shared could not have been contained in one night.

"I knew you were trouble, but that didn't stop me. No, quite the opposite." She shook her head in self-disgust. "And, let's face it, you weren't thinking about forever after one night with me."

Hafiz wearily rubbed his hands over his eyes. "All I knew is that I couldn't stay away."

"And you kept coming back. I would count the days until we could see each other again. I thought you felt the same way, too."

"I did." The anticipation that burned in his veins, the excitement pressing against his chest had never waned.

"No, it's only been recently when I realized we had approached this affair very differently. I was so happy in love that I wanted to share it with the whole world. You wanted to keep this relationship secret because you were ashamed."

"For the last time, Lacey, I am not ashamed—"

"No, not of me." Her jaw trembled as she tried to hold her emotions in check. "You were ashamed that you couldn't stay away. After all those years of resisting temptation, of demonstrating your willpower, your strength, you couldn't stay away. An ordinary woman, a nobody, was your weakness."

He closed his eyes, momentarily overwhelmed. She was right. He didn't like how Lacey saw right through him. Understood him better than he understood himself.

"I am Prince Hafiz ibn Yusuf Qadi," he said quietly. "I have spent the last ten years proving that I am worthy of that name. I had purged every wild impulse, and nothing could tempt me off the straight and narrow path. And then I met you."

"You make me sound like I'm a vice. Something you need to give up to be a better person."

Hafiz was too deep into the memory to reply. "And then I see you at the piano in a hotel lobby. I didn't even stop to think. I was drawn to your singing as if I was a sailor listening to the sirens."

"Being attracted to me does not show weakness of character. Falling for me is not a sin."

"It is if you are a prince from the Sultanate of Rudaynah."

She crossed her arms and stared at him. "And yet, you asked me to live here. I thought it was because you loved me. No, it's because you see me as some kind of bad habit that you couldn't give up."

Fury flashed through him, and he held it in check. "You don't have that kind of power over me. No one does."

"Especially a young woman who doesn't understand the royal court politics or influential people. That's why you felt safe to bring me over here."

He scoffed at her statement. "Having you here was never safe."

"I thought you trusted me. I thought that made me different from everyone you knew. It made me special to you. But that's not it at all, is it? It's that you contained the situation. You made sure I wasn't in a position to break your trust."

"Not a lot of good it did me," he muttered.

Lacey's fingers fluttered against her cheeks as if she was brushing something away. "I wish I didn't know any of this. I wish I could have left Rudaynah the night I found out about your engagement."

Hafiz remained silent. He knew he should feel the same way. She was his weakness, his vulnerability, but he didn't want her to go.

"That night had been magical," she said softly. There was a faraway look in her eyes. "It was the right way to say goodbye. I would have left here believing that…what we had was special. That I had been special."

Hafiz clenched his hands. He wanted to tell Lacey how special she was to him. But what purpose would it serve? What they had was over. It could not continue.

"You think I'm bad for you," Lacey said. "That I'm proof of your bad judgment, or that I symbolize all of those wild impulses you couldn't get rid of. One of these days you're going to realize that I was the best thing that had ever happened to you." She pointed her finger at him. "Someday you'll realize that everything I've done was to protect you."

"I don't need your protection, Lacey." He shook his head. "It was my job to protect you."

Lacey blinked rapidly as if she was preventing

more tears from falling. "I wanted to be your confidante. Your partner. My goal was to help you be the best prince you could be."

"And in return, you would become a princess." Hafiz grimaced. Even as he said it, he knew that wasn't her true motivation.

"If you believe that, you don't know me at all." Her shoulders drooped as if she didn't have the energy to fight anymore. "I thought you knew everything about me," Lacey announced dully as she pulled her hair away from her face.

"And you know everything about me," Hafiz said. "I confided in you when I shouldn't have."

Lacey jerked at his harsh tone and slowly turned to meet his gaze. "Why do you continue to believe that I would betray you?"

Her question was carried out with a wispy puff of air. The wounded look in her eyes threatened to shatter him inside. He drew from the dark edges that hovered around him, knowing he had to be callous, and knowing he was going to regret it.

"Because you are a mistress. A fallen woman. Betrayal is your only power against me." Hafiz knew what he said hurt her where she was most vulnerable, but it was his only guarantee. That cold response would prevent Lacey from trying to hold on to him and what might have been. He had to protect her even if it meant tearing down the love she felt for him.

The darkness surged through Hafiz, and he struggled against the cold bitterness invading his body. He'd battled it before, only this time he had to do it alone. In the past, Lacey was the only person he knew who could stem the flow.

"If I'm a fallen women, you shouldn't be seen with me. So, why are you still here?" Lacey asked in a withering tone. She folded her arms more tightly and crossed her legs. Hafiz wondered if it was an attempt to get as far away from him as possible. "Stop the car and I'll get out."

"That's enough." Hafiz's tone held a steely edge. "I'm making sure you get on that helicopter."

She gave a haughty tilt of her chin. "I'm perfectly capable of finding my way."

"I'm sure you could, but you don't have access to the palace."

"Palace?" Hafiz saw her tense as a sound of panic rumbled in the back of her throat; she turned abruptly to her window. When she didn't see anything on her side of the limousine, she frantically searched out his window.

He knew the minute she saw the towering mud brick walls that surrounded the palace. The historical site was constructed as more of a fortress than the home of a sultan. It wasn't opulent or majestic. The curved buildings, domed roofs and large archways were made out of clay. The buildings were functional and cool against the desert heat.

It was also designed to intimidate the enemy. Lacey had a look of unease as they passed through the guarded gates, and she got the first good look of the palace. Hafiz held back his assurances. He needed her to focus on leaving without looking back.

"I can't see you again," he began.

Her eyes dulled with pain. "I don't want you to."

Hafiz scowled at her statement. "I mean it, Lacey."

"I do, too. I'm not really big on sharing." Her chin

wobbled, and she blinked back the moisture from her eyes. "Don't contact me unless you've changed your mind and only want me."

That wasn't going to happen, Hafiz thought. It couldn't.

The limousine lurched to a stop next to the helicopter pad. Hafiz immediately stepped out of the car and reached for Lacey's hand. When she hesitated, he grasped her wrist. Fierce sensations scorched his skin from the touch. He grimly ignored the way his pulse tripped and assisted her outside.

Her long hair blew in the desert wind, and he escorted her to the pilot who was waiting by the helicopter. After Hafiz yelled instructions over the noise, Lacey climbed in. He tried to assist her, but she batted him away. He flashed a warning look at her.

The warning dissipated as he looked into her eyes. Even after what had happened, after everything they'd said, he wished for one more kiss. He was desperate for it and felt the pull. His mouth craved her taste and her softness. The yearning pierced at him like swift jabs of a knife, because he knew after this moment, circumstances would snatch Lacey away from him.

He looked away. The darkness inside him eclipsed the pain of knowing this was the last time he would see her. Their paths would never cross, and he could never contact her again. He wouldn't know where she lived or if she was safe. She would disappear but linger in his mind as he worried and wondered.

"Your Highness," the pilot shouted, breaking through Hafiz's thoughts. "We need to leave now."

Hafiz hesitated. He couldn't make a clean break

from Lacey, no matter how much he wanted to. How much he needed to, for both their sakes.

He glanced at her and met her gaze. No tears escaped her eyes. She didn't speak. Didn't move, but he knew she struggled for composure. He knew her poise was for his benefit. It was her way to prove that she would be fine.

She looked so beautiful and elegant. Regal. Hafiz thought his heart was going to blast through the wall of his chest. Lacey was more beautiful than when he first saw her. He was fortunate to have known and loved her, and she would never know. His throat closed shut as his strength seeped out of his bones.

He had to tell her. He had thought it would be kinder not to say anything. Not to give her the answer because it would have given her hope. Something to fight for. But he could not let her go with the belief that she didn't matter.

"I love you, Lacey."

Her lips parted, and she stared at his mouth. She frowned as if she had heard incorrectly. As if she had heard what she wanted to hear.

"You may think I hate you or I'm ashamed of you," he said over the whine of the helicopter, "but it isn't true. I took all of these risks because I love you. I will always love you."

She began to reach out as the helicopter started to lift off. Hafiz wanted to grab her hand, but he forced himself to back away.

He watched her, unblinking, as the helicopter rose into the sky and turned, taking his love, his last chance of happiness, away from him.

But he didn't deserve happiness. He didn't deserve a life with Lacey.

Hafiz remained where he stood when every instinct screamed for him to run after Lacey. A ragged gasp escaped his raw throat as he watched the helicopter fly off until it was no longer a speck in the air. The silence sliced deep into his dreams and wishes until they lay tattered at his feet and darkness descended in his heart.

CHAPTER NINE

"Lacey, my work shift is about to start," Priya shouted over the music. "Are you going to be okay? I feel weird leaving you alone."

"That's sweet of you, but you don't have to worry." Lacey smiled at her roommate. She felt bad that Priya felt the need to mother her. And drag her to this party so she would get out of the apartment. "I'm going to be fine. It's been a while since I've been to a party, but it's all coming back to me."

"Good," Priya said with a nod. "I know you've been mending a broken heart, but you are too young to spend all your time working at the hotel and staying in bed."

"You're right," she said as her roommate walked away. Taking a small sip from the beer bottle she had been nursing for an hour, Lacey stood at the sidelines and watched her coworkers mill around the pool room located in their housing complex. It was an eclectic mix of young people in swimwear and colorful sundresses. While some splashed around in the pool and others danced to the blaring music, most of the guests nibbled on the spicy snacks and drank the boldly colored concoctions.

Once Priya left the party, Lacey closed her eyes and exhaled. She would stay another five minutes and then leave.

She still wasn't sure why she'd chosen to stay in Abu Dhabi, but it had proven to be a good decision. The rich nightlife had allowed her to find a job performing at the hotel lounge. She'd also managed to make a few friends within the month she arrived. She was determined to get out and meet more people. Forget the past and make up for lost time.

Sometimes determination wasn't enough. Her time in Rudaynah had changed her. Marked her in ways she hadn't considered. Lacey glanced down at the purple bikini she wore and the wispy sarong around her hips. These days she wasn't comfortable showing too much skin. She preferred the modest dress code she had to follow once she was outside the housing complex.

"Lacey!" Cody, another American who worked in the hotel, was at her side. His wide smile, unbuttoned shirt and bright red swim trunks conveyed his casual attitude toward life. He liked to flirt with her, and while she knew it didn't mean anything, she tried to discourage it.

"You haven't danced once the whole time you've been here." He held out his hand. "We need to fix that."

She hesitated for a second. She knew the invitation wasn't going to jump-start her love life, but the idea of dancing with another man—touching another man—felt wrong.

It's just a dance. It's no big deal. But she knew Cody would try for more. How could she explain to him that she didn't feel whole or intact? That she was definitely not strong enough to even expose herself to a lighthearted fling or a one-night stand?

Looking into Cody's face lined by the sun rather than by hardship, Lacey realized falling in love again was impossible. She felt the corners of her mouth quirk as she considered her foolishness. What was she worried about? She was safe with Cody and every other man. No one could measure up to Hafiz.

"Okay, sure. Why not?" She set down her beer and took his hand. Lacey didn't feel any thrill of anticipation when he placed his other hand on the curve of her hip or when her fingers grazed his bare skin. She felt no excitement, no awareness. Nothing.

But, quite honestly, she hadn't felt a thing since the helicopter touched down in Abu Dhabi a month ago. She went through the motions of living, but she felt dead inside. She had a feeling it was going to be like that forever. And still she didn't worry over the possibility.

As Lacey danced in Cody's arms, she wondered how long the song would last. She knew that if Hafiz had been her dance partner, she would have wanted the music to go on forever.

Hafiz. She had to stop thinking about him. Lacey abruptly pulled away just as the song changed into something harsh and angry.

Cody motioned for her to keep dancing, but she wanted to go home. No, that wasn't true. She wanted to find Hafiz.

But that was not going to happen, Lacey reminded herself. He didn't want her near him. She was a vice. A sin. Hafiz's words ricocheted through her head.

Nothing had changed. Nothing ever would. She had to move on.

"Don't hold back, Lacey!" Cody yelled as he jumped up and down to the drumbeat.

Move on. Start now. Fake it until you make it. Lacey swayed to the music. She wished it had the power to make her forget everything. But the music didn't reach her heart or fill her soul like it used to.

She needed to feel it again. Music was part of who she was. It was more than her livelihood; it was how she expressed herself and how she found solace. She couldn't let Hafiz take that away from her, too.

Lacey pushed harder as she danced. She moved her shoulders and swished her hips to the beat of the drums. The music still didn't reach her.

She pulled and pushed her body to move as far as it would go, wishing that the numbness that held everything back would break. That the music would grow louder until it seeped inside her. If that didn't work, then she hoped the dancing would exhaust her so she could sleep without dreaming.

From the corner of her eyes, Lacey saw that someone wore all black. A jacket…no, a suit. The formality was at odds with the party. The darkness was out of place among the bright rainbow colors. But there was something familiar about the person's movement. What was it that… Her heart lurched, and she went still.

Hafiz. She froze as the wild hope and surprise ripped through her. Hafiz was here? No, that was impossible. She blinked, and he was suddenly gone. Lacey rubbed her eyes. Was she now having hallucinations about him along with her dreams?

Her pulse skipped hard as she quickly scanned the crowd. Why did he seem so real? Shouldn't her memory become hazier as time went on?

She frowned as she resumed her dancing. Her memory was definitely playing tricks. Lacey didn't understand why she envisioned him in a black linen jacket, collarless shirt and black trousers. Usually she remembered him in a pinstripe suit, in traditional robes, or in nothing at all.

Lacey squeezed her eyes shut as she tried to discard the images of Hafiz in various stages of undress flickering through her mind. *Forget about him,* she decided as she forced herself to dance. *It's time to start living again.*

Hafiz watched Lacey dance, her body moving with the same earthiness as when they shared a bed. It had been four weeks since he'd seen Lacey. Since he had declared his love. It felt like an eternity. He shouldn't be here, and yet he couldn't stay away.

Now he wished he hadn't given in to the impulse. Anger and indignation swirled inside him, ready to explode. From what he could see, Lacey was the center of the party. She wasn't laughing or smiling, but her intense expression suggested that nothing mattered more than exploring the music.

He glared at the bikini and sarong she wore. It flaunted her curves instead of hiding them. The bikini top lovingly clung to her breasts. Her nipples pressed against the fragile fabric. The sarong hung low, emphasizing her tiny waist and the gentle swell of her hips.

His gaze traveled down her taut stomach. The ivory

skin was sun-kissed, but she had lost weight. Pining for him? Hafiz glanced around the party and scoffed at the idea as he crossed his arms. He wished. More like too much partying.

The brightly colored sarong teased his senses, and he couldn't drag his gaze away from her bare legs. He remembered how they felt wrapped around his waist as he drove into her.

When Lacey rolled her hips, Hafiz's restraint threatened to shatter. Where was a voluminous caftan when you needed one? He was beginning to see the advantages.

Lacey was surrounded by cheering men, and she unknowingly taunted them with the thrust of her hips. Hafiz swore she was more sensual than any belly dancer without even trying. Did she know that these men would do anything to get her into bed? They couldn't hide the desperation to take his place in her life.

Had they already?

The possibility fueled his bitter jealousy. He could not hold back any longer. He stepped through the circle of the men posturing for Lacey's attention and reached for her. Hafiz grasped her wrist and was painfully aware of the heat coursing through him from the simple touch.

Lacey opened her eyes just as he slid her against him. Blood sang through his veins as her soft breasts pressed against his hard chest. He shuddered as his control slipped. After a month without her, every primal instinct told him to pounce and never let her go.

"Miss me, Lacey?" he murmured in her ear.

He watched as she blinked at him. His chest ached

as he waited, wondering how she would greet him. Would she push him away? Would she welcome him with the same cool friendliness she'd welcome an old acquaintance? Or would she treat him with indifference?

"Hafiz?"

He drew her closer as the people and the noise faded around them. He had eyes only for Lacey. She pressed her hands to his face. "I can't believe you're here," she whispered.

He held her hand and pressed his mouth against her palm. "You did miss me," he said, purring with satisfaction.

"Of course I did." She wrapped her arms around his neck and held him fiercely. "How can you ask?" she asked against his chest.

"Let's get out of here," he insisted as he drew her away. He was too impatient to taste Lacey's mouth on his. He needed her more than his next breath. "I want you all to myself."

Hafiz held her hand tightly as he guided her out of the party as if he couldn't risk losing her. As if she might break away. He was striding to the elevators that would whisk them to her apartment when he abruptly turned and pulled her into a shadowy corner.

It had been too long. He wasn't going to wait anymore. He pressed her back against the corner and braced his arms against the walls, trapping her. "Show me how much you missed me."

Lacey didn't hesitate and claimed Hafiz's mouth with hers. The one touch, one kiss, was all it took for the numbness to disappear. Her skin tingled, her heart pounded against her chest, and blood roared in her ears as she violently came back to life.

She still couldn't believe it. Hafiz had come for her. He chose her over his fiancée and his duty. Over his country. He chose *her*.

Lacey pulled away and stared at Hafiz. She searched his face, noticing how much he had changed in a month. His features were harsher, the lines and angles more pronounced. The sexual hunger in his eyes was ferocious.

She trembled with anticipation and grabbed his jacket lapels. Hafiz wrapped his hands around her waist and ripped off her sarong. He tossed it on the ground with an impatience she'd never seen in him.

She knew Hafiz was almost out of his mind with lust. He was desperate to touch her. To taste her. She understood this driving need, but the intensity was almost painful. She felt as if she could explode from it.

Hafiz pushed the bikini top away and exposed her breasts. They felt heavy under his hot gaze. Lacey almost wept as Hafiz captured one tight nipple in his mouth. She raked her fingers through his hair, encouraging him closer.

Lacey gasped at the primal, almost savage way he stripped her bikini bottoms from her hips. She could tell that his control was slipping. He couldn't hold back. This reunion was going to be hard, fast and furious.

She couldn't believe she had this power over him. That they had this power over each other. Lacey liked how his fingers shook as he tore the flimsy piece of fabric from her trembling legs. She bit her lip when he roughly cupped her sex.

"Now," she muttered. "I need you in me now."

Hafiz didn't follow her demands. Instead he dipped his fingers into her wet heat. Lacey panted hard as her flesh gripped him tight and drew him in deeper.

As Hafiz stroked her with his fingers, Lacey pressed her mouth shut to prevent a throaty moan from escaping. They were hidden as the party continued around them. No one could hear them, no one could see, but old habits died hard. She couldn't risk being discovered, but she couldn't bear the idea of stopping.

Lacey dove her hands under his shirt and slid her fingers along his hot, flushed skin. She wanted to rip his clothes off his perfect body, but that would take too much time. She smiled when his breath hitched in his throat as his muscles bunched under her touch. He countered with the flick of his finger inside her. She shuddered as the fiery sensations swept through her body.

"Now, Hafiz. I can't wait any longer." She heard the metallic sound of his zipper and rocked her hips with impatience. She gulped for air and inhaled the musky scent of his arousal. Her chest ached with excitement as he lifted her up and hooked her legs over his hips.

He entered her with one smooth thrust. Hafiz's long groan rumbled from his chest, and he didn't move as if he was savoring this moment. His penis stretched and filled her, but Lacey couldn't stay still. She wanted more—needed everything Hafiz had to give her. She rolled her pelvis slowly and was rewarded with a warning growl before he clenched his fingers into her hips. Hafiz withdrew and plunged into her again and again.

She eagerly accepted each wild thrust. Lacey held on to Hafiz tightly and closed her eyes as her climax forked through her. Her heart faltered as the fury rushed through, taking the last of her strength. Her mind grasped on the only thing that mattered—he had chosen her above all else.

"This bed is too small," Hafiz complained in a murmur as he held Lacey in his arms. She lay on top of him, naked and warm. She rested her head against his chest, and he threaded his fingers through her long hair.

He was right where he wanted to be.

"It's fine," she said sleepily.

Fine? He shook his head at the thought. His feet dangled off the edge, and his shoulders were almost too wide for the bed. The mattress was as thin and cheap as the sheets.

It was too dark to see all of Lacey's bedroom, but he could tell that it was tiny with just a few furnishings. It was nothing like the apartment she had in Rudaynah.

"We should go to my hotel suite," Hafiz suggested. "It's more comfortable. Bigger." *Better.* He felt Lacey deserved more. How did she wind up here?

"Mmm-hmm." Lacey made no move to get up.

He slid his hand down and caressed her spine. He felt her shiver of pleasure under his palm. "Do you like Abu Dhabi?" he asked.

"Mmm-hmm."

"Why did you choose to live here?" He had been astounded when he discovered she was still in the UAE. He thought she had gone home. Back to St. Louis. "Did you know someone? Had business contacts?"

"I didn't know anyone," she said with a yawn. "But I applied for some jobs, did the necessary paperwork, and I got this one at the hotel."

"Adventurous of you," Hafiz said as he cupped the base of her head and held her close. He didn't like the idea that she was all alone in the world. That there was no one looking out for her. Protecting her.

"You sound surprised," Lacey said. "May I remind you, I moved to Rudaynah sight unseen? Some people consider that adventurous. My friends thought it was crazy."

"That was different. You had me to take care of you."

"I've been looking after myself for as long as I can remember."

"You let me take care of you," Hafiz said. The words echoed in his mind. She *let* him. She had given her trust in so many ways, and he took it for granted.

"It wasn't easy for me," Lacey admitted as she pressed her mouth against his chest and gave him a kiss. "I didn't want to be dependent on you."

Lacey Maxwell wasn't cut out to be a mistress, Hafiz decided. Most women took the role because they wanted to be taken care of.

"What's wrong with depending on me?" he asked. "On anyone?"

"I remember what it was like when I had to rely on my parents. They really didn't want to deal with me."

His fingers tightened against her. Anger flared inside him as he imagined a young Lacey, ignored and neglected. "You don't know that."

"I do." There was no sadness in her voice. She spoke as if she was giving the facts. "They have not reached out to me once I've been on my own. It's better this way. I know I made the right decision to cut them out of my life."

A cold chill swept through Hafiz. *"You're* the one that walked away?"

"I tried for years to be the daughter they wanted and needed. But I couldn't earn their love or attention. I walked away and didn't look back."

His heart started to race. He had always thought Lacey was tenacious. It was one of her most admirable traits. He had seen her practice a piece of music until she got it right or talk him through a work problem even if it took all night. But even she had limits. "But…they're your parents."

"And that's why it took me so long to walk away. I kept thinking circumstances would change. But they didn't see any need to change. They weren't being malicious. They were extremely selfish. It took me years to forgive them, but I'm not trying to make them love me anymore."

Hafiz couldn't shake the fear that gripped his chest. He had always felt that Lacey's love was unconditional. It was the one thing he could count on. Yet Lacey had walked away from the strongest bond a person could have. He thought that once Lacey loved someone, it was forever.

This changed everything.

"Lacey." She felt a large hand cupping her shoulder, rousing her out of the best sleep she'd had in a long, long time. "Lacey, wake up."

She peered through bleary eyes. A whisper of a smile formed on her lips when she saw Hafiz looking down at her. Last night hadn't been a dream. "Come back to bed," she mumbled drowsily and patted the mattress next to her.

"It's time to get up, Sleeping Beauty," he said with a smile.

She looked at him and noticed for the first time that he was already dressed in his black T-shirt and trousers. His hair gleamed with dampness from a recent shower.

Lacey sighed and stretched, murmuring in protest at the twinges in her muscles. "Sleeping Beauty isn't my favorite fairytale princess," she said as she rubbed the sleep from her eyes.

"You prefer Rapunzel?" he asked. "I finally read that fairy tale you kept talking about."

"Really?" She slowly sat up in bed and pushed her hair away from her face. "What did you think of it?"

Hafiz's mouth set in a grim line. She suspected he was going to ask something but wasn't sure if he would like the answer. "Did you see me as the prince who saved the day, or did you see me as the witch who trapped Rapunzel in the tower?"

Lacey blinked, startled by the question. The corners of her lips tilted into a sad smile as she wrapped the bed sheet around her nude body. "It took me a while before I realized that you were the Rapunzel in the story."

Hafiz jerked his head back. "That's not funny."

"I'm serious. Think about it," she said. She knew she should have kept her opinion to herself. What man would want to be compared to Rapunzel? But it was too late, and she needed to explain her way of thinking. "Rudaynah was your tower and you were trapped."

"I am not trapped," he said stiffly. "I have duties and obligations, but that is not the same thing."

"Those expectations were holding you back. The sultan was more interested in how you acted than what you accomplished."

"I don't want to talk about that right now." The flash of annoyance in Hafiz's eyes indicated that the topic would be discussed at length later.

"It doesn't matter. It's the past. You're free now," she said with a wide smile. "You escaped the tower. Although I'm sure you would want to visit the sultanate every once in a while. It is your homeland."

Hafiz tilted his head and stared at her with incomprehension. "Lacey, what are you talking about?"

"You left Rudaynah. Didn't you?" she asked slowly. "We agreed that we wouldn't see each other unless you chose me and only me."

"I never agreed to that."

She tried to remember what had been said that night. Hafiz had said he loved her. It was the one thing that held her together when she wondered what it all had been for.

"You love me. You found me," she said softly. "But you're not staying?"

Hafiz sighed. "No."

She flinched as his answer clawed at her. It tore her to shreds before she had a chance to ward off the pain. "And you're still…"

"Getting married. Yes."

Those three words ripped away the last fragment of hope. She closed her eyes and hunched her shoulders. Hafiz hadn't chosen her. He hadn't chased her across the world to get her back.

CHAPTER TEN

HE WAS STILL getting married to Nabeela. The stark truth sliced through her. He'd failed to mention that important piece of information before he possessed her body and soul throughout the night. The rat. The snake.

She couldn't believe he would do this to her. Again. How many times would she fall for this routine? "Get out," she ordered hoarsely, clutching the sheet against her.

"What?" Arrogant disbelief tinged his voice.

"I thought you chose me. I'm such a fool," she whispered, gently rocking back and forth. It felt as if she was bleeding inside. She was going to drown in it.

Hafiz exhaled sharply. "I am choosing to be with you."

"Temporarily," she said. "You came here for sex." She stiffened and looked at the bed before scrambling off of the mattress. She gave a fierce yank to the bed sheets that covered her body. Her body, which she'd freely given to him with her love hours before.

He splayed his hands in the air. "I didn't plan it."

"Right." This from a man who was in control of everything and everyone around him. "You didn't plan to travel to Abu Dhabi. You didn't plan to search for me. You didn't plan to take me against a wall minutes after you found me."

He rolled his shoulders back as if he was bracing himself for a direct hit. "I traveled here for a meeting. I'm staying at this hotel, and I didn't know you were still in Abu Dhabi until I saw the poster at the hotel lounge about your performance."

Just when she thought she couldn't feel any worse. He hadn't come here just to find her. He didn't go out of his way to seek her. She stared at Hafiz, not sure if she was going to burst into tears or start laughing maniacally at the unfairness of it all.

She needed to cover herself. Protect herself. Lacey grabbed her robe that had fallen on the floor. "You needed to scratch an itch. Why? Your fiancée won't sleep with you until the wedding night?"

His eyes darkened. "I have no contact with my future bride because it is an arranged marriage. It is not a love match."

As if that was supposed to make her feel better. The muscle in her cheek twitched with fury. "It's probably best that way. You don't want her to find out how rotten to the core you are until after the vows are exchanged."

"Lacey, I apologize for the misunderstanding."

"Misunderstanding? There was no misunderstanding. You withheld that information because if I knew you were still engaged, I wouldn't have welcomed you with open arms."

"Don't be too sure. We have a connection that is too—"

"Connection?" She gave a harsh laugh. "No, we have

a past. That is it. You severed that connection when you got me out of your life as quickly as possible."

"We still have something," he argued. "That's why I came to check up on you and—"

"You came to have sex because you're not used to going without." Lacey thrust her arms through the sleeves of her robe. The fiery orange silk felt like needles across her sensitive skin. "And you knew I wouldn't deny you. Especially since you had lied to me and said you loved me."

Hafiz drew back. "That wasn't a lie."

She glared at him, fighting the urge to strike out with her nails unsheathed. "Your timing was suspicious."

He placed his hands on his hips. "Suspicious?"

"You tell me that you love me the moment before I was out of your life forever. Was it a way to keep me dangling on your hook? That way, when you looked me up, you didn't have to work too hard to get back into my bed."

"I told you in a moment of weakness," he said in a low growl. "I didn't want you to look back and think the year we spent together meant nothing."

Their time had meant everything to her. It had been the one time when she felt safe and wanted. She had honestly believed during the months in Rudaynah that they had been growing closer and that their relationship could weather anything.

"You could have told me you loved me at any time, but you didn't. Why?" She took a step closer and pointed her finger accusingly at him. "Because saying those words at the last minute meant you didn't have to do anything about it."

He raked his fingers through his hair. Lacey had the feeling he wanted to grab her by the shoulders and shake her. She took a prudent step back.

"If you don't believe me," Hafiz said in a clipped tone, "that is your problem."

Lacey glared at him. Wouldn't a man in love want to express his emotions? Wouldn't he show it with grand gestures and small, intimate moments?

But not this man. No, not Prince Hafiz. He wasn't going to lower himself and try to convince her. He wasn't going to waste his energy on proving something that didn't exist.

"You want to forget everything I did for you? For us? Go right ahead," Hafiz said. "I love you and nothing is going to change that."

"What am I supposed to think? You say you love me when you are engaged to another woman." She tied the sash of her robe with enough force that it could have ripped.

Hafiz ground the heels of his palms against his eyes. "I'm not replacing you."

"Of course not," Lacey said as she walked out of the bedroom. "I would have had to be part of your life for Nabeela to replace my role."

Hafiz followed her into the main room with long, brisk strides. His presence made the apartment feel smaller, as if it couldn't contain him. Lacey wished Priya had not had the night shift. She wanted him to leave and could have used some backup right now. Knowing what kind of man he was, Hafiz wouldn't leave until he got what he was after.

"You made sure I wasn't part of your world," Lacey continued. "I thought I needed to earn that privilege because I was a foreigner and a nobody. Now I realize that nothing I did would have made a difference. It just wasn't going to happen."

She was done trying to earn love. It didn't work. She had twisted and bent herself into knots, determined to give her all and make her relationships work. She had made Hafiz the most important part of her life, and he could not do the same. He had accepted her love as if it was his due, but he did not see her as a priority in life.

No more. Hafiz did not value her role in his life, and he wasn't going to. From now on, she would put herself first because no one else would. She would not settle or compromise.

She heard Hafiz's cell phone ring. Lacey whirled around and saw him retrieve it from his pocket. "Don't you dare."

He frowned as he glanced up from the touch screen. "I'm just—"

"No, you are not answering that phone. I don't care if Rudaynah suddenly disappeared from the face of the earth. It can't be as important as what's going on here."

"Lacey, don't be—"

"I'm serious, Hafiz. For once, I am your top priority. The most important person in your life is right in front of you, so put the phone away."

Hafiz's austere face tightened, clearly holding his anger in check.

"If you'd rather take the call," she said coldly, "then leave and don't come back."

Her heart was pounding as the phone continued to

ring. Hafiz silently turned off the ringer and returned the phone to his pocket as he held her gaze.

Lacey tried to hide her surprise. She had never given him an ultimatum like that. She had always been reluctant, always knowing that he held the power in the relationship. She'd believed that if she made any demands, placed any expectations on him, he would exchange her for another woman.

It turned out that he'd done it anyway.

"I am marrying Nabeela, but the marriage is in name only," Hafiz assured her.

"What exactly does that mean?"

"It means that we will not live in the same suite of rooms in the palace. It means that we will see each other on official occasions, and, even then, we won't stand next to each other."

Lacey's eyes narrowed as she listened to his explanation. "And this is what you want?"

"It's not about what I want to do. It's about meeting my obligations. Meeting the expectations of my country and my family."

"Will you consummate the marriage?"

His nostrils flared as he reined in his patience. "It is required by law."

The idea of him in bed with another woman made her sick to her stomach. How would he feel if she chose to sleep with another man? Claimed it was required? Hafiz would do everything in his power to prevent that from happening. Why did he think she wouldn't respond in the same way? Because she was a woman? Because as a mistress she had no claim on him?

"Will you have children?" she asked.

The muscle in his jaw twitched. "As the second in line to the throne, I am not required to have an heir."

She noticed he didn't answer her question. "But you won't be second in line," she reminded him. "You will be the crown prince if you marry Nabeela."

"That is the sultan's promise, but I don't know if or when it will happen. I need to be the crown prince," Hafiz admitted. "I didn't expect to get a second chance, and I have to take it."

"It's what you want most," she said in a matter-of-fact tone. He wanted it more than he wanted her. "It's what you strove for all these years."

"I had abused that power ten years ago. If I get the title back, I can make amends. I can show that I'm different. That I am the leader that they need."

Power. It was all about the power. "But the sultan has the ultimate power. And he can strip your title whenever he sees fit."

"That is true, but I won't let that happen. I know how to protect what is mine. This time no one will intimidate or harm those who are important to me. This time I have the power to fight back."

Lacey shook her head with resignation. That sounded like the Hafiz she knew and loved. "You already have that power," she pointed out. "You don't need to be a prince to use it."

He reared his head back as if she had said something blasphemous. "I disagree. Taking care of Rudaynah is my purpose in life. I can't do that if I'm not their prince."

Lacey tried to imagine what Hafiz would be like without a royal title. He would still be arrogant and influential. People would continue to clamor for his attention and advice. But would his countrymen allow him to represent the sultanate if he wasn't a prince, or would they treat him as a celebrity? She didn't know.

"I may not agree with you every time, Lacey, but I always listened. You made me look at the world differently. I missed the way we used to talk," Hafiz said.

Lacey looked away. "We didn't talk. I was your mistress, not your girlfriend. We had sex. Lots and lots of sex."

"Don't," Hafiz said harshly. "Stop rewriting our history."

Was she guilty of that? Lacey sank her teeth into her bottom lip. She had felt loved and adored when she was with Hafiz. He had been generous and caring. Maybe it wasn't just about sex.

"Think about the times you listened to the troubles I had on a project or my concerns for the sultanate," Hafiz said quietly. "You gave me advice and ideas. I knew I could count on you to give me honest feedback. Your opinion always mattered to me."

"And now you have Nabeela for that."

"Nabeela won't look after my best interest. She can't drive me wild. She can't love me the way you do."

"Then break the engagement," she whispered.

He froze and turned his head away. "No, Lacey," Hafiz said as he took a step back.

"You don't have to do this to redeem yourself. You have made up for your mistakes years ago."

"I don't deserve forgiveness."

"You don't deserve a loveless marriage," she insisted. "I know what it's like to be unloved. To be surrounded by indifference. It chips away at you until you become a shadow of yourself."

"I can't break the engagement. It's too late."

Lacey closed her eyes as the pain flashed through her. "And you can't walk away from me. So, what do you plan to do?" She slowly opened her eyes as it occurred to her. "You plan to have both of us?" she asked in a scandalized whisper.

Hafiz remained silent as he watched her closely.

She felt the blood drain from her face. "You need to leave right now. I can't believe you would insult me this way."

"I told you, my marriage would be in name only. It's not a real marriage. It's not even a relationship."

She thrust her finger at the door. "Get out," she said, her voice trembling with outrage.

Hafiz sighed and went to collect his jacket. "Give me one good reason why this won't work."

"I don't want to be your mistress." At one time in her life, she gladly accepted the role. It had been the only way she could be in his life. She'd gratefully accepted the crumbs he offered, but now she knew she deserved more.

"But you can't be my wife," he murmured.

"You made sure that couldn't happen. Even if you didn't accept Nabeela as your bride, I still wouldn't be your wife. Because I was a mistress. *Your* mistress."

"That's not the only reason."

"Because you don't think I'm worthy of the title."

"That's not true," he said, grabbing her wrists with his large hands, forcing her to stand still as he towered over her. "I love you and I want to spend the rest of my life with you. This is the best compromise I can make."

"Compromise." Her lips curled with disgust as she said the word. "I'm done compromising."

"There are rules," he said in an impatient growl.

"Break them," she suggested wildly. "You've done it before."

"And I regret it every day. This is different."

"Here's a thought. Stop hiding me from the world and present me to your family with pride. Show them that it's not a sin to love me. Tell them that I am everything you need and that I'm the one you will marry."

"That isn't going to happen. Ever."

Lacey looked down at her bare feet. She had gone too far. She had made an ultimatum that showed the limit of his love for her. She should have known, should have been happy with what he offered, but she couldn't. She wasn't going to take a smaller and demeaning role just to stay in his life. That wasn't love. That was the first step on the path to her destruction.

She had to protect herself. She suddenly felt weak, so much so she couldn't raise her head to meet his gaze. Lacey took a deep breath, the air hurting her raw throat and tight chest.

"And this, what we had together, isn't going to happen again," she said in a low rush. It took all of her strength to raise her head and meet his gaze. "I need you to leave now."

She saw the calculating gleam in his eye just as she heard a key fumbling in the lock of the front door. Lacey turned just as her roommate rushed in.

"Lacey! Why haven't you been answering your texts?" Priya asked as she slammed the door closed.

Priya looked flustered. Her topknot threatened to collapse, and her name tag was crookedly pinned on her black blazer. She appeared out of breath, and her face gleamed with sweat.

"Are you all right?" Lacey asked as her roommate openly studied Hafiz. "Priya, this is—"

Priya raised her hand. "Prince Hafiz, the guy who broke her heart."

Lacey straightened her spine and clutched the lapels of her robe. "How do you know that? I never told you his name."

"No need." Priya swiped her finger against the screen of her phone. "It's all right here in full color."

"What are you talking about?" The lethal tone in Hafiz's low voice made Priya hesitate.

"This." She turned the phone around to show a picture of Hafiz and Lacey in a hot embrace at the party. It was a good quality picture from someone's phone. There was no denying that Prince Hafiz was the man in the picture. Lacey's face was partially hidden, but her identity didn't matter. The fact that her bikini-clad body was plastered against Hafiz was damning enough.

The sharp twist of dread in Lacey's stomach almost made her sick. She clapped a shaky hand against her mouth.

"How many pictures are there?" Hafiz asked.

Lacey's gaze clashed with his. Her eyes widened as she remembered those stolen moments in the corridor outside the party. They hadn't been aware of their surroundings as they made love. What if their recklessness had been caught on camera?

Oh, God. What had they done? It had been madness. Lacey watched Hafiz's gaze harden, no doubt considering the repercussions.

"I've only seen this one so far."

So far. Lacey wanted to sit down before she tumbled to the floor. Hafiz was right. She was his vice. No, she was his poison. She was going to ruin everything for him.

"Who sent it to you?" Lacey asked. "Maybe we can get them to delete it from their camera." Maybe they would luck out. Maybe one of their friends had no idea who Hafiz was and sent it to Priya because she was in the picture.

"I don't know," Priya said as she pressed the screen. "One of our friends was sharing pictures of the party. But it's only a matter of time before someone finds out Hafiz is the playboy prince. Once that happens, there's no containing this."

CHAPTER ELEVEN

HAFIZ STARED AT the image on the small screen. The picture revealed everything. He had greeted Lacey with an intensity that indicated they were more than acquaintances. The passion, the love, the desperate yearning was evident in his expression.

Why? Why hadn't he been more careful? He knew the risks. Did he think the rules only applied when he was home?

He hadn't been thinking. The moment he had seen Lacey's picture in the hotel lounge he had been on the hunt for her. He should have resisted the urge. He had not contacted Lacey for a month and managed to get through each day. But that didn't mean he hadn't thought of her constantly.

"Hafiz?"

He jerked at the sound of Lacey's voice. His gaze slammed into hers. He saw the concern and the tears. But it was the defeat in her eyes that slayed him. Lacey always looked at him as if he was invincible. That he could achieve the impossible.

Now she wasn't so sure. Not when it looked as if he would lose everything over a damning photo.

Priya cleared her throat and only then did Hafiz remember she was in the room. He was always like this when he was around Lacey. Nothing else mattered. It was becoming a major problem.

"I'm going to give you guys some privacy," the roommate said as she started to back away. "Lacey, text me when the prince is ready to return to his hotel suite."

"Why?" Lacey asked.

"If this picture gets out, other photographers will try to find me. A picture of me is worth a lot of money, especially if it includes you," Hafiz explained.

He remembered how this worked. It was humbling that he was in the same predicament that he'd found himself in ten years ago. It didn't matter how much he had tried to control his wilder impulses, he had not changed at all.

Priya nodded. "I can get you to your room unseen."

"Thank you." He returned his attention to Lacey. She crossed her arms tightly against her body and began to pace.

The moment Priya closed the door, Lacey whirled around to face him. "I had nothing to do with this."

Hafiz narrowed his eyes. He wasn't sure what Lacey was talking about, but he often found being silent was the best way to get information.

"I did not set you up," Lacey said. "I know you think that I'm out to sabotage your wedding, but I wouldn't do that."

"You wouldn't?" he asked softly. The thought hadn't crossed his mind. He knew his appearance had been unexpected, and Lacey's attention had been focused on him from the moment they had reconnected. He knew he could trust Lacey about this.

The fact that she immediately leaped to the conclusion that he would suspect her bothered him. He didn't trust easily, and yet he trusted Lacey more than anyone. But since his trust wasn't blind or absolute, Lacey thought he didn't trust her at all.

"Of course, I wouldn't. Do you think all mistresses are manipulative schemers who would do anything to maintain their lifestyles?"

"You aren't like any other mistress." Lacey hadn't been motivated by money, status or power.

"I wouldn't know. I have nothing to compare," Lacey said as she continued to pace. "But, believe me, I am not interested in returning to Rudaynah and maintaining the lifestyle of secrets and hiding."

"Hate Rudaynah that much?"

"I don't *hate* it," she corrected him. "There were parts of it that I found intolerable, but I also saw the beauty and wonder."

Hafiz doubted she could list what she found beautiful. "No, you hated it."

"I hated that I was separated from you," she said. "I hated that we had to hide our relationship."

"Our relationship is about to be brought out into the open," he murmured. He would have to deny it, but no one would believe him. It was clear in the photo that he was intimate with Lacey. And if they had photos of what happened immediately after that embrace... He would protect Lacey from the embarrassment, no matter the cost or the consequences.

"Do you think I forced your hand?" Lacey stopped pacing and stood directly in front of him. "I didn't. I don't know how to convince you that I have nothing to do with this picture. I don't have any proof. But once I find the person who is responsible…"

Hafiz was momentarily fascinated as he watched her shake her fist in the air. He hadn't seen her like this. She was in full protective mode. Of *him*. He took care of Lacey, not the other way around.

"I know you don't have anything to do with it," Hafiz said.

She lowered her fist and gave him a sidelong glance. "You do?" She said the words in a slow drawl.

Hafiz nodded. "It's not your nature." He knew that, but it hadn't stopped him from accusing her in the past. He had let his past experiences with women cloud his judgment.

"Just like that?" She snapped her fingers. "A month ago I couldn't have lunch with a few friends without you accusing me of betrayal."

"I had jumped to conclusions," he admitted. "I thought…"

"That I would retaliate because I was kicked out of your life with little ceremony?"

He felt his mouth twitch with displeasure at her description. Their relationship ended abruptly, but he did not kick her out.

"Something like that," he admitted. "I'm sorry I considered that was a possibility. I know you're not that kind of person. You are loyal and sweet. Innocent about the world, really."

"That's an unusual choice of words for a mistress."

He raked his fingers through his hair and exhaled. "Stop calling yourself a mistress."

She looked at him with surprise. "Why? That was my role in your life. We weren't a couple. We weren't partners. We led separate lives during the day and spent the nights together. Only you didn't stay all night."

"No, I didn't." It had been a test of willpower every night to get out of Lacey's bed and return to the palace.

"Where is this coming from?" Lacey asked as she planted her hands on her hips. "You don't have to pretty up the past, Hafiz."

"I don't want people to think the worst about you." He should have considered that before he brought her over to Rudaynah, but all he had cared about was having her near.

"You don't want them to know that I was a mistress?" She tilted her head as she studied his expression. "Or is it that you don't want people to know about your role?"

Those words were like a punch in the stomach. Was that the real reason he didn't want Lacey to wear that label? He was a prince, was held to a higher standard, but he had brought Lacey to his world by any means necessary.

"Because deep down that goes against what you believe in, doesn't it, Hafiz? You don't want to be the playboy prince, but you had a kept woman. Instead of making a commitment or having a relationship based on mutual feelings, you made arrangements with a woman so you could have exclusive access to her body."

"Our relationship was more than just sex," Hafiz said in a growl. Not that anyone would see it that way.

"The palace may have some questions about that if they see that picture." Lacey dragged her hands down her face. "What are we going to do about it?"

Hafiz went still. "*We?* No, you aren't getting involved with this."

Lacey rolled her eyes. "We're in this together, and we're going to get out of it together."

He was conflicted. Hafiz had always appreciated it when Lacey was ready to fight alongside him, but he didn't want to drag her into this battle.

"No one can see your face in the picture," Hafiz insisted. "You can't be identified. Let's keep it that way."

"It's only a matter of time," Lacey said. "Someone at the party is going to remember what I wore and how you dragged me out of the party."

"It was late, and people had been drinking. No one can be too sure what happened."

"Anyway," she continued, "I don't care if people know it's me."

Why didn't Lacey care about her reputation? A public scandal never died. He hadn't thought much about his until he destroyed his reputation and took the slow, hard road to repair it. He knew it would be much worse for a woman.

"I care." Hafiz knew his voice sounded harsh, but he had to get Lacey to understand. "If you get caught up in a scandal with me, it will cling to you for the rest of your life. You will always be known as the woman who slept with the playboy prince."

Lacey lifted her chin. "I've done nothing to be ashamed about."

"Nothing?" he asked with a tinge of incredulity. "We lost control. We made compromises and excuses even when it went against everything we've been taught. Everything we believe in." He turned away from Lacey. "And even though we swear that we won't meet again, that we won't think about what might have been, we break our promises. The moment we see each other, we destroy everything we tried to create."

The silence pulsed between them.

She made him dream about a life he had no right to pursue. Hafiz winced as resentment shot through his chest. He took in a deep sigh, and he realized nothing had changed. No, that wasn't true. When he was with Lacey, everything he felt was sharper and stronger. Life after Lacey was going to be excruciating.

He needed to be strong and not give in to his wants. He had done that for years until he met Lacey. After disappointing a nation, he had sacrificed his happiness to make amends. He could do it again, but he had to stop teasing himself with the fantasy of life with Lacey.

"Hafiz," Lacey said in a husky voice, "there are many reasons why I love you. You have worked hard to make up for your mistakes. You try to be a good man, a good son and a good prince. I have always admired your willpower and your strength. But your one weakness is me."

Hafiz wanted to deny it.

She slowly shook her head. "All this time I've hated the idea that I'm your one and only vice. Your weakness. But it's true. I am making you into the man you don't want to be."

"That's not true. I like who I am when I'm with you."

"You like sneaking around?" she asked. "Breaking

promises? Feeling guilty because you shouldn't love a woman like me?"

"No," he admitted gruffly.

"Would you have acted this way with another woman? Would you make love to her in public?"

Hafiz wanted to lie and say yes. But even when he was known as the playboy prince, he had always been aware of his surroundings. But when he was with Lacey, nothing else mattered. It wasn't just a weakness. It was a sickness.

"You know what kind of woman I want to be?" she asked.

He knew. She never said it out loud, but he knew of her plans and dreams. Lacey wanted to be a woman surrounded by love and family.

"I can tell you that I didn't grow up thinking I wanted to be a femme fatale. I didn't want to be the kind of woman who ruined lives."

"You're not ruining my life. My—" He stopped. He wasn't going to think it. Voice it. His royal status was part of his identity and the one true constant in his life. It was not an obstacle that kept him from being with Lacey.

"I'm a problem for you, Hafiz. What do you think is going to happen if this photo gets out? What will the sultan do?"

Hafiz gritted his teeth. He wasn't going to tell Lacey. She would try to protect him and keep him in Abu Dhabi. "I can take care of myself."

"No, that's the wrong way to go around it," Lacey said. "That's expected. You'll probably use the words that every powerful man has used when denying an affair. I will take care of this."

Hafiz's shoulders went rigid. "No, you will not."

"Why not?" Lacey's eyes lit up, and she held up her hands. Hafiz knew that look. Lacey had a plan. "This is what we're going to do. If the picture gets published, I'll take the blame."

"Not a chance."

"Listen to me, Hafiz." She placed her hand on his arm as she pleaded. "It's so simple. I'll tell people that I saw you at this party, and I came onto you. You rejected my advances."

He wasn't going to let anyone think that his woman was an indiscriminate seductress. "The picture says otherwise."

"Pictures lie." She dismissed his words with the wave of her hand. "No one knows what happened before or after. It's very possible that I propositioned you. It's just as possible that you declined my offer."

Hafiz gave her a disbelieving look. He couldn't remember a time when he refused Lacey. "No."

She squeezed his arm. "It will work."

He placed his hand over hers. "No, it won't. I am not hiding behind a woman."

She jerked her hand away. "Excuse me?"

He leaned closer. "And no one is going to believe you."

"Yes, they will."

"Not when every gossip site is going to drag up my playboy past and follows up with my former lovers."

He felt the weight of his past on his shoulders. Why had he thought he could erase those moments? And why did it all have to be dug up now?

"Lacey, there is a very real chance that someone

took a picture of us after the party." He was furious at himself that he'd put her in this position.

She blushed a bright red. "If they had a picture, they would have already used it, right?"

"No, they would hint that something even more scandalizing is coming out," Hafiz said. "Stir up interest and sell it to the highest bidder."

"Hafiz, I'm sure there aren't any more pictures," she said in a shaky voice. "We would have seen someone."

He wasn't so sure. They had been lost in their own world. "I need to call a few people and find out if someone is shopping the pictures," he said as he turned on his cell phone and walked to the door.

"Good. And I—"

He halted and turned around, stopping her with one warning look. "You will stay here."

She glared at him. "You have no say in the matter. Anyway, I have to go to work in a couple of hours."

"Promise me that you won't try to fix this," Hafiz said in a low tone. "I need you to trust me on this. Let me handle it."

"But—"

"I won't let you down."

She hesitated, and Hafiz knew what she was thinking. He had let his former mistress down. Back then, he had abandoned his woman when she was vulnerable and in need. At that time, he didn't have the power to protect what was his from the sultan. Now he did, and he wasn't going to let anything happen to Lacey.

"Fine," she said through clenched teeth. "I will hang back…for now. But if I see that you are in trouble, I am—"

"No, you won't." He didn't care what she was planning to do. He wasn't going to let it happen. Hafiz grabbed the door handle and was about to cross the threshold when he turned around. "And, Lacey, one of these days you will realize that I don't need saving."

CHAPTER TWELVE

LACEY LOOKED OUT on the audience and gave a warm smile as she played the last note on the piano.

Why am I wasting my life doing this? she wondered. *Why do I still feel as if my life is on hold?*

Her smile tightened. The spotlight above her felt extraordinarily hot as sweat trickled down her spine. There were only a few people in the hotel lounge on the weekday afternoon.

That was not unusual, Lacey decided as she rose from the bench and bowed to the smattering of applause. It was common to see a few businessmen sitting in the audience at this time of day. They all had a dazed look from back-to-back meetings or constant travel.

She knew they weren't really listening to the music. If asked, they wouldn't remember her or describe her hair in a tight bun or her black lace dress. They were here because they didn't want to return to their quiet hotel rooms. They didn't want to be alone.

Lacey knew how they felt. She had struggled with loneliness before she had met Hafiz. It permeated her life and had been the theme in all the songs she had performed. .

And when she met Hafiz, she had felt a connection between them. It had excited and frightened her. She didn't want to lose it. She didn't want it to end.

She glanced around the lounge and noticed Hafiz was not there. He knew when she was going to perform but he didn't stop by. Hafiz had always claimed that he enjoyed listening to her music, but now she wondered if that was just an empty compliment. Or perhaps he enjoyed it when she performed only for him.

She knew he wouldn't be there, but yet she still couldn't stop the disappointment dragging her down. Did he not show up because he was too busy or because he didn't want to be seen in the same room with her?

It shouldn't hurt. She was used to Hafiz not being part of her life. If he had shown up, she would have been unreasonably happy. Thrilled that he graced her with his presence.

And even with the decision that she wasn't going to let him treat her this way anymore, Lacey knew she would weaken her stance. She wanted him in her life no matter how little time she got with him.

Her dreams were not as grand as Hafiz's goals. Her plans for her life wouldn't lead her on the road to glory. At times what she wanted in life seemed impossible. But that didn't mean her dreams were less important than Hafiz's dreams. She needed to remember that.

What she wanted in life was to be with Hafiz. Build a life together and have a family. Create a home that was filled with love, laughter and music.

Lacey quickly got off the stage and glided between the empty tables. There was no use yearning for that kind of life. She wasn't going to get it. Not while she was on this path, waiting, hoping for Hafiz to change his mind.

Maybe she was Rapunzel. Lacey's footsteps slowed as the thought crashed through her. Oh, hell. She *was* the one who was stuck. She kept following the same pattern, waiting for a different outcome.

This was why she felt like her life was on hold. She was waiting for Prince Hafiz to reach out, take her away from her tower, and carry her away with him.

Not anymore. As much as she loved Hafiz and would greedily accept whatever he could spare, she didn't want a part-time love. She couldn't agree to sharing him.

She wanted a love that was exclusive and one that would last. She was willing to work for it, willing to give up a lot to make it happen. But she would not be his mistress or long-distance lover. She deserved more than that.

Lacey hurried through the hotel and headed for the staff housing. An enclosed garden separated the employee residences from the hotel. She usually found it peaceful walking past the fountains and ponds, inhaling the fragrance of the brightly colored flowers. Today the formal garden seemed too big.

"Lacey?"

Her pulse gave a hard kick when she heard the familiar masculine voice. She whirled around and saw Hafiz. Her heart started to pound as she stared at him. He was devastatingly handsome in his black suit. The severe lines of his jacket emphasized his broad shoulders and lean torso. He looked powerful and sophisticated. She was very aware of her cheap lace dress and secondhand shoes.

"Hafiz?" she whispered and frantically looked around the garden. "What are you doing here?"

"What do you mean?" he asked as he approached her. "I'm staying at this hotel."

"I mean you shouldn't be seen speaking to me. The last thing you need are more pictures of us together."

"The picture has been deleted," he said.

"Oh." Lacey knew that it was the wisest course of action, but getting rid of the picture bothered her. She realized it was because she had no pictures of them together. It was as if all evidence of them together had been erased.

"Why do you look upset?" Hafiz asked. "I took care of it just like I said I would."

"I had no doubt that you would be successful." Hafiz always got what he wanted. Except her. It made her wonder just how much he really wanted her in his life.

"You don't have to worry about it being released."

"I wasn't worried," she said, crossing her arms as a gentle breeze brushed against her skin. "I don't care if people know I'm with you."

Hafiz frowned. "You don't care if people know that you were a mistress?"

Did she care that people knew she didn't hold out for a wedding ring? That she accepted whatever Hafiz offered so she could be with him? No, she didn't regret those choices, but she knew she couldn't make them again.

In the past she'd thought accepting his offer to live in Rudaynah was one step toward a future together. Now she understood the rules. She either got to be his mistress, or she didn't get to be with him at all.

If he asked her to be his mistress now, she would decline. Even if he was unattached, even if he moved out of Rudaynah. It would be hard to say no, but these days she placed more value on herself and her dreams.

"I just finished working," Lacey said as she took a few steps away.

"I know," he said as he moved closer.

"I didn't see you in the lounge." Lacey bit down on her lip, preventing herself from saying anything more.

He frowned at her sharp tone as if he sensed an emotional minefield. "I wanted to be there."

"Something more important came along?" she asked with false brightness. "Something better?"

"You know why I couldn't be there."

"No, I really don't." She had automatically accepted the belief that they couldn't be seen together, and yet, here they were alone in a garden, deep in conversation. It felt as if he chose when he could and could not see her. "Explain it to me. Why were you not there to support me?"

"Did you need my support?" he asked.

"Yes." She never asked because she didn't want to set herself up for rejection. Her parents had not taken the time to see her perform while she was in school or early in her career. Hafiz had only seen her a few times early in their relationship.

"You have performed on stage countless times," he pointed out.

"Doesn't matter. I was always there for you, behind the scenes and in the shadows. I didn't stand next to you during ceremonies and events, but I supported your work. Why don't you support mine?"

His eyes narrowed. "Where is this coming from?"

"You wouldn't understand," she said as she closed her eyes. She realized she surprised him with her demand. It was rare to demand anything from him. She had spent so much energy trying to be part of his life that she didn't expect him to take part in hers.

"Lacey, the next time I'm here, I will sit in the front row and watch your entire performance," he promised.

She went still. "The next time you're here?"

"I'm leaving Abu Dhabi in a few hours," he said. "It's time for me to home."

He was going back. Lacey shouldn't be surprised, but she was struggling not to show it. "You are returning to Rudaynah?"

"I have to go back." His tone suggested that there had never been a question. "I'm still the prince. I have obligations."

"And a wedding?" she bit out.

Hafiz tilted his head back and sighed. "Yes, I am getting married."

"Why?" Lacey asked as the hopelessness squeezed her chest. "I've seen what kind of marriage you're entering. It's bleak and lonely. There is no happiness, no partnership and no love. Why are you doing this?"

"Because this is what I deserve!" he said in a harsh tone.

She gulped in air as she stared at Hafiz. "You're still punishing yourself for something you did over ten years ago," she said in a daze. "Hafiz, your countrymen have forgiven you. In fact, they adore you."

"It's not about my country. Yes, I accepted an arranged marriage because it is my duty. But I don't deserve a love marriage. Not because I'm a prince. It's because of what I did to Elizabeth."

"Your mistress who had become pregnant?" she asked. "I don't understand."

"I discarded her and I denied my son. I had a chance to take care of them, but instead I abandoned them. I treated them worse than how your parents treated you."

"Don't say that," Lacey whispered. "You are nothing like my parents. You value family. Your children will be your highest priority."

"I don't deserve to become a father after what I did. I neglected my responsibilities because I had been selfish. One day my brother will have a son, and he will become the heir to the throne."

She was stunned by his words. Lacey had always known that Hafiz would make a good father. He would be attentive but allow his children to forge their own paths and make their own mistakes.

"All this time," Lacey said, "you've been avoiding a love marriage and creating a family because of the way you treated Elizabeth?"

"Yes," he said. "It's only right."

"No, it's not. I'm sure Elizabeth has moved on."

"That doesn't matter," Hafiz replied. "My suffering doesn't end because she can accept what happened in the past. What I did was unforgivable."

"You have suffered enough," Lacey declared. "You have sacrificed your happiness for years while you've taken care of Rudaynah. You did everything you could to be the dutiful son and the perfect prince. When is it going to stop?"

"I don't know. What if the selfish and spoiled prince

is the real me? What if the playboy prince is underneath the surface, ready to break free?"

"It's not," Lacey insisted. "What I see before me is the real you. Caring and loving. Strong and protective. This is the man you're supposed to be."

"I want that to be true, but I can't take that risk. I am going back to Rudaynah and marry Nabeela, who understands that this marriage is nothing more than a business arrangement."

"This is crazy!"

"But I promise, Lacey, I will be back one day."

"How? When?" She frowned. "Why?"

"Why? Because I'm not giving up on us."

Her eyes widened. "Are you saying that you want a long-distance relationship?"

"Yes," he said as he reached for her. "We did it before when you lived in St. Louis."

She snatched her hands back. "That wasn't what it was. You kept visiting me because you couldn't stay away."

"It started out that way."

"And then you visited more frequently. Your trips were longer. But you never made the commitment."

"I was faithful to you." His eyes flashed with anger. "I haven't been interested in another woman since I met you."

"We weren't living together. Your main residence was somewhere else. And it was the same in Rudaynah. We were in the same country, the same city, but we lived separately."

"So what?"

Lacey crossed her arms and hesitated. She wasn't asking for marriage, and she wasn't asking for forever, but she knew she might be asking for too much. "If you want to be with me, then you have to make the commitment. You have to live with me."

"We can't." His answer was automatic.

"You mean, *you* can't."

"I just explained why I can't," Hafiz said. "If you expect a commitment from me, you are setting yourself up for disappointment."

"And I don't mean living in the same town or in the same hemisphere," she continued. "We will share a home and live as a couple."

"You can't return to Rudaynah."

"I know." She rolled her shoulders back and met his gaze. "You will live elsewhere."

"You mean leave the sultanate?" He angrily barked out the word, but she could see the fear in his eyes. The fear of losing her again. "Do you understand what you are asking of me?" He splayed his hands in the air.

"Yes, I'm asking to you to make a choice." And she had a feeling that she was setting herself up for rejection. "You asked me to make the same choice when I moved to Rudaynah."

"That is different. You didn't have obligations that tied you down to one place."

"It's not different. I made a choice of staying home or being with you. I chose you."

Hafiz took a deep breath. "Lacey," he said quietly, "I wish I could live with you. You are the only woman I've ever loved."

"But you don't want anyone to know it." She felt the first tear drip from her eyelashes, and she dashed it away with the side of her hand. "You love me as long as nothing is expected of you."

"That is not true." Hafiz's voice was gruff. "I want to take care of you. I want to be with you. Share a life together."

"You mean share *part* of your life," Lacey said. "You want to give me the occasional day or weekend. That's not good enough. I want it all."

He splayed his hands in the air. "You are asking me to do the impossible."

"Then there is nothing you can do but—" her breath hitched in her throat "—walk away."

Hafiz stared at her with incredulity. "I tried to do that, but I can't. I won't!"

"You have to," she pleaded, her tears falling unchecked. "If you really love me, if you really want the best for me, you will."

"What's best?" He flinched as if she slapped him. "Suddenly I'm not good for you?"

"You have to set me free." She didn't realize how hard it would be to say those words. Hafiz's devastated look made her want to snatch them back. It took all of her courage to continue. "Let me find a life where my needs are equal to everyone else's."

"What do you—" Hafiz's eyes lit with brutal understanding, and he recoiled from her. "You mean you want to find another man," he spat out.

"If it comes to that." Lacey knew it wasn't possible, but she couldn't let Hafiz know that, or he would continue to pursue her. "I need someone in my life who will put me first, just like I place him first. I can't have that kind of life with you."

"I have always put you first," he said in an angry hiss. "I took care of you the best way I knew how.

I—" He covered his face with his hands. "I would die for you."

Lacey believed him, and it bruised her heart. She didn't want him to die for her. She wanted to share her life with him. The thought speared her chaotic mind. Everything became clear.

She swept her tongue across her lips as her jittery heart pounded against her chest. "If it was between living with me or dying for the good of Rudaynah, which would you choose? The ultimate shame of loving me or the highest honor of serving your country?"

Hafiz was frozen in silence. She held her breath in anticipation as Hafiz dragged his hands from his face. She saw all of the emotions flickering in his ashen face. Shock. Pain. Hesitation.

"That's what I thought." She dragged the words out of her aching throat as hope shriveled up and died inside her. Hafiz might have loved her and he might have trusted her, but he couldn't be proud of her. He couldn't respect himself for loving her.

Nothing she could do would change that. She wasn't going to make the mistake of trying to earn her way. She wasn't going to think that being patient and uncomplaining would be rewarded.

"You need to leave and never come back," she said as she marched away. "Right now."

He shook his head. "I am not leaving. Not until you listen."

"I've listened, and I know nothing is going to change. I need to leave to protect myself. Goodbye, Hafiz," she said, her voice breaking as she fled.

CHAPTER THIRTEEN

SHE HAD TO protect herself. Hafiz silently leaned back in his chair and listened to the business presentation given in his conference room, but he turned Lacey's words over and over in his head. *I need to leave to protect myself.*

From him. Hafiz clenched his jaw as the hurt stung through his chest. It was that thought that had kept him up at night for the past week. Why did she think he was harmful to her? He would never touch her in anger or deny her anything. Everything he did for Lacey was to support her. Protect her.

Hadn't he proved it in Abu Dhabi when he'd kept the pictures from being released? Hadn't he spent lavishly on her throughout their affair? How did her life get worse because of him?

He was the one who needed to protect himself. He could have lost everything if their relationship had been revealed. He was addicted to Lacey Maxwell and risked everything for her. Why didn't she see that?

But instead she cut off all contact. She gave up on them. She abandoned *him*.

Hafiz wanted to believe it was for the best. She was a distraction he couldn't afford. He had almost everything he worked for just within his grasp. His work to improve the lives in the sultanate was making progress. He had made Rudaynah a wealthy country. He would regain the title of crown prince that had been stripped from him.

So why did he feel as if he had failed Lacey?

I need someone who will place me first.

Lacey's words echoed in his head. He was a prince. He could not make a person more of a priority than his country.

Because he was a prince, he was not the man she needed. The knowledge devastated him. Most women would have accepted that. Most women would have been thrilled with the arrangement he offered Lacey.

But not Lacey. She wanted the one thing he couldn't give her. No, *wouldn't* give her. His duty to the sultanate may have sounded noble, but she understood him too well. All this time he thought he was trying to make up for his past sins, but he was just as driven hiding the fact that he was a man who couldn't meet the high standards placed on him.

All he managed to prove was that he was not worthy of Lacey Maxell.

He had worked hard to make up for his mistakes, and he was a prince who was respected and admired. But was he the man he wanted to be? No. He was making the same mistakes.

Despite the punishment he had received for having a kept woman in the past, Hafiz had made Lacey his mistress. Not his girlfriend or wife. He hadn't thought she needed that status. He had treated her as a sexual convenience instead of the woman he loved.

Hafiz had known about Lacey's upbringing, but he

had done nothing to make her feel safe in the relationship. She had been neglected and abandoned. Marginalized in her family. Instead of showing how grateful he was that she was in his life, he had kept her on the sidelines of his life.

Hafiz frowned as he gave a good look at his affair with Lacey. He thought their relationship had been perfect. A dream. A fantasy. He thought he had been generous and good to Lacey, but he had failed her.

He had to fix this. Somehow he would show Lacey that she was the most important person in his life. She thought it could only be demonstrated by marriage, but that was wrong. Marriage was about alliances and property. It was about lineage and power.

He would prove to Lacey that marriage had nothing to do with love.

Lacey sighed as she tiredly unlocked the door to her apartment. The stupor that had encased her almost a week ago when she left Hafiz now felt cracked and brittle. Exhaustion had seeped in. She couldn't wait to tumble into bed, regardless of the fact that it would be cold and lonely.

She pushed the door open and stumbled to a halt as she was greeted by Damask roses everywhere. Lacey inhaled the heavy fragrance with her gasp of surprise. The front room looked like a garden with red and pink flowers.

An image splintered through her mind. St. Louis, in the hotel's penthouse suite. Hafiz dragging a rose bud along her naked body. Longing swept through her as a flush of red crept under her pale skin.

"Lacey, I have to know," her roommate Priya said

as she strolled into the room, wearing wrinkled pajamas. "What have you done to deserve all these flowers?"

"They're for me?" Her stomach clenched. She'd sensed they were. Only one person would send her flowers. Only one man would make such a grand gesture. Trust Hafiz to disregard her demands and to this extent. Suddenly she was a challenge that he had to overcome. "Uh...nothing."

Priya cast a disbelieving look. "No guy goes through all this trouble without a reason," she said as she walked over to one oversized bouquet and stroked the fragile petals. "And this one is very sure he has no competition. He didn't sign the cards."

Lacey felt her mouth twist into a bittersweet smile. Hafiz didn't need to say anything because the flowers said it all. He wanted to remind her of the passion between them, the love they shared and of what she was turning her back on.

As if she was in a trance, Lacey walked from one bouquet to the next. The shades of pink and red thawed the coldness inside her. She felt the vibrant flowers questioning her choice to exist without Hafiz. Lacey sighed, knowing she should have ignored the bouquets and gone straight to bed.

"Prince Hafiz doesn't want you to forget him," Priya said with a sigh and placed her hands on her hips. "As if you could."

"I'm not getting back together with him."

"If you say so," her roommate said softly.

She bent her head and brushed her cheek against the soft petals. "I've learned that being with him wasn't worth the tears," she lied.

"No guy is," Priya muttered.

Lacey pressed her lips together. Hafiz was worth it. What she had really learned was that he didn't think *she* was worth the sacrifice or the struggle. Hafiz desired her, he may even believe that he loved her, but he didn't love her enough.

"I should call…and tell him to stop," Lacey said. She needed to let him know that she couldn't be wooed like the first time. She understood the rules now. Another affair with him would destroy her.

"Uh-huh." Priya rolled her eyes. "Right."

Was she kidding herself? Lacey wondered as she grabbed her cell phone from her purse and headed for her bedroom. Maybe those flowers stirred up a longing she didn't feel strong enough to deny. Maybe she was desperate to hear from Hafiz, and she was jumping on to this weak excuse. Lacey knew she should talk herself out of it, but instead she paced the floor as she called, wondering why she hadn't deleted his number. She held the phone to her ear with shaky fingers.

"Hello, Lacey."

She halted in the middle of her room. "Hafiz." She closed her eyes, tears instantly welling. Her heartbeats stuttered as a shiver swept through her. He sounded so close to her, as if his mouth was pressed against her ear, ready to whisper sweet nothings. Lacey curled her head into her shoulders, wanting to hold on to the feeling, wanting it to be real. "Thank you for the flowers, but I don't think you should be sending me presents," she said huskily. She gritted her teeth. She needed to be firm.

"Why?" His voice was silky and smooth, heating her body from the inside out.

Lacey frowned. Why? Was he kidding? Wasn't it obvious? "Because it's not—" she resumed pacing as she searched for the word "—appropriate."

"When have we ever been appropriate?" Hafiz's sexy chuckle weakened her knees.

She had to follow through and tell him to stop. She had to be strong. "I mean it," she said sternly, hoping he didn't catch the slight waver. "I don't want anything from you."

"That's not true."

She closed her eyes as his low voice made her skin tingle. It wasn't true. She wanted everything from him. But why would he give it to her? After a year of eagerly accepting whatever he offered, she knew Hafiz thought he could wear her down. That this was some sort of negotiation.

She couldn't live that way anymore. She deserved more. She deserved everything. She refused to settle.

"I've already told you that I'm not interested in married men."

Hafiz was quiet for a moment. "What if I broke the engagement?" he asked.

Her breath hitched in her throat. "Would you?" Her knees started to wobble. Was it because of her? Was he going to give the palace an ultimatum? "Could you?"

"I'm not interested in marriage."

"Oh." She sank on the bed. So many emotions fought inside her, struggling to surface, that they felt as if they would burst through her skin. Hope soared through her, and realization pulled her down. He may no longer be the playboy prince, but he also had no interest in marriage. With her, with anyone.

As much as she didn't want him to get married, she

also wanted to weep because she couldn't be with him and never would. "But it's only a matter of time before the palace can prove why marriage is necessary."

"I don't need a wife to be a good prince."

"Now, there you are wrong," Lacey said as she lay down on the bed and drew her knees to her stomach. "You need a woman at your side. A family of your own."

"I had that with you," he reminded her, his voice filled with such tenderness that she ached. "But Rudaynah wouldn't recognize it like that. The palace would never accept it."

And the ties that bound him to Rudaynah were too powerful for her to cut. Hafiz might withstand the burdens placed on him, but not if he held on to her. Lacey winced with pain as she had to make a decision, her face already wet with tears. She had to be the strong one, or they both were headed for destruction.

She took a deep breath. She could do this. She had to do this and take the brunt of the fall. Even if it meant she would wither and die, she would do it, as long as Hafiz thrived and flourished. "What we had was good." She choked out the words. "But we can never recapture it."

"Lacey?" Hafiz asked in an urgent tone.

"No more presents." She thought she was going to gag on her tears. "No more trying to… No more…." She disconnected the call and turned off the phone.

Lacey curled up into a ball as her spirit howled with agony. She clutched the phone, the last tangible connection she had with Hafiz, to her chest. Her weary body convulsed as she cried.

She wished she could disintegrate. But she knew

the ramifications of her decision were just beginning. She had to live without Hafiz, and she had to
be ruthless about it. Starting now. It meant leaving
Abu Dhabi. Tonight. Without a trace. Without hope.

Hafiz stood at the arched window and watched the
laborers set up the decorations along the route to the
palace. The colorful flags and banners celebrated his
upcoming nuptials while street vendors displayed wedding souvenirs.

He wished he could be as excited about the weeklong ceremony. Maybe, if it had been a different bride.
A woman with copper hair and a smile that warmed
his heart. A woman he loved and who fiercely loved
him in return.

"Having second thoughts?"

He turned to the sound of his brother's voice. From
the concern lining the crown prince's face, Hafiz knew
he must look like hell.

Ashraf strode down the open hallway, the desert
morning wind tugging his white robe. His younger
brother looked how a crown prince should. Hafiz felt
scruffy and tarnished in comparison in his tunic and
jeans.

That was no surprise. Ashraf was the perfect son.
The perfect prince. And did it all effortlessly when
Hafiz failed spectacularly.

While Ashraf embraced tradition, Hafiz always
questioned it. Hafiz was tempted by the world outside of Rudaynah, and Ashraf preferred to stay home.
Hafiz couldn't resist the charms of an inappropriate
woman. From all accounts, his brother lived like a
monk, nothing distracting him as he fulfilled the role

of the heir apparent. One day he would be the benevolent sultan this country needed. Rudaynah would be in good hands with Ashraf on the throne.

"I was thinking about something else," Hafiz said.

"*Someone* else. A woman," Ashraf guessed. "And from the look in your eyes, not the woman you are about to marry."

Hafiz nodded. "Her name is Lacey Maxwell."

No recognition flickered in his brother's eyes. "Who is she?"

"She's my…" Mistress? The term bothered Hafiz. It had been Lacey's status, but the word minimized her place in his life. She was not a sexual plaything. The label of mistress didn't describe her generous spirit or inquisitive mind. It didn't explain how important she had been in his life.

"She's yours," Ashraf said simply.

"She should be my bride." It hurt to say it. He hadn't said it to Lacey, and now it was too late. He gave voice to the idea, even though he knew it couldn't happen. And yet…Hafiz pushed away from the window.

"I know that look," Ashraf said. "Whatever you're thinking, just forget about it."

"You don't know what's going through my mind," Hafiz said with a scowl.

Ashraf grabbed Hafiz's arm. "Back out of this wedding and you could lose everything."

Okay, so his brother was a mind reader. "I've already lost everything," Hafiz replied.

"Not quite. This is just wedding nerves," Ashraf said, his fingers biting into Hafiz's arm. "Marry the sultan's choice and keep this Lacey Maxwell on the side."

"No, she deserves better. She should be the one who should have my family name. I don't want to hide how I feel about her anymore."

"Listen to me, Hafiz. I'm giving you advice even though it's against my best interest," Ashraf said. "I understand you will be made crown prince once you marry."

The pause between them sat uncomfortably on Hafiz. "Does everyone know about that agreement?" he finally asked. "Don't worry, Ashraf. Knowing the sultan, he will find a loophole to prevent that from happening."

"Typical Hafiz," Ashraf muttered. "You always think someone is going to betray you. That they are destined to fail you."

"I'm cautious," Hafiz corrected. "The more I know of this world and the more I understand people, I become more cautious."

"That shouldn't include your family." The shadows darkened on his face. "Despite what you may think, I didn't betray you when I became crown prince. I had to preserve the line of succession."

Hafiz drew back, astounded by the guilt stamped on his brother's face. "I don't blame you. I blame myself. I'm sorry you were dragged into this. In fact—" Hafiz tilted his head as a thought occurred to him "—you were affected most of all by what happened."

"You have the chance to redeem yourself and reclaim the title of crown prince."

"Maybe I don't want it anymore," Hafiz said. "Maybe I found something better."

"Like the title of Lacey's husband?" Ashraf asked in disbelief.

He wasn't worthy of that title. He had disappointed Lacey too many times. But he was willing to spend the rest of his life earning the right to be with her.

"You are very close to regaining your birthright," his brother said. "Don't ruin it now."

He was very aware of completing his ten-year quest, and yet he didn't think it was going to happen. He didn't believe it should happen. "Sometimes I think ruling Rudaynah was never my destiny."

"What has gotten into you?" Ashraf asked. "This isn't you talking. This is Lacey."

Lacey made him look at his life differently. She showed him what really mattered. "Perhaps I was only supposed to hold on to the crown prince title temporarily."

Ashraf gave him a suspicious look. "Do you really believe this, or are you trying to talk yourself into giving it up again?"

"I was holding on to the title until you were ready."

"You were born a crown prince," Ashraf said, his voice rising with anger. "You were destined to take care of this country, just like you were destined to marry for duty."

"I marry tomorrow," Hafiz said, grimacing.

His brother studied him carefully. "If you don't marry, you will be exiled. For life."

Hafiz flinched. He lifted his head and allowed the cool breeze to glide across his skin. Inhaling the scent of palm trees and sand warmed from the sun, he felt the land beckon his Bedouin blood. He opened his eyes and stared at the dunes in the distance, feeling the depth of his connection to his ancestors.

"Marry their choice of bride." Ashraf gave him a

firm shake. "You were going to before. What could possibly have changed?"

"I found out what life was like without Lacey." Life without any contact with his woman was slowly destroying him. Hafiz returned his attention to the horizon, wondering where she could be. She'd vanished, sending her message loud and clear. *Don't follow me. Don't find me. Get on with your life.*

"Do you have any idea what life will be like without Rudaynah?" Ashraf asked.

Living away from the land he loved was a misery all of its own. No matter where he had been and how much he enjoyed his travels, his heart always heard the call from the land of his people. Sometimes the ancient call brushed against him like a haunting song. Other times, it crashed against him with the beat of tribal drums. "I've lived elsewhere," Hafiz finally said.

"But always knowing that you could return in an instant," Ashraf pointed out.

Hafiz closed his eyes, and his shoulders sagged. Was he wrong to consider life with Lacey when she'd made it clear she'd moved on without him? Was it foolish to hope for the impossible or was his faith in his love being tested?

"No matter what happens, you are my brother, and that will never change."

Hafiz inhaled sharply as the emotion welled in his chest. Ashraf would never know how important it was to hear those words. He stepped forward and embraced his brother.

Ashraf returned the embrace. "And when I reign," he promised fiercely, "you will be invited back to Rudaynah with open arms."

"Thank you." His words were muffled into his brother's shoulders.

Ashraf stepped away and met his brother's gaze. "But our father could reign for years. Decades. Are you willing to risk exile for that long?"

Hafiz realized he couldn't answer that. What did that say about him and the strength of his love for Lacey? "I don't know."

"Rudaynah is a part of you," his brother reminded him. "You can't deny that."

"But Lacey is a part of me, as well." To deny that was to refuse the man he was. The man he could potentially be.

"Then for the next twenty-four hours you need to decide which one you can live without." Ashraf pressed his lips together as his stark face tightened with apprehension. "Because this time, my brother, there's no second chance."

CHAPTER FOURTEEN

THE ELEGANT SURROUNDINGS in the lounge seemed a world away from the trendy nightclubs and blues bars of her past. She *was* a world away, Lacey decided as her fingers flew over the piano keys. Istanbul was a culturally diverse city, but it wasn't home.

Home. Lacey gave a slight shake of her head. A simple word but a complicated idea. Home wasn't St. Louis. She had no family or connection there. Nor was it Abu Dhabi. While she had friends in the beautiful city, she didn't feel as if she had belonged.

She chose to move to Istanbul because it felt like a bridge between Hafiz's world and hers. She tried to take the changes in stride, but she felt the loss of everything familiar. Of everything she'd left behind.

The only time she had felt at peace was in the penthouse apartment in Rudaynah. Lacey didn't know why she missed that place so much. She had been hidden and isolated. She couldn't count on the basic necessities. She'd had difficulty living in the sultanate, but that apartment had been the one place where she and Hafiz could be together.

She wondered what had happened to the apartment. Hafiz undoubtedly got rid of it. He no longer needed a hideaway, since he would live in the palace with his wife.

Lacey's fingers paused on the piano keys for a moment as the pain ripped through her. She continued to play, her touch a little harder, as she imagined Hafiz as a newlywed.

The last news she read about Rudaynah was about the preparations for his wedding. After that, she stopped searching for information about the sultanate. It didn't matter if his marriage was arranged or if his bride was incompatible. Hafiz would do whatever it took to make the marriage work. Even give up the woman he loved.

When the audience applauded while the last mournful note clung to the air, a uniformed waiter approached the piano. "A request." He presented his silver serving tray with a flourish.

The Damask rose lying on the cream card caught her attention. The sight of the pale pink flower was like a punch in the stomach. They were just like the roses Hafiz used to send her.

Lacey swallowed and hesitated before she took it from the waiter. Her hands trembled as she nestled the fragrant flower between her fingers before picking up the card.

She stared at bold slashes in black ink. Lacey blinked, scrunching her eyes closed before opening them wide. She stared incomprehensively at Hafiz's handwriting.

It couldn't be. It looked like Hafiz's scrawl only because she was thinking of him. She was always thinking of him. But the request was for the song Hafiz always wanted her play. It had been their song.

The clink of stemware clashed in her ears. The murmur of different languages boomed in her head. She wet her suddenly dry lips with the tip of her tongue. "Where did you get this?" she asked huskily. She felt as if she was paralyzed with shock.

"That man." Lacey's heart leaped into her throat as the blood roared in her ears. From the corner of her eyes, she saw the waiter pointed in the direction of a window that offered a breathtaking view of the Bosphorus strait. "Well, the man who had been over there," he said with a shrug and left.

Lacey's shoulders tightened, and her pulse continued to pound a staccato beat. Had it been Hafiz? If so, then why did he leave once he found her? Had he given into temptation to see her one more time and thought better of it? She couldn't stop the pang of betrayal even when she wanted him to stay away.

Lacey cast a furtive glance around the lounge, ignoring the disappointment that flooded her bones. She didn't understand how Hafiz had found her. She thought she had made it impossible for him to follow, but then the prince never gave up on a challenge. The more difficult the test, the more determined he was to conquer.

She returned her attention to the rose in her hands. She thought she would never hear from Hafiz again. She had been his vice and the one thing in the way of his goals. No matter what she did, she could never give him what he needed.

This time he had stayed away longer. She knew it was because of his upcoming wedding. It had been ridiculously easy to avoid all news sources after that tidbit of information. She wouldn't have been able to look at his wedding pictures or cope with comparing herself and his chosen bride. But why did he seek her out? Was the pull just too strong to deny?

Rubbing the rose petals with short, agitated strokes, Lacey gave into temptation and brought the exquisite flower to her nose. Inhaling the delicate fragrance, she relived everything from the instant Hafiz invaded her life to the moment she'd retreated from his.

Regret seized her heart until the last of her strength oozed out. With clumsy fingers, Lacey set the pink flower aside on the grand piano. She couldn't cope with the sweet ache of remembering.

Her gaze fell upon the card again, wincing at the song title. The lyrics had captured how she felt about Hafiz. About them. She'd had so much faith in their love. She had believed anything was possible.

Now she knew better. Lacey wanted to crumple the card in her fists and toss it away. She knew the song by heart, had sung it to Hafiz countless times, but she no longer had the resilience to play the song. It held a glimpse of her innocent, carefree days. It was a testament of her naïve love.

And she still loved Hafiz. That was how naïve she truly was. Even though he was forbidden, married and out of reach, she still loved him.

Her love was actually stronger than when she first played the song. It might be as battered and bruised as her heart, but her feelings reached a depth she couldn't have even imagined a year ago.

Lacey paused at the thought, her fingers curved over the ivory keys. She couldn't play it. Not now, not here. This was a song just for him, not for a roomful of strangers. She would only bare her soul for Hafiz.

She *wouldn't* play it, Lacey decided, despite his request. Even if he were here, she wouldn't cave. If he were watching over her, she would play him a different song, one that offered another message but still held a poignant memory. The song she played when they first met.

Her determination wavered as the first few chords twanged deep in her heart. She would have stopped altogether, but an inner need overrode her misery, guiding her through the song. Her smoky voice was coaxed out of her raw throat, occasionally hitching and breaking with emotion. She closed her eyes, fighting back the tears as the last note was wrung out of her, depleting her remaining strength.

The enthusiastic applause sounded far away when she felt a shadow fall over her. Lacey froze, instinctively ducking her chin. She knew who was standing next to her before she inhaled a trace of the familiar scent of sandalwood.

Lacey was reluctant to look up. She wasn't strong enough to see Hafiz and let go of him again. But she also wasn't strong enough to deny herself one more glance.

Cautiously opening her eyes, Lacey saw the expensive leather shoe on the traditional Persian rug. Her chest tightened as her gaze traveled along the black pinstripe trousers. She remembered every inch of Hafiz. The crimson red tie lay flat against his muscular chest, and the suit jacket stretched against his powerful shoulders.

Her pulse skipped hard as she looked at Hafiz's face. Her skin flushed as she stared at his harsh, lean features. When she looked into his eyes, Lacey felt the full force of his magnetic power crash over her.

Hope and devastation escaped her fractured heart.
Hafiz.

She couldn't turn away. "What are you doing here?"
Her voice croaked.

"Why didn't you play my request?" he asked softly.
His voice skittered across her skin, blanketing it with
goose bumps.

Lacey gnawed her bottom lip. She didn't expect
the gentleness. His reticence was surprising. In fact,
it bothered her. Where was the primal man who made
a fierce claim on her?

She cringed as she remembered how she'd misun-
derstood his motives the last time he sought her out.
She wasn't going to repeat that mistake. "That's not
an answer," she said as she reached for the flower.

Hafiz's watchful eyes made her feel awkward. Her
simple black dress suddenly felt tight against her chest
and hips. The silky fabric grazed against her sensitive skin.

"When are you taking your break?" he asked.

"Now." She covered the keys and stood up
abruptly. How could she work when he was nearby?
At the moment, she didn't care if she received a reprimand for her boss or got docked in pay. "What are
you doing here?" she repeated as she stepped away
from the piano.

He arched his eyebrow in warning. "I'm here for
you."

Lacey's brisk stride faltered when she heard the
words she craved. But she knew better. There had to
be a catch, a dark side to her deepest wish. She kept
walking and sensed him following her.

"Hafiz, we've been through this," she said, grateful for her firm tone that came out of nowhere. "I am not available every time you're in town. I'm not a one-night stand. And I don't sleep with married men."

"I'm not married."

Lacey whirled around and stared at Hafiz. "What? How is the possible?"

"Is that why you didn't play my request?" his voice rumbled.

The rose threatened to snap, and she relaxed her grip. "No. Why are you not married? You were sup-posed to have your wedding after Eid."

"I refused." A shadow flickered in his dark eyes. Lacey had a feeling his refusal wasn't as easy as he made it sound.

"When? Why? I don't understand. You had to. There was no way out of it."

"I found a way." Hafiz dipped his head next to hers. "Why didn't you play my request?" He was so close, sending a burst of sensations spraying through her veins. "Because you thought I was married?"

Lacey stopped in front of the lounge's entrance and folded her arms across her chest. He wasn't mar-ried. The relief swirled inside her, only to be pulled down by a heavy sadness. One day Hafiz would have to marry, and she wouldn't be the bride.

"Did you forget the words to the song?" he asked softly. "Like you tried to forget us?"

She didn't know if it would be wise to explain any-thing. To encourage a love that was impossible. "You wouldn't understand," she finally said.

"You don't know that," he said as he placed his large hand against the gentle swell of her hip. The contact nearly undid her. Lacey stiffened, fighting the urge to sway into his body and melt against his heat.

She needed to calm down before her heart splintered. Lacey cleared her throat. "I don't play that song anymore. It reminds me of our time together."

His fingers flexed against her spine. "And you regret what we had?" Hafiz's penetrating eyes made her feel vulnerable and exposed. "Do you regret loving me?"

Lacey exhaled wearily. Nothing could be further from the truth. In a way, her life would be so much easier if she regretted her love. "I told you that you wouldn't understand," she said as she strode away.

She didn't get very far. Before she knew it, her back was pressed against one of the alabaster columns. The Damask rose fluttered to the champagne-colored carpet as Hafiz barricaded her with his strong arms. Her eyes widened anxiously as he leaned into her. "Make me understand," he growled.

The anguish deepened the lines of his stark face, and she struggled with the wrenching need to erase it from him altogether. Lacey tilted her head in the direction of the piano. "I don't play that song because it's about you. How you changed my life, how you changed me. How much you mean to me and what I would do to keep you." She pressed her clammy palms against the column, but they streaked against the cool, slick surface. "And that is why it belongs *only* to you."

Comprehension flashed through his bronze eyes. "Ah." Hafiz straightened and removed his hands from the alabaster.

Lacey frowned at his sudden retreat. She'd revealed more than she was comfortable with, and this was how he responded. "Ah, what?" she asked defensively, doing her best not to feel slighted. Why was he pulling away? "I knew you wouldn't understand."

"No, I do." The corner of mouth slowly slanted up. "It's how I feel when I give you this."

She watched with growing alarm as he removed his royal ring from his finger. The gold caught the light. Lacey stared at it, transfixed, unable to move until Hafiz grasped her wrist.

Lacey bunched her hand up into a fist. "What are you doing?" she asked in a scandalized whisper. She struggled to keep her arm flat against the column.

"I'm giving you my ring." He easily plucked her hand and moved it closer to him.

Her knuckles whitened as her tension grew. There was no way she was going to let him. She knew the rules, but she could only imagine the consequences of breaking them. "But, but—it's a royal ring." She gestured wildly at it. "Only someone born into royalty is allowed to wear it."

"And," Hafiz added as he leisurely caressed her fingers, enticing them to unfurl, "I'm allowed to give it to the woman I want to marry."

Lacey's hand tightened, her short fingernails digging into her palm. Her mouth gaped open as the remainder of her argument dissolved on her tongue. "Marry?"

"Yes." His gaze ensnared her. The depths challenged. Tempted. Pleaded. "Marry me, Lacey."

"I—I—" she spluttered, unable to connect two words together. Her heartbeat drummed painfully against her breastbone. "I…can't."

"Why not?" Hafiz didn't sound crestfallen. His

taunting tone indicated that he was primed and ready to argue. And win.

Her gaze clung on to the ring. It looked big and heavy. It belonged on Hafiz's hand, not hers.

"I'm not from the right family," she blurted out. She knew her shortcomings.

"I disagree," Hafiz said confidently. "You are the only family I need. Together we will create the home we always wanted."

And he would give it to her. He would be loving and protective. Hafiz would do everything in his power to make her feel safe and secure.

She felt herself weakening, but she couldn't let that happen. She had to be strong. Strong enough for the both of them. Lacey struggled to voice another reason. "I'm your mistress."

"You are my heart," he corrected in a husky voice. "Marry me."

"I can't marry you." Her firm statement trailed off in a whimper. She frowned ferociously and tried again. "I can't return to Rudaynah."

His hand stilled against hers. "Neither can I," he confessed.

His words froze her racing thoughts. Hafiz couldn't return to Rudaynah? What was he saying? "What?" The startled question tore past her lips as she stared at him with horror.

"I've been exiled." He broke eye contact, the frown lines burrowing into his forehead. "Banished for life."

Her hand fell from his. "Why?" she cried out, but instinctively she knew. "Because of me?" She sagged against the column as tears burned her throat and eyes.

Her body threatened to collapse into a broken heap on to the floor.

"Because I refuse to give you up again," Hafiz said, his voice rough with emotion. "I was given the choice to remain in my homeland or be with you. I chose you."

Hafiz chose her. He gave up everything he wanted for her. It didn't make her feel triumphant. The news destroyed her. Lacey struggled to contain the sob rising in her throat. "You shouldn't have done that."

"I don't want to stay in Rudaynah if I can't have you at my side."

She wanted to be at his side, but not if it cost him his world. "You say that now, but one day you're…"

"I refuse to hide how I feel about you, Lacey," Hafiz said in a low voice as his eyes flashed with determination. "I have nothing to be ashamed about."

"How can you say that? After all you did, you didn't get the respect you deserve. Your father exiled you." Lacey cringed as she said those words. She knew how important his status was to Hafiz.

She'd sacrificed everything, but she wasn't able to give Hafiz the one thing he needed. He hadn't redeemed himself in the eyes of his family. He would never gain the recognition that belonged to him.

Lacey covered her face with her hands. She didn't want this to happen. She had done everything in her power to prevent Hafiz from losing the world he fought so hard to keep.

"Hafiz, you can't give up being a prince," she begged. "Not for me. Not for anyone. It's who you are."

"No, it's not." His voice was clear and steady. "I am myself, I am who I want to be, when I am with you."

"No… No…"

"I'm not fully alive unless I'm with you," he said as he wrapped his fingers around her wrists and lowered her hands. "I'm not myself when you are not around. I love you, Lacey."

Tears dampened her eyelashes. "That can't be," she whispered. "It's impossible."

He cupped his hand against her cheek. The gentle touch contrasted with the demand in his eyes. "All I know is that this ring belongs only to you. *I* belong only to you." He held the glittering royal ring in front of her.

She slowly shook her head. "Hafiz…" Her eyes widened when he bent down on one knee in front of her.

"Lacey Maxwell, will you do me the honor of marrying me?"

EPILOGUE

"LACEY, WHERE ARE you?" Hafiz looked over the assembly of dignitaries that crowded the throne room and spotted his wife lurking in the shadows. As she turned, the diamonds in her hair shimmered under the chandelier lights.

Pride swelled in his chest as she made her way through the sea of evening gowns and military uniforms. Hafiz watched statesmen and socialites respectfully lower their heads when she passed, but his attention was focused on his woman.

It amazed him how Lacey's regal image concealed her passionate nature. Just thinking about it, he was tempted to sink his fingers in her copper red hair and pull down the sophisticated chignon. The rose taffeta caftan encrusted with iridescent pearls teased his senses as it skimmed her curves with each step she took.

When Lacey drew close, he captured her hand. "The coronation is about to start," Hafiz informed her and entwined his fingers with hers.

Lacey's uncertain smile tugged at his heart. He swore it gleamed more brightly than any jewel or medal in the room. "I'm sure the vizier said I'm not supposed to be here."

"You are right where you belong." He made a mental note to give the adviser a more explicit explanation of the new protocol. No one was going to hide his woman. No one was going to separate him from his wife.

The first few notes of the procession march filtered through the throne room. Exhilaration pressed against his chest. Soon Ashraf would be crowned sultan, and then he and his brother would bring Rudaynah to its full glory. The revitalizing plans that Hafiz dreamt for years could now be realized.

Lacey cast a troubled glance at the empty throne. "Do you regret—"

He shook his head. "No, I have everything I want," he replied truthfully. Most importantly, he had Lacey. He shared a life with the woman he loved and trusted.

She also helped him realize that he didn't need a royal title to take care of his countrymen. In fact, he was more successful without the restraint of royal protocols and rituals. For the past few years they'd traveled worldwide while promoting the Sultanate of Rudaynah's resources to other countries and international businesses.

And now with the passing of his father, Hafiz could return to Rudaynah any time he wanted.

It had been a bittersweet homecoming. Hafiz had felt like a stranger in his own country until Lacey lured him to the dunes. She knew that once he visited the desert, he would reconnect with the land.

The corner of his mouth kicked up in a wicked smile as he remembered how he and Lacey had spent those cold desert nights. His mind buzzed with anticipation as he rested his hand on her stomach. It was fate to have his first child conceived in Rudaynah.

Lacey's eyes widened from his possessive touch. "Stop that!" she whispered fiercely as she tried to dislodge his hand with a subtle push. "The formal announcement isn't until the end of the month. People will speculate."

Hafiz lowered his head and brushed his mouth against hers. "Let them talk."

* * * * *

TEMPORARILY
HIS PRINCESS

OLIVIA GATES

To everyone at Mills & Boon, RWA, RT Book Reviews, NINC and CataRomance who helped me realise a dream and get to a much better place. No thanks are enough.

Prologue

Six years ago

Vincenzo froze as he heard someone fumbling open the door.

She was here.

Every muscle turned to rock, every nerve fired like a high-voltage cable. Then the door slammed with an urgent thud and frantic footsteps followed, each jarring his equilibrium with the force of an earthquake.

There'd been no alert from his guards. No doorbell had announced her arrival. She was the only one he'd ever given unlimited access and keys to his penthouse.

But he'd given her more than access to his personal space—he'd given her dominion over his priorities and passions. She'd been the only woman he'd fully trusted, believed in. Loved.

And it had all been a lie.

The spear embedded in his gut twisted. Rage. Mostly at himself.

Even after he'd gotten proof of her betrayal, he'd clung to the belief that it would be explained away. She'd had him that deeply in her power.

That alone should have alerted him something was seriously wrong. It wasn't in his nature to trust. He'd never let anyone come that close or become anywhere near that vital. As a prince of Castaldini, he'd always been suspicious of people's intentions. After he'd become *the* rising-star researcher in the cutthroat field of energy alternatives, he'd believed any hope of a genuine relationship was over.

Until her. Until Glory.

From the first glance, he'd reeled at the attraction that had kept intensifying. From the first conversation, he'd sunk into a well of affinity, the deepest he'd ever known. It had been magical, how they'd hungered, connected. She'd aroused his every emotion, appeased his every need—physical, intellectual and spiritual.

But he'd just been a means to an end. An end she'd achieved.

After the first firestorm of agony had almost wrecked him, logic had doused it with its sobering ice. Seeking retribution would have only compounded the damage. He'd decided to let pain consume him, rather than give her more than what she'd already snatched from him. He'd walked away without a word.

Not that she'd let him walk away.

Her nonstop messages had morphed from worried to frantic. With each one, his heart had almost exploded, first with the need to soothe her, then with fury at falling for her act yet again. Then had come that last message. A heart-stopping simulation of a woman going out of her mind fearing for her loved one's safety.

The pain had been so acute it had seared him with clarity.

He'd realized there could only be one reason behind her desperate persistence. Her plan must not be concluded yet. Even if she thought his avoidance meant he suspected her, she seemed to be willing to risk anything to get close to him again, to pull the strings of his addiction to her for the opportunity to finish what she started.

So he'd let her find out he'd returned. He'd known she'd zoom right over to corner him.

But though he'd planned this face-off, he wasn't ready. Not for the sight of her, or for what he had to do.

Mannaggia! He shouldn't have given her the chance to invade his life again for any reason. He just wasn't *ready....*

"*Vincenzo!*"

A pale creature, who barely resembled the vibrant one who'd captured him body and heart, burst into his bedroom.

She stumbled to a halt, eyes turbid and swollen with what so convincingly looked like incessant weeping, and stood facing him across the bedroom where they'd shared unimaginable pleasures for the past six months.

Before another synapse could fire, she exploded across the room. Before he could draw another breath, her arms were around him, clinging like a woman would to a life raft.

And he knew. He'd missed it all, every nuance of her. He'd yearn for her, the woman he'd loved but who didn't exist, until the end of his days.

His mind unraveled with the need to crush her back, breathe her in so he could breathe again. He struggled not to bury his aching hands in her hair, not to drag her face to his and take of her breath. His lips went numb, needing to feel hers, just one last time....

As if sensing his impending capitulation, she surged up, pulled his head down and stormed his face in kisses.

Temptation tightened around his throat like a noose. His hands moved without volition.

They stopped before they closed around her, his body going rigid as if guarding against a blow as what she'd been reiterating in that tremulous, strangled voice sank into his fogged awareness.

"My love, my love."

Barely suppressing a roar, he clamped her arms before she sucked him dry of will and coherence.

She reluctantly let him separate them, raised the face that had embodied his desires and hopes. Her heavenly eyes were drowning in those masterfully feigned emotions.

"Oh, darling, you're all right." She hugged him again, seamlessly changing from overwrought relief to agitated curiosity. "I went insane when you answered none of my calls. I thought something…terrible must have happened."

So that was her strategy. To play innocent to the last.

"Nothing happened."

Was that his voice? That inhuman rasp?

Pretending not to notice the ice that encased him, dread entered the eyes that hid her soullessness behind that facade of guilelessness. "Did you have another breach? Did your security isolate you this time until they could identify the leak?"

Was she that audacious? Or did she believe she was too ingenious to be exposed? If she *were* still secure in his obliviousness, she wouldn't conceive of any other reason he'd stay away while his security team investigated how his research results kept being leaked in spite of their measures.

Good. He preferred to play it that way. It gave him the perfect opportunity to play the misdirection card.

"There haven't been any breaches." He pretended a calm that had to be his greatest acting effort. "Ever."

Momentary relief was chased away with deepening confusion. "But you told me…" She stopped, at a loss for real this time.

Si, that was a genuine reaction at last. For he *had* told her—every detail of the incidents and the upheavals he'd suffered as his life's work was being systematically stolen. And she'd pretended such anguish at his losses, at her help-lessness to help him.

"Nothing I told you was true. I let decoy results get leaked. I had great pleasure imagining the spies' reactions when they realized *that,* not to mention imagining their punishment for delivering useless info. No one knows where or what my real results are. They're safe until I'm ready to disclose them."

Every word was a lie. But he hoped she'd relay those lies to her recruiters, hopefully making them discard it without testing it and finding out it *was* the real deal.

That chameleon hid her shock, seamlessly performing un-certainty with hurt hovering at its edges. "That's fantastic… but…why didn't you tell *me* that? You thought you were being monitored? Even…here?" She hugged herself, as if to ward off invasive eyes. "But a simple note would have saved me end-less anguish, and I would have acted my part for the spies."

He gritted his teeth. "Everyone got the version I needed them to believe, so my opponents would believe it along with them. Only my most trusted people got the truth."

She stilled. As if afraid to let his words sink in. "And I'm not among those?"

Searing relief scalded through him, that she'd finally given him the opening to vent some antipathy. "How could you be? You were supposed to be a brief liaison, but you were too clingy and I had no time for the hassle of terminating things with you. Not before I found an as-convenient replacement, anyway."

If he could believe anything from her anymore, he would have thought his words had stabbed her through the heart.

"R-replacement…?"

His lips twisted. "With my schedule, I can only afford sexual partners who jump at my commands. That's why you were so convenient, being so…compliant. But such accommodating lovers are hard to come by. I let one go when I find another. As I have."

Hurt blossomed in her eyes like ink through turquoise waters. "It wasn't like that between us…"

"What did you think it was? Some grand love affair? Whatever gave you that impression?"

Her lips shook, her voice now a choking tremolo. "You did… You said you loved me…."

"I loved your…performance. You did learn to please me exceptionally well. But even such a…malleable sex partner only…keeps up my interest for a short while."

"Was that all I am…was…to you? A sex partner?"

His heart quivered with the effort to superimpose the truth over her overwhelming act. "No. You're right. A partner indicates a somewhat significant liaison. Ours certainly wasn't that. Don't tell me that wasn't clear from day one."

He could have sworn his words hacked her like a dull blade. If he didn't have proof of her perfidy, the agony she simulated would have torn down his defenses. Its perfection only numbed him now, turning his heart to stone.

He wanted her to rant and rave and shed fake tears, giving him the pretext to tear harder into her. She only stared at him, tears a precarious ripple in her eclipsed eyes.

Then she whispered, "If—if this is a joke, please, stop…"

"Whoa. Did you actually believe you were more to me than a convenient lay?"

She jerked as if he'd backhanded her. His trembling hold on restraint slipped another notch. He had to get this over with before *he* started to rant, exposing the truth.

"I should have known you wouldn't take the abundant hints. From the way you believed my every word it was clear you lack any astuteness. You sure didn't become my executive projects manager through merit. But you're starting to anger me, acting as if I owe you anything. I already paid for your time and services with far more than either was worth."

Her tears finally overflowed.

They streaked her hectic cheeks in pale tracks, melting the last of his sanity, making him snarl, "Next time a man walks away, let him. If you'd rather not hear the truth about how worthless you were to him…."

"Stop…please…" Her hands rose, as if to block blows. "I know what I felt from you…it was real and intense. If—if you no longer feel this way, just leave me my memories…."

"Is that obliviousness or just obnoxiousness? Seems you've forgotten who I am, and don't know the caliber of women I'm used to. But it's not too late to give you a reality check. Your replacement is arriving in minutes. Care to hang around and get a sobering, humbling look at her?"

Her disbelief finally disintegrated and resignation seeped in to fill the vacuum it left behind.

She was giving up the act. At last. It was over.

He turned away, feeling like he'd just kicked down the last pillar in his world.

But she wouldn't let it be over, her tear-soaked words lodging in his back like knives. "I…loved you, Vincenzo. I *believed* in you…thought you an exceptional human being. Turns out you're just a sleazy user. And no one will ever know, since you're also a flawless liar. I wish I'd never seen you…hope one of my 'replacements' pays you back…for what you've done to me."

When his last nerve snapped, he rounded on her. "You want to get ugly, you got it. Get out or I won't only make you wish you'd never seen me, but that you'd never been born."

His threat had no effect on her; her eyes remained dead.

Then, as if fearing she'd fall apart, she turned and exited the room.

He waited until a muted thud told him she'd left. Then he allowed the pain to overwhelm him.

One

The present

Vincenzo Arsenio D'Agostino stared at his king and reached the only logical conclusion.

The man had lost his mind.

He must have buckled under the pressure of ruling Castaldini while steering his multibillion-dollar business empire. *And* being the most adoring and attentive husband and father who walked the planet. No man could possibly weather all that with his mental faculties intact.

That must be the explanation for what he'd just said.

Ferruccio Selvaggio-D'Agostino—the bastard king, as his opponents called him, relishing it being a literal slur, since Ferruccio *was* an illegitimate D'Agostino—twisted his lips. "Do pick your jaw off the floor, Vincenzo. And no, I'm *not* insane. Get. A. Wife. ASAP."

Dio. He'd said it again.

This time Vincenzo found himself echoing it. "Get a wife."

Ferruccio nodded. *"ASAP."*

"Stop *saying* that."

Mockery gleamed in Ferruccio's steel eyes. "You've got only yourself to blame for the rush. I've needed you on this job for *years,* but every time I bring you up to the council they go apoplectic. Even Leandro and Durante wince when your name is mentioned. That playboy image you've been diligently cultivating is now so notorious, even gossip columns are beginning to play it down. And that image won't cut it in the leagues I need you to play in now."

"That image never hurt *you.* Just look where you are today. The king of one of the most conservative kingdoms in the world, with the purest woman on earth as your queen."

Ferruccio shrugged amusedly at his summation. "I was only known as the 'Savage Ironman' in reference to my name and business reputation, and my reported…hazard to women was beyond wildly exaggerated. I had no time for women as I clawed my way up from the gutter to the top, then I was in love with Clarissa for six years before she became mine. But your notoriety as one of the world's premier womanizers won't do when you're Castaldini's emissary to the United Nations. You've got to clean up your act and spray on some respectability to clear away the stench of the scandals that hang around you."

Vincenzo scowled up at him. "If it's depriving you of sleep, I'll tone things down. But I certainly won't 'get a wife' to appease some political fossils, aka your council. And I won't join your, Leandro's and Durante's trio of henpecked husbands. You're all just jealous you can't have my lifestyle."

Ferruccio gave him that look. The one that made Vincenzo feel hollow inside, made him feel like putting his fist through his king's too-well-arranged face. It was the pitying glance of a man who knew bone-deep contentment and found nothing more pathetic than Vincenzo's said lifestyle.

"When you're representing Castaldini, Vincenzo, I want the media only to cover your achievements on behalf of the kingdom, not your conquests' surgical enhancements or tell-alls after you exchange them for different models. I don't want the sensitive diplomatic and economic agendas you'll be negotiating to be overshadowed or even derailed by the media circus your lifestyle generates. A wife will show the world that you've changed your ways and will keep the news on the relevant work you'll be doing."

Vincenzo shook his head in disbelief. "*Dio!* When did you become such a stick in the mud, Ferruccio?"

"If you mean when did I become an advocate for marriage and family life, where have you been the last four years? I'm the living, breathing ad for both. And it's time I did you the favor of shoving you onto that path."

"What path? The one to happily ever after? Don't you know that's a mirage most men pursue to no avail? Don't you realize you've beaten impossible odds in finding Clarissa? That not a man in a million will find a fraction of the perfection you share with her?"

Ferruccio pursed his lips. "I don't know about those odds, Vincenzo. Durante found Gabrielle. Leandro found Phoebe."

"Only two more flukes. You all had such terrible things happen during your childhoods and youths, unbelievably good stuff has been happening later in life in compensation. Having lived a blessed life early on, I seem to be destined to have nothing good from now on, to even out the cosmic balance. I will never find anything like the love you all have."

"You're doing everything in your power *not* to find love, or to let it find you—"

Vincenzo interrupted him. "I've only accepted my fate. Love is not in the cards for me."

"And that's *exactly* why I want you to get a wife," Ferruccio interrupted back. "I don't want you to spend your life without the warmth and intimacy, the allegiance and certainty only a good marriage can bring."

"Thanks for the sentiment. But I can't have any of that."

"Because you haven't found love? Love *is* a plus, but not a must. Just look at your parents' example. They started out suitable in theory and turned out right for each other in practice. Pick someone cerebrally and once she's your wife, the qualities that logically appealed to you will weave a bond between you that will strengthen the longer you are together."

"Isn't that an inverted way of doing things? You loved Clarissa first."

"I thought I did, with everything in me. But what I felt for her was a fraction of what I feel for her now. Going by my example, if you start out barely liking your wife, after a year of marriage you'll be ready to die for her."

"Why don't you just acknowledge that you're the luckiest bastard alive, Ferruccio? You may be my king and I may have sworn allegiance to you, but it's not good for your health to keep shoving your happiness in my face when I already told you there's no chance I'll find anything like it."

"I, too, once believed I had no chance at happiness, either, that emotionally, spiritually, I'd remain vacant, with the one woman I wanted forever out of reach while I was incapable of settling for another."

Was Ferruccio just counterarguing with his own example? Or was he putting two and two together and realizing why Vincenzo was so adamant that he'd never find love?

Suddenly, bitterness and dejection ambushed him as if they'd never subsided.

Ferruccio went on, "But you're pushing forty…"

"I'm thirty-eight!"

"*...and* you've been alone since your parents died two *decades* ago..."

"I'm not alone. I have friends."

"*Whom* you don't have time for and who don't have time for you." Ferruccio raised his hand, aborting Vincenzo's interjection. "Make a new family, Vincenzo. It's the best thing you can do for yourself, and incidentally, for the kingdom."

"Next you'll dictate the wife I should 'get.'"

"If you don't decide on one on your own, *ASAP,* I will."

Vincenzo snorted. "Is that crown you've been wearing for the last four years too tight? Or is your head getting bigger? Or is it the mind-scrambling domestic bliss?"

Ferruccio just smiled that inexorable smile of his.

Knowing the kind of laserlike determination Ferruccio had, Vincenzo knew there was no refusing him.

Might as well give in. To an extent he found acceptable.

He sighed. "If I take the position..."

"*If* implies this is a negotiation, Vincenzo. It isn't."

"...*it* will be only for a year..."

"It will be until I say."

"A *year.* This isn't up for negotiation, either. There will be no more 'scandals' in the rags, so this wife thing..."

Ferruccio gave him his signature discussion-ending smile. "Is also nonnegotiable. 'Get a wife' wasn't a suggestion or a request. It's a royal decree."

Ferruccio had eventually buckled. On Vincenzo's one-year proviso. Provided that Vincenzo chose and trained his replacement to *his* satisfaction.

He hadn't budged on the "get a wife" stipulation. He'd even made it official. Vincenzo still couldn't believe what he was looking at. A royal edict ruling that Vincenzo must choose a suitable woman and marry her within two months.

This deserved an official letter from his own corporation telling Ferruccio not to hold his regal breath.

There was no way he'd choose a "suitable woman." Not in two months or two decades. There was no suitable woman for him. Like Ferruccio, he'd been a one-woman man. Unlike him, he'd blown his one shot on an illusion. After six years of being unable to muster the least interest in any other woman he was resigned to his condition.

Though he knew *resigned* wasn't the word for it. Not when every time her memory sank its inky tentacles into his mind, his muscles felt as if they'd snap.

He braced himself until this latest attack passed....

A realization went off in his head like a solar flare.

All these years...he'd been going about it all wrong!

Fighting what he felt with every breath had been the worst thing he could have done. After he'd realized none of it was going away, he should have done the opposite. He should have let it run its course, until it was purged from his system.

But it didn't matter that he hadn't done that before. Now was the perfect time to do it. And to let all those still-seething emotions work to his advantage for once.

A smile tugged at his lips, fueled by what he hadn't felt in six years, what he'd thought he'd never feel again. Excitement. Anticipation. Drive. Challenge.

All he needed now were some updates on Glory to use in this acquisition. He already had enough to make it a hostile takeover, but more leverage wouldn't hurt.

Wouldn't hurt *him*.

Now, *her*—that was a totally different story.

Glory Monaghan stared dazedly at her laptop screen.

She couldn't be seeing this. An email from *him*.

She drew a shaky hand across numb lips, shock reverberating in her every nerve.

Slow down. Think. It must be an old one….

No. This was new. She'd deleted his old emails. Though she had only two months ago. And by accident, too.

Yep, for six years, those emails had migrated from one computer to another with all of her vital data. She hadn't clicked a mouse to scrub her life clean of his degrading echoes. She hadn't gotten rid of one shred of him. Not his scribbled notes, voice messages or anything he'd given her or left at her place.

It *hadn't* been as pathetic as it sounded. It had been therapeutic. Educational. To analyze the mementos and the events associated with each, to familiarize herself further with the workings of the mind of a unique son of a bitch.

The lessons gained from such in-depth scrutiny had been invaluable. No one had ever come close to fooling her again. No one had come close again, period. No one had surprised her, let alone shocked her, since.

Leave it to that royal bastard to be the one to do it.

She resisted the urge to blink in hope that his email would disappear. She did squeeze her eyes, but opened them to find it still staring back at her. His unread message, somehow bolder and blacker than the other unread ones. As if taunting her.

The subject line read An Offer You Can't Refuse.

Incredulity swept inside her like a tornado.

But wait! Why was she thinking it was an actual email from Vincenzo? Some spammer with some lewd scam must have hacked into his account. Yeah. That was it. With a subject line like that, this had to be the only explanation.

Still…it was strange that Vincenzo hadn't deleted her from his list of contacts.

Whatever. This email belonged in the trash.

But before she emptied it, her hand froze on the button, an

internal voice warning, *Do that and go nuts wondering what that email was really all about.*

Okay. She had to concede that point. Knowing herself, she wouldn't be able to function today if she didn't know for sure.

But what if she opened it, only to find some nasty surprise? In the name of her quest for peace of mind, she should delete the damn thing.

God. That bastard was reaching through time and space, tugging at her like a marionette. Just an email with an inflammatory subject line had her spiraling down a vortex of agitation as if she'd never exited it.

Maybe she never had. Maybe she'd only been bottling it up, pretending to be back to normal. Maybe she did need some blow to jolt her out of her simulated animation. Maybe if this *was* an email from him, it would trigger some true resolution so she'd bury his memory once and for all.

She clicked open the email.

Her gaze flew to the bottom. There was a signature. His. This *was* from him.

All the beats her heart had been holding back spilled out in a jumbled outpour. And that was before she read the two sentences that comprised the message.

I can send your family to prison for life, but I'm willing to negotiate. Be at my penthouse at 5:00 p.m., or I'll turn the evidence I have in to the authorities.

At ten to five, Glory was on her way up to Vincenzo's penthouse, déjà vu settling on her like a suffocating cloak.

Her dry-as-sand eyes panned around the elevator she'd once taken almost every day for six months. The memories felt like they belonged to someone else's life.

Which wasn't too far-fetched. She'd been someone else then. After a lifetime of devoting her every waking hour to excelling in her studies, she'd reached the ripe age of twenty-three with zero social skills and the emotional maturity of someone a decade younger. She'd been aware of that, but hadn't had time to work on anything but her intellectual growth. She'd been determined she wouldn't have the life her family had, one of precarious gambles and failed opportunity hunting. She'd wanted a life of stability.

She'd worked to that end since she'd been a teenager, forgoing the time dump others called a social life. And she'd believed she'd been achieving her goal, graduating at the top of her class and obtaining a master's degree with the highest honors. Everyone had projected she'd rise to the top of her field.

But though she'd been confident her outstanding qualifications and recommendations would afford her a high-paying and prestigious job, she'd applied for a position in D'Agostino Developments not really expecting to get it. Not after she'd heard such stories about the man at the helm of the meteorically rising enterprise. In his corporation, Vincenzo D'Agostino had grueling standards. He interviewed and vetted even the mailroom staff. Then he had vetted her.

She still remembered every second of that fateful meeting that had changed her life.

His scrutiny had been denuding, his focus scorching, his questions rapid-fire and deconstructing. His influence had rocked her to her core, making her feel like a swooning moron as she'd sluggishly answered his brusque questions. But after only ten minutes, he'd risen, shaken her hand and given her a much more strategic position than she'd dared hope for, working at the highest level, directly with him.

She'd exited his office reeling at the shock of it all. She hadn't known it was possible for a human being to be so beautiful, so overpowering. She hadn't known a man could have her hot and wet just looking at her across a desk. She hadn't even been interested in a man before, so the intensity of her desire after one meeting had had her in a free fall of confusion.

But while she'd gotten a job she'd thought impossible, she'd thought the real impossibility would be him. Even if he hadn't had an absolute rule against mixing work and pleasure, she couldn't imagine he'd be interested in someone like her. Cerebrally, she knew she was pretty, but a man like him had stunning and sophisticated women swarming all over him, and she'd certainly been neither. Something he'd confirmed when he kicked her out of his life.

She'd been determined to stifle her fantasies so she wouldn't compromise her fantastic position. At least she had until he'd called an hour later, inviting her out to dinner.

Silencing her misgivings about his change of M.O. and its probable negative effects on her career, she stumbled over herself saying yes. She'd thrown discretion to the wind and hurtled full force into his arms, allowing her existence to revolve around him on every level, personal and professional.

Yeah, she'd hurtled all the way off the cliff of his cruelty and exploitation. And she could only blame herself. No law, natural or human-made, protected fools from their folly.

But there'd been one thing she'd learned from that ordeal. Vincenzo didn't joke. Ever. He was as serious as the plague.

In her eyes, it had been the one thing missing from his character back then. Of course, her eyes had been so filled with the plethora of his godlike attributes, she'd given the deficiency nothing but a passing regret. But that fact forced one belief on her. His email had been no prank.

She'd reached that conclusion minutes after she'd read it. After the first shock had passed, she'd gone through the range of extreme reactions until only rage remained.

A ping yanked her out of her murderous musings.

Forcing stiff legs to move, she stepped out into the hall leading to that royal slimeball's floor-spanning penthouse.

Nothing had changed. Which was weird. She'd thought he would have remodeled the whole building to suit the changing trends and his inflating status and wealth.

He'd once told her this opulent edifice in the heart of New York was nothing compared to his family home in Castaldini. He'd pretended he couldn't wait to take her there. His desire to take her there, and the prospect of visiting his home, had kept her in a state of constant anticipation and excitement.

But she hadn't been able to imagine anything more lavish than this place. His whole world had made her feel what Alice must have felt when she'd fallen into Wonderland. It *had* alerted her to how radically different they were, how it made no sense that they'd come together. But she'd ignored reason.

Until he'd thrown her out of his life like so much garbage.

Another wave of fury crashed over her as she stopped at his door.

He must be watching her through the security camera. He always had, barely letting her enter before sweeping her away on the rapids of his eagerness. Or so she'd thought.

She glared up at where the camera was hidden. She still had the key. Another memento she hadn't thrown away. He probably hadn't changed the lock. Why should he have? With enough guards to stop an army, she wouldn't have gotten here without his permission.

He probably expected her to ring the bell. Yeah, right. He might have dragged her here, but she was damned if he'd leave her waiting until he deigned to open the door.

She stabbed the key in, imagining the lock was his eye.

Her breath still hitched as the door clicked open, then again as she stepped inside.

He stood facing her at the end of the expansive sitting area, in front of the screen where he'd once displayed their video-taped sessions of sexual delirium as he'd drowned her in more.

Her heart clamored out of control as his steel-hued eyes struck her with a million volts of sexiness and charisma across the distance.

He'd once been the epitome of male beauty. Now he'd become impossibly more, his influence enhanced, his assets augmented.

Dressed in all black, he seemed taller than his six foot five, his shoulders even wider, his waist and hips sparser in comparison to a torso and thighs that had bulked up with muscle. His face was hewn to sharper planes and angles, his skin a darker, silkier copper, intensifying the luminescence of his eyes. The discreet silver brushing his luxurious raven hair at the temples added the last touch of allure.

But she wasn't only checking off his upgrades against what she'd known…too intimately. She was reacting to him in the same way, with the same intensity she had when she'd been younger, inexperienced and oblivious of his reality.

Weird, this disconnect between mental aversion and physical affinity.

She could barely breathe, and that was before he spoke, his voice deeper, strumming hidden places inside her with each inflection, with that trace accent, those rolling *r*'s…

"Before you say anything, yes, I do have evidence that would send your father and brother to prison from fifteen to life. But you must already be certain of that. That's why you're here."

Her momentary incapacitation cracked.

She moved steadily toward him, roiling rage fueling each step. "I know you're capable of anything. *That's* why I'm here."

His eyes smoldered as they documented her state. "I'll

dispense with the preliminaries then and get to the point of my summons."

She stopped feet away, scoffing, "Summons? Wow. Your 'princehood' has gone to your head, hasn't it? But then, you must have always been this pompous and loathsome, and I was the one who was too blind to notice."

Those sculpted lips that had once driven her to insanity twisted. "I don't have time now for your scorned-woman barbs, Glory. But once my objective is fulfilled, I might accommodate your need to vent. It will be…amusing."

Bringing herself under control, she matched his coolness. "I'm sure it will be. Sharks do relish blood. And that, along with anything I say to you or about you, isn't a barb. Just a fact. So let's stop wasting calories and get to the point of your 'summons.' What will it take so you won't destroy my family? If you want me to steal some top secret info from your rivals, I no longer work in your field, as I'm sure you know."

An imperious eyebrow rose. "Would you have, if you were?"

Her answer was unhesitating. "No."

Something streaked in his eyes, something that looked like…pain? What made it even more confusing was that it was tinged with…humor? Humor? Vincenzo? And now of all times?

"Not even to save your beloved family?"

She wanted to growl that they were no such thing.

Oh, sure, she loved them. But they drove her up the wall being so irresponsible. They were why she was now at this royal scumbag's mercy. He must have acquired some debts of theirs. And if he could send them to prison using those, they must be *huge*.

"No," she said, more forcefully this time. "I was just analyzing the only thing you might think I have to offer in return for your generous amnesty."

"That's not the only thing you have to offer."

For heart-scrambled moments it felt as if he meant…

No. No way. He'd told her in mutilating detail what an exchangeable "lay" she'd been. He'd discarded her and moved on to a thousand others. And he was known to never return to an already pollinated flower. He wouldn't go to these lengths, or any, to have her in his bed again.

Her glare grew harder. "I *can* offer you a much deserved skull fracture. Apart from that, I can't think of a thing."

This time, the humor filling his eyes and lips was unmistakable, shaking her more than anything else had.

"I'll pass on the kind cranial-reconstruction offer. But there is another alteration you can offer me that I vitally need." His lips quirked as if at a private joke. "ASAP."

"Will you stop wasting my time and just spit it out? What the hell do you 'need'?"

Unfazed by her fury, he calmly said, "A wife."

Two

"A wife?"

Glory heard herself echoing what Vincenzo had said.

But he couldn't have said *that*.

He only nodded, confirming that she'd parroted him correctly.

Dazed, she shook her head. "How can I offer you a wife?" A suspicion hit her between the eyes. "You're interested in someone I know?"

That lazy humor heated his eyes again. "Yes. Someone you know very well."

Nausea twisted her stomach as every woman she knew flashed through her mind. Many were beautiful and sophisticated enough to qualify for Vincenzo's demanding standards. Amelia, her best friend, in particular. But she was newly engaged. Was that why Vincenzo had her here, because he wanted her help to break up her friend's relationship so he'd…?

He interrupted the apoplectic fit in progress. "According to my king, I need an emergency reputation upgrade that only a wife can provide."

Her mind burned rubber calibrating the new info. "Your sexual exploits are giving Castaldini a bad name? That must be why King Ferruccio had to intervene. Did he issue you a royal decree to cease and desist?"

He gave a tranquil nod of that leonine head of his. "What amounted to that, *si*. That's why I'm 'getting a wife.'"

"Who knew? Even the untouchable Vincenzo D'Agostino has someone he bows down to. It must have stung bad, standing before another man, even if he is your lord and liege, being chastised like a kid and told what to do, huh? How does it feel to be forced to end your stellar career as a womanizer?"

One of those formidable shoulders jerked nonchalantly. "I'm ending nothing. I'm only getting a wife temporarily."

So he wasn't even pretending he'd change his ways. At least no one could accuse him of hiding what he was. No one but her. He'd hidden his nature and intentions ingeniously for the duration of their…liaison—what he'd made her believe had been a love affair to rival those of literature and legend.

She exhaled her rising frustration. "Of course she'd have to be temporary. All the power and money in the world, which you do have, wouldn't get you a woman permanently."

His uncharacteristic amusement singed her again. "You're saying women wouldn't fall over themselves to marry me?"

"Oh, I bet there'd be queues across the globe panting at the prospect. What I'm saying is any woman would end up paying whatever price to get rid of you once she got to know the real you. There's no way a woman would want you for life."

"Isn't it lucky then that I don't want one for anywhere near that long? I just need a woman who'll follow every rule of my temporary arrangement to the letter. But my problem isn't in finding the woman who'll accept my terms. It would be difficult to find one who won't."

"You're that conceited, you think all women would be so desperate for you, they'd accept you on any terms, no matter how short-lived and degrading?"

"That's not conceit. That's a fact. You being a case in point. You accepted me on no terms whatsoever. *And* clung so hard, I ended up needing to pull your tentacles out of my flesh with more harshness than I've ever had to employ before or since."

She stared at him, shriveling with remembered shame and again wondered…why all this malice? This fluency of abuse? When all she'd ever done was lose her mind over him….

He went on, his eyes cold. "But any woman, once she's carrying my name, might use my need to keep up appearances, the reason that drove me to marriage in the first place, to milk the situation for more. I need someone who can't even think it."

"Just hire a…mercenary then," she hissed. "One practiced enough to pretend to stand you, for a fixed time and price."

"A…mercenary is exactly what I'm after. But one who's not overtly…experienced. I need someone who's maintained an outwardly pristine reputation. I am trying to polish mine, after all, and it wouldn't do to put a chipped jewel in my already tarnished crown."

"Even an actual immaculate gem would fail to improve your gaudiness. But you should have called ahead. I certainly don't know anyone, well or not, who fits the category of… mercenary, let alone one so…experienced she simulates a spotless past. I don't even know someone reckless or desperate enough to accept you on any terms, for any length of time."

"You do know someone who fits all those criteria. You."

Vincenzo watched Glory as his last word drained every bit of blood and expression from her face. The face that had haunted him for six years. It was still the same, yet so different.

The last plumpness had vanished, exposing a bone structure that was a masterpiece of exquisiteness. It brought her every feature into stark focus, in a display of harmony and gorgeousness. Her complexion, due to her new outdoorsy lifestyle, was tanned a perfect honey, only shades lighter than her magnificent waterfall of tawny hair. Her skin gleamed with health, stretching taut over those elegant bones. Her eyebrows were denser, their arch defined and decisive, her nose more refined, more authoritative and her jaw cleaner, stronger.

But it was still those summer skies she had for eyes that struck him to his core. And those flushed lips. They looked fuller, as if they'd absorbed what had been chiseled off her cheeks. They were more sensuous even in their current severity. Just looking at them made every part of him they'd once worshipped and owned tense, tingle, clamor for their touch. Everything about her had him fighting to ease an arousal that had hardened to steel. And that was before his appraisal traveled down to her body.

That body that had held the code to his libido.

It was painfully clear it still did, now more than ever. But while her face had been chiseled, her body had filled out, the enhanced curves making her the epitome of toned femininity, a woman just hitting the stride of her allure and vigor. Her newly physical lifestyle really agreed with her.

Her navy pantsuit was designed to obscure her assets, but he had X-ray vision where she was concerned. And he couldn't wait until he confirmed his estimates with an unhindered visual and hands-on examination.

For now, he just wondered how those eyes of hers didn't display any tinge of the cunning the woman who'd once set him up should have. They only transmitted the indomitable edge of a warrior used to fighting adversaries who surpassed her in power a hundredfold. As she knew he did.

Or, at least they had until he'd said "You."

Her eyes now displayed nothing but absolute shock. If he didn't know better, he'd think she hadn't even considered that he'd been talking about her.

But of course she had. She was just in a class of her own when it came to spontaneous acting.

She blinked, as if coming out of a trance, shock giving way to fury so icy it burned him. "I don't care how big a debt my father and brother have. I'll pay it off."

He didn't see *that* coming. "You think what I have on them is a debt? You really think I'd have leverage so lame it could be nullified with money?"

"Quit posturing, you loathsome jerk. What *do* you have on them?"

He paused, testing, even tasting, his reaction to her insult. It felt like exhilaration, tasted tart and zesty. He immediately wanted more.

Dio. If he was hankering for more of her slurs, he must be queasier than he thought with all the deference he got in his official and professional roles. Not that he could imagine himself reveling in anybody else's verbal abuse.

His lips tugged as he contemplated his newfound desire to be bashed by her, knowing it would inflame her more. Which was just what he was after. "Oh, just a few crimes."

Her jaw dropped. "You'd go as far as framing them to get me to do your bidding?"

"I'm just exposing them. And only a fraction of their crimes at that. To save posturing on *your* end, read this." He bent, swiped a dossier off the coffee table between them and held it out to her. "Verify my evidence any way you like. I have more if you want. But that would be overkill. This is quite enough to see both in prison for embezzlement and fraud for maybe the rest of your father's life, and most of what's left of your brother's."

Her hand rose as if without volition, receiving the dossier. With one more dazed look, she relinquished his gaze, turned unsteadily and sank down onto the couch where he'd once taken her. He'd made love to her in every corner of this place. At least, *he'd* been making love. Love, or anything genuine, hadn't been involved on her end.

He watched her as she leafed through the pages with unsteady hands, that amazing speed-reading ability engaged, letting memories sweep through him at last.

How he'd loved her. Now he needed to exorcise her.

It felt as if hours had passed before she raised her gaze back to his, her eyes reddened, her lips trembling. What an incredible simulation of disbelief and devastation.

When she talked, her voice was thick and hoarse, as if she were barely holding back tears. "How long have you had… that?"

"That particular accumulation of damning evidence? Over a year. I have much older files retracing the rest of their crimes, in case you're interested."

"There was more?"

Anyone looking at her would swear this was the shock of her life, that she'd never suspected the men in her family could possibly be involved in criminal activities.

He huffed his disgust at the whole situation, and everyone involved in it. "They're both extremely good, I'll give them that. That's why no one else has caught them at it yet."

"Why have you?"

She was asking all the right questions. If he answered them all truthfully, they'd paint her the real picture of what had happened in the past. Which wouldn't be a bad idea. He was sick and tired of the pretense.

So he told her. "I've been keeping them under close scrutiny since the attempts to steal my research."

Her eyes rounded in renewed shock. "You suspected them?"

"I suspected everyone with access to me, direct or indirect."

A stricken look entered her eyes, as if she was just now realizing he must have suspected her, too. Of course, she was still under the impression that nothing of value had been stolen. When everything had been.

It had been so sensitive, even with all his security, he'd documented his results in bits and pieces that only he could put together. But they'd still been accessed and reconstructed and appeared in the hands of his rivals. Then he'd been given proof that the breach had originated from Glory.

But he'd insisted it must have been someone who had total access to Glory. Only her family had that. Needing to settle this without her knowledge, only thinking of her heartache if she found out, he'd confronted them. They'd broken under his threats, begged his leniency. He'd already decided to show them that, for Glory, but he'd said he'd only consider it if they gave him the details of their plan, their recruiters and any accomplices. If they didn't, he'd show no mercy. And they'd given him proof that it had been Glory. She'd been their only hope of getting to him.

And how she'd gotten to him.

She'd played him like a virtuoso. It hadn't even occurred to him to guard himself against her like he did with everyone else.

But a lengthy, highly publicized court case would have harmed more than helped him. Worse, it would have kept her in his life. So he'd groped for the lesser mutilation of cutting her off from his life abruptly, so the sordid mess wouldn't get any bigger.

Then something totally unexpected had happened. Also because of her.

As he'd struggled to put her out of his mind, he'd restarted his work from scratch, soon becoming thankful he had. What he'd thought was a breakthrough had actually been fundamentally flawed. If he hadn't lost the whole thing, he would have cost his sponsors untold billions of wasted development financing. But the real catastrophe would have been if the magnitude of confidence in his research had minimized testing before its applications hit the market. Lives could have been lost.

So her betrayal had been a blessing in disguise, forcing him to correct his mistakes and devise a safe, more cost-effective and streamlined method. After that, he'd been catapulted to the top of his field. Not that he was about to thank Glory for the betrayal that had led to all that.

Glory's choking words brought him out of the darkness of the past. "But they had nothing to do with your leaked research. And according to you, there *was* no leaked research."

"Not for lack of trying on the culprits' part. That I placed false results for them to steal doesn't exonerate them from the crime of industrial espionage and patent theft."

Her sluggish nod conceded that point. "But if you didn't pursue them then, they must have checked out. So why did you keep them under a microscope all this time?"

So she was still playing the innocence card. Fine. He'd play it her way. He had a more important goal now than exhuming past corpses. He'd get closure in a different way, which wouldn't involve exposing the truth. If she still believed she'd failed in her mission, he'd let her keep thinking that.

His lips twisted on ever-present bitterness. "What can I say? I follow my gut. And it told me they were shifty, and to keep an eye on them. Since I could easily afford to, I did. And because I was already following their every move, I found out each instance when they stepped out of line, even when others couldn't. I also learned their methods, so I could anticipate them. They didn't stand a chance."

A long moment of silence passed, filled with the world of hurt and disillusion roiling in her eyes.

Then she rasped, "Why haven't you reported them?"

Because they're your family.

There. He'd finally admitted it to himself.

Something that felt like a boulder sitting on his chest suddenly lifted. He felt as if he could breathe fully again, after years of only snatching in enough air to survive.

So this was how it felt to be free of self-deceptions.

It *had* sat heavily on his conscience, that he'd known of her family's habitual crimes and not done anything about it. He'd tried to rationalize why he hadn't, but it had boiled down to this: after all she'd done to him, he still hadn't been able to bring himself to damage her to that extent. He had been unable to cause her the loss of her family, as shoddy as they were. But even more, he couldn't have risked that they might have implicated her.

In spite of everything, he hadn't been able to contemplate sending her to prison.

Not that he was about to let her realize that she'd always had control over every irrational cell in his body.

He gave her one of the explanations he'd placated himself with. "I didn't see any benefit to myself or to my business in doing so." At her widening stare, he huffed. "I'm not just a mad scientist, not anymore. And then, scientists are among the most ruthless pragmatists around. Since the incidents six years ago, I've learned it always pays to have some dirt on everyone, to use when needed. Now the time has come for that nugget to deliver its full potential."

"And you think you can coerce me into marrying you, even temporarily, using their crimes?"

"Yes. It would make you the perfect temporary wife. You're the only woman who wouldn't be tempted to ask for more at the end of the contract's terms, or risk any kind of scandal."

Another silence detonated in the wake of his final taunt.

With eyes brimming, she sat up and tossed her head, making her shimmering hair shift to one side with an audible hiss.

He struggled not to swoop down on her, harness her by those luxurious tresses, ravage those lush lips, crush that voluptuousness under his weight and take her, make her writhe her pleasure beneath him, pour all of his inside her.

She exacerbated his condition with the lash of her challenge. "What if I told you I don't care what you do with said 'nugget'? If they did the things this file says they did, then they deserve to be locked up to pay for their crimes, and learn a lesson nothing else could teach them."

Elation at her defiance and disgust at the whole situation mingled in an explosive mix, almost making him lightheaded. "They may deserve it, but you still won't let them get locked up for a day, let alone years, if you can at all help it."

All anger and rebellion went out of her, dejection crashing in its place. Her shoulders slumped and her eyes dimmed.

He attempted to look unaffected by her apparent upheaval and defeat. *Apparent* being the operative word. In reality she must be rubbing her hands at the unexpected windfall and what she could negotiate out of it.

He exhaled. "It's a beneficial arrangement all around. Though your father and brother deserve to be punished, their punishment wouldn't serve any purpose. I…will compensate those they've embezzled from and defrauded." He'd nearly slipped and told her that he'd *already* compensated their victims, each in a way that made up for their losses, without connecting his actions to those, or to her family. "You will be spared the disgrace and heartache of having them imprisoned. My king and Castaldini will have me where they need me. And I will have the temporary image cleansing necessary for the job."

Her gaze froze on his face for a fraught moment until his heart started to thunder in his chest. And that was before a couple of tears arrowed down her flushed, trembling cheeks.

She wiped them away, as if pissed off with herself for letting him witness her weakness. Her turmoil seemed so real he felt it reverberating in his bones. But it couldn't be real. It had to be another act. But how could it be so convincing?

He should stop wondering. As far as his senses were concerned, her every breath and word and look were genuine. So he'd better stop pitting their verdict against that of his mind before they tore him down the middle in their tug-of-war.

She finally whispered, "How temporary is temporary?"

He exhaled heavily. "A year."

Her face convulsed as if at a stab of pain.

After swallowing with evident difficulty, she asked, "What would be the…job description?"

So she'd moved from rejection to defiance to setting terms. And somehow, though he was holding all the cards, it felt like she was the one setting the pace of this confrontation, steering its direction. No wonder. She'd been the best negotiator he'd ever had on his team, the most ordered, effective executive. He *had* loved her for her mind and abilities as much as everything else. He'd respected them, believed in them. Relied on them. Her loss had damaged every pillar in his world.

Pushing aside the bitterness that kept derailing him, he said, "I will be Castaldini's representative to the United Nations. It's one of the most exalted positions in the kingdom, and it is closely monitored and rated by Castaldinians before the rest of the world. My wife will need to share all of my public appearances, act as the proper consort in all the functions I attend, the gracious hostess in the ones I give, and the adoring bride in everything else."

Her incredulity rose with his every word. "And you think I am qualified for those roles? Why don't you just get someone from Castaldini, a minor princess or something, who'd jump at the chance for a temporary place in the spotlight, and who's been trained from birth in royal and diplomatic pretense? I'm sure no woman will cling or cause scandals when you want to cast her aside. You cast me aside without as much as a wrinkle in your suit."

No. Just a chasm in my heart. "I want no one else. And yes, you are qualified and then some. You're an unequaled expert in all aspects of the executive life with its due process and formalities. You're also quite the chameleon, and you blend perfectly in any situation or setting." Her eyes widened at that, as if she'd never heard anything more ridiculous in her life. Before she could voice her derision, he went on. "The jump to court and diplomatic etiquette and 'pretense' should be a breeze. I will tutor you in what you'll say and how you'll behave with dignitaries and the press. I'll leave the other areas of your education to Alonzo, my valet. And with your unusual beauty, and your…assets—" his gaze made an explicit sweep of said assets before returning to her once again chagrined eyes "—once Alonzo gets his hands on you, the tabloids will have nothing to talk about but your style and latest outfits. Your current occupation as a humanitarian crusader will also capture the imagination of the world, and add to my image as a clean-energy pioneer. We'll be the perfect fairy-tale couple."

What he'd once thought they could be for real.

His summation seemed to have as brutal an effect on her as it had on him. She looked as if regret that this could never be real crushed her, too.

Suppressing the urge to put his fist through the nearest wall, he gritted out, "I am also offering a substantial financial incentive to sweeten the deal. That's part of the offer I've already said you can't refuse."

She kept staring at him with what looked like disappointment pulsing in the depths of her eyes. She didn't ask how much. Still acting as if money meant nothing to her.

"Ten million dollars," he said, suppressing a sneer of disillusion. "Net of deductions or taxes. Two up front, the rest on completion of the contract term."

He bent, picked up the other dossier on the coffee table and came to stand over her where she sat limply on the couch. "That's the prenuptial agreement you'll sign."

When she didn't take the volume, he placed it on her lap.

"I'm giving you today to read through this. You're free to seek legal counsel, of course, but there's nothing in it to impact you whatsoever, if you abide by the letter of the terms. I will expect your acceptance tomorrow."

Without looking up from the dossier in her lap, she said, "Take it or take it, huh?"

"That about sums it up."

The gaze fixed on his filled with fury, frustration and… vulnerability.

Dio. Just a look from her and his whole being surged with need. To devour her, to possess her. To protect her.

Seemed his weakness where she was concerned was incurable.

And to think he'd hoped he'd realize that everything he'd felt for her was an exaggeration, that seeing her again would only make him wonder at how he'd once thought himself attracted to her. He'd hoped it would purge the memories that circulated in his system like a nondegradable mind-altering drug.

Instead, he'd found that what he remembered of her effect on him had been diluted by time. Either that or her effect had multiplied tenfold. He'd been aroused since he'd laid eyes on her again, was now in agony.

His only consolation was that she wanted him, too.

Si, of this he had no doubt. Not even she could have faked her body's responses. Their memory had controlled his fantasies all these years. Every manifestation of her desire, the scent of it, the taste of its honey on his tongue, the feel of its liquid silk on his fingers and manhood, the rush of her pleasure at the peaks that had rocked her beneath him, squeezed her around him and wrung him of explosive releases.

What would it feel like having her again with all their baggage, maturity and changes?

No need to wonder. For he'd made up his mind.

He *would* have her again.

Might as well make his intentions clear up front.

He caught her arm as she heaved up. Jolts arced from every fingertip pressing into firm flesh.

At her indignant glare, he bent and whispered in her ear, "When I take you to my bed this time, it will be far better than ever before."

Her flesh buzzed in his hand, her breath becoming choppy, her pupils dilating. Her scent rose to perfume the air, to fill his lungs with the evidence of her arousal.

Still, she said, "I will never sign to that."

"And I'd never ask you to. This has nothing to do with the deal. You have full freedom on this front. I'm only letting you know I want you in my bed. And you will come. Because you want to. Because you want me."

Her pupils fluctuated, her cheeks flushed. Proof positive of his claims.

She still scoffed, even if in a voice that had deepened to the timbre that used to arouse him out of his mind, as it did now. "You really have to see someone for that head of yours, before it snaps off your neck under its own weight."

He tugged on her arm, brought her slamming against him. A groan escaped him at the glorious feel of her against him from breast to knee. A moan of stimulation issued from her before she could stifle it.

The bouquet that had been tantalizing him since she'd walked in—her unique brand of femininity, that of sunshine-soaked days and pleasure-drenched nights—deluged his lungs. He had to get more, leave no breath unmingled with it.

He buried his face in her neck, inhaled her, absorbing her shudder into his. "I don't want you in my bed. I *need* you there. I've craved you there for six long years."

The body that had gone limp at contact with his stiffened, pushing away only enough to look confusedly up at him.

Feeling he'd said too much, he let her go before he swept her up and carried her to bed here and now.

Her face was a canvas of every turbulent emotion there was, so intense he felt almost dizzy at their onslaught.

And he found himself adding, "Passion was the one real thing we shared. You were the best I've ever had. I only ended it with you because you—" he barely caught back an accusation "—seemed to expect more than was on offer." He injected his voice with nonchalance. "But now you know what is on offer. You have every choice in becoming my lover, but none in being my princess."

Her gaze dropped to the dossier in her hand, which regulated their temporary relationship's boundaries and how it would end with a cold precision he was already starting to question.

Then she raised her eyes, the azure now dull and distant. "Only for a year."

Or longer. As long as we both want, he almost blurted out.

Catching back the impetuousness with all he had, he nodded. "Only for a year."

Three

"How long?"

Glory winced at her best friend's shrill stupefaction.

She was already regretting telling Amelia anything. But Glory had felt her head and heart might explode if she didn't tell someone. And it couldn't have been her mother. Glenda Monaghan would have a breakdown if she knew what her husband and son had been up to. Or what they were in danger of if Glory didn't go through with Vincenzo's "deal." The "take it or I send your family up the river for life" deal.

Glory smirked at her best friend's flabbergasted expression. "Don't you think you're going about this in reverse? You keep asking me a question right after I answer it."

Amelia rolled her long-lashed golden eyes. "Ex*cuse* me, Ms. Monaghan. We'll see how you'll fare when I come to you saying *I* was once on mouth-to-mouth-and-way-more terms with a prince of freaking Castaldini, who happens to be the foremost scientist and businessman in the clean-energy field, and that he now wants to marry me."

"Only for a year," Glory added, her heart twisting again.

Amelia threw her hands, palms up, at her. "There. You've said it again. So don't get prissy with me while I'm in shock. I mean…Vincenzo D'Agostino? Whoa!"

Glory emptied her lungs on a dejected sigh. "Yeah."

Amelia sagged down on the couch beside her. "Man. I'm trying to compose this picture of you with Prince Vastly Devastating himself, and I'm failing miserably."

Glory's exhalation was laced with mockery this time. "Thanks, Amie, so kind of you."

"It's not that I don't think you're on his level!" Amelia exclaimed. "Any man on any level would be lucky to have you look his way. But you haven't been making any XY chromosome carriers lucky since the Ice Age. You've been such a cold fish…." She winced then smiled sheepishly. "You *know* how you are with men. You radiate this 'do not approach or else' vibe. It's impossible to imagine you in the throes of passion with any man. But now I'm realizing your standards are just much higher than us mere mortal women. It's either someone of Vincenzo's caliber or nothing. Or—" realization seemed to hit Amelia, making her eyes drain of lightheartedness, then fill with wariness "—is it because it's Vincenzo or nothing? Is he the one who spoiled you for other men?"

Glory stared at her. She'd never thought of it this way.

After the brutal way Vincenzo had ended their affair, she'd been devastated, emotionally and psychologically. For the next year, she hadn't thought beyond stopping being miserable. After that, she'd poured all of her time and energy into changing her direction in life.

It had taken Vincenzo's kicking her out of his life, and out of her job, to make her realize the fatal flaw in her unwavering quest for security and stability. She'd known then that there could be neither, emotional or financial. If the man she'd thought to be her soul mate could destroy both with a few words, she wouldn't count on anything again. She'd decided to give her heart and skills to the world and hope they'd do it more good than they'd done her.

The more she'd achieved, the more in demand she'd been. For the past five years, she'd been constantly on the go, living out of a suitcase, setting up and streamlining multiple humanitarian operations across the globe. If she'd wanted intimacies, they would have had to be passing encounters. And those just weren't for her.

But now, after Amelia's questions, she had to pause and wonder. Had one of the major attractions of that whole lifestyle been the legitimate and continuous way of escaping intimacies?

Glory loved her job, couldn't ask for anything more fulfilling on a personal or professional level. But it *had* given her no respite, no time or energy for self-reflection or reassessment. Had she unconsciously sought that flat-out pace to make herself too unavailable? Too consumed to even sense anything missing? So she didn't have to face that she'd always be a one-man woman? That for her, it *was* Vincenzo or nothing?

Amelia must have read the answer in Glory's silent stare, for she, too, exhaled. "Did he break your heart?"

"No. He…smashed it."

Amelia frowned, expression darkening. "Okay, now I hate the guy. I saw him a few times on TV, and I don't know how I didn't peg him for a slimeball! I thought he sounded like a pretty decent guy, no airs, and even with his reputation, I remember wondering how he demolished the stereotype of the royal playboy. I thought being a scientist saved him from being a narcissistic monster. But I stand corrected."

The ridiculous urge to defend him overpowered Glory. "He isn't…wasn't like that. He's—he's just… I don't know." She shook her head in confusion. "It's like he's two—no, three people. The man I fell in love with was like you describe

him—honorable, sincere and grounded in his public life, focused, driven and brilliant in his working one, and sensitive,
caring and passionate in person. Then there was the man who
ended things with me, cold and callous, even vicious. And
finally there's the man I met today. Relentless and dominat-
ing, yet nothing like the man who took everything seriously,
or the man who relished humiliating me."

"Humiliating you?" The edge to Amelia's rising fury was
a blade against Glory's inflamed nerves. "And now he's asking you to marry him to fix his reputation? And don't say
'only for a year' again or I may have to break something. I
can't believe I was excited at first! Tell him to take his short-
term-lease-marriage offer and go to hell."

Glory had always thought Amelia as magnificent as a
golden lioness. She now looked like one defending her cub.
Her reaction warmed Glory even through the ice of her despondency. "You mean you wouldn't have told me to tell him
that anyway?"

"No, I wouldn't have. I mean, you're not in the market
for a regular marriage anyway, then comes Prince Very Delicious offering you a year in a fairy tale with a ten million
dollar cash bonus. If he wasn't a scumbag who seems to have
crippled you emotionally for life, I would have thought it a
super deal for you. Now what I want to know is how *dare* he
approach you of all people with his offer?"

Glory hadn't shared Vincenzo's reason for picking her. As
the one "convenient"—not to mention compromised—enough
for his needs. Again. She exhaled and escaped answering.

Amelia harrumphed. "But it doesn't matter what he's
thinking. If he bothers you after you say no, I'll have my
Jack have a word with his teeth."

Imagining Jack, a bear of a man and a bruiser, pitted
against the equally powerful but refined great feline Vincenzo suddenly brought a giggle bursting out of her.

Pulling back from the edge of hysteria, Glory's laughter died on a heavy sigh. "I'm not looking for an intervention here, Amie. I only wanted to…share. I—" she barely swallowed back *have to* "—already decided to say yes."

Amelia gaped at her. Glory hadn't told her of Vincenzo's ultimatum, either. If she did, Jack and his whole rugby team would be after Vincenzo. Then Vincenzo would gather all those hulking wonders he had for cousins and it would probably lead to a war between the U.S. and Castaldini.…

She suppressed the mania bubbling inside her, and focused on overriding Amelia's vehement objections. "It'll only be for a year, Amie. And just think what I can do for all the causes I'm involved in with ten million dollars."

Amelia snorted. "Not much. That would barely supply a few clean-water stations. If you're foolish enough to put yourself within range of the man who hurt and humiliated you, I'd ask for a *hundred* million. He can afford it, and he's the one who needs to scrape a mile-deep of dirt from his image with your shining one. At least you'd be risking annihilation for a good enough cause."

Glory smiled weakly at the firebrand she had for a best friend. She'd met Amelia five years ago while working with Doctors Without Borders. They'd hit it off immediately—two women who'd worked all their lives to become professionals, then discovered, each through her own ordeal, that they needed a cause, not a career. As a corporate and international law expert, Amelia had made it possible for Glory to accomplish things she'd thought impossible. Amelia always insisted Glory's business and economic know-how were more valuable than law—in a world where money was a constant when everything else was mercurial.

"I wanted you to take a look at this.…" She reached for the hardcover prenuptial agreement as if reaching for a bomb. She dropped it in Amelia's lap as if it scalded her and attempted a wink. "That's mainly why I told you. To get your legal opinion on this little gem."

Amelia stared at the heavy volume in her lap with the gilded inscription proclaiming its nature. "I'd say this is a huge one. And from the looks and weight of it, I'm not sure *gem* is the right word for it, either. Okay, let's see what Prince Very Disturbing has to offer."

Unable to sit beside her as she read Vincenzo's terms, Glory got up and went to the kitchen.

While she searched for something to do, she tried telling herself that, considering the situation, the prenuptial shouldn't disturb her. She'd never seen one, and she had no knowledge of marriage laws. Maybe this language was standard within every marriage where one party outranks the other in position and wealth a thousandfold.

She wasn't poor, but financial ease had ceased to be a goal to her. She'd settled for having no debts, and a few inexpensive needs. But in comparison to Vincenzo with his Midas touch, she guessed she would rank as destitute. Maybe he had to consider his investors when he dealt with anything that could affect him financially. Maybe even his board of directors had a say in his financial decisions, and in today's world, marriage was one.

But did he have to go that far with the prenup, as if he was safeguarding himself from a hardened criminal? Or was it she who didn't know what was too far?

She'd made apple pie from scratch and baked it by the time Amelia entered the kitchen with the volume tucked beneath her arm, and a thundercloud hanging over her head.

Amelia slammed the prenup on the island with a huff of disgust. "The only thing he left out was the number of cutlery pieces that have to be accounted for before he gives you the 'latter portion of the monetary settlement at termination of contract term'!"

Glory's heart kicked her ribs. "It's that bad, huh?"

"Worse. This guy is making provisions for provisions, as if he's dealing with a repeat offender known for 'stealing kohl from the eye,' like I heard they say in Castaldini."

Just what Glory had been thinking.

Now that Amelia had confirmed her suspicion, her confusion deepened. Why all this? So a man in his position had much to lose, but *he* was forcing her to serve a sentence in lieu of her family. Could he really think she'd want to prolong it, or try to bribe him or cause any trouble at its end?

But those extensive precautions said that he did. Why? Because of her family's history? Didn't he already know she had nothing to do with her father's and brother's actions and choices? With his surveillance and investigations, he must know she'd had very little to do with them in the past years. She maintained close relations with her mother, who had nothing to do with her husband's and son's transgressions and stupidities. Or was Vincenzo just this paranoid with everyone?

He had been very cautious with people in general. She'd thought she'd been the exception, that he'd been totally open and trusting with her. Yeah, sure. Just like she'd thought he'd felt anything for her.

It had all been a lie. A mirage. This was the reality. That he'd never bothered to know anything about her. No, worse, that he thought the worst of her.

Amelia's harrumph brought Glory out of her musings. "You wanted my opinion? Based on a prenup like that, and the rest of this man's pattern of behavior? Go for a *billion* dollars, Glory. Up front. And right after the wedding, go for his balls."

After Amelia had given her verdict on Vincenzo's offer and Vincenzo himself, she'd insisted on going over the "submission contract." She'd spent the rest of the night dissecting it, and writing down in lawyer-speak what Glory would ask for instead. It was past two in the morning by the time Amelia left, and not of her own accord. Glory had to pretend to fall asleep on the couch to convince her she couldn't take anymore.

Not that she'd wanted to sleep. In fact, she'd known sleep would be an impossibility tonight. Maybe every night from now on. As long as Vincenzo was back in her life.

Her sleeping patterns had already been irrevocably changed since she'd first met him. First, with nights of longing, then ones interspersed with repeated lovemaking, then memories and miseries. She'd only had a measure of her old sleeping soundness restored when she'd maintained a schedule that knocked her out for the five or six hours she allotted for rest.

Right now she felt she was back in the bed of thorns of post-Vincenzo devastation. Even worse. Now she was caught in his maelstrom again, in a far more ambiguous relationship than ever before; she felt she was lying on burning coals.

But apart from the shock of her family's crimes and Vincenzo's outrageous "offer," what really shook her were those last minutes at his penthouse.

Everything inside her had surged so fiercely in response, it had incapacitated her. Outraged her. That after all the heartache and humiliation, he only had to touch her, to tell her he wanted her, that she'd been the best he'd ever had, to have her body come to life, proclaiming him its master...

A classic ringtone sundered the stillness of the night.

Jerking up in bed, her heart thundered, unformed dreads deluging her. Her mother. She'd been fragile since her last round of cancer treatments months ago. Something had happened....

She fumbled for the phone, almost dropping it when she

hit the button to answer. A deep-as-night voice poured into her brain.

"Are you awake?"

Gulping down aborted fright, anger flooded in to replace it, dripping into her voice. "It figures. You had to be one of those unfeeling, self-absorbed people who wake up others to ask if they're awake."

Dark amusement tinged his fathomless voice, making her almost see, taste, the smile that tugged at his lips. "You sound awake."

"I am now, thanks to a royal pain."

A bone-liquefying reverberation poured right into her brain, yanking at her responses. "So you still wake up ready."

He didn't say for what. He didn't need to. She'd been always ready for anything with him, on waking up in his arms. Even now, when her mind wanted only to roast him slowly over an open fire, her body obeyed his inexorable influence, readying itself with a languid throb of remembrance and yearning.

And that was before his voice dropped another octave as he whispered, "If I woke you up, I'm glad. I shouldn't be the only one who can't sleep tonight."

"Your conscience weighing on you?" Her voice, to her dismay, was rough and thick, aroused, nowhere as demolishing as she intended it to be. "Or have you long had that removed? Or has it always been genetically missing?"

His chuckle was louder this time, more enervating. "Its deployment hasn't been required in our current situation. As I mentioned before, my offer is beneficial to everyone, starting with you. Now enough of that. What did you decide?"

"You mean I *can* decide? Now, that's a new development."

"It's a few-hours-old one. I already made it unquestionable that it's up to you. I just couldn't wait till morning for your verdict."

"Good thing that you called, so *I* wouldn't have to wait to tell you that I never want to see or hear from you again."

"That's not on the menu of options open to you. Being my temporary princess is a done deal. And as such, you'll see plenty of me. I'm only inquiring if you've decided to see *all* of me."

Her huff was less exasperated with him than disgusted with the clench of longing at his lazy, overpowering seduction. "I guess you decided to develop a sense of humor and you had to start from scratch. I must have your late blooming to thank for this juvenile double-talk."

"I apologize for my trite attempts at euphemisms." He sounded serious all of a sudden. Just as she wondered if she'd finally managed to offend him, his voice plunged into the darkest reaches of temptation. "So when will you let me strip you naked, worship and own and exploit every inch of your mind-blowing new curves for my pleasure and yours? When will you let me kiss and caress you within an inch of your sanity, suckle and stroke you to a few screaming orgasms before sinking inside you and riding you into oblivion?"

Breath sheared out of her lungs, heartbeats fractured against her ribs. The surge of images crowded her mind's eye with memories of her desperation for his touch and assuagement.

She'd asked for that when she'd taunted him. Not that she'd thought he'd say…

"Mind-blowing new curves?"

She almost groaned. She couldn't believe that was what she'd latched on to in all the mind-melting things he'd just said. Seemed body-image issues were so hardwired that they'd override even the heart attack he'd almost given her. But she *had* put on weight she wasn't happy about and couldn't believe he found it appealing.

"Ah, *si, bellissima,* every inch of you has…appreciated.

You were always gorgeous down to your toes, but the years have ripened you into something impossibly...more. I ached the whole time you were at my penthouse to test and taste every remembered wonder, every new enhancement. I am now in agony to explore and devour every part of you. And I know you need every part of me, too, on you, in you. I can feel your arousal echoing mine even at this distance. But if you think you're not ready yet, I'll come...persuade you. I'll remind you what it was like between us, prove to you how much better it will be now we're both older and wiser and certain of what we want."

Fighting another surge of response and haywire heartbeats, she said, "Now that I'm older and wiser, you think I'll let you have me without guarantees, like when I was young and stupid?"

"You want a ring first? I can bring it with me right now."

"*No*. That's not what I meant...." She gulped, her head spinning. This was zooming beyond warp speed. Just a few hours ago she'd never thought she'd see him again. Now he was almost seducing her, over the phone no less, and she was a breath away from telling him to just hurry the hell over. "I didn't mean material guarantees. I meant guarantees of being treated with respect when you decide I'm no longer 'convenient.' I don't even have the advantage or excuse of obliviousness like I did when I believed you valued me."

A silent moment followed. Then an expressionless drawl. "Let's leave the past buried. We're different people now."

"Are we? Maybe you are, whatever the hell you are. But unlike you, I have one basic character, and I'm pretty much the same person I was six years ago. Just older and wiser, as you pointed out, and aware that what you're suggesting would cause long-term damage. And mentioning that, if I become your 'princess,' temporary or not..."

"*When* you become my princess. Very soon. Though, with

the necessary preparations, not soon enough. But say the word, and I'll be worshiping your glorious body within the hour—"

She cut him off before she combusted. "I demand to have a say in the details, since I have no choice in the fundamental stuff. If part of this charade is a ring, then I want to choose it. You'll have it back in the end, but I'm the one who's going to be wearing it, and 'only a year' is still a long time."

His voice suddenly lost the mind-scrambling sexiness and filled with a different passion. "Then you will choose your ring. And everything else you want. As my princess you can and will have everything you wish for."

Her heart squeezed into her throat. "Weird. I have a two-hundred-page volume detailing how I can't have anything."

Silence stretched over long seconds.

A forcible exhalation followed. "That volume is only to…" He stopped again. As if he couldn't find the right words. Which was even weirder. Vincenzo was never at a loss for words.

She decided to help him out. "Only to protect you from any opportunistic ideas I might develop at contract termination. So it's strange you're willing to be wide-open for those same ideas at its start. Not that I want anything from you, but I'm just observing the contradictions."

Another long silence answered her.

Then another heavy exhalation. "I changed my mind."

He did? He was taking back his offer of "everything"? Figured. That must have been his need to have sex talking. She must have managed to douse his desire and he was back to thinking straight, and taking back his reckless concessions.

Then he went on. "You don't have to sign if you find it excessive. And you don't have to make a decision now. And you *are* free to say no. Of course, I won't stop trying to persuade you. But for now, you can go back to sleep. I'll come for you tomorrow at five to pick the ring. Sorry if I woke you up."

The line went dead.

She pulled the phone from her ear, staring down at it.

What was that all about? Had that been a fourth man inhabiting his body?

What was she walking into? And with which man? Or would it be with all of them? With him changing from one to the other until he drove her mad with confusion, insane with wanting him—whoever he was—and self-destructing in the process?

Not that she had any choice. She'd enter his den, and wouldn't exit it for the next year. It was doubtful she'd exit in one piece.

No. Not doubtful.

Impossible.

Four

"Impossible!"

Vincenzo cocked his head at his valet's stupefaction. The fondness Alonzo always stirred in him relaxed lips that had been spastic with tension since his conversation with Glory last night.

Even over the phone, she'd seeped under his skin and into his system and confounded his common sense. He shouldn't have called her in the first place. But he'd been unable to stop. The indiscretion alone had been enough to expose his condition, but he hadn't left anything to her imagination, had told her in exhaustive detail he was burning for her.

Then at the first tinge of disappointment and indignation in her voice, he'd offered anything at all in hope of erasing it. He'd taken back every precaution his mind—not to mention his attorney—insisted were indispensable to protect him.

He jerked back to the moment as Alonzo, in a totally uncharacteristic action, grabbed him by the shoulders.

"Are you teasing me? Because I was lamenting the other day that it seemed both of us would end up shriveled-up bachelors? But…you never joke." Alonzo's vivid green eyes widened. "*Dio.* You mean it. You *are* getting married."

He hadn't told Alonzo why, or how. For reasons he wasn't up to facing, he wanted Alonzo to think this was real. And to treat the whole thing accordingly. To treat Glory accordingly.

"When? *How?*" Alonzo grabbed his own head in dramatic disbelief. "You met a woman, fell in love with her, decided to marry her, asked her and had her agree without my knowledge?"

That would have been an impossibility, indeed. Alonzo was almost his shadow, had been indispensable to him since his teens, even before he lost his parents, smoothing out his daily life, anticipating his needs and providing him with hassle-free, meticulous support and problem solving in everything that didn't involve work and most things that did. He'd only gotten Glory's visit under Alonzo's radar because he'd sent him on some needless errand. Not that Alonzo would have recognized her. In a weird coincidence, Alonzo had taken his one and only prolonged leave of absence during Vincenzo's affair with Glory. It was probably the reason she'd been able to breach him that totally.…

Oh, who was he fooling? He'd been the one and only reason. He'd left himself wide-open to her. And as she'd shrewdly commented, he was doing it again.

Clearly unaware of his turmoil, Alonzo pursued his own perplexity. "But most important, who?" Alonzo grimaced as if at an unsavory thought. "Please, don't tell me it's one of those women you parade for the paparazzi!"

This was another of the privacies that only Alonzo was privy to. That Vincenzo's reputation had been manufactured. By him. To keep hopeful and gold-digging women away. To keep women away, period. He'd found a ruthless playboy's image much more effectively off-putting than a reclusive scientist-prince's. Around a year after breaking up with Glory, he'd started hiring "escorts" wherever he went, to paint the image he wanted.

Not that he hadn't been with women outside his propaganda campaign. He'd tried. If not for long. After a few encounters had ended with him being unable to…rise to the occasion, he'd given up. Alonzo had even once asked if Vincenzo had changed his mind about his orientation, asking if he could take the glad tidings to the gay community that Vincenzo might be on the market soon.

Alonzo had been scandalized when Vincenzo had told him he'd just decided to take an open-ended leave of absence from sex. According to Alonzo, that was the most unnatural thing he'd ever heard. A virile man in his prime owed it to the world to give and receive pleasure to and from as many people as possible. Since he had no partner, of course.

But that had been the problem. While Vincenzo didn't have a partner, his body didn't know that. It had already been imprinted with Glory's code. And though his mind had rejected her, there'd been no reprogramming his body.

Now he decided to tell Alonzo what would appeal to the hopeless romantic in him. What had been true, if he didn't mention the parts that made it also ugly and painful.

"Her name is Glory Monaghan. She's an American who was once my executive consultant, and now she's consulting for major humanitarian operations. I fell in love with her during that time you went with Gio to Brazil. It ended…badly. Then Ferruccio slammed me with a royal decree to get married to clean up my image so I can be Castaldini's representative to the United Nations. And after all these years, and in spite of the way we parted, she was the only one I could think of. I sought her out again and found her hold on me is stronger than ever. Things…developed, and now…I'll marry her."

Alonzo's eyes, which had been reddening as he listened, now filled. "Oh, *mio ragazzo caro!* I have no words...no words..."

Vincenzo wondered if he'd ever get used to Alonzo calling him "dear boy." And he wondered if he was making a mistake by hiding the nature of his impending marriage.

Alonzo interrupted his heavy musings by doing something he hadn't done since Vincenzo was twelve. He pulled Vincenzo into a fatherly hug. Alonzo *had* been that to him, even more than his real father, though Bernardo D'Agostino had been an exceptional father, too.

Vincenzo accepted Alonzo's distraught joy, only wishing it was founded on something genuine, already starting to regret that he'd misled him.

Before he could make qualifications that would temper Alonzo's delight and expectations, and his subsequent letdown when things came to an inevitable end, Alonzo pulled back with a look of absolute anxiety on his face.

"Please tell me you're giving me enough time to prepare!"

Vincenzo shook his head, his lips once again tugging at how passionately Alonzo felt about everything. "Anyone hearing you would think it's your wedding, Alonzo."

"If only!" Alonzo's eyes filled with mockery and not a little resignation. "If Gio hasn't popped the question in fifteen years, he isn't about to do so now."

And for that, Vincenzo considered Giordano Mancini a major ass. Everyone knew Alonzo was his partner, but Giordano seemed to think that if he didn't openly admit it and didn't live with him he would avoid the prejudices that plagued same-sex relationships. As a businessman who came from a deeply traditional family, everyone turned a blind eye to his sexual orientation as long as he wasn't blatant about it.

Which outraged Vincenzo to no end. He considered Giordano a coward who shortchanged Alonzo to protect himself.

So same-sex marriages were still not accepted in Castaldini, but Vincenzo had told Gio he'd stand up for them, make sure everyone showed them every respect and courtesy, personally and professionally. His assurances hadn't been enough for Gio, and he'd convinced Alonzo that they didn't need a certificate or the world's acceptance to be happy. Or at least, Alonzo pretended to be convinced so he could stay with the man he loved. But his reaction now proved that he still yearned for the validation of his beloved's public proclamation, and the delight of preparing a ceremony to celebrate their bond.

Vincenzo's gaze settled heavily on Alonzo. Everyone thought Vincenzo couldn't be more different from the man, fourteen years his senior, who'd been his closest companion since he was ten. Only he knew how similar they were where it mattered. They were both detail-oriented and goal-focused. But most important, they suffered from the same fundamental ailment. Monogamy. The one thing stopping him from telling Alonzo to kick that guy out of his life was that Gio was equally exclusive.

At least so far. Vincenzo had made certain. If that ever changed, Gio wouldn't know what hit him.

"But it's worse." Alonzo's exclamation interrupted Vincenzo's aggressive thoughts. "It's *your* wedding. Do you know how long I've waited for this day?"

"I can subtract, Alonzo. Since you started droning that I should get married when I wasn't yet twenty. It's been two decades since you started longing to plan the elusive day."

"But it's elusive no more! I could kiss King Ferruccio for pushing you to make the decision."

"You just want to kiss Ferruccio under any pretext," he teased.

After that, Alonzo deluged him with questions, milking him for info on dates, preferences, Glory and everything besides, so he could start preparing the "Wedding of the Century," as he was adamant it would be. He insisted he'd have to get his hands on Glory ASAP so he'd get her input, and construct the perfect "setting" for Vincenzo's royal jewel.

Alonzo only left him alone when he told him of his ring-picking mission, for which he'd yet to prepare.

Alonzo almost skipped out of the room in his excitement about the million things he had to arrange and the prospect of his prince getting a princess at last.

Once alone, Vincenzo attacked planning the perfect ring rendezvous with as much single-mindedness as he did his most crucial scientific or business endeavors. But even with his far-reaching influence, it still took hours to prepare things to his satisfaction, leaving only two before his self-imposed appointment with Glory.

He rushed into his bathroom, ticking off the things he needed to do. To get ready for her.

Lust and longing seethed in his arteries as he entered the shower cubicle, letting the hot water sting some measure of relief into his tension. Not that it worked. He felt about to explode, as he had when he'd called Glory. He'd felt he might suffer some lasting damage if he didn't spend the rest of the night all over her, inside her, assuaging the hunger that had come crashing to the fore at renewed exposure to her.

But although he was still in agony, he was glad she'd resisted him, and that he'd backed off. And he was fiercely satisfied that his domineering tactics had made her push back. This was how he wanted it, wanted her, giving him the elation of the struggle, the exhilaration of the challenge. And she'd done that and more. She'd asked to pick her ring.

Suddenly, something that had been clenched inside him since he'd lost his dream of a life with her unfurled. The plan he'd started executing only twenty-four hours ago had been derailed. It had taken on a life of its own. He no longer had the least control over it or himself.

And he couldn't be more thrilled about it.

She's bewitched you all over again.

He smirked at that inner voice's effort to jolt him out of his intentions. It failed. He didn't care if she had. All his caution and self-preservation had only brought him melancholy and isolation. He was sick of them, of knowing that without her, he'd feel this way forever. It had taken seeing her again to prove that she was the only thing to bring him to life.

It might feel this way, but it's an illusion. It has always been.

He still didn't care. If the illusion felt that good, why not succumb to it? As long as he knew it was one.

What if knowing still won't protect you when it ends?

He frowned at the valid thought.

But no. Anything was better than the rut he was in. Apart from those months he'd had with her, all he'd done since he could remember was research, perform his business and royal duties, eat, exercise and sleep. Rinse and repeat in an unending cycle of emotional vacuum. Alone.

But when he had her again, he wouldn't be alone anymore. And he'd slake that obdurate sex drive of his with the only one who fueled and quenched it, who satisfied his every taste and need. For a year.

What if it isn't enough? What if you start this and sink so deep you can't climb out again? Last time you almost drowned. You barely survived, with permanent damage.

So be it. He was doing this. Letting go and gorging on every second of her. At whatever risk. He'd never have a real marriage, anyway. His only chance of that had been with her. Now that he'd already experienced the worst, he'd be prepared. At the end of the year, if he still wanted her as unstoppably as he did now, he'd negotiate an extension. And another, and another, until this unquenchable passion died out. It *had* to be extinguished at some point.

What if it only rages higher until it consumes you?
No, it wouldn't.
You're only hoping it won't. Against all evidence.
So what if it did consume him? After six barren years of safeguarding his emotions until they atrophied, of expanding his achievements until they'd swallowed up his existence, not to mention being bored out of his mind and dead inside, maybe it was time to live dangerously. Maybe being consumed wasn't such a bad idea. Or maybe it was, but so what?

He couldn't think of a better way to go.

And as long as he took her with him, he couldn't wait to hurl himself into the inferno.

Though she'd been counting down seconds, Glory's heart still rattled inside her rib cage like a coin inside an empty steel box when her bell rang at five o'clock sharp.

Smoothing hands damp with nervousness over the cool linen of her pants, she took measured steps to the door.

The moment she pulled the door open, she felt like she'd been hit by a car. And that was before she realized how Vincenzo looked. Exactly how he had looked the first time he'd shown up on her doorstep.

Her head spun, her senses stampeded with his effect now, with the reliving of his influence then.

A deepest navy silk suit, offset with a silver-gray shirt of the same spellbinding hue as his eyes, hugged the perfection of his juggernaut body. The thick waves of his hair were brushed back to curl behind his ears and caress his collar, exposing his virile hairline and leonine forehead. He even smelled of that same unique scent. Pine bodywash, cool sea-breeze aftershave, fresh minty breath and the musk of his maleness and desire. His scent was so potent, she'd once believed it was an aphrodisiac. Her conviction was renewed.

Had he meant this? To show up on her doorstep like he

had that first day, only a minute after she'd said yes, making her realize he'd been already there? Dressed and groomed exactly like he had been then? The only difference was the maturity that amplified his beauty.

But there was another difference. In his vibe. His glance. His smile. A recklessness. A promise that there would be no rules and no limits.

Vincenzo? The man who had more rules and limits than his scientific experiments and developments? The prince who was forcing her to marry him to abide by his kingdom's social mores?

Maybe her perception was on the fritz. Which made sense. Vincenzo had always managed to blow her fuses. In spite of everything, all she wanted now was to drag him inside and lose herself in his greed and possession, have him reclaim her from the wasteland he'd cast her into, devour her, finish her…

"*Ringrazia Dio* for that way you look at me, *bellissima*…." He walked her back until he had her plastered against the wall. The sunlight slanting into her tiny but cheery foyer dimmed as his breadth blocked out the sun, the world. His aura enveloped her, his hunger penetrating her recesses, yanking at her. "As if you're starving for a taste of me. It would have been excruciating being the only one feeling this way."

Exactly what he'd said to her that first time.

He *was* reenacting that day.

That…that…*bastard!* What was he playing at?

Fury jerked her back from her sensuous stupor, infusing her backbone and voice with steel as she glared up at him. "You would have saved yourself the trip if you'd read my messages."

His hand moved, making her tense all over. His lips tugged as he touched her hair, smoothing it away from her cheek until she almost snatched his hand and pressed it against her flesh.

Then he made the feeling worse, bending to flay her with

his breath and words. "Oh, I read them. And chose to ignore them."

"Your loss." She almost gasped. "Their contents stand, whether you sanction them or not. I'm not going anywhere with you. Just give me whatever ring you have."

He withdrew to pour a devouring look down on her. "I would have gotten one if you'd said yes early this morning."

"Fine. When you get one, send it with one of your lackeys. And email instructions when you require I start advertising your image-cleansing campaign and wearing your 'brand.'"

His gaze melted her on its way down her body, taking in her casual powder-blue top and faded jeans, appreciation coloring the hunger there. "I see you believe you won't go out with me as you're not dressed for the occasion."

"There is no occasion, so I'm dressed in what suits a night at home. Alone."

This time, when his hand moved, it made contact with her flesh. A gossamer sweep with the back of his fingers down her almost combusting cheek. "You need to know that there are column A matters that are not open for negotiation. And then there are column B ones, where we either negotiate, or you can have whatever you like. Picking your ring is smack dab in column A."

Struggling so she wouldn't sink her teeth in his hand before dragging it to her aching breasts, she said, "Wow. You can even make a supposedly gallant gesture coercion."

"And reneging on our agreement is passive aggression."

"What agreement? You mean my stunned silence at your audacity in making an appointment without asking if I'm free?"

His pout was the essence of dismissal. "You're on vacation. I checked."

"I have a life outside of work. A personal life."

His self-satisfied grin made her palm itch for a stinging

connection with his chiseled cheek.. "Not anymore. At least, none that doesn't involve me. Do get done with this tantrum so I can take you to pick your ring."

"It's you who's throwing a tantrum by insisting I pick it. Far from casting doubt on your impeccable taste when I asked to pick it, I was just trying to make a point, which I now see is pointless. I don't have any choice and pretending to have one in worthless stuff is just that—worthless. I've admitted it and moved on. So you don't have to prove your largesse by letting me grab a bigger rock, which is clearly what you think this is about."

All teasing evaporated from his eyes. "That didn't even cross my mind. I only want your taste not mine to dictate everything that will be intimate and personal to you."

"Wow. How considerate of you," she scoffed. "We both know you don't give a fig's peel about my opinion. And what intimate and personal things? This ring, and anything else you provide me with, is just a prop. What do I care what you deck me in? It's my role's costume and I'm returning everything at the end of this charade. And speaking of returning stuff, just so you're not worried I might 'lose' anything, or that you'll have to pay a steep premium on insuring it, just get me imitations. No one will dream anything you give me isn't genuine. And it would befit the fakeness of the whole setup."

The darkness on his face suddenly lifted. His eyes and lips resumed their provocation. "I must have been speaking Italian when I said this is nonnegotiable. Must be why we're having this breakdown in communications."

"Since I speak decent Italian—" she ignored his rising eyebrows; she wasn't telling him how and why she did "—it wouldn't have mattered which language you used. No is still my answer. It's the same in both languages."

His contemplation was now smoky, sensuous. "No is unacceptable. Are you prodding me into...persuading you?"

Knowing what kind of persuasion he'd expose her to, she slipped past the barrier of his bulk and temptation, staggered to her foyer's decorative storage cabinet and picked up the prenup. Her hands trembled as she turned and extended it to him.

He took it only when she thrust it against his chest, didn't even look at it, instead staring at her in that incapacitating way of his, his eyes like twin cloudy skies.

"I signed." Her voice was too breathless for her liking.

"I gave it to you to read. Signing would have been in duplicates, with both our legal counsels present."

She shrugged, confused at the note of disapproval—or was it disappointment?—in his voice. "Send me your copy to sign."

His gaze grew ponderous, probing. "Does that mean you didn't find it excessive?"

She huffed bitterly. "You know your Terms of Submission leave *excessive* in another galaxy. You only stop short of making provisions that I turn over the tan I acquire during my time in Castaldini."

"Then why did you sign? Why didn't you ask for changes?"

"You said it was nonnegotiable."

"I thought you'd have your attorney look at it, who'd tell you there's nothing in the world that isn't negotiable. I expected an alphabetized list of deletions and adjustments."

"I don't want any. I don't want *anything* from you. I never did. If you thought I'd haggle over your paranoid terms out of indignation or challenge or whatever, then you know nothing about me. But I already know that. You didn't consider me worth knowing, and I don't expect you to start treating me with any consideration now, when I'm just your smokescreen. So no, I don't care how far you go to protect yourself. This is what I want, too. It makes sure I'm out of your life, with no lingering ties whatsoever, the second the year is up."

Silence crashed in the wake of her ragged words.

Then he drawled, deep and dark, "A year is a long time."

Her pent-up breath rushed out. "Tell me about it. I just want to start serving my sentence with as little resistance as possible, so it will pass with as little damage as possible."

This time his gaze seemed to drill into her, as if to plumb the depths of her thoughts and emotions.

And she felt that he *could* read and sense everything she was thinking and feeling. Which was another new thing.

In the past, she'd always felt this…disconnection, except in the throes of passion. He'd been the classic absent-minded scientist, with his research occupying his fundamental being, only his superficial components engaged in everything else. Now it felt as if his whole being was tuned in to her. And that only deepened her confusion. What was he after?

Just as she tried to activate a two-way frequency to read him, he turned away, laying the prenup on her cabinet before turning back to her in utmost grace and tranquility.

"I'll wait while you put on something suitable for this momentous occasion. Any more stalling and I'll do it myself. I probably should since it's for my pleasure. I can also undress you first, for *our* pleasure. I remember in vivid detail how you used to enjoy both activities."

The avid look in his eyes said he'd carry out his silky threat at the slightest resistance. She couldn't risk it, since she might end up begging him not to stop at undressing her.

Exasperated with both of them in equal measure, her glare told him what would give her utmost pleasure now. Giving his perfect nose some crooked character.

Mumbling abuse, she stormed to her room, with his laughter at her back, sending her temperature into the danger zone.

Half an hour later, when loitering drove *her* to screaming pitch, she exited her room. She found him prowling her living area like a caged panther.

He stopped in midstep, taking in her new outfit. Or her old

one. The cream skirt suit with a satin turquoise blouse was…
adequate. Even with stilettos and a purse coordinating with
her blouse, it was nowhere near glamorous. But it was the only
outfit she'd kept from her corporate days. Her wardrobe now
consisted of a minimum of utilitarian clothes. Otherwise she
would have never picked this suit. It was what she'd worn to
her job interview with him. What she'd gone out with him in
when he'd insisted on not wasting time changing. Fate was
conspiring for her to take part in his déjà vu scenario.

She couldn't tell if he remembered the suit, since that devouring look he'd had since they'd met again remained un-
changed.

Before he could say anything, she preempted him. "In
case you find this lacking, too, tough. This is my one and
only 'momentous occasion' outfit. You're welcome to check."

"It is a 'momentous occasion' outfit indeed. If only for
being…nostalgic of one." So he remembered. Figured. He
had a computer-like mind. Their time together must be ar-
chived in one of his extensive memory banks. "But we must
do something about your wardrobe deficiencies. Your incomparable body must be clothed in only the finest creations. The
masters of the fashion world will fall over each other for the
chance to have your unique beauty grace theirs."

She just had to snort. "Uh…have you been diagnosed
with multiple personality disorder yet? Incomparable body?
Unique beauty? What do you call the persona that thinks
that?"

He started eliminating the distance between them, intent
radiating from him. "If I never told you how I find you breathtaking down to your pores, I need to be punished. Which you
are welcome to do. In my defense, I was busy showing you."

"Yeah, before you showed me the door, and told me how
interchangeable you found me with any female who wasn't
too hideous but meek and willing enough."

"I lied."

His gaze was direct, his words clear, cutting.

Disorientation rolled over her. "You—you did?"

His nod was terse, unequivocal. "Through my teeth."

"Why?"

His lids squeezed, before he opened them, his gaze opaque. "I don't want to go into the reasons. But nothing I said had any basis in truth. Let's leave it at that."

"And to hell with what *I* want. But then, you're getting what you want no matter what I desire or what it costs me. Why do I keep expecting anything different? I must be insane."

He seemed to hold back something impulsive. An elaboration on his cryptic declarations?

But she *needed* something. *Anything.* If what he'd said to her, the words that had torn into her psyche like shrapnel all those years ago, had all been lies, why had he said them? To push her away? Had she been clinging so hard that he'd panicked…?

No. She wasn't rationalizing that son of a bitch's mistreatment. There was no excuse for what he'd done to her. And now he was doing worse. Reeling her closer even as he pushed her away. Confounding her then leaving her hanging. Depriving her of the stability of hating him, the certainty of why she did.

His eyes were blank as he took her coat from her spastic grip, disregarding her bitterness. "We'll have dinner first."

She sullenly let him help her on with her coat, moving away as his arms started to tighten around her. "You're not worried about putting cutlery in my reach?"

His gaze melted with an indulgence that hurt and confused her more than anything else. "I'll take my chances."

"You really expect me to eat after…all this?"

"I'll postpone serving dinner until you're very hungry. By

then, I also hope your appetite for food will overpower that of poking me in the eye with a fork."

With a look that said fat chance, she preceded him out of her condo.

She ignored him as he tried to hand her into the front passenger seat of a gemlike burgundy Jaguar he had parked in her building's garage. He gave up acting the gallant suitor and walked around to take the wheel.

So. No driver, no guards. He wasn't making their liaison public yet. Because he hadn't expected her to sign the prenup, hadn't considered it a done deal? No doubt he'd planned to coerce her some more during this "momentous occasion" until she did. She wondered what recalculation was going on inside that inscrutable mind now that she'd made further manipulation unnecessary.

During the drive, she sat barely breathing or moving so his scent and presence wouldn't scramble her senses even more. Then observations finally seeped into her hazy mind.

They were leaving the city.

When she was certain this was no roundabout way to any restaurant or jeweler, she forced herself to turn to him.

"Where are we going?"

Still presenting her with the perfection of his profile, he smiled. "To the airport."

Five

"The airport?"

At her croak, Vincenzo's smile widened. "We're going to have dinner on the jet. We'll fly to where the most exclusive collection of jewelry on the planet awaits you, so you can pick your ring, and anything else that catches your fancy."

He was so pleased with himself for stunning her again.

She was more than stunned. She was working on a stroke.

"And it didn't occur to you to ask if I'd agree to this hare-brained scheme of yours?"

His lips twitched at her venom. "A man going out of his way to surprise his fiancée doesn't tell her in advance of the details of his efforts."

Her jaw muscles hurt at his mention of *fiancée*. "Do save your 'efforts' for when you have a real fiancée."

"But you already said I can't have a real one for all the money and power in the world."

"Who knows? Lots of women have self-destructive tendencies. And I didn't say you couldn't get one, I said you wouldn't keep her."

His eyes twinkled with mischief before he turned onto a route she'd never seen into the airport, and she'd been here countless times. "Well, you're real enough for me. And for as long as I keep you, I get to go all-out to surprise you."

She harrumphed. "Save your energy. And save me from a stroke. I hate surprises. I haven't met one that wasn't nasty. Certainly never any from you."

He sighed. "I assure you, this trip is anything but."

"I don't care what it will be like. It's the concept I can't stand." She exhaled exasperatedly. "And to think I once thought you were part bulldozer."

He slowed down as he took a turn, his eyebrows rising in amused query. "You changed your mind?"

"Yes. You're the pure breed."

And he did something that almost made her head explode.

He threw *his* head back and let out a hearty guffaw.

When she felt he'd scrambled her nervous system forever, he turned to her, chuckles still reverberating deep in his endless chest, his smile wider than she'd ever seen it.

"Watch it with the laughter, Vincenzo," she mumbled, hating it that he affected her to extremes no matter what he was doing. "Doing something so unnatural to you can be dangerous. You'll dislocate a brain lobe or something."

His laugh boomed again. "*Dio,* I can get used to this."

"Your highness hasn't been exposed to sarcasm before? Figures, with all the syrupy ass-kissing you have everywhere you turn. Since you've been exposed to it from birth, you must have always had social juvenile diabetes."

"I was wrong. I'm already too used to getting lashed with your delightful tongue. I hope you won't ever hold it."

"I think it's a physical impossibility with you around."

He chuckled again, this time doing something even more

distressing. He reached out for her hand and brought it to his lips.

His lips. Those lips that had enslaved her with their possession, that had taught her passion and the pleasure her body was capable of experiencing. The moment they touched the back of her hand, her heart almost ruptured.

She snatched her hand back as if from open fire, agitation searing her insides. "I don't know what you're playing at…"

"I already told you my game plan." His eyes turned serious as he brought the car to a stop and turned to her. "But I've also come to a new decision. I no longer care how this started…"

"I do."

"…I only care that when I'm with you I feel…great. I haven't felt like that in… I don't even remember if I ever felt like that. You invigorate me. Your every word and look thrills me, and I don't intend to keep holding back and not show it. If you tickle my humor, and you do, constantly, I'll laugh. And I want you to do the same. Forget how we got to be here…"

"Because you blackmailed me."

"…and just make the best of it. If you enjoy my company…"

"I'm not a fan of Stockholm syndrome, thank you."

"…just allow yourself the enjoyment, don't stifle it and don't keep telling yourself why you should hold it back."

"Easy for you to say and do. You're not the one being threatened with your family's imprisonment and taken hostage for a year. *And* being kidnapped right now."

His eyes grew coaxing. "You are my partner in an endeavor I'm undertaking to serve my kingdom." The word *partner*, the term he'd once said would never apply to her, scratched like a talon against her heart. "You will help me bridge its distance from the world to benefit its people and the coming generations. And you're the fiancée I'm taking on a surprise trip. I will do everything in my power so you will enjoy it."

The wish that all that could be true overwhelmed her, closing her throat. "That's the facade hiding the ugly truth."

"It *is* the truth, if you don't dwell on the negative aspects."

"Negative aspects? Now, that's an innovative euphemism for *extortion*."

He didn't segue into a rejoinder this time. His gaze lengthened, grew distant, as if he was looking inward.

Seeming to come back to her, he exhaled. "Would you marry me if I took your family out of the equation?"

It was her turn to stare. "You mean I can say no and you wouldn't report them?"

"Yes."

He looked and sounded serious. Yeah. Sure.

"I don't believe you."

"Understandable. I don't believe myself, either." His head-shake was self-deprecation itself. "But I do mean it."

"Is this a ploy to put me at ease? So I'll stop giving you a much deserved, not to mention much needed, hard time? So I'll stop resisting and 'come to your bed'?"

"Yes. No. Definitely." At her frown, he elaborated. "Yes, I want to put you at ease, though it's not a ploy. No, I don't want you to stop bashing me on the head. With the way I'm relishing it, I'm realizing how much I do need it. And I'm definitely anticipating you in my bed…." His arm snaked around her, pulled her into his heat and hardness, enervating her with the delight of his feel and scent. "I'm willing to do whatever it takes to have you racing me there as you used to."

Her head fell back as she stared at him, sounding as faint as she felt. "Even if it means not using your winning hand?"

"I already said it had nothing to do with our intimacies."

"How can I be sure you won't hurt my family if I say no?"

"How were you sure I wouldn't after you said yes? I guess you'll have to trust me."

"I don't." She'd trusted him before. Look where it had gotten her.

"We're even, then."

What? What did that mean?

Before she could voice her puzzlement, he pressed her harder, cupped her face, and her questions combusted at the feel of the warm, powerful flesh cradling hers. "Don't say anything now. Let's forget everything and go with the flow. Let me give us tonight."

Tonight. The word reverberated between them, sweeping through her, uprooting the tethers of her resolve and aversion. His lips were half a breath away, filling her lungs with his intoxication.

She hated that she yearned for his taste and urgency and dominance, but she did. How she did. The need screwed tighter, squeezing her vitals, strangling them. Everything that would assuage the craving gnawing her hollow was a tug away, on his lapel, his hair. Then he would give her everything she needed.

But she couldn't do it. Literally. She couldn't move a muscle. And he was giving her the choice of the first move. He wouldn't take that out of her hands, too. When that was where she needed him to leave her no choice.

Leave it to him to do the opposite of what she wanted.

Annoyance spurted, infusing her limpness with tension.

With a look acknowledging that he wouldn't get a ceasefire that easily, and with a last annihilating stroke across her stinging lips, he pulled back.

In moments he'd stepped down from the car and come around to her door. She almost clung to him for support as he handed her down. The coolness of twilight after the warmth of the vehicle sprouted goose bumps all over her, adding to her imbalance.

Then every concern evaporated as she gaped. Up.

They were beneath a massive jetliner that looked like a giant alien bird of prey. This was his jet?

The next moment left no doubt as he took her elbow and led her to the Air Force One–style stairs that led from the tarmac to the inside of the jet.

Once inside, her jaw dropped further. She'd been on private jets before, though never his. Another proof of how marginal she'd been to him, when he'd been the center of her universe. But any other jets she'd seen paled in comparison.

She turned sarcastic eyes up to him. "It's clear you believe in going the extra hundred million in pursuit of luxury."

He smiled down at her. "I wouldn't say I go that far."

She looked pointedly around. "I'd say you go beyond."

His smile remained unrepentant. "I travel a lot, with staff. I have meetings on board. I need space and convenience."

"Tell me about your need for those." She waited until she got a "so we won't stop dredging up the past, eh?" look, then added more derision. "And you must have yet another castle in the sky to accommodate both 'needs,' huh?"

"My family's being the first one on terra firma?"

"And the third being the futuristic headquarters in New York. Next, I'll find out you have a space station and a couple of pyramids. Hang on…"

She got out her phone.

He gave her a playful tug, plastering her to his side. "What are you doing now?"

Squeezing her legs tighter against the new rush of heat, she cocked her head up at him. "Just estimating how many thousands of children this sickeningly blatant status symbol could feed, clothe and educate for years."

He tipped his head back and his laughter boomed, sending her heartbeats scattering all over the jet's lush carpeting.

"*Dio,* will I ever come close to guessing what you'll say next?" He still chuckled as he led her through a meeting area, where staff hovered in the background, to the spiral staircase leading to the upper deck. "So you consider this jet too pretentious? A waste of money better spent on worthy causes?"

"Any personal 'item' with a price tag the length of a phone number ranges from ludicrously to criminally wasteful."

"Even if it's a utility that I use to make millions of dollars more, money I do use to benefit humanity at large?"

"By advancing science, protecting the environment and creating jobs? Yeah. You forget how I started my working life. I've heard all the arguments. And seen all the tax write-offs."

"But you started your working life with me, so you know I'm not in this to make money or to flaunt my power or status."

"Do I? Solid experience has taught me that I know nothing about the real you."

He didn't answer that as he walked her across an ultrachic foyer and through a door that he opened via a fingerprint-recognition module. It whirred shut as he let her lead him into what had to be the ultimate in airborne private quarters.

The sheer opulence hit her with more evidence of the world he existed in. The world he now maintained she could choose to enter, or not.

He guided her to one of the tan leather couches by huge oval windows and tugged her down with him. She hit the soft surface and it shifted to accommodate her body in the plushest medium she'd ever sat on. Not that she could enjoy the sensation with his body touching hers, making her feel split down the middle, with the half touching him burning and the other half freezing.

She tried to ignore him and her rioting senses by looking

around the grand lounge drenched in golden lights, earth tones and the serenity of sumptuousness and seclusion. At the far end of the huge space that spanned the breadth of the jet, a wall was decorated in intricate designs from the blend of cultures that made up Castaldini: Roman, Andalusian and Moorish. A double door led to another area. No doubt a bedroom suite.

A ghost of a touch zapped through her like a thousand volts. His finger feathering against her face, turning it to his.

"Regarding the 'real me,' as you put it," he said, his eyes simmering in the golden lighting. "If you insist you don't know him, let me rectify this." He sank deeper into the couch, taking her with him until their heads leaned on the headrest, their faces close enough for her to get lost in the pattern of his incredible irises. "The real me is a nerd who happens to have been born in a royal family then inherited lots of money. He owes not squandering said fortune on his research and impractical ideas to the teachers he's been blessed with, who tutored him in business practices, and directed his research and resources into money-making products and facilities. He, alas, never had the temperament or desire to become a corporate mogul."

"Yet 'he' became one, and as ruthless as they come." To her chagrin, her denunciation sounded like a cooing endearment.

"'He' basically found himself one. And I must contest the ruthless part. Though 'he' makes too much money, it's not by adopting cold-blooded bottom-line practices. It just happens that the methods those people taught him are that efficient."

Her own fundamental fairness got the best of her. "No one could have helped you make a cent, let alone such a sustained downpour, if you hadn't come up with something so ingeniously applicable and universally useful."

"And I wouldn't have gotten any of that translated into reality without those people."

Her heart hammered at his earnest words. At the memories they exhumed.

She'd once poured all her time and effort into providing him with a comprehensive plan for his future operations. He'd already had an exceptional head for business when he applied his off-the-charts IQ to it, but it hadn't been his specialty or his focus. And he *had* had some unrealistic views and expectations when it came to translating his science into practice. So she'd insisted on educating him in what would come after the breakthrough, how his R&D and manufacturing departments would sync and work at escalating efficiency and productivity to streamline operations and maximize profit.

That had been another of the injustices he'd dealt her as he'd discarded her, evaluating her only based on her sexual role, as if she'd never offered him anything else. That had cut deeper into her the more she'd dwelled on it. It had taken her a long time to recover her sense of self-worth.

She bet he didn't count her among those teachers fate had blessed him with.

A finger ran gently down her cheek. "You're at the top of the list of those people."

She blinked. He admitted that?

"I owe you for most of the bad decisions I didn't make before the good ones I did make."

Her heart stumbled, no longer knowing how hard or fast to beat, thoughts and emotions yo-yoing so hard she felt dizzy.

She shook her head as if to stop the fluctuations. "Is this admission part of your efforts to 'put me at ease'?"

"It's the truth."

"Not according to you six years ago. Or forty-eight hours ago."

His eyes misted with something like melancholy. "It's not the whole truth, granted." Now, what did *that* mean? "But I'm sick and tired of pretending this didn't happen, that there were no good parts. There were…incredible parts. And no matter why you offered me this guidance, you did offer it, and I did use it to my best advantage, so…*grazie mille, bellissima.*"

This time she gaped at him for what felt like an hour.

What did this confounding man want to do to her? Was he truly suffering from a multiple personality disorder? What else could explain his contradictions?

But he'd already said he wouldn't explain. So there was no use pursuing it.

Deciding not to give him the satisfaction of a response to his too-late, too-little thanks, she cast a look around. "I still think this level of luxury is criminal."

His smile dawned again, incinerating all in its path. "Sorry to shoot down your censure missiles, but this isn't my jet. It's the Castaldinian Air Force One." So her earlier observation was true! "Ferruccio put it at my disposal as soon as I told him of you, in his efforts to see me hitched…ASAP."

As he grinned as if at a private joke, something inside her snapped.

She whacked him on the arm, hard.

His eyebrows shot up in surprise that became hilarity, and then he was letting out peal after peal of laughter.

"Had your joke at my expense?" she seethed.

"I was actually basking in your abuse," he spluttered.

"Why didn't you say you developed masochistic tendencies in your old age? You don't need to manipulate me into obliging your perversion. The desire to shower abuse on your unfeeling head is my default setting." She'd bet her glare would have withered rock. That hunk of unfeeling male perfection only chuckled harder. She attempted a harder verbal volley. "That this jet isn't yours doesn't exonerate you. You probably have your own squadron that puts it to shame. But apparently you're so cheap you'd rather use state property and funds."

"Damned if I do and if I don't, eh?" He didn't seem too

upset about it, but looked like she'd just praised him heartily as he picked up her hand and brought it to his lips. "Sheathe your claws, my azure-eyed lioness."

She gritted her teeth as his lips moved against her knuckles. "Why? Didn't you just discover that you relish being ripped to shreds?"

He sighed his enjoyment. "Indeed. But it works better when you're slamming me over my real flaws. Being pretentious and exploitative isn't among my excesses and failings. If you think so then you haven't kept abreast with my pursuits."

That made her snort. "You mean you think it's possible to avoid those? When your face and exploits are plastered everywhere I go? You even come out of the faucet when I turn it on. My building has turned to your services for heating."

His laugh cracked out again.

In spite of wanting to smack him again, that sense of fairness still prodded her to add, "But among all that obnoxious overexposure, I do know your corporations have substantial and varied aid programs."

That seemed to surprise him. "The world at large doesn't know about this side of my activities. I wonder how you knew."

Her smirk told him two could play at withholding answers. "It's I who wonders what you're after with all the discreet philanthropy. Are you playing at being Bruce Wayne? If you are, all that's left is for you to don the cape, mask and tights..." She paused as his laughter escalated again then mumbled, "Since making you feel great is nonexistent on my list of priorities, I'll shut up now."

He leaned closer until his lips brushed her temple. He didn't kiss her, just talked against her flesh. "I'd beg you not to. I don't think I can live now without being bombarded by the shrapnel that keeps flying out of your mouth."

She kept said mouth firmly closed.

To incite another salvo—she was sure—his lips moved to the top of her cheekbone, in the most languid, heart-melting kiss.

She jumped to her feet, nerves jangling.

He was somehow on his feet before her, blocking her way. "If you're not going to abuse me, how about you use your mouth for something else?" He waited until her chagrin seethed and blasted out of her in a searing glare before adding in provocative pseudo innocence, "Eat?"

"It's safer for you if I'm not near cutlery tonight."

"Nonsense. I'm not in the least worried. What's the worst you could do with disposable ones?"

This was beyond weird. Had he always had a sense of humor, but just hadn't turned it on in her presence? Why did he have it perpetually on now?

Giving up trying to understand this baffling entity, yet refusing to give him an answer, she turned away, headed to the lavatory. She needed a breather before the next round.

When she came out, she faltered, trying to breathe around a lump that materialized in her throat.

He'd taken off his jacket. And had undone a few buttons on his shirt. And rolled up his sleeves.

It probably wouldn't affect her any more if he'd taken off all his clothes. Okay, it would, but this was bad enough. The imagination that was intimate with his every inch was filling in the spaces, or rather, taking off the rest of his clothes.

He smiled that slow smile of his, no doubt noting the drool spreading at her feet. Then he extended that beautifully formed—and from experience, very talented—hand in invitation.

She covered the space between them as if by his will alone, unable to stop devouring his magnificence.

Reality again outstripped imagination or memory. The breadth and power of his shoulders and chest had owed nothng to tailoring. They were even magnified now that they were covered only in a layer of finest silk. His arms bulged with strength and symmetry under the material that obscured and highlighted at once. Those corded forearms dusted with black hair tapered to solid wrists. His abdomen was hard, his waist narrow, as were his hips, before his thighs flowed with strength and virility on the way down to endless legs.

Magnificent wasn't even a fitting description.

He sat back down on the couch, patting where he wanted her to sit. On his lap.

She wanted to. To just lose her mind all over him, let him seduce her, own her, drain her of will and blow her mind with pleasure, again and again and again, for as long as it took him to have enough of her this time, and to hell with caution and the lessons of harsh experience.

Before she decided to take a flying jump into the abyss, he engulfed her hand in the warm power of his and gave a tug that was persuasion and urgency itself. She tumbled over him, her skirt riding up as her thighs splayed to straddle him.

The moment she felt him against her, between her legs, the rock hardness and heat of his chest and his erection pressing against her breast and core, arousal surged so fiercely she almost fainted. Then his lips opened over her neck, and she did swoon, melting over him.

His hands convulsed in the depths of her hair, harnessing her for his devouring as his mouth took pulls of her flesh, as if he'd suck her heartbeats, her essence into him. Her head fell back, arching her neck, giving him fuller access, surrendering her wariness and heartache to his pleasuring.

She needed this, needed him, come what may.

"You feel and taste even better than all the memories that tormented me, *Gloria mia*."

She jerked and moaned when he said her name the way he used to, Italianizing it, making it his. It inflamed her to hear

it, maddened her. The way he moved against her, breathed
her in, touched and kneaded and suckled her…it was all too
much. And too little. She needed more. Everything. His mouth
and hands and potency all over her, inside her.

"Vincenzo…"

The same desperation reverberating inside her emanated
from his great body in shock waves. Then he heaved beneath
her, swept her around, brought her under him on the couch,
bore down on her with all of his greed and urgency. Spreading her thighs, he hooked them around his hips, pressed
between them, his daunting hardness grinding against her
entrance through their clothes. Her back arched deeply to
accommodate him, a cry escaping from her very recesses
at the yearned-for feel of him, weight of him, sight of him
as propped himself above her, his eyes molten steel with the
vehemence of his passion.

"Gloriosa, divina, Gloria mia…"

Then he swooped down and his lips clamped on hers,
moist, branding, his tongue thrusting deep, singeing her with
pleasure, breaching her with need, draining her of moans and
reason. Pressure built—behind her eyes, inside her chest, deep
in her loins. Her hands convulsed on his arms, digging into
his muscles, everything inside her surging, gushing, needing
anything…anything he'd do to her. His fingers and tongue
and teeth exploiting her every secret, his manhood filling the
void at her core, thrusting her to oblivion….

"We'll be taking off in five minutes, *Principe.*"

The voice rang in a metallic echo, not registering in the
delirium. It was only when he stopped his plundering kisses
that it crashed into her awareness, that it made sense.

He froze over her for a long moment, his lips still fused to
hers. He moved again, took her lips over and over in urgent,
clinging kisses as if he couldn't help himself, as if he was
gulping what he could of her taste before he could have no

more. Then muttering something savage under his breath, he severed their meld, groaning as if was scraping off his skin. It was how she felt, too, as his body separated from hers.

She lay back, stunned, unable to move. Dismay at the barely aborted insanity drenched her, even as need still hammered at her, demanding his assuagement. His heavy-lidded gaze regarded her in denuding intensity, as if savoring the sight of what he'd done to her. Then he reached for her, caressed and kneaded her as he helped her up on the couch.

He secured her seat belt before buckling his as the engines, which she realized had been on for a while now, revved higher and the jet started moving.

They were really taking off.

Everything was going out of control, too far, too fast.

And she had no idea where they were going. Figuratively and literally.

The latter had a definite answer. And in an existence that had no answers, past or future, she had to have at least that.

"Where are we going?"

At her unsteady question, he pulled her closer, his eyes blazing with unspent desire. "How about we keep it a surprise?"

"How about I go demand that your pilot drop me off?"

He tutted. "I see I have to surprise you with no warning next time."

"Since you can't take me somewhere without warning unless you develop teleportation, too…"

"Or kidnap you for real and keep you tied up and gagged on the way."

"…then get a *real* surprise when you finally untie and ungag me. Something broken or bitten off or both."

Looking even more aroused and elated, he gathered her tighter, put his lips to her ear, nipped her lobe and whispered, "We're going to Castaldini."

Six

Glory had one thought. That she wasn't going to repeat his words. No matter how flabbergasted she was that he'd said...

"Castaldini."

God. *No.* He was making her echo his declarations like a malfunctioning playback.

She pushed out of his arms, whacked him on both this time, as hard as she could.

"No, we're *not* going to Castaldini," she hissed.

He caught his lower lip in beautiful white teeth, wincing in evident enjoyment at her violence, rubbing the sting of her blow as if to drive it deeper, not away. "Why not?"

She barely held from whacking him again. "Because you conned me."

"I did no such thing."

"When you said we were flying, I assumed it would be to another city or at most another state."

"Am I responsible for your faulty assumptions? I gave

you all the clues, said I'm taking you where the most exclusive jewelry on the planet awaits you. Where did you think that was?"

"I didn't realize you were playing Trivial Pursuit at the time. And why go all this way for a ring? What's that hyperbole about Castaldinian jewelry? Is that exaggerated national pride where you claim everything in Castaldini is the best in history?"

"I don't know about everything, but I'm pretty sure Castaldini's royal jewels are as exclusive as it gets."

"Castaldini's royal j—" Her teeth clattered shut before she completed parroting this latest piece of astounding info. Shock surged back a moment later. "You can't be serious! I can't wear a ring from Castaldini's freaking royal jewels!"

"*You* can't be serious thinking my bride would wear anything else."

"I'm not your bride. I'm your decoy. And that only for a year. But as you said, a year can be a very long time. I can't take the responsibility for something that…that priceless…." She pushed his hands away when they attempted to draw her back into his embrace. "For God's sake, during the height of Castaldini's economic problems, before King Ferruccio was crowned, people were saying that if only Castaldini sold half of those jewels, they'd settle the national debt!"

"Oh, I did propose the solution. But Castaldinians would rather sell their firstborns."

"And you want me to wear a ring from a collection that revered, for any reason, let alone a charade? You expect me to walk around wearing a kingdom's legacy on my finger?"

"That's exactly what you'll do as my bride. In fact, you yourself will be a new national treasure. Now that's settled…"

"Nothing's settled," she spluttered, feeling she was in a whirlpool that dragged her deeper the more she struggled. "I won't go to Castaldini. Now tell your pilot to turn back."

A look came into his eyes that made her itch to hit him again. One of *such* patient reasonableness. "You knew you'd go to Castaldini sooner rather than later."

"I thought you said I could say no to your blackmail."

His nod was equanimity itself. "I said I wouldn't expose your family if you said no. But if you say yes, I'll make sure they will never be exposed."

Ice crept into her veins again. "Wh-what do you mean?"

"They've committed too many crimes. It's only a matter of time before someone finds out what I have. Marry me and I'll do everything in my power to wipe their trail clean."

"That's just another roundabout blackmail."

"Actually, it's the opposite. Before, I said I'd hurt them if you say no. Now I'm saying I'll help them if you say yes."

Her head spun, her thoughts tangling like a ball of twine after a wicked cat had gotten to it. He was the feline to her own cornered mouse.

"I don't see how that's different. And even if I say yes…"

He caught her hands, pressed them into the heat of his steel muscles. "Say it, *Gloria mia*. Give me your consent."

"Even if I do…"

"Do it. Say you'll be my bride."

She squirmed away from his intensity. "Okay, okay, yes. Dude, you're pushy."

He huffed mockingly. "Such eagerness. Such graciousness."

"If you think I owe you either, you're out of your zillion-IQ mind. And this doesn't mean anything's changed. Or that's it's not still under duress. It certainly doesn't mean I consent to going to Castaldini now."

He sat back, all tension leaving his body, a look of gratification sweeping across his breathtaking face. "Give me one reason why you're so against going."

She had to blink to clear the glaze of hypnosis from her eyes. "I can give you a volume as thick as your prenup."

"One incontestable reason should suffice. And 'because I don't want to' doesn't count."

"Of course what I want doesn't count. You made *that* clear."

His pout made her want to drag him down and sink her teeth into those lips that had just reinjected his addiction into her system. "I made it clear that I changed my mind, about many things. Be flexible and change yours."

"I don't owe you any flexibility, either. I let you steamroll me by letting me think this was going to be a short trip inside my country. I didn't sign on to leave it."

"As my bride, you will leave it. Though not forever."

"Yeah, only for a one-year term. But I get to choose when that will begin."

"I meant you'd always be free to return, to go anywhere. This time, you can go back to New York tomorrow if you wish."

"I don't want to leave New York in the first place. I can't just hop to another country!"

"Why not? You do that all the time in your work."

"Well, this isn't work. And speaking of work, I can't drop everything with no notice."

"You're on vacation, remember?"

"I have other things to do besides work."

"Like what?" He met her fury with utmost serenity.

"Okay, I changed my mind, too. You're not a bulldozer. You're an ocean. You'd erode mountains. No, a tsunami. You uproot everything, subside only with everything submerged under your control."

He chuckled. "As much as I enjoy having you dissect and detail my vices, food is becoming a pressing issue. I had the chef prepare favorite dishes from Castaldini for you to sample."

Her hands itched to tweak that dimpled cheek, hard. "Don't change the subject."

Ignoring her, he undid his seat belt, then leaned into her, undoing hers. "You really shouldn't risk me getting any hungrier—in every way."

Her gaze slid to the evidence of one hunger and…whoa.

She tore her gaze up, only to slam into his watchful, knowing, enticing one. Gasping with the need to explore him, she said, "Even in food you're giving me no choice."

He separated from her lingeringly, pushing buttons in a panel by the couch. It was still only when he stood up that she realized they were cruising steadily.

"I am. *My* choice is to feast on you and to hell with food. I'm giving you the choice to avoid what you really want by choosing food, for now."

She bit back a retort. It would be silly to deny his assessment, when only the pilot's announcement had saved her from being wrapped around him naked right now, begging for—and taking—everything.

Exasperated with both of them, she ignored his inviting hand to rise and walk to where he indicated. Behind a screen of gorgeous lacelike woodwork at the far end of the lounge by the closed quarters was a stunning table-for-two setup.

Though everything in the compartment felt like authentic masterpieces, with the distinctive designs of seventeenth- or eighteenth-century Castaldini, the furniture was discreetly mounted on rails embedded in the fuselage. Exquisite, delicately carved, polished mahogany chairs were upholstered in burgundy glossy-on-matte floral-patterned silk. The matching round table was draped in the most intricate beige tape-lace tablecloth she'd ever seen, set over longer burgundy organza, with its pattern echoing the stunning hand-painted china laid out on top. Lit candles, crystal glasses, a vase with a conflagration of burgundy and cream roses, linen napkins, silver cutlery and a dozen other accents—all monogrammed with the royal insignia of Castaldini—completed the breathtaking arrangement.

She looked up at him as he slid the chair back for her. "I somehow can't imagine King Ferruccio here."

His eyebrows rose as he sat across her. "You mean you still think it's my jet?"

It hadn't occurred to her to doubt that or anything else he'd said. She'd believed his every word, declaration and promise.

Which was only more proof that fools never, ever learned.

She sighed. "It's not that. The rest of the jet is so grand, befitting a king and then some. But *this* setting is too…"

"Intimate?" he chimed in when she made a stymied gesture around the dreamily lit space. "Your senses are on the money. This section was designed by Clarissa as her and Ferruccio's mile-high love nest."

Glory's simmering heat shot up, imagining all the pleasure that could be had here, and feeling she was intruding on someone's privacy. "You sure he's okay with you invading it?"

"He scanned my fingerprint into the controls."

"Let me put it this way, then. Are you sure he cleared it with Queen Clarissa?"

"What I'm sure of is if he didn't, he'd love to be punished for his unsanctioned actions."

Her lips twitched as she imagined the regal figure of King Ferruccio being spanked by his fair queen. "Another D'Agostino with a fetish for female abuse?"

"Ferruccio would let Clarissa step dance all over him and beg for more. But since she's part angel, she doesn't take advantage of his submissive affliction where she's concerned."

His expression softened as he talked about his queen and cousin. Though she'd been a princess first, the previous king's daughter, not much had been known about Clarissa before she became the illegitimate king's queen. Ever since their marriage, she'd become one of the most romantic royal figures in history. Glory had heard only great things about her.

It still twisted her gut to feel Vincenzo's deep fondness for the woman, to witness evidence that he was capable of such tender affections. What he hadn't felt for her. What she hadn't aroused in him.

Oblivious to her sudden plunge in mood, he smiled. "And speaking of access…"

He pushed a button on a panel by the huge oval window to his side. The door of the lounge whispered open. In moments, half a dozen waiters dressed in burgundy-and-black uniforms, with the royal emblem embroidered on their chests in gold, walked in a choreographed queue into the dining compartment.

She smiled back at them as they began arranging their burdens on the table and on the service station a few feet away. Even though domes covered the trays, the aromas struck directly to her vacant-since-she-read-Vincenzo's-email stomach, making it lament loudly.

His lips spread at the sound, his beauty supernatural in the candlelight. "Good to know you've worked up another appetite." The word *another* came out like a caress to her most intimate flesh. He was playing her body like the virtuoso he was. "Bodes well for your being more interested in food than using me for target practice."

"I see you failed to acquire harmless tableware. But you like living dangerously, don't you?" She picked up a fork, gauging its weight and center of gravity as if to estimate a perfect throw. "I mean, silver? Isn't that deadly to your kind?"

He sat back in his chair, spreading his great body, as if to let her to take aim wherever she pleased. "If I was the kind you refer to, wouldn't I be 'undying' dangerously?"

And she realized something terrible.

She was…enjoying this. This duel of words and wills. She found it exhilarating.

It shocked her because she'd never experienced anything quite like it. Certainly never with him. She'd once loved him with all her heart, lusted after him until it hurt, but she'd never really *enjoyed* being with him. Enjoyment necessitated ease, humor, and those and so much more had been missing from his life. He'd been too tense, too *in*tense, in work and in passion. She'd felt only towering yet turbulent emotions while he was around.

Now, this new him was just plain…*fun*.

Fun? The man who was more or less kidnapping her and making her marry him temporarily under terrible conditions and for all the wrong reasons while seducing her out of her mind just because he could?

Yeah. He was doing all that. And was still fun with a capital *F*. It made everything she felt for him even fiercer.

Had she caught his masochistic tendencies? Or maybe she was developing Stockholm syndrome after all?

Again unaware of her turmoil, he pursued their latest topic. "In the interest of not turning to dust if you fling something my way while you attempt to crack open the crab…" He took the fork from her, gathered the rest of her cutlery and placed them on the tray of a retreating waiter.

Admitting that there was no denying, or fighting, the enjoyment, she decided to go with the flow. As he'd recommended earlier, in what felt like another life.

She eyed him in derision. "You could have left me the spoon. It poses minimal danger, certainly a lesser one than the mess I'll make as I slurp soup directly from the bowl and wipe sauce off the plate with my fingers."

"Mess away." Another button had his chair circling the table, bringing him a breath away. "I'll lick you clean."

Leaving her struggling with another bout of arrhythmia, he leaned across her then lifted silver covers bearing Castaldini's royal insignia in repoussé, uncovering serving plates and bowls simmering over gentle flames. Her salivary glands gushed with the combination of aromas—his and the food's. He filled a bowl with heavenly smelling soup, garnishing it with dill and croutons. Then he reached across the table for his spoon.

Dipping it in the steaming depths, he scooped a spoonful then brought it to his lips. Pursing them slowly, sensuously, he blew a cooling breath over the thick creaminess. It rippled, just like the waves of arousal inside her.

Her nerves reverberated like plucked strings as he drew her to his side, no longer knowing if she felt her heart or his booming inside her rib cage. Then he lifted the spoon to her lips. They opened involuntarily, accepting his offering. She gulped down the delicious, rich liquid, moaning at the taste, at his ministrations. *Vincenzo was feeding her.*

Then he was kissing her, plumbing her depths with wrenching possession, as if he'd drink her up, gulping down her moans as they poured from her, growling the fervor of his endearments and enjoyment inside her. *"Meravigliosa, deliziosa..."*

Her stomach made another explicit protest.

He pulled back, his eyes on fire, his smile teasing. "So the flesh is willing, but the stomach is even more so. Will you stop looking so delicious so I can feed you?"

Unable to do anything but keep her head against his shoulder and her body ensconced in the security and delight of his, she sighed. "So, it's my doing now?"

"Everything is your doing, *gloriosa mia.* Everything."

For all the indulgence in which he'd said that, it confused her. For it didn't feel like a joke. Yet all she could do was surrender to his pampering and marvel at what a difference a few hours could make. She'd started this bent on resisting to the end. Now look at her. Her mind was shutting down, her will raising the white flag. And why not?

This, whatever this was, wouldn't last. But she knew that this time. She'd been forewarned, should be forearmed against any pain and disillusion. And it felt so good. The best she'd ever felt. Why not just revel in it?

Even at the cost of untold damages later? Maybe it couldn't be survived this time?

She gazed into his gorgeous eyes, let his spell topple the last pillar of her sanity, and had to face what she'd never wanted to admit. She'd missed him like she would a vital organ. The accumulated longing was only exacerbated by the new appreciation that was taking her over.

So yes. She'd take this journey with him. At any cost.

"We'll be landing in minutes, *Principe.*"

The announcement made Glory do a triple take over Vincenzo's shoulder at the wall clock in the distance.

It was nine hours since they'd come on board already?

Time had never flown so imperceptibly. So pleasurably. She hadn't felt sleepy all through the flight, only deliciously languorous yet energized at once, each passing minute electrified, alive.

And here they were. Landing in a place she'd never been, and till forty-eight hours ago had thought, for too many reasons, she'd never be. His homeland. A land of vivid legend and unique tradition.

Castaldini.

She'd been so engrossed in Vincenzo and their newfound affinity she hadn't once looked outside the window as the pilot had periodically announced the landmarks they were flying over. She was now draped half over Vincenzo, one leg held in a possessive hand over his thighs, her face inches from his as they lay back on a now-reclined couch, gazing at each other, luxuriating in chatting and bickering and just relishing the hell out of each other.

Giving her thigh a gentle squeeze, he leaned in for another of those barely leashed kisses that had been scrambling her coherence, then withdrew with a regretful sigh. "Though I think some fuses inside me will burn out when I do, I have to take my hands off you. You need to see this. Castaldini from the air is breathtaking."

He untangled them and took her with him as he sat up, opening the shutter on the window behind them. He stood behind her as she rose to her knees and bent forward to peer down at his homeland. But she registered nothing but him as he pressed against her, one hand pulling her back into his hardness, the other moving the mass of her hair aside to caress her back and buttocks. All she wanted was to thrust back at him, beg him to end the torment that had been building for hours, years, plunge inside her as she knelt like that, vulnerable, open. She wished he would plummet them into delirium as they descended into his domain and the limited time they'd have together.

He bent over her until he was covering her back then suckled her earlobe, pouring his seduction right into her brain. "See this, *gloriosa mia?* This is where I'm going to make you mine again, this land that's as glorious as you are."

Everything inside her throbbed like an inflamed nerve, screaming for his invasion, his domination. "So you took your hands off me, only to substitute them with your whole body."

"Don't tell me, tell your body." His hand twisted in her hair, harnessing her as he suckled her neck, thrust against her, mimicking the act of possession. "It's operating mine remotely. It must want to keep my fuses intact, needs them fully functional." She was way past contesting this. With the way she'd been responding to his every touch, inviting more, she wondered how he hadn't taken her yet. Or why. He nipped her jaw, which sent another shock wave of need spasming in her core. "Now look."

It took moments to focus on the sight beneath her through the crimson haze of arousal. The place where she would come to life again, in his arms, in his orbit, however briefly.

And it was as he'd said. Breathtaking. Glorious.

The island gleamed like a collection of multifaceted jewels in the early afternoon sun. Jade masses of palm and olive trees, ruby and garnet rooftops on amber and moonstone houses, obsidian roads. White-gold beaches surrounded everything and were hugged in turn by the gradations of a turquoise-and-emerald Mediterranean.

Her chest tightening with elusive longing, she turned amazed eyes to him. "How can you leave this place, and stay away so long?"

Relief flared in his eyes, as if he'd been worried about her response. As if she could feel anything but wonder at beholding this magnificence.

"Wait until you see it at ground level." He turned her around, sat both of them down, buckled them in and brought her hands to his lips with a contemplative sigh. "But you're right. I was here too little for too many years."

"And now you're taking the UN post, you're going to be anywhere but here." And they wouldn't be here for their year of marriage.

As if feeling her disappointment, he shook his head. "We'll come here often and stay as long as possible each time. We can stay for a good while now. Would you like that?"

Vincenzo was asking her if she'd like to stay? When he hadn't bothered to ask if she'd like to come in the first place? Was that part of his "put her at ease" campaign?

If it was, it was succeeding. Spectacularly.

She melted back, luxuriating in his solicitude, no matter

its motives. She hadn't worked up the courage to take an active part in this seduction, but having him this close made her dizzy with the need to touch and taste him. His skin made her drool, polished as bronze, soft as satin. And it was like that everywhere. She knew. She'd once explored him inch by inch. She couldn't wait to binge on his flawlessness again.

But having taken the decision to give in to the insanity, she knew she'd have the mind-blowing pleasure soon. Sighing with the relief of surrender, she looked into his expectant eyes, loving the anxious expectation she saw there.

"As long as I can get a better toothbrush than the one in the jet's welcome pack."

Elation blazed in his eyes before he crushed her lips in an assuaging yet distressing kiss, groaning inside her. "Next time we're here, or on my jet—yes, I have only one—we're going to do our dueling and eating and bantering in bed. I hope you know what it cost me to not take you there this time."

"Because it's your king and queen's bed?"

"*Bellissima,* I'll have to refresh your memory that when it comes to taking you, I don't care where we are."

As if she needed her memory refreshed. She'd spent years wishing it erased. He'd once taken her at work, in the park, in his car, everywhere—the only uncharacteristic rule breaking he'd done back then. But...

"Then why didn't you?"

Winding a thick lock of her hair around his hand, he tugged her closer, whispered against her cheek, "Because I want to wait. For the ring. For our wedding night."

After that she had no idea what she said or what happened. Agitated all over again at being hit with the reality of what she was doing, she functioned on auto as they landed in what must have been the royal airport and disembarked.

A Mercedes was awaiting them at the bottom of the stairs.

The driver saluted Vincenzo with a deep bow, gave him the key then rushed to another car. Then Vincenzo was driving them out of the airport on a road that ran by the shore.

She gazed dazedly at the picturesque scenery as the powerful car sped on the smoothest black asphalt road she'd ever been on. She didn't ask where they were going. Now that she'd given up resisting, she wanted him to surprise her, and she had no doubt he'd keep doing that. This time she'd enjoy it. Having no expectations, knowing the worst was to come, freed her, allowing her to live in the moment.

For someone who worried every single second she was awake, and most of the moments she slept, too, it was an unknown sensation. Like free fall. And she was loving it more by the second.

Vincenzo bantered with her nonstop, acting the perfect tour guide, pointing out landmarks and telling her stories about each part of the island. He said he'd take her to Jawara, the capital, and the royal palace, later. For now, he wanted to show her something else.

Letting the magic of this land with its balmy weather and brilliant skies seep through her, she soaked up his information and consideration. Then coming around a hill, in the distance there was…

She sat up straight, her heart hammering.

This…this was his home. His ancestral home.

She'd researched this place in her greed to find out everything about him. She'd read sonnets about it, written by Moorish poets, sonnets about the princes who inhabited it, and defended and ruled the countryside at its feet. Back when she'd thought she'd meant something to him, she'd ached for the time he'd take her there, as he'd promised.

Now she knew she meant nothing to him, and he hadn't promised anything, and yet he'd just taken her there.

Life was truly incomprehensible.

Photos had conveyed a complex of buildings overlooking a tranquil sea with gorgeous surrounding nature. But its reality was way more. Layer upon layer of natural and man-made wonders stretched as far as her vision did, drenched in the Mediterranean sun and canopied by its brilliant skies.

The centerpiece of the vista was a citadel complex that crouched high on a rocky if verdant hill like something out of a fantasy. At its foothills spread a countryside so lush and a town so untouched by modernity, she felt as if they were traveling through time as they approached.

The complex sprawled on multiple levels over the rugged site, the land around it teeming with wildflowers, orange trees and elms. As they approached, Vincenzo folded back the roof so she could hear the resident mockingbirds filling the afternoon with songs. He told her they were welcoming her.

Then they were crossing an honest-to-goodness moat, and she did feel she'd crossed into a different era.

Driving through huge wooden gates, Vincenzo drove around a mosaic-and-marble fountain in a truly expansive cobblestone courtyard, parking before the central tower. He hopped out without opening his door and ran around to scoop her into his arms without opening hers.

Giggling at his boyish playfulness, she glanced around embarrassedly at the dozens of people coming and going, no doubt the caretakers of his castle, all with their gazes and grins glued on her and Vincenzo.

He climbed the ancient stone steps with her protesting that she was too heavy all the way. By the time they arrived at a stone terrace at the top, he'd proved she wasn't, for him. He was barely breathing faster. He'd always been fit. But he must have upped his exercise regimen. She couldn't wait to test his boosted stamina....

The moment he put her down on her feet, she rushed across the terrace and came up against the three-foot-high balustrade looking over the incredible vista that sprawled to the horizon. Well-being surged through her in crashing waves, making her stand on tiptoe, arch her back and open her arms wide as if to encompass the beauty around her.

Vincenzo came up behind her, stopping less than a whisper away, creating a field of screaming sensuality between them, his lips blazing a path of destruction from her temple to the swell of her breasts. By the time he took the same path back up, she was ready to beg for his touch.

She didn't have to. He finally pulled her against him, arms crisscrossing beneath breasts that felt swollen and heavy. His murmur thrummed inside her in a path that connected her heart and core, melting both. "*Dea divina mia,* my divine goddess, now I know what this place lacked in my eyes. Your beauty gracing it. I won't be able to think of this place again except as a backdrop to showcase and worship you."

That was…extravagant. When had he learned to talk like that? With the women who flowed in and out of his bed?

A fist squeezed her heart dry of beats.

Steady. She had no right to feel despondent or disillusioned. Vincenzo wasn't hers. He never had been.

But the thought still didn't sit right. Those women had always seemed as if they'd been there to serve his purpose. She couldn't see him serenading them. So where did the poetry come from? Why was he so free with it? She'd already promised him the pretense *and* the passion.

So was he only going all-out to make her feel better about both?

Yeah. That had to be it.

But he'd said his passion had always been real. Whatever his reasons for his past cruelty, it didn't matter. For now, she could have heaven.

"If you think I add to the scenery that much, I'll pose for a photo shoot if you ever need to put the place up for sale. I can see the ad with the title 'Property in Paradise.'" She turned in his arms. "But seriously, now I've seen it up close, I'm wondering how you don't live here most of the time."

"Maybe now I will." His tone remained that tempting burr. But she felt it. An earnestness. A query. One he couldn't be asking. This was a fake marriage, with a nonexistent future. He wouldn't be considering her or soliciting her endorsement before he made plans for his own future.

Ignoring a pang of regret, she pretended she didn't hear the subtext in his comment. There was probably none, anyway.

"So, what now?"

"We start preparing for next week."

"What's next week?

He pressed her against the balustrade and spanned her rib cage with his large hands, the translucence of his eyes bottomless reflections of the vivid sky. Then he said, "Our wedding."

Seven

"Our wedding?"

Vincenzo's heart dipped in his chest at the frown on Glory's face as she echoed his words.

Was she angry again? After the magical flight here, when she'd gradually relaxed, seeming to accept their situation and then enjoy being with him, he'd almost forgotten how resistant she'd been. But what if her acquiescence had been a lull, and now she'd come to her senses and would start antagonizing him again? He couldn't stomach a return to friction, would give anything for their newly forged harmony to continue. Even if it meant letting her make the decisions from now on.

She threw her hands in the air. "God, I was determined to stop repeating your words like an incredulous parrot. Then you go and say something that forces me into being one!"

She *had* sounded and looked deliciously startled frequently in the past couple of days. Was that all? She was annoyed at herself for parroting his declarations?

He watched her intently, considering his response so he wouldn't trigger a relapse into hostilities. "Why is what I just said worthy of incredulous parroting?"

"When you talk you don't hear yourself? Or was it one of the other Vincenzos who said our wedding is next week?"

Her smirk blanked out his mind with the memory of having those sassy lips beneath his, soft and pliant, burning with urgency, spilling moans of pleasure. He needed to devour them again. But he had to settle this first.

He backed her up against the balustrade, his gaze sweeping her from her piled-up hair to her turquoise stilettos, hunger an ever-expanding tide inside him. "That was the one and only Vincenzo talking. So is a week too long? I can make it sooner. I probably should. We probably wouldn't survive a week."

She picked up her dropping jaw and replaced it with a more bedeviling smirk. "It's okay, this happens with a newly installed sense of humor. Sometimes you can't turn it off. Or you're such a new user, you don't know how to. Let's hope you get the hang of it soon."

This wasn't the first time she'd made comments to that effect. Had he been that much of a humorless boor before?

He guessed so. He'd been too focused on what he'd thought paramount he'd forgotten to lighten up.

But back then he'd thought his behavior suited her, the driven, dead-serious woman he'd thought her to be. Serious about work and passion. A delightful, challenging wit hadn't been among the things he'd thought she possessed, what he'd told himself he'd have to live without, with so many qualities to make up for the deficiency. Now he realized being a sourpuss had made her turn her humor off, making him miss knowing this side of her.

How much more had he missed? Was it possible other things he'd believed about her would turn out to be as totally wrong? How, when he'd had proof of them?

No. He was leaving this alone. This bomb had already detonated once and destroyed his world around him. He wasn't lighting its fuse again.

What mattered now was that she seemed to relish his new lightheartedness. He'd never dreamed they could have anything like the time they'd spent on the flight, filled with not only mounting hunger, but escalating fun, too.

He wanted more.

He went after it.

"You're right. It's a joke thinking I can wait a few days. We'll have the wedding today."

It was exhilarating. Teasing her, soaking up her reactions, opening himself wide for her retaliations, every barb targeting his humor triggers.

She obliged him with another bull's-eye. "This is worse than anything I feared. That humor program had a virus that scrambled you up. We'll have to uninstall everything in your brain and reformat you."

He pulled her into him, groaning at the electric thrill that arced between their bodies. "I like me all scrambled up like that. So shall I rush the delivery of the catering, minister and guests? I can have everything ready by eight tonight."

She arched to look up, pressing her lushness closer to him. He'd never remained that hard, that long. And he loved it.

"So he first hits his opponents with a ludicrous offer, then, as they gasp in disbelief, he follows up with an insane one, making them grab for the ludicrous lesser evil."

"You're not an opponent."

At her raised eyebrow, though it was mocking and not cynical, he felt that nip of regret again. One that made him wish he could erase the past, both distant and recent. What he'd give to restart everything from this point, with them who they were today, with no yesterdays to muddy their enjoyment of each other, and no tomorrows to cast shadows over it.

He caressed that elegant, dense eyebrow. "Put that down before someone gets hurt. Namely me. At least more than I'm already hurting." He ground his beyond-pain hardness into her, showing her she should have mercy on him. The eyes that rivaled Castaldini's skies darkened, her body yielding, shaping itself to his seeking. Her response, as always, heightened his distress, his delight. He groaned with them both. "So you want to postpone the wedding till next week."

A choppy laugh shook those globes of perfection against his chest. How he didn't have them free of their restraints and in his hands and mouth already, he had no idea. "And *then* he makes it all sound like his opponent's decision."

"'He' has no opponents here. He's just negotiating."

"I can sniff out the faintest scent of negotiating a mile away. I can't even detect a trace now."

"It must be because I learned the undetectable negotiation method at the hands of a mistress of the art."

"Seems I didn't teach you but transferred it to you. That skill has been nowhere to be found when I most needed it."

He tugged a loose glossy lock from the satin hair that shone in his homeland's sun like burnished copper. "But 'your' decision to postpone is well-advised. Next week's forecast says it will be a perfect day for a wedding."

She curled that dewy, edible lip. "Every day is a perfect day on Castaldini. But…" Something like panic spurted in her eyes. "You're serious, aren't you?" At his nod, she grabbed his lapels. "And what do you mean *wedding?*"

It was his eyebrows' turn to shoot up. "The word has more meanings than the one agreed on since the dawn of humanity?"

She shook her head, something frantic creeping into her eyes. "I thought we were just going to get a ring, sign a marriage certificate and report to the king so he can officially send you to your UN post."

It pained him that she expected only a cold ritual to befit the barren deal he'd proposed forty-eight hours ago.

Sorrow filled him for what should have been with this woman his heart and body had chosen, but wasn't and wouldn't be.

Suddenly, all levity drained from him, loosening his embrace.

Unable to remain in such intimate contact with her anymore, he stepped away. And saw it. A quiver of insecurity. A crack in the veneer of confidence and cheek.

He should have felt that was the least she deserved. To suffer some uncertainty and trepidation. But he didn't. It hurt him to see her looking so…bereft. He hated to see vulnerability in those indomitable eyes.

He forced himself to smile at her, to reach a soothing hand to her cheek. "If you didn't think I was talking about a wedding with all the trimmings, why were you surprised at all when I said next week? Or today? The ceremony you describe could have been concluded in a couple of hours."

"Forgive me if I'm boggled by the idea of *any* brand of ceremony. I was never married before, you know, for real or for pretense, and a date, let alone one so soon, makes me feel this is actually happening."

He watched her lips shaking, attempting a smile of bravado and failing, and could no longer deny it.

His gut was having a fit, sanctioning no evidence but what it sensed. It insisted she wasn't the hardened manipulator he'd once thought her. That person would have grabbed his deal, would now be working his evident eagerness to milk more from him. But she wasn't. She was really shaken.

And for the first time, he put himself in her place. Taken away from everything she knew to a strange land, her choice stripped away, her family not only unable to come to her aid, but the reason for her predicament. Her only company and precarious support was the man behind it all. And he kept blowing hot and cold, to boot. She must be feeling lost, helpless. And to a woman who'd been mistress of her own fate for so long, that must be the scariest thing she'd ever experienced.

His gut finally communicated with his brain, reaching a decision.

If he took out the terrible blot of her betrayal from their lives, he could connect the woman he'd once loved with this woman he laughed so easily with, the woman he now wanted more than he'd known he was capable of wanting. And he didn't want that woman to be under any form of compulsion.

Taking another step back, severing any intimacy, he exhaled. "It doesn't have to happen."

More uncertainty flooded her eyes. "What do you mean?"

"I mean you don't have to marry me."

Glory wondered if the sun had overheated her brain.

That would explain feeling and hearing things that couldn't be real. When Vincenzo had stepped away, she'd felt as if she was teetering on a cliff without his support. Then, because of the distance that had come over him, she'd felt she'd fallen into the abyss of the past, discarded all over again.

That remoteness couldn't have been real. Not after all his pursuit and passion. And he couldn't have just said...

"I don't have to marry you?" There she went, parroting him again. She swallowed the knot of anxiety that rose in her throat. "Just a minute ago you wanted me to marry you in seven hours or seven days, and now... Just what are you playing at?"

He stuffed his hands into his pockets. "Nothing. No more games, Glory. But don't worry. I'll still help your family. Of course, they can never again as much as forge a note to your nephew's kindergarten or take a cent from a tip dish."

Her heart slowed, as if fearing every beat would make

this real. "Y-you mean that?" His slow nod, his solemn gaze cleaved into her. "Wh-what will you do about King Ferruccio's decree?"

"I don't know. I'm thinking on the fly here. Maybe I'll ask someone else."

Her heart boomed now, each beat almost tearing it apart.

She couldn't bear thinking he'd marry someone else, even in pretense. "Why?"

His shrug was heavy; his spectacular face gripped in the brooding she hadn't seen there since she'd met him again. "It just suddenly hit me, how wrong this whole thing is."

It suddenly hit her, too. That he wasn't only confounding. He was nerve-racking. Heartbreaking. And he probably did suffer from a severe bipolar disorder. What else explained the violent pendulum of his mood swings?

He forced out an exhalation. "You can go back as soon as you wish. If you want me to escort you, I will. If not, the royal jet is at your disposal."

Feeling as if her whole world was being swept from under her, she leaned back on the balustrade before she collapsed.

He meant it. He was setting her free.

But she didn't want to be free.

She no longer knew what to do with her freedom.

Before he'd reinvaded her life, she'd spent years nurturing the illusion of steadiness. His hurricane had uprooted her simulated peace and exposed the truth of her chaos, the bleakness of her isolation.

But she'd already succumbed and had woven a tapestry of expectations around this time she would have had with him. She'd anticipated its rejuvenation, thought it would see her through the rest of her life. In her worst estimations she'd never thought it would all end before it began.

But it had. He'd suddenly cut her loose, letting her plummet back into her endless spiral of nothingness.

She pushed away from the balustrade as if from a precipice and past the monolith who stood brooding down at her.

She looked around her stunning surroundings, every nerve burning with despondency.

In a different life, Vincenzo would have brought her here because he wanted to share his home with her. If not permanently, then at least sincerely, passionately, for as long the fates let them be together.

In this life, he'd brought her here for all the wrong reasons, only to send her away before she got more than a tantalizing taste of the place that had forged him into the man she loved.

Yes, in spite of the insanity and self-destructiveness of it all, she still loved him.

Now she'd only gotten enough of a glimpse of him in his element to live with their memory gnawing at her, to mourn what hadn't and could never have been.

Needing to get it over with, she turned and found him still standing where he had been, his back to her, looking up at the sky. Thunder filled her ears as her gaze ached over the sight of his majestic figure…then she realized.

The din didn't come from her stampeding heart. It was coming from above.

It took a moment to realize its direction then see its origin. A helicopter.

"The Castaldinian Air Force One, rotorcraft edition." Vincenzo gazed at her over his shoulder, his eyes grave. "Seems Ferruccio couldn't wait to meet my future bride."

Hot needles sprouted behind her eyes. She didn't want to meet anyone. She wasn't even a counterfeit bride now.

He turned, expression wiped clean. "Please say nothing while he's here. I'll resolve things with him later."

She only nodded numbly, making no reaction when he took her hand and led her from the terrace and down the stairs he'd carried her up what felt like a lifetime ago.

By the time they exited the castle, the helicopter was landing in the courtyard, the revolving blades spraying the fountain water at them. Glory shuddered at the touch of the warm mist, cold spreading in her bones.

As the rotors slowed down, a man stepped down from the pilot's side. She recognized him on sight. So the king flew himself here. And without guards or fanfare. It said so much about him and his status in Castaldini.

But all photos and footage hadn't done him justice. He'd looked exceptional in those. But the man was way more than that. He was on par with Vincenzo in looks and physique. He could even pass for his brother.

King Ferruccio rushed in strides laden with urgency and power to the passenger side as it opened. In moments, his arms went around the waist of a golden vision of a woman, lifting her down as if he was handling his own heart.

"And the king has brought his queen," she heard Vincenzo mutter over the rotor's dying whirs. "Or maybe it's the other way around. She must be thrilled to see me entering the gilded cage at last."

Glory's heart contracted on what felt like thorns on hearing his words, and more as she watched the regal couple advance hand in hand, their bond blatant in their every nuance.

What attention they didn't have focused on each other, they had trained on her. She looked from one to the other, feeling like a specimen under a microscope.

Queen Clarissa was what Glory had always imagined fairy queens to look like. In a sleeveless floor-length lilac dress and high-heeled matching sandals, she stood maybe an inch or two taller than Glory, with the body of a woman who'd been ripened by the satisfaction and pampering of a powerful man's constant passion, by bearing his children. From the top of her golden head to her toes, she glowed in the afternoon sun as if she was made of its radiance. Glory could easily believe she had angels in her lineage.

King Ferruccio was as tall as Vincenzo, another overpoweringly handsome D'Agostino. There was no doubt the same blood ran in their veins. They had almost identical coloring, too. But that was where the similarities ended.

While Vincenzo was imposing, Ferruccio was intimidating. If his wife was the benevolent breed of angel, he was the avenging variety. And it had nothing to do with the way he looked. It was in his eyes. His vibe. This was a man who'd seen and done unspeakable things…and had those things done to him. Which made sense. He'd grown up an illegitimate boy on the streets, one who'd dragged himself from the dirt to the very top. She could only imagine what he'd been through, what had shaped him into the man who was now undisputedly the best king in Castaldini's history. She felt no one could know the scope of his depths, and those of his sufferings and complexities.

No one but his wife, that was.

They seemed to share a soul.

It hurt to see them together, to feel the love arcing between them in a closed circuit of harmony. What she'd once thought she'd had with Vincenzo.

Vincenzo, who was still holding her hand as they stopped two feet away from the couple, making her feel as if he couldn't let go of it. When he was letting her go completely.

Hand still entwined with hers Vincenzo bowed before his king and queen, his other hand flat palmed over his heart, in the Castaldinian royal salute.

What was she supposed to do? Bow, too? Curtsy?

Before her muscles unlocked, Vincenzo straightened, his face softening on a smile that she'd only seen before when he'd been talking about Clarissa.

With an arm going around her waist, he gave Queen Clarissa a tender hug with his other arm, kissing her gently on her cheek, before raising one eyebrow at King Ferruccio. "I see you've brought your husband with you."

So he was on teasing terms with his king. Figured. It was clear that though he observed the king's status officially, he was on the same level personally.

Clarissa chuckled, her thick, long hair blowing around her face in the breeze like strands of sunlight. "You know me, I can't say no to him."

Vincenzo's lips twisted. "I can train you."

Her chuckle turned to a snicker. "Like *you* can say no to him."

Vincenzo teased. "I'm not the woman who has the power to make a yo-yo out of His Majesty. It's your duty as his queen to save his subjects from his implacability, and as his wife to counteract the toxic level of yeses in his blood."

Clarissa gave her husband a look full of all they had between them. "I like him intoxicated." She turned teasing eyes on Vincenzo. "Now shush, Cenzo, and let me meet your much better half."

Then she turned those eyes on Glory. They were so unbelievable, Glory involuntarily stepped closer to find out if they were contacts. They weren't. She'd seen so-called violet eyes before, always blue with a violet tinge. But Clarissa's were pure, luminescent amethysts. Eyes to stare into for hours. Ferruccio evidently wanted to do nothing else for life.

Glory's lips trembled on a smile in response to Clarissa's exquisite one as she clasped her in a warm, fragrant embrace.

Already on the brink of tears, Clarissa's words almost made them escape. "Welcome to Castaldini and to the family, Glory. I'm thrilled to have another friend my age, especially since I hear we have so much in common, our professional training—" she pulled back, her smile becoming mischie-

vous "—and being married to one of our impossible yet ir-
resistible D'Agostino men."

In spite of her upheaval, her lips moved of their own accord. "Your Majesty…"

Clarissa held out a warning finger. "Stop right there! No
YMs and not the Q word, either. Away from all the court
stuff, I'm just Rissa—my husband claims exclusivity on Clarissa—" another melting look at her husband "—and I'm just
part of a brigade around here, with the other members being
Gabrielle, my brother Durante's wife; Phoebe, my cousin Leandro's; and Jade, my cousin Eduardo's. We used to call ourselves the Fabulous Four. Now we'll be the Fabulous Five."

Glory swallowed, at a loss on how to answer. Seemed Vincenzo's advice about saying nothing was the best one to follow in this mess. She smiled weakly at Clarissa, wishing the
earth actually opened and swallowed people.

"You're real."

The deep, dark burr had goose bumps storming across her
body. King Ferruccio.

Without coming closer, he made her feel his presence had
enveloped her, immobilizing her for analysis as he cocked
his head in contemplation. "I thought Vincenzo was pulling
one over on me until I was forced to send him off to his new
post, only to discover too late that you were a figment of his
very creative mind."

Her bones tightened under his scrutiny. He felt something
wasn't right. His eyes said he *knew* it. Shrewd man. That must
be how he'd raised himself from destitute illegitimacy to become not only one of the world's most hard-hitting magnates,
but the king who'd brought Castaldini back from the brink of
ruin and into unprecedented prosperity in under four years.
The intelligence she felt radiating from him was almost frightening, and he must possess all the additional qualities that
made others follow him.

Under his probing, words formed on her lips. "I am real, I assure you, Your Majesty. Forgive me if I won't call you Ruccio, if that's your name in informal setting, according to the abbreviations I observed your names undergo."

A ghost of a smile played on Ferruccio's uncompromising lips. "Come to think of it, that contraction should have been my name's fate. Seems no one was bold enough to attempt it. But you can call me Ferruccio like everyone is free to, since my wife has her own exclusive names for me. But Your Majesty is certainly not something you're allowed to use."

Her smile attempted a semblance of steadiness. "It might be impossible to call you by your name just like that."

Ferruccio's gaze leveled on her. "In her incurable kindness, Clarissa has made it a request, but I have no such qualms. Away from the court I order you to call me Ferruccio. As your future king, that's a royal decree."

"See what I have to put up with?"

That was Vincenzo, his tone light and teasing, but his eyes made her feel he was following her breaths.

Ignoring him, Ferruccio maintained his focus on her. "But you're not only real, you're nothing like I expected. As soon as I had a name to his alleged fiancée, I investigated you." At Clarissa's silent reprimand, he caressed the hand that discreetly poked at him, his eyes on Glory. "And now I'm left with an unsolvable question. How was he able to get a woman of your caliber not only to take him seriously, but to agree, and so fast, to take on the onerous task of marrying him?"

Vincenzo snorted a laugh. "And that's what you say when you're trying your best to marry me off? What would you have said if you wanted to send her running away screaming?"

Clarissa tugged on her husband arm, her color high with embarrassment. "He must have done exactly what you did to make me undertake the same task with you." Her eyes turned apologetically on Glory. "Now you see the *impossible* part I was talking about."

Suddenly deciding to throw herself into the part Vincenzo expected her to play until his king and queen left, Glory quirked her lips at Clarissa. "And now that I do, I actually feel better about Vincenzo's exasperating tendencies. I now have proof they're genetic and therefore beyond his control."

Clarissa whooped with laughter. "I *knew* it! I liked you on sight, but now I know I'll *love* you! You're exactly the addition we need to our brigade!"

Ferruccio cast an indulgent look at his wife, then raised an eyebrow at Glory, clearly approving the comeback that bundled him and Vincenzo and put them firmly in their places.

Vincenzo's arm tightened. "How about we call it quits, Ferruccio, before we're cut down to an even tinier size?"

Ferruccio gave a tiny bow of his regal head. "By all means. Not that I'll quit being flabbergasted at your phenomenal luck anytime soon."

Vincenzo sighed. "Your flattery knows no bounds. Now before you have Glory rethinking her hasty and ill-advised decision to marry me, how about you go do some kingly stuff and leave me to resume what I was about to do before your... surprise inspection? I was about to take Glory to explore the place before dinner." He turned his eyes to Clarissa. "You, of course, are more than welcome to join us."

Clarissa looked up into her husband's eyes, exchanging what Glory had once thought she'd shared with Vincenzo. Such allegiance. Such understanding. Such adoration.

Clarissa pinched her husband's hard cheek. "See what you've done? Now make nice so you can stay for the tour and dinner, too."

Catching her hand to bury his lips in its palm, Ferruccio looked over at Vincenzo challengingly. "Why make nice when I can order him to invite me? Or better still, invite myself?"

Vincenzo raised him a pitying glance. "Seems you haven't lived on Castaldini long enough to realize how provincial it remains, don't realize what power I wield in my ancestral region. Here, I rule supreme. King or no, Ferruccio, one more word and I sic my whole province on you."

Ferruccio's eyes gleamed with devilry. "Let's not start a civil war over the dinner you've been cornered into feeding me. Now lead the way, Vincenzo. And try to do your 'ancestral home' justice as you act as the guide."

Grumbling something about getting Ferruccio later when he wasn't under Clarissa's protection, Vincenzo did lead the way.

And how he did. He detailed everything with the thoroughness of someone who took the utmost pride in the place that had been in his family for generations. As he should. This place was phenomenal.

And it would be the first and last time she was here. Why not just enjoy the experience while it lasted?

"The architecture of all the buildings is a symbiosis of every culture that makes up Castaldini—Roman, Andalusian, Moorish and some North African influences," Vincenzo said, his explanations all for her. "Geometric patterns rule, with accessory-heavy decoration, from mosaic to plaster carving to worked metal. The main castle is circular but the other annexed buildings and towers are quadrangular, with all rooms opening onto inner courts."

It was all right out of a fairy tale. Far grander and better preserved that any of the architectural wonders she'd visited all over the world.

She asked, "How long has this place been in your family?"

"Over five hundred years."

Wow. That really put into perspective the difference between them. Her family tree was known only three or four generations back on both sides. And there hadn't been a "family home" in her life, let alone an ancestral one.

Vincenzo underlined the unbridgeable gap between them. "My umpteenth great-grandfather was Castaldini's founder, King Antonio D'Agostino."

"*Our* umpteenth great-grandfather," Ferruccio put in.

Vincenzo countered, "*My* line is that of one of his grandsons, who started building this place, but it reached its present size by gradual additions of more quadrangles over two centuries. Leandro, a slightly less obnoxious cousin, inherited a similar place, which King Antonio himself had built. When we were young, we always liked to brag about which is bigger and better."

Glory's blood tumbled as her imagination flew on a tangent, to other bigger and better…things.

"You still do," Ferruccio said, his tone condescending. "I always leave you boys to squabble over size and quality. Mine is the undisputed best of all."

"But the royal palace isn't yours, my liege," Vincenzo calmly retorted. "As per Castaldini's laws, you're just the resident caretaker. You really should start building or acquiring a place to pass on to your children."

Ferruccio suddenly threw his head back and guffawed. "See that, Vincenzo? That's the take-no-prisoners attitude I want you to have when you're representing Castaldini."

Clarissa's eyes rounded. "You mean you've been poking him to get him to bare his fangs?"

Ferruccio grinned down at her. "He's been getting soft of late. Now that he has Glory, I was afraid he'd turn to putty and be no good to me in the war zone I'm sending him to. I had to do something to remind him how to use his fangs."

Vincenzo huffed. "Have I told you lately how much I love you, Ferruccio?"

"You're welcome to renew your oath of allegiance any-time, Vincenzo."

Clarissa spluttered as she smacked her husband and cousin playfully, and Glory had to join in the laughter.

After that the day flowed, filled with many unprecedented experiences with the most exciting people she'd ever met.

It was past midnight when she and Vincenzo stood in the courtyard, watching the regal couple vanish into the night.

Her heart twisted at the symbolism. This place and Vincenzo would soon disappear from her life as if they'd never been.

The moment she turned to Vincenzo, he turned to her, too, taking a leashed step closer, practically vibrating with intensity.

And she realized. That he was sending her away because he no longer wanted to coerce her. But he still wanted her. And she'd already decided that this passion was worth any risk.

Closing the gap between them, taking both his hands in hers, she took the plunge into the path to eventual heartache.

And she whispered, "I'll marry you for the year you need, Vincenzo. My choice this time."

Eight

"What did you say?"

As the exclamation rang in her ear, Glory sighed. "You heard right, Mom. I'm getting married. To Vincenzo."

Silence expanded on the other end of the line.

Which was to be expected. She herself still couldn't believe any of this was really happening.

After she'd told Vincenzo last night that she'd marry him of her own free will, she hadn't known what to expect.

Or she had. She'd expected him to be elated, or relieved, or best scenario of all, to resume his mind-melting seduction.

He'd done none of that. He'd just taken her hands to his lips, murmured a cell-scrambling *"Grazie mille, gloriosa mia"* then he'd silently led her to her guest quarters and bid her good-night.

After a night of tossing and turning and pacing her quarters, which looked like something out of a fairy tale, he'd come knocking with a breakfast tray. He didn't stay, said he had too many things to prepare. He asked her to invite everyone she wanted and to make lists of what she needed for the wedding. It *would* be in a week's time.

The first person she'd thought of had been her mother.

And here she was, pretending this was real to the person she was closest to in the world. But there was nothing to be gained by telling her mother the truth. Her mother had suffered too much, and God only knew how long her remission would last this time—or if it would. She would do and say anything to make her mother as happy as possible for as long as she could.

Glenda Monaghan's silence thickened until it weighed down on her. "Mom, you still there?"

A ragged exhalation. "Yes, darling. I'm just…surprised."

Her mother had been apprehensive about her first liaison with Vincenzo. She had feared Glory would end up plummeting into the huge gap in power and status between them. But on meeting Vincenzo, Glenda had thought him magnificent and later waxed poetic about the purity and clarity of his emotions for Glory. She suspected her mother had entertained dreams that her daughter would become a princess and had looked devastated when Glory had informed her that the relationship was over.

Glenda must be stunned her dream was coming true after all these years, and so suddenly. When they'd talked four days ago, none of this had been on the horizon.

Glory gave her mother a pretty little story about how she and Vincenzo had met again, rediscovering how they'd once felt about each other and resolving the issues that had separated them. This time, he'd popped the question and wanted to get married right away so he could start his new post with them as husband and wife.

By the time she'd told all those lies, Glory was almost panting, but she forced herself to go on. "Vincenzo will send his private jet for you. If you can come right away, I'd love it! If not, come a couple of days before the wedding if possible, to help me with all the last-minute things. All you need to do is buy something pretty to wear and pack a bag for two weeks or so. You should enjoy Castaldini at least that long."

When she finished, silence stretched again.

Then her mother whispered, "Is it only me you're inviting?"

Glory had known that question would come yet still wasn't ready to answer it.

From the time Glory was a little girl, her mother had tried all she could to defuse her dissatisfaction with her father and brother. Then, in the past few years, she'd fought to reinstate the relationship that Glory had escaped, always ready with an excuse for their latest damaging decisions or exasperating actions. Now the situation was reversed and it was Glory who had to hide the true extent of her father's and brother's transgressions from her mother. And she wasn't sure she could do that if she saw them again now.

But her established disapproval wasn't grave enough to warrant not inviting them to her wedding. If she didn't invite them, she'd have to give her mother an explanation why. She couldn't tell the truth. And she'd already told her enough lies.

But then, why not just have them here? She doubted she'd have enough mental or emotional energy to register their presence. And Vincenzo had stressed she could invite anyone. By "anyone" she believed he sanctioned her father's and brother's presence. And she did want to please her mom.

She forced lightness in her voice. "You're the one I can't wait to have here, but of course Dad and Daniel are invited." That didn't sound as welcoming as she'd tried to make it. Well, her father and brother would just have to make do with that level of enthusiasm.

"Don't you want your father to give you away, darling? I

know it's been a long while since you thought he was the best dad in the world, but he does try."

Yeah, he tried so hard his efforts could send him to prison for life. "I'm almost thirty, Mom. I'm perfectly capable of walking down that aisle on my own."

"I know you can do anything on your own, darling, but your father has dreamed of this day for so long, and—" her mother broke off, as if swallowing tears "—it'll break his heart."

Glory gritted her teeth on the surge of familiar guilt she suffered every time she felt she'd been too hard on her father. But once the sentimental reaction subsided she always realized that she hadn't been. If only she'd been harder, had known the truth earlier, she could have stopped him and Daniel from spiraling that far that they risked their freedom. There was one way out of this for now.

"Listen, Mom, I'm marrying a prince from a kingdom steeped in history and tradition and giving me away might not be part of the ritual here. If it is, I'll let Dad give me away."

Another fraught silence greeted her prevaricating promise. For an otherwise shrewd woman, her mother had a rationalizing disease where her husband and son were concerned. Glory barely suppressed her need to tell her mother to open her eyes and see her husband and son for the lost causes they were.

The one thing that had always held her back was knowing how much they loved her mother. Glory had no doubt they'd die for her mother in a heartbeat.

What an inextricable mess everyone was tangled up in.

Sighing, she soothed her mother. "Just pack your men up and bring them here, Mom. It'll all work out."

After that, she diverted her mom into talking about the guest list and wedding plans.

By the time Glory ended the call, she felt she'd run a mile. Now on to the marathon of the next week.

* * *

After sunset, just as she was getting restless having nothing to do, Vincenzo came into her suite. He introduced the tall, graceful and extremely chic man with him as his valet and right-hand man, Alonzo Barbieri. After greeting her in utmost delight and kissing her hand as if she was his long-lost princess, Alonzo ushered in four other people, two men and two women, each carrying a heavy, ornate antique chest. They opened them on the coffee table then promptly left, leaving her gaping at the contents.

The freaking royal jewels of Castaldini.

She'd thought they would be— No, she couldn't have thought anything that could come close to—to…*that.*

Each piece on its own would have been jaw-dropping, but having them piled together—from hefty necklaces, bracelets and tiaras to intricate earrings, brooches and rings—the treasure was literally dazzling. There were even some scepters and goblets and ornamental pieces not for wearing. And were those…those…

"The royal crowns! What are those doing here?"

As she turned stunned eyes between the two men, it was Alonzo who supplied an explanation. "I applaud your knowledge of our history, *Principessa!*" Before she could wince at the title, he went on, "Those are indeed the crowns that had been worn by kings and queens of Castaldini until King Benedetto and his wife—Queen Clarissa's father and mother. But since their lives were marked by tragedy, King Ferruccio had new crowns made, with personalized changes, so the past wouldn't throw the least shadow on his and Queen Clarissa's lives."

More proof of how total Ferruccio's love for Clarissa was.

With that strange reticence that had come over him still subduing his eyes, Vincenzo said, "As my princess you're entitled to any piece you'd like. After last night, Ferruccio and Clarissa insist you should have as *many* as you'd like."

Alonzo chuckled. "They're ready to offer the whole treasure to you as the one who'll save *Principe* Vincenzo from unremitting bachelorhood. I am also offering whatever your heart desires for that Herculean achievement."

So Vincenzo hadn't even taken his closest person into his confidence. Alonzo clearly believed this was a grand love story with a happily ever after.

"Ferruccio is also putting the royal palace and everyone inside it at your service," Vincenzo said.

"He wants us to have the wedding there?"

Vincenzo nodded. "Being the control freak that he is, he insists I take my vows under his supervision."

"Can't we…" She stopped, swallowed. "Can't we have the wedding here?"

A flare of surprise then intentness incinerated the deadness in Vincenzo's eyes. "Is this what you want?"

Feeling suddenly shy and awkward, wanting to smack herself for behaving as if she was a real bride, she murmured, "It's just this place is magnificent, and it's your family home…"

Vincenzo spoke over her, his tone urgent. "If it's what you want, then we certainly will have the wedding here."

Alonzo looked scandalized. "But what about King Ferruccio's decree? And all this talk about being a knight in his round table and doing anything he commands?"

Vincenzo had said that about Ferruccio? Watching those two together, you'd never have guessed he felt that way about him.

Vincenzo twisted his lips at Alonzo. "That's until my bride says different. Then it's her desires that I follow, nobody else's, no matter who they are."

Alonzo whooped. "*That's* what I waited two decades to

hear. *Principessa,* you're a miracle worker. A miracle, period."

Feeling tears too near the surface, she wanted to get this over with. "Will you please do the honors, Vincenzo? I'm almost afraid to look at those pieces, I'm not about to go rummaging through them and chip or crack something."

Vincenzo's expression hovered on the smile she'd been missing, had even gotten dependent on basking in it. "Rummage away. Those pieces have weathered the test of hundreds of years. Choose whatever you want."

"I want you—" her voice trembled, holding back *only you* "—to choose the ring for me."

A moment of probing stillness. "Are you sure?" A tinge of teasing said *after all the fuss?* Then his lips spread. "I do have one ring, one collection in mind. I always felt it was made as a tribute to the beauty of your eyes."

He gave Alonzo a nod, and as if Alonzo knew exactly which pieces Vincenzo was talking about, Alonzo started sorting through the treasure. In minutes, without letting her see what he'd selected, Alonzo placed the pieces in a rectangular box he'd had under his armpit all along then handed it to Vincenzo.

Coming to stand above where she sat feeling as though she'd fall apart any moment, Vincenzo suddenly dropped down on one knee in front of her.

Holding her stunned gaze with eyes roiling like thunderclouds, he opened the navy blue velvet box. She relinquished his gaze to its contents…and the gasp that had caught in her chest when he'd knelt before her escaped.

A seven-piece set—necklace, bracelet, ring, earrings, tiara, armlet and anklet—lay on the dark velvet like a brilliant constellation of stars set against a night sky. They were all made from the most delicate filigree yellow gold she'd ever seen, and studded with magnificent white and blue diamonds in ingenious patterns. But it was the ring that her eyes couldn't leave. A flawless, vivid blue diamond of at least ten carats, the color of her eyes at night, with emerald-cut white diamonds on both the sides.

Vincenzo singled it out, turned his hand up, asking for hers. She placed it there without volition or hesitation.

The moment he slipped the ring on her finger, she knew what a huge mistake she was committing. She wouldn't survive losing him this time.

His watchfulness intensified as he singed her hand in a kiss, then with a long groan, he stabbed his other hand into the depths of her hair and hauled her against him, kissing her so deeply, so hungrily, she felt he might finish her.

Surrendering to his passion, her need, her panic subsided as she accepted that if she wasn't careful, he *would* finish her.

"We have only one hour left to go."

Glory turned her head at Alonzo's declaration. The man was the most outstanding organizer she'd ever seen. He'd marshaled everyone's efforts to get the most efficient operation going. And in just one week, he'd managed to plan a wedding more incredible than any in storybooks.

Alonzo took exception to her saying that. The wedding hadn't happened yet, and would she stop jinxing it?

If only he knew a jinx wasn't needed to spoil anything. Everything would self-destruct in a year.

But a year was a long time.

The week had passed faster than she could catch her breath. Now the wedding was an hour away.

Her mother had arrived only yesterday with her father and brother, and Alonzo had promptly swept them off their feet and into the rush of preparations, for which Glory was grateful. No one had time to think of any relationship issues. Amelia, who'd arrived the day after Glory had invited her, had been running interference for her whenever any awkward moment arose.

Clarissa and Gabrielle—Clarissa's sister-in-law—were now flitting about doing Alonzo's last-minute bidding. He'd already sent Phoebe and Jade, the other two in the Fabulous Five brigade, on errands. Though they were his queen and princesses, in those wedding preparations, he ruled supreme.

Everything around the castle and the town below now echoed the themes of Glory's dress and accessories. Everything was swathed in glorious white, gold and a whole range of vivid blues. Vincenzo had already told her that *she* was made of Castaldini's hues, her hair of its soil, her skin of its sunlight, and her eyes of its skies.

"You do look like a princess, darling."

Glory looked at her mother in the Andalusian-style full-length mirror before shifting her gaze to stare at her reflection. She had to admit her mother was right.

So clothes did make the woman. This dress made her feel like a different person. The person a dozen designers had turned her into as she'd stood for endless hours for them to mold this creation on her.

During the stages of its creation, she hadn't imagined how it would look finished. She'd last seen it when it had yet to be embroidered. The end product was astounding.

In sweeping gradations of brilliant blues on a base of crisp white, it looked like something made in another realm, from materials and colors that defied the laws of nature. Its fitted, off-the-shoulder bodice with a heart-shaped plunging neckline accentuated her curves and swells to beyond perfection, nipping her waist to a size she hadn't believed achievable—and without a breath-stealing corset.

Her one request had been that the dress not have a mushrooming skirt. But it was only when Clarissa had backed up her request that the designers had backed down. On hearing that they hadn't taken her request as a command, Vincenzo had fired them and gotten new ones who'd been doing everything she said before she finished saying it.

Now the dress had a skirt that molded to her hips before flaring gently in layers of chiffon, tulle and lace overlaying a base of silk. The whole dress was adorned in thousands of sequins and diamonds that echoed the colors of her jewelry, in patterns that swept around her body and down the dress and formed the crest of Vincenzo's province, where he was the lord.

Alonzo finished adjusting the layered veil from the back of her high chignon, then the tiara just behind her coiffed bangs, while Amelia hooked her twenty-foot train.

As they all pulled back to exclaim over her perfection, her mother neared, tears running down her thin cheeks. "Oh, darling, I can't tell you how happy…how happy…"

A surge of poignancy threatened to fill Glory's eyes, too, as her mother choked. She blinked it back. The last thing she wanted was to go to Vincenzo with swollen eyes and reddened nose. But there was something in her mother's eyes that gripped her heart in anxiety. Something dark and regretful.

Gathering herself, her mother continued, "I'm so happy I lived to see this day, to see you with the man who loves you and who will protect you for the rest of your life."

Alarm detonated in Glory's chest. Had her mother had a relapse and not told her? She'd always said the worst thing about having cancer was how it pained Glory and disrupted her life as she'd dropped everything and rushed to her side.

Before she could blurt out her worries, a burst of music shook the chamber.

"Ferruccio has brought out the whole royal brass orchestra to your door, Glory." Clarissa chuckled at her astonishment. "It's a royal tradition in all huge occasions, playing the anthem to herald the beginning of ceremonies. And Vincenzo getting married is certainly huge."

Another wave of anxiety drenched her. This was really happening. She had to walk out now and marry Vincenzo in a legendary ceremony in front of thousands of people.

She turned away from everyone, inhaling a steadying breath as she faced herself in the mirror one last time. She wondered if everyone saw what she saw. A woman lost in love but resigned that love would remain lost to her forever?

No, they didn't. Everyone behaved as if they had no doubt this was a match made in heaven, and made forever.

Alonzo touched her shoulder gently. "Are you ready for your groom?"

She wasn't ready. For anything. Yet she was ready for nothing else, ready for everything. She nodded.

Alonzo rushed to the table where he'd arranged the blown-glass bottles filled with the aromatic oils he'd rubbed on her pulse points as Castaldinian custom dictated. He picked up one of the oils and also took the crystal pitcher filled with the rose water he'd given her earlier to drink as another part of the ritual before rushing to open the door.

Her heart clanged, expecting to see Vincenzo. The father giving the bride away wasn't done in Vincenzo's province, thankfully. Instead, the groom came to take his bride from among her family and friends, to claim her as his, and take her from her old life to the new one with him.

Everything inside her stilled as she stared at the empty doorway. Vincenzo wasn't there, and Alonzo was pouring water in his hand and sprinkling it across her doorstep carefully, once, twice, three times.

"That's to ward away evil spirits that might try to enter with your groom and conspire to come between you later," Gabrielle explained, a red-haired beauty whom the matron-of-honor dress suited best, with her eyes reflecting its sapphire and cerulean colors. She grinned sheepishly at Glory's wide-eyed stare. "I've been investigating the myriad provincial traditions around here. I'm thinking of writing a book."

"You should," Clarissa exclaimed. "You'd be even more of a national treasure if you do!"

Amelia, who was having the time of her life rubbing shoulders with a posse of princesses, chuckled. "Make it a royal decree that she must, Clarissa. With all the fascinating stuff Alonzo introduced us to during the preparations, I can't wait to read that book. I want to adopt all of those traditions in my own wedding!"

Glory barely heard their banter, all her senses focused on the threshold as Alonzo stood to one side, pumping his chest in deference and pride and called out, *"Avanti, Principe."*

And Vincenzo appeared.

His gaze slammed into hers, compacting the dozens of feet between them, making her feel him against her, his breath hovering a gasp away from her inflamed flesh.

Air vanished from the world. Fire flooded her limbs.

And that was before she really looked at him.

Her heart emptied its beats in a mad rush.

This was Vincenzo as he was born to be. As she'd never seen him before. The prince whose blood ran thick with nobility and entitlement. The man who inhabited a realm she should have never seen, let alone entered. But she had entered it once, tangentially. Now she was stumbling all the way in, even if for only a year.

Her ravenous gaze devoured his every detail. His lavish costume complemented her dress, magnifying his height, breadth and bulk, worshipping his coloring and lines. A mid-high jacket in royal-blue silk, embroidered with Castaldinan designs, opened over a crisp white satin shirt and golden sash. His black fitted pants disappeared into knee-high shining black leather boots. A gold cape embroidered in blues and white flowed at his back down to his calf and completed the image of an otherworldly prince.

She'd always thought no description did him justice. Seemed there were always new heights to the injustice. Of his beauty. Of his escalating effect on her.

And he was hers. Tonight. And for a whole year.

Alonzo gave him the same water he'd given her to drink, and Gabrielle whispered that now the evil spirits couldn't come between them from the inside.

Vincenzo strode in, a predator who had his prey standing before him. His eyes swept her before returning to her face with a promise that turned her into a mass of tremors.

And that was before he stopped before her and said, "I'll kick these helpful ladies out and take the edge off so I can survive the torturous festivities ahead."

The wild gleam in his eyes told her he wasn't joking. He wanted to take her now, hard and fast.

Her lungs emptied on a ragged gasp. "Vincenzo…"

"Don't stand there devouring your bride with looks and intentions." That was Clarissa, her voice merry. She must have guessed what Vincenzo was saying. "The sooner you're done with the ceremony, the sooner you can devour her for real."

Unable to blush any deeper, she watched Vincenzo turn to his queen with a glare, felt him vibrating with control as he offered her his arm.

She clung to it as if to a raft in a stormy sea, felt his power moving her legs and his support holding her up as they exited the chamber after another water-sprinkling ritual.

It felt as if she was outside her body watching the whole spectacle unfold as they passed through the castle's torch-lit corridors to the courtyard where the ceremony would be held. Her dazed gaze swept the magical setting that had become even more so with extensive decorations and ingenious lighting. Alonzo had turned the main building, its satellites and the grounds into a setting for a dream.

They passed through hundreds, maybe thousands, of smiling faces, only a few registering a spark of recognition in her stalled mind. Princes Durante and Eduardo, Gio, Alonzo's partner, and other relatives of Vincenzo's whom she'd met in the past week. Her gaze hiccupped and lingered only once, on her father and brother. They looked so dashing in their fineries, so moved, looking at her so lovingly. Her resentment crumbled and her heart trembled with that affection that had and would always defy logic.

Then Vincenzo swept her away and to the stage that now blocked the doors of the central tower, facing the courtyard where guests milled in concentric semicircles of tables.

As soon as they took the last step up the royal-blue satin-covered stairs, where a sumptuously dressed minister awaited them between King Ferruccio and Crown Prince Leandro, who would be their witnesses, the live medley of regal music stopped. Silence and sea breeze lamented in her ears as Vincenzo handed her down so she could kneel on the velvet cushion before the minister, then he followed her, keeping her molded to his side.

The minister of the province's main church—a jovial man who'd told her how delighted he was to be finally marrying the confirmed bachelor lord of his province—gave a little speech then recited the marriage vows, in Italian then in English, for the bride's guests' benefit. As per Vincenzo's province and family traditions, bride and groom didn't repeat those vows or exchange ones of their own.

She welcomed that. She had nothing to say to Vincenzo. Nothing but the truth of her feelings. And those should not and would never leave her heart to pass through her lips.

Ferruccio came forward with their rings, blessing them

and their union as their king, accepting their bows with that still-pondering smile. This guy was just too astute.

His assessing eyes spiked her agitation so much it made her keep missing Vincenzo's finger as she tried to slip his wedding band on. Vincenzo took hold of her hands and branded them with a kiss that rendered them useless before guiding them through the achingly symbolic ritual. The imaginary pins holding up her smile started to pierce into her flesh.

Then it was Leandro's turn as the second witness to perform the last ritual, coming forward with a crystal goblet. Vincenzo clasped her to his side as he leaned down, plastering his cheek against hers as Leandro held the goblet to their lips for them to simultaneously sip the bloodred liquid that tasted and smelled of an elusive amalgam of spices, fruits and flowers. He recited the words that would "bind their blood" so that they'd never be complete without the other.

Then Vincenzo turned her to face the crowd, who were now on their feet in a standing ovation, holding up their similarly filled glasses and toasting the couple in unison.

This was really happening. She was standing with the man she'd thought she'd lost forever, before his family, friends and followers, before the world, as his bride and princess.

Acting as his bride and princess. *Never forget that, and you might yet survive this.*

Just when she thought the worst was over, Vincenzo made everything infinitely worse.

His magnificent voice rose, carrying on the deepening night's breeze. "My people, my family and friends, everyone blessed to call Castaldini home. I give you your new princess. The glory of my life. Gloria D'Agostino."

If he hadn't had her firmly tucked into his side, she would have folded to the ground.

The canopy of moonlit sky at his back blurred as he looked down at her with an intensity that flayed her already inflamed senses. He brought her back into her body, crushing it to his, and swooped down to claim her lips, reclaiming her wasteland of a soul, feeling like bliss, tasting like life.

The crowd roared its approval accompanied with a storm of clinking glasses as the orchestra played a joyful tune this time, with the majority of the crowd joining in, a song celebrating the newlyweds' future happiness.

As the festivities escalated into the night, she lost herself in the creativity of Alonzo's efforts and the enthusiasm of everyone present. The fantasy of it all deepened until she felt she'd never resurface, until her ordinary, solitary life blipped out from her memory.

Everything became replaced by the wonder of Vincenzo's nearness, by that of his world, and all the wonderful people who populated his life.

And her resolve was resurrected.

Nothing mattered but having this time with Vincenzo. And she would drain every single second of it dry.

Nine

"The ordeal is finally over."

Tremors drenched Glory at Vincenzo's deep purr.

It came from the darkness that enveloped the doorway of her hideaway.

At midnight, as per tradition, Vincenzo's friends had held him back while she'd been "spirited" away by hers. It was supposed to whet the groom's appetites even further, searching for his bride in the castle, until he caught her and carried her back to their marital quarters.

The ladies had deserted her somewhere she'd never been in the castle what felt like an hour ago.

She'd felt like someone in a movie who'd been suddenly left behind somewhere mysterious and otherworldly, filled with whispers of temptation beckoning to an unknown fate.

She'd felt his approach long before she'd heard his voice. She now felt his eyes on her as she stood in the dancing light of a flame-lit brass lantern. Her heart no longer had distinct beats, buzzing like a hummingbird's wings, failing to pump blood to her vitals. The world started to blotch crimson....

His voice brought her jackknifing back to focus. "While being forced to share you with every single person I've known in my life, I've been pretending sanity and civilization for the crowd and the cameras. Now the wait is over."

He appeared as if separating from the darkness, a piece of its endlessness taking the form of the epitome of manhood. The need radiating from him violently strummed her, the reverberations deepening her paralysis.

She could only hurl herself at him, climb him, tear him out of his clothes and devour him in her mind.

Then he was there, against her, pressing her into the wall. Her cry echoed in the almost empty chamber as he ground himself against her. Moans and groans filled her head, high and deep, the sounds of suffering. He was in agony, too. His flesh burned her with his torment.

"Ti voglio tanto...tanto, Gloriosa mia."

Her nod was frantic. "I want you too much, too.... Take me to our room...." She didn't know where that was. Another tradition of the nobility around here. The groom picked the quarters for his bride and prepared them for pampering and pleasuring her. Just imagining it made her plead, *"Please, Vincenzo...now."*

He roared as she sank her teeth in his neck to stress her plea. He snatched her off her feet, hurtled with her through the now-deserted winding corridors of his fairy tale domain.

Doors opened into a place set up like an erotic dream. The vast chamber opened onto a semicircular balcony with wide-open ten-foot doors. The balmy sea breeze wafted in with the scent of jasmine and sandalwood incense, making sheer white curtains dance like gossamer spirits. The flames of a hundred candles undulated like fiery beings. A bed bigger than any she'd thought possible occupied the far end of the room. It was spread in satin the color of her eyes and covered in white and gold rose petals.

But instead of taking her there and putting an end to the torment, he only put her down on her feet.

She stood swaying with the loss of his support and watched him move to stand framed against the moonlit balcony door, her Roman god come to life.

Before she could ask why he'd walked away, his voice cascaded over her, intertwining with the music of the night. "Though I'm dying to end our suffering, there's one thing I want to do first. A wedding night ritual that used to be done here before modernism took over and people started taking too many shortcuts, even in passion. Something I never thought I'd have the chance to do, but always wished I could."

She groaned, louder inwardly. Not another thing to prolong her waiting! "What's that ritual?"

"A striptease. Of sorts."

Okay. Sounded good. Exactly what she wanted to do. Though she wasn't sure her system could withstand watching him strip at this point.

"It has rules, though."

Not so good. He expected her to follow rules, or do anything that required coherence now?

"Would you hurry up and say what those rules are before I liquefy completely?"

His chuckle was pure male pride. "We play a game. The winner gets to dictate the intimacies we share, until the other wins a next one."

"And the rules of the game, dammit?"

His laughter deepened. He loved watching her come apart. "Each says the most audacious thing that has ever crossed their mind about the other, confessing every uninhibited fantasy. According to the enormity of each confession, we shed one or more pieces of clothing."

Now, that wasn't good *at all.* She wasn't ready to expose her most private yearnings.

Which was stupid, when she was begging him to expose *her* to every intimacy he could think of.

But it was one thing for him to do it, for her to revel in having it done to her, another to put her needs into words. She'd been hoping he'd give her what she needed with nothing but surrender on her part, as he'd always done.

But that was exactly what this was about. Making her own her needs heard. Taking pride in them and responsibility for them. An opportunity to be on equal footing with him, at least in this.

And that wasn't bad. Also, she could see he believed he'd win without breaking a sweat, that he would have her writhing in submission before he was through.

He probably would. Didn't mean she'd make it easy for him, or that she would go down without a fight. Dictating intimacies was a hefty prize. Just the idea of having him doing her sensual bidding was worth any risk.

She took the first one. "The first time I saw you, before you ushered me into your office for my interview, you were in your meeting room among all those stuffy suits. All I could think as I shook your hand was whether you tasted as incredible as you smelled. I wanted to know if you looked even more heart-stopping in the throes of pleasure. I wanted to tell the others to get out so I could find out, right there and then. My fantasy went even further, that if they didn't leave, I wouldn't stop, even if it meant giving them a show."

His eyes had darkened with her every word, becoming obsidian pools. His lips belied his eyes' ferocity, spreading wider with approval as he clapped, lazily, sensuously. "I thought you'd balk. Well done."

He took off his sash and slid his cape off his shoulders in an arc, aborting its momentum with a tug that spooled it around his forearm before he let it pool to the ground.

"Taking off pieces of clothing should be simultaneous."

She jerked from her mesmerized gawking, fumbling with her train, almost tearing it off in her haste.

Then it was his turn. "The moment you walked into the room that first day and looked at me with those incredible eyes, I wanted to push you back on my desk, whether anyone remained in my office or not, spread your silky legs and devour you to a screaming orgasm before I even knew who you were."

The fire in her loins was spreading, consuming her, flowing down her thighs. And all he'd done was expose her to his visual and verbal desire and make her confess hers.

He prowled toward her, giving her a hormone-roaring show of contained power and inbred poise as he slipped off his jacket. By the time it thudded to the ground in his wake, she'd torn off her veil, tumbling her chignon in disarray.

"When you showed up on my doorstep that night," she panted, "I thought it would be the first and last time I had you alone. I fantasized about seizing the opportunity, dragging you in, tearing you out of your clothes and losing my mind all over you, even if you fired me for it."

He unbuttoned his shirt, exposing his Herculean torso and abdomen, shrugged the shirt off then yanked off his boots and socks. "All those licentious thoughts when you were a virgin, too."

As she bent to take off her stilettos, a warning finger stopped her. She straightened, swaying in place. "Being a virgin made my fantasies even more licentious. I had no expectations or experience to water them down."

His zipper slid down with a smooth hiss that made her start to shake in earnest.

He let his pants fall then kicked them aside. "Whatever happened to the fantasies after you experienced me?"

Her zipper was undone in a far less assured fashion. Her dress peeled off her swollen breasts under its own weight, sighing in a rustling mass around her ankles. She struggled not to stumble as she stepped out of it.

She stood facing him, in her white lace thong, jewelry and four-inch stilettos, her gaze glued to the erection stretching his boxers.

"They ended." At his frown, she elaborated, "I realized they were actually modest, almost pathetic. You surpassed any fantasy I was creative enough to have."

A shock wave of lust blasted off of him.

Her lips trembled in triumph. "Do I win?"

His chest was heaving now. "All those years, I fantasized about going back for you, dragging you away wherever I found you, taking you somewhere where there was only us, only ever us. I would be in my lab, or in a board meeting or at a summit and I'd sit and plan everything I'd do to you touch by touch. I planned whole nights of arousing you and taking you to the edge again and again until you were begging me to take you over it, to do anything and everything to you, with you. I mapped out the number of orgasms I'd give you, their variations and method before I had mercy on you, took you, rode you until I drained your magnificent body of every spark of sensation it was capable of. Then I planned how to keep you in my power, how to have you beg to be my pleasure slave, and a slave to my pleasure."

"Vincenzo, pietà...have mercy now...you win." She stumbled the last steps between them, crushed her breasts against his hard chest, assuaging the pain, accumulating more. "Now dictate. Any intimacy. And just do it."

He grabbed her head in both hands. "I always started our intimacies as the hunter, the seeker. Even when you did anything to me, it was at my request, my prodding. But I always fantasized that you'd take the initiative, do anything you want to me. This is what I dictate. That you show me *your* desire, *Gloria mia.*" His hands stabbed into her hair, pulling her away by its tether, demand vehement in his eyes. "Do it."

Vincenzo watched Glory as she pulled away. Her eyes were eclipsed with hunger as she started demonstrating her fantasies.

She touched him all over, explored and owned and worshipped him, in strokes and caresses, in suckles and kisses, in nips and kneads—his chest and abdomen, his arms and hands, his neck and face—telling him how she'd always wanted to do that, every second of every day, how she'd thought nothing, real or imagined, touched him in beauty, in wonder.

He reveled in feeling his mind unravel with her every touch and confession, in feeling her craving cocooning him, claiming him. Then, without warning, she dropped before him, wrapping her arms around his thighs, burrowing her face into his erection.

His eyes glazed over at the sight of her as she knelt before him. The ripe swell of her buttocks, the graceful curve of her back, the gleaming luxury of her hair, her unbridled expression as she drew deep of his feel and scent, as she pulled his boxers down. His engorgement rebounded against his belly, throbbing, straining.

Then she was showing him in glorious sight and sound and touch. And words. Feverish, explicit, uncensored words, confessing all. Exposing the true extent of her desire.

His body hovered on the edge of detonation with every touch, yet plateaued in the most agonizing arousal he'd ever experienced. He felt his life depended on, and was threatened by, prolonging this. His groans merged as her hands owned and explored him, her breath on his flesh a furnace blast, her tongue as it swirled and lapped the flow of his desire a sweep of insanity. Then she engulfed all she could of him, poured delight and delirium all over him. And his mind snapped.

"Enough."

Then she was hauled over his shoulders, gasping and moaning as he hurtled across the room. Her teeth sank into his shoulder blade, unleashing a roar from his depths as he swung her over and down on the bed. He stood back for one more fractured heartbeat, looking down at her, a goddess of abandon and decadence lying open and maddened with need among the petals, her satiny firmness sparkling in his kingdom's treasures, trembling arms outstretched, bidding him come lose his mind. He first rid her of jewels, leaving only the ring, then he lost the last shred of the civilized man and let the beast claw its way out of his skin.

He came down on top of her, yanked her thighs apart and crushed her beneath him. She surged back into him, grinding herself against him, her legs spreading wider, her fingers and nails digging into him, her litany of "don't wait, don't wait, fill me, fill me" completing his descent into oblivion.

Incoherent, he gripped her buttocks, tilted her, bore down on her, then, in one forceful stroke, he plunged inside her, invading her to her recesses. She engulfed him back on a piercing scream, consuming him in her vise of pure molten pleasure.

His bellow rocked him, and her beneath him. *"Glory... at last."*

Her head thrashed, tossing her hair among the petals, her back a steep arch, her voice a pulse of fever. "Yes, Vincenzo, yes...take me, take me back, take all of me..."

But before he did, he rested his forehead on hers, overcome by the enormity of being inside her again. She arched beneath him, taking him all the way to her womb, her eyes streaming, making him feel she'd taken him all the way to her heart like he'd once believed she had.

On a fervent prayer that it was true, he withdrew all the way out of her then thrust back, fierce and full.

Then he rode her. And rode her. To the escalating rhythm of her satin screams, his frenzied rumbles echoing them. It could have been a minute or an hour as the pleasure, the intimacy, rose and deepened. Then, with relief and regret, both of them extreme, he felt his body hurtling to completion. Needing her pleasure first, he held back until her almost unbearable tightness clamped down on his length, pouring a surplus of red-hot welcome over his flesh as she convulsed beneath him, her orgasm tearing through her, wrenching her core around him.

Seeing her lost to the pleasure he'd given her hurled him after her into the abyss of ecstasy. His buttocks convulsed into her cradle as he poured himself inside her, surge after surge of blinding, scorching pleasure. Her convulsions spiked with every splash of his seed, her cries were stifled against his shoulder as she mashed herself into him. He felt her heart boom out of control along with his as the paroxysm of release wiped out existence around them....

"Dio, siete incredibile."

Glory thought this had to be the most wonderful sound in existence. Vincenzo cooing to her. That he was telling her she was incredible didn't hurt, either.

She hadn't slept, not for a second. The first time had also been like that, leaving her with the experience still expanding inside her, awake but in the stasis of stunned satisfaction.

She tried to open her eyes, but they wouldn't cooperate. They were swollen. Just like every inch of her, inside and out. From Vincenzo's ferocious possession, and her fierce response. A numb hand flew to her head, surprised it was still there. He'd almost blown it off with pleasure, discharging the accumulated frustrations and cravings of six years in one annihilating detonation.

And he'd only managed to whet her appetite sharper. She wanted him again, even more than before. Her addiction was fully resurrected and would keep intensifying. Until it ended again.

But now it was just starting. She wanted every second of it before she had to relinquish it all again.

Succeeding in opening her eyes at last, she found him propped over his elbow, draped half over her, his eyes smoldering down at her. "*Dio,* what have you done to yourself? How could you be even more beautiful than before? How could you give me even more pleasure?"

"Look who's talking." She dragged his head down to her, twisting beneath him, bringing him fully on top of her.

He started to kiss her, caress her, but she was too inflamed. She clamped her legs around his waist, thrusting herself against his intact arousal.

He eased her down, unlocked her legs and rose between her splayed thighs, probing her with a finger, then two. Her flesh clamped around their delicious invasion, but it was him she needed inside her. She was flowing for him. He attempted to soothe her frenzy, clearly wanting to take it slower this time. She wouldn't survive slower. Her heartbeats felt as if they'd race each other to a standstill.

"Just take me, Vincenzo," she cried, undulating beneath him, her breasts turgid and aching, her core on fire. "I've needed you inside me for so long…so long…and having you once only made me want more…."

"After six endless years without this, without you, you'll have more, as much as you can survive." He bore her down into the mattress, driving air from her lungs. "Now I take my fill of you. And you take your fill of me. Take it all, *Gloria mia*."

And he plunged inside her.

Her scream was stifled with that first craved invasion, that elemental feeling of his potency filling her, like a burning dawn, scorching everything away as it spread. He kept plunging deeper, feeling as if he'd never bottom out. Then he did, nudging against what felt like the center of her being. He relented at her scream, resting against the opening of her womb and stilling inside her, overfilling her, inundating her with sensations both agonizing and sublime.

Then the need for him to conquer her rose. Her legs clamped around his back; her heels dug into his buttocks, urging him on; her fractured moans begged for everything, insane for the assuagement of his full power and possession. And he answered, drowning her in a mouth-mating as he drove her beyond ecstasy, beyond her limits, winding that coil of need inside her tighter and tighter with each thrust.

Then he groaned for her to come for him and all the tension spiked and splintered, lashing out through her system in shock waves of excruciating gratification. His tongue filled her, absorbing her cries of pleasure as he filled her with his own, jet after jet of fuel over her fire.

He kissed her all through the descent, rumbling her name again and again, throbbing inside her until the tide receded and cell-deep bliss dragged her into its still, silent realm.

Glory had been awake for a while now.

She kept her eyes closed, regulating her breathing even as her heart stumbled.

From the flickering dimness illuminating her closed lids, she knew it was night again. Twenty-four hours or more had passed since Vincenzo had carried her into this chamber of pleasures. He had said he wasn't coming up for air for at least that long. And he'd kept his promise. How he'd kept it.

After the first two times he'd made love to her, he'd carried her to the adjoining bathroom, an amalgam of old Castaldinian design and cutting-edge luxury. By the time he'd carried her back to bed, he'd melted her into too many orgasms to count. Then they'd spent hours reviving every sensual bond they'd formed years ago. He claimed they'd never loosened their hold over him.

Then he'd let her have him at *her* mercy as she fulfilled her fantasy of losing her mind all over him. Riding him to the most explosive release in her life was the last thing she remembered before waking up minutes ago.

There was a problem, though. She'd woken up so many times, too many, from abandoned nights to feel him wrapped around her like that. Then she'd opened her eyes and he'd dissolved into the emptiness of reality. She was afraid if she opened her eyes now, he might disappear again.

"Gloria mia?"

She'd heard him crooning her name in her waking dreams before. Logically speaking, everything that had culminated in their wedding night had to be some lovelorn hallucination....

Every nerve in her body fired in unison as the hand cupping her breast started caressing it to the fullness of need again.

Okay. None of her tormenting phantasms had felt that real. That good. That meant that even if it made no sense whatsoever, Vincenzo *was* really wrapped around her after a night of magic beyond her wildest fantasies.

Then his silk-covered leg drove between hers, pressing just where she needed. He must have sensed she was awake. Or her heart must have been shaking the whole bed.

No use pretending to be asleep now.

She opened her eyes. The best sight in existence filled her

vision. Vincenzo. His every line thrown into relief by stark shadows and the illumination of the gibbous moon pouring from the open window. But it was his expression that had her on the verge of crushing herself against him and weeping.

She must be seeing what she longed to see. Or she was superimposing what *she* felt on him. He couldn't be looking at her as if he couldn't believe she was in his arms again. As if he was afraid to blink and miss one nuance of her, one second with her. As if he loved her. As if he'd always loved her.

As if responding to her need to escape the impossible yearnings, his expression shifted to another kind of passion as he weighed and kneaded her breast. "I think I will fulfill my fantasy, after all. I'll keep you here as my pleasure slave." She moaned, arched, pressed her breast harder into his big palm. Something elemental rumbled in his gut. "The way you respond to my every word and touch is pure magic. What you do to me by just existing is beyond even that."

Her hips moved to yield to the erection that she was still stunned she could accommodate. Her moan grew louder as he expanded and hardened even more. "It's only fair that I turn you inside out like you do me."

Indulgence smoldered in his eyes. "So we're even."

"*Not* unless we play musical slaves."

"After what you did to me last night, I might cheat and let you sit on the chair every time. I'll let you sit anywhere you want, as many times and as long as you want."

"Oh, I want. I *want,* Vincenzo."

Unable to bear the emptiness inside her that only he could fill, she tried to drag him over and inside her. He resisted her, slid down her body, looking up as she twisted in his hold.

"I have a six-year hunger that I need to appease, *gloriosa mia.* Surrender to me, let me take my fill."

And she collapsed, could do nothing but submit to his will and let him take everything he wanted, let him drive her to

madness, over and over until he'd drained her dry of reason.
Of worries. Of anything that wasn't him.

When next she woke, it was night again, and she was alone.

Before dismay could register, the door creaked open and
in Vincenzo walked with a huge, piled tray in his hands. In a
molded gray shirt and pants, he looked like a god come down
to earth to mess with mortals' wills and jeopardize their souls.

His smile was indulgence itself as he put the tray aside to
pull her up to a sitting position. The sheet fell off, exposing
her breasts. As if he couldn't help it, he bent and saluted each
nipple with soft pulls, soothing the soreness she'd literally
pummeled him to inflict on her.

He pulled back reluctantly. "No more temptation, princess." He chuckled at her pout. "I'd do nothing but service
and pleasure Your Royal Voluptuousness nonstop, but I have
to refuel you so you can withstand the week ahead."

She sighed her pleasure as she sifted her fingers through
the thick, silky depths of his hair. "I've been holding up pretty
well for the past two days. What's so different about the week
ahead?"

"First, for the past two days you haven't even left this
room. You have been mostly flat on your back—or belly—
and apart from a couple of memorable instances, I've been
doing all the work." She smacked him playfully, giggling, her
body priming itself again at the memory of all the "work"
he'd done. "But I'm going to demand more of your partici-
pation over the next week, as it's all the time I have for our
honeymoon. My post back in New York starts next week."

Her heart plummeted. That soon?

She must have looked as crestfallen as she felt. He
smoothed her tousled bangs out of her eyes, his tone urgent.
"I'll only work by day. The nights, I'm all yours."

She smiled, hating that she'd made him feel bad for having to work. "It's okay. I need to get back to work myself."

His eyes flared with possessiveness as he slid the sheet totally off her. "During the days only, *Gloriosa mia*. The nights are mine."

She nodded dreamily as she squeezed her breasts and thighs together to mitigate their aching throb. "Yes."

His eyes glazed over as he pushed her thighs apart, sliding two fingers between her soaked folds. "And afternoons and lunch breaks and whenever I can squeeze you in."

Her legs fell apart, inviting his fingers inside; her breasts jutted for him to squeeze away. "Oh, yes."

Her response tore away any intentions to prioritize food as he fell on her breasts again, suckling, his fingers plunging inside her, pumping. She poured fuel on his fervor, kneading his erection, sinking her teeth into his shoulders.

"*Dio, Gloria mia,* you make me insane…."

His growl was driven as he descended over her, pushed her flat on her back, impacting her with his full weight and rising between her spread legs only enough to free himself.

Then, without preliminaries, he drove into her, tearing a shriek from her depths. He rammed inside her in a furious rhythm, plunging deeper with every thrust, growling like a beast. The expansion inside her around his girth and length, the feeling of being totally dominated and mastered, had her sobbing, pleasure twisting tighter inside her until she feared she'd unravel once it snapped.

He rose on outstretched arms. "Look at us, *Gloria mia,* look what I'm doing to you, look how you're taking me…."

She looked, and the sight of the daunting column of flesh disappearing inside her, spreading her, joining them, made her thrash at the carnality of it, the beauty.

Then the tightness was quickening inside her, the familiar crescendo, her flesh fluttering around his girth.

He felt it, fell on her breasts, suckling hard, biting, triggering her. "Come for me, *gloriosa,* come all over me. Finish me with your pleasure as I finish you."

Everything snapped inside her like a high-voltage cable, writhing and lashing out and wreaking devastation. He drove the deepest he'd ever been inside her, roaring as he rested against her womb and razed her in the ecstasy of his release.

But feeling his seed splashing her intimate walls, filling her, branding her, spread regret along with the pleasure. Regret that his seed wouldn't take root. She'd made sure it wouldn't.

He collapsed on top of her, his breathing as harsh as hers. She wrapped herself tighter around him, relishing his weight. Without him covering her like this, anchoring her in the aftermath of devastation, she felt she might dissipate....

He drew up, supporting his weight on one elbow, fusing them in the evidence of their mutual satisfaction, his other hand securing her head for a deep, luxurious kiss.

The moment he felt her quickening beneath him again, he rumbled a self-deprecating laugh, then groaned as he separated their bodies. "Have mercy, *bellissima.* Now it's I who needs to refuel. I'm not a spry teenager anymore."

Her gaze clung to his undiminished manhood. "Are you kidding me? I've been wondering if you've hooked yourself to your inexhaustible energy source."

"I am hooked, all right, on a perpetually renewable source of passionate madness whose name is but a description of her." Before she could lunge at him, he jumped up, stuffing himself with difficulty into his pants. "*We're* refueling. Then I'm taking you sailing. We'll continue this session on board. Ever made love rocking to the undulations of a tranquil sea?"

Before she said no, since he hadn't taken her sailing before, jealousy sank into her gut.

He grinned. "Neither have I. Another fantasy I'll fulfill.

I wrote a list of one hundred and ten items while you slept. I intend to make serious headway into all of them during the next week."

Her tension deflated. He hadn't done it before. He hadn't done so many things, but he wanted to do them all with her. Because she was the only one who made him want them. Just like he was the only one who made her want everything and anything.

She arched sensuously, smoothing her hands down her breasts, her tummy, delighting in the soreness inside and out. "I thought we were going to take turns playing out fantasies."

He tugged her up by the hand, this time making sure not to come too close and be snared back. "*Incantatrice mia,* I just played one of yours now. Taking you with no foreplay, just rough domination and explosive satisfaction."

So he could read her like a hundred-foot billboard.

He brought back the tray, placed it across her thighs and bent for one last kiss before he withdrew quickly, making her bite him in her effort to cling.

He laved her bite with a wince of enjoyment. "Eat something else for now, *amore mio.* I have to go prepare the rest of the day, then the week. I promise your fantasies are going to be heavily featured and meticulously taken care of."

With one last wink, he turned and strode out.

She watched him go, everything on pause.

Had he said *amore mio?*

My love?

Ten

Amore mio.

The words rang in a loop inside Glory's head as she stood staring around her condo. *Amore mio, amore mio*—crooned in Vincenzo's voice, soaked in his passion.

He'd been calling her that constantly, among all the other endearments he kept lavishing on her. At least he had for the first six weeks after their wedding. It had been over a week now that he hadn't been around to call her much of anything.

They'd been back to New York after their honeymoon ended. Vincenzo had extended their time away to two weeks at a hefty cost to all the people who'd arranged their schedules counting on his presence a week earlier.

A wave of oppression descended over her as images from those two weeks in paradise bombarded her. At their end, she'd thought that if she died then, she would have certainly died the most fulfilled, pleasured and pampered woman on earth.

Then they'd gone back to New York. He'd started his position and she'd gone back to work, and instead of everything slowing and cooling down, it had gotten better, hotter. He'd kept his promises and more, making time for her, for them, always, but even better, making a place for her in his working life, and asking for and taking a place in hers.

He'd taken her with him to every function, showing her off as if she was his most vital asset. He'd come to her like he used to with his work issues, taking her opinion and following her advice. He'd thrown his full weight into making difficulties in her work disappear and making far-fetched hopes achievable, without her even asking.

And through it all he'd been saying *amore mio.* My love.

He'd called her that in the past. She'd believed he'd meant it. Then everything had happened, and she'd known the name had just been an empty endearment. Now, she no longer knew what to believe. After he'd confessed he'd lied about his reasons for leaving her. After the past weeks in his arms, in his life.

So what had it meant to him then? What did it mean now?

The need to ask, to understand everything that had happened in the past, mushroomed daily. She'd tried more than once to broach the subject, but he'd always diverted her, unwilling to talk about it, as if he hated to bring up the past, fearing it would taint the present.

She could understand that. He appeared to have decided to live in the moment, without consideration for the past or the future. And she tried to do that, too, succeeding most of the time. At least, when he was with her. The moment she was out of his orbit, obsessions attacked her, and questions that had never been answered preyed on her. And it was all because she'd done an unforgivable thing.

She'd let herself hope. That this wouldn't be temporary, that it couldn't be, not when it was so incredible.

At least it had been incredible until last week when he'd suddenly started becoming unavailable. Even though he'd apologized, blamed work problems, swore it would only be temporary, his absence had plunged her into a nightmarish déjà vu. Though he still came home, still made love to her—not like before when he'd cut her off suddenly—it still made her feel this was the beginning of the end. She tried to tell herself that the "honeymoon" was over, that it happened with everyone, that there was no way he could have sustained that level of intensity. It didn't mean anything was wrong.

Tell that to her glued-back-together heart.

But all her upheaval had one origin. The missing piece that could explain how the noble man she was now certain Vincenzo was could have been so cruel to her.

Her eyes fell on the prenup he'd left on her entrance cabinet what felt like ages ago, and something turned in her head, clicked.

Her eyes jerked up, slamming into their reflection in the mirror above as that missing piece crashed into place.

Her family.

God, how hadn't it occurred to her before? This had to be the explanation. He'd said her father and Daniel had been perpetrating crimes for a long time. What if it had been as far back as six years, and he'd discovered it when he'd been investigating them during his espionage crisis?

Then another idea whacked her like an uppercut.

Even if he'd found it out of the question to be involved with someone with a family of criminals, there had been no reason to be vicious with her over her family's crimes. That meant one thing. He'd thought she'd been involved in those crimes. Or worse, he'd thought she'd embezzle or defraud him, too, and had thought to preempt her, cut her off before she had the chance.

Gasping as suspicions solidified into conviction, she staggered to the nearest horizontal surface, sitting heavily.

Then another realization pushed aside the debris of shame and anguish.

He'd believed her an accomplice to her family, a danger to him, and he'd simply walked away. He'd turned vicious only when she'd cornered him. That meant one thing—he *had* felt something for her. Something strong enough that it stopped him from prosecuting her even when he'd thought she deserved it.

Following that same rationalization, the way he was with her now, even with his new evidence of her family's crimes, meant that he believed she couldn't be party to those. As for what she'd been seeing in his eyes, the way he said *amore mio,* this could mean...

In the next moment her trembling hope was shot down like a bird before it could spread its wings.

Even if he didn't think she was involved in illegal activities now, he would never think her worth more than a fleeting place in his life. And who could blame him?

She couldn't.

Her aching eyes panned around her condo. She'd come here to empty it, to end its lease. Vincenzo had asked her to do so a couple of weeks ago. She'd felt alarmed at what that implied and had groped for a reason to dismiss his request, arguing she needed a place to entertain family and friends away from their own private quarters. But he'd already thought of that, producing a lease to another condo, far more lavish, and a minute's walk from his building. It looked as if he was thinking of her all the time, going out of his way to provide her with anything that would make her life easier, fuller.

But she couldn't count on anything from him, or with him. She wouldn't do this to herself again. She had to live with the expectation that this would end, and after last week, it appeared that the end would be sooner rather than later. She had to be ready to fade back into her own life once he pulled away completely. But to do that, she had to make sure she had a life to fade back to.

She rose, headed back to the suitcases she'd packed, opened them and started putting everything back in its place.

An hour later, on her way out, she stopped by the entrance cabinet. After a long moment of staring at the prenup, she picked it up.

Vincenzo whistled an upbeat tune as he exited the shower.

He caught his eyes in the steamed-up mirror and grinned widely at himself. He felt like whistling all the time now. Or singing. He'd been struggling not to do either in all those stuffy meetings and negotiations he'd been attending. He'd had the most important one so far today, what he'd been working toward since he'd gone back to New York with Glory after their honeymoon six weeks ago.

The memory of their honeymoon cascaded through him again. He'd extended it for a week and had representatives of a dozen countries scrambling to readjust their schedules. When they'd complained, he'd told them they instead had to thank his bride for putting their agendas ahead of her rights and consenting to cut short her honeymoon for them. He'd seen to it that each and every one *had* thanked her, in all the functions to which she'd accompanied him.

A thrill of pride spread through him. She'd been beyond magnificent. A consort of a caliber he couldn't have dreamed of. Though she'd gone back to her own hectic schedule, she always made time for him. She aided, guided and supported him with her counsel, honored, soothed and delighted him with her company. Every moment with her, in and out of bed, had been better than anything he'd dared plan or hope for.

He'd never known happiness like this existed.

Just as he thought that, a frown invaded his elation.

He hadn't been able to have her with him for over two weeks now. With back-to-back meetings and unending follow-up work, he'd had to leave her behind, cancel dates and generally have no time for her. He hadn't even come home for the past three days.

He was paying the price for taking too much time with her during the first weeks of their marriage. Work had accumulated until it had become unmanageable, and resolving the mess had been like digging in the sea, with new chores only pouring over the unfinished ones. He'd needed to clean out his agenda then start fresh using the system Glory had set up for him.

So, for the past two weeks, he'd worked flat out to get this phase, the groundwork his whole mission was built on, out of the way once and for all.

Though it had been agonizing being without her, at least he'd succeeded in fixing the problem he'd caused by being too greedy for her. He was now out of the bottleneck and the first phase of his mission here had been concluded.

And before he entered the next phase, he had a prolonged vacation with Glory planned. A second honeymoon. He intended to have another one every month.

Grinning to himself again, luxuriating in the anticipation, he entered the office he hadn't used for weeks.

He saw it the moment he stepped inside and recognized it for what it was at once.

The prenup agreement.

Was his mind playing tricks on him? He'd left it in Glory's condo over two months ago.

A surge of trepidation came over him as he neared it, approaching it as if it was a live grenade. A quick, compulsive check ended any doubt. That *was* the copy he'd given her.

Why was it on his desk, as if Glory was loath to hand it

to him face-to-face? If she was, why put it there at all? After all this time? All this intimacy?

What was she trying to tell him?

Was she reinforcing his original conditions, telling him this was still how she viewed their marriage? As a temporary hostile takcover? But that had stopped being true almost from the start. He'd told her he'd changed his mind after *hours* of being with her again. She hadn't changed her mind after weeks of being with him? But she'd agreed to marry him of her free will, then proceeded to blow his mind with passion and pleasure ever since. He'd thought she'd been showing him that she'd forgotten how this had started, that she'd been demonstrating with actions how she now viewed their relationship, that she wanted it to continue. He sat down, staring at the offensive volume as if it was his worst mistake come back to haunt him. Which it was.

And it was his fault it was haunting him. He'd avoided a confrontation about the past, with her, with himself. He'd just been so scared it might spoil the perfection they had now.

But here was what avoidance had led to.

He now had to admit to himself what he'd been thinking and feeling all along.

He'd at first thought she'd changed her ways. But when he couldn't find a trace of subterfuge in her—something that couldn't be wiped so totally from someone's character—he'd been able to sanction only one thing. That she'd always been what he'd believed her to be from the start, the upstanding human being and the incredible woman he'd fallen in love with. And this had led him to one conclusion. That she'd been forced into her past betrayal.

There was only one scenario that made sense. As soon as he'd employed her, those who always looked for chinks in his armor got to her family, and through them, to her. Younger, vulnerable to her family's needs, she'd been forced to do their bidding, probably under fear of losing them to imprisonment through their crippling debts. That *had* been the first thing that had occurred to her when *he'd* threatened to imprison them.

But she must have hated doing it and soon realized there'd been no excuse for what they'd forced her to do. She *had* struck out as far away from them as possible, becoming the magnificent force for good she was now.

But after observing her with her family, with her mother especially, he was now certain Glory had no idea that he'd discovered her betrayal, or she would have understood why he'd kicked her out of his life. Her mother clearly hadn't told her of the climactic confrontations with him. Probably out of shame that she'd exposed her daughter to buy the rest of her family's salvation.

Or he might be all wrong and there might be another explanation. But whatever it was, he was certain she hadn't set him up in cold blood, or pretended emotions she hadn't felt. Everything in him just *knew* that her involvement with him had been real, and predated whatever she'd been forced to do. And that was the one thing that mattered to him.

Where he was concerned, from the moment he'd told her she was free not to marry him, that past had been wiped out from his mind and heart. Nothing remained in him now but that he wanted her, *loved* her, far more than he ever had.

But it was clear she had no idea this was how he felt. This must be why she was offering him the prenup. Showing him that he was free to keep his original pact if he wanted.

It was time to make a full admission, to leave her in no doubt what he wanted. Her. As his wife, for real and forever.

He heaved up to his feet, excitement frothing inside him, and swiped the prenup off the desk.

He'd take that piece of paranoid crap he'd regretted ever since it had passed from his hands to hers and tear it to pieces. He'd throw it at her feet along with his heart and his life. He'd…

His phone rang.

Gritting his teeth at the interruption, he answered the call. A moment later, he wished he hadn't.

A deep, somber voice poured into his ear, and everything inside him tightened, as if to ward off a blow.

Now what?

"Thanks for seeing me on such short notice, Prince Vincenzo."

Vincenzo's unease rose. Brandon Steele never asked to see him unless there was some catastrophe brewing.

"We're alone now so drop the titles, please, Brandon."

The man inclined his head silently, looking, as always, like a strange cross between a suave celebrity and a linebacker. He had a quietly menacing aura hanging over him like a cloak.

Vincenzo had hired him seven years ago to protect his research and businesses against sabotage and intellectual property theft. The agency Brandon owned and ran, Steele Security, had come highly recommended by Vincenzo's cousin Eduardo as the most effective undercover agency to handle financial fraud and industrial espionage.

Brandon held a spotless track record, had uncovered dozens of masterful infiltrations and conspiracies, saved Vincenzo and his cousins untold millions and smoothed the course of their rise to the top of their respective fields.

But it was one particular achievement that always made Vincenzo loath to see him, more now than ever.

He'd been the one who'd gotten proof of Glory's espionage six years ago.

Getting to the point as always, Brandon exhaled. "I don't know how to say this, Vincenzo, but what were you thinking? You married the woman who once spied on you?"

Was that it? Brandon was here to scold him?

"Things aren't as simple as they look to you, Brandon."

Brandon cocked one disbelieving eyebrow. "Aren't they?"

Vincenzo had no time for skepticism. If not for Brandon's untimely call, he could have been with Glory right now, resolving everything with her.

Vincenzo exhaled. "Did you detect another leak in my operations? And you jumped to the conclusion that the only new thing in my life is Glory, again, so she must be involved somehow?"

Brandon stared at him as if he'd grown a third eye. "I see you're not concerned about the prospect of a leak."

It was strange, but he wasn't. Or if he was, it was only mentally, for all logical reasons and considerations. But there was no trace of the all-out agitation and anger he'd once experienced, when his work had been the central thing in his life. His priorities *had* changed irrevocably. They all revolved around Glory now.

He sighed. "I thought your security system was now impenetrable."

Brandon gave a curt nod. "It is. And there is no leak."

"So you just want to reprimand me for marrying Glory? You don't know much about who she is now if you're even worried."

Brandon gave him a long-suffering look. "It's my business to know everything about everyone. I know exactly who she is and what she does. The body of work she's amassed over the past five years is nothing short of phenomenal."

He exhaled. "Just spit out the 'but' you're here to say."

"*But* I think this might be a far more elaborate facade than the one she had six years ago."

He waved the man's words away. "I don't care about the past anymore, Brandon."

"I'm not talking about the past."

Everything inside Vincenzo hit pause. "You just said there's been no leak."

"Not in *your* operations, no. But you are deep in negotiations with multinational interests on behalf of Castaldini. I caught leaks of vital info that only you could know, that could end up costing Castaldini the projects and investments you're on the verge of securing on its behalf."

Vincenzo's temperature started to rise, his muscles turning to stone. "The sides I'm negotiating with are privy to the same info, and the leak could be on their side."

"It isn't."

At the curt final statement, he found himself on his feet, agitation no longer in check. "Why on earth are you suspecting Glory when she had no part in any of this?"

"You mean she isn't privy to the details of your dealings and the innermost workings of your mind this time around?"

He shook his head, felt his brain clanging against his skull. "No—I mean, I *do* consult with her—you know there's no one better than her when it comes to negotiations—and she has been advising me, and I've used every shred of advice she gave me to my advantage, but that doesn't mean she—"

Brandon interrupted his ramblings. "*Do* you observe all the security measures I devised in your shared space?"

Vincenzo hadn't even given security a thought around her. But... "*No.* Stop right there. This isn't Glory's doing. I'm certain. Whatever happened in the past, it must have been against her will. She's worked so hard ever since to make good, to turn her life around. With only the power of her benevolence and perseverance she's done more for more people than I've done with all my power and money. I'm never suspecting her again."

Brandon gave him the look of a disapproving parent. "May I remind you it wasn't 'suspicion' last time? I gave you proof, proof you yourself verified, from her closest people."

Vincenzo's voice rose, no longer under his control. "I *told* you the past has nothing to do with the present. And then it turned out she actually saved me from making the worst mistake of my life."

"So you should forgive someone because she didn't succeed in killing you, but inadvertently made you jump and save yourself from falling into a pit? How far are you willing to stretch to make excuses for her, Vincenzo?"

"As far as I need to. When all is said and done, I'm in a much better place now and it is because of what happened."

"Even if it turns out for the best, a failed attempt at a crime still deserves punishment."

"And I *did* punish her," he bellowed. "I passed sentence on her without a trial, without even giving her the chance to defend herself. And what did all that righteousness get me? Six years of hell, without her. Now I have her back, and I'm never losing her again."

Brandon gaped at him for a long, long moment.

Then he grimaced. "God, this is worse than I thought. You're totally under her spell."

"I *love* her."

"And she betrayed you again. What a mess."

Vincenzo barely held back from punching him. "Stop saying that and look elsewhere, Brandon. You're not infallible, remember? You made a mistake with Eduardo's wife."

"It wasn't a mistake. Jade *was* hacking into his system."

"Under duress," he gritted out. "And she was doing that in order to fortify it, so no one could infiltrate it again. As I said, everything isn't always as it seems. You were right, but you were also wrong. You're wrong again now. I don't only love Glory, I *know* her."

Brandon pinned him with a conflicted gaze before he finally squared his shoulders and held out the dossier he had with him. It had the Steele Security insignia on it. Vincenzo knew from experience those were only used for final reports and verified evidence.

Trepidation overwhelmed Vincenzo as he looked at it. He snatched his gaze back to Brandon's, as if to escape an image that would sear his retinas if he gazed at it a second more.

Brandon looked at him like someone would look at a patient before amputating a limb. "I can't tell you how sorry I am, Vincenzo, but this is a compilation of all emails and text messages leaking the info. The originating addresses were expertly hidden, just not expertly enough to hide them from me. Everything was traced back to Glory's phone and computer."

Eleven

Vincenzo had no idea what he'd said to Brandon or when the man had left.

He found himself sitting in the bedroom he had only ever used with Glory. He'd bought this place six years ago when she'd consented to be his. He'd left it when he sent her away, but hadn't been able to sell it off. He'd only come back when he'd decided to have her back in his life.

The life that was falling apart all over again.

This couldn't be happening. Not again.

And he refused to believe it was. There had to be some explanation other than the obvious, other than what Brandon sanctioned. But Vincenzo couldn't think what it was. So he wouldn't even try to think. He'd stop everything, his very heartbeat if need be, until she told him what to think.

He sat there for what might have been hours until he heard her coming into the penthouse. The sense of déjà vu almost overwhelmed him, of that day more than six years ago when he'd waited for her in this room, listening to her advance and feeling that every step was inching toward the end of everything worth living for.

Then she entered the room. For the moment she didn't notice him as he sat to her far right on the couch by the floor-to-ceiling windows, her expression was subdued, pensive. Suddenly she started, her head jerking around, as if his presence electrified her.

Her uncensored reaction the split second she saw him was a smile that felt like a flare of light and warmth in the cold darkness that was spreading inside him.

Her rush toward him felt as if life itself was rushing back into his veins. Her eagerness flooded him, submerged him as she straddled him on the couch.

He let her deluge him in her sweetness, drink him dry in the desperation of her need.

Her kisses grew wrenching, her gasps labored. "I missed you...missed you, darling...Vincenzo..."

And how he'd missed her. Three days and nights without losing himself in the depths of her and drinking deep of her pleasures had him raving mad with starvation.

Her hands fumbled with his clothes, and he knew. The moment she touched his flesh he'd go up in flames, and he owed it to her to settle this before he let her drag him into their realm of delirium. His hands covered hers, stopping her.

She stiffened. Then slowly, as if afraid something would shatter if she moved too fast, she took her lips away from his neck. After a harsh intake of breath, she turned her head away and her rigidity increased as her gaze fixed on a spot on the couch. The security report file lay close to him. He knew she'd recognize it for what it was. But her gaze was fixed farther away, on the prenup.

She spilled off him, staggering up only to take two steps before slumping down on the opposite armchair. She looked at him as if waiting for a blow.

He had to hear her reasons from her own lips. "Why did you put this on my desk today, Glory?"

"Today?" Her eyes rounded. "I—I put it there over a week ago. I thought you'd long seen it, and when you didn't mention it I thought…"

"What did you think?"

A spasm seized her face. "I didn't know what to think."

"What did you want me to think when I saw it? What were you telling me?"

The pained look deepened; her voice sounded strangled. "I was offering you my answer to what I thought you were telling me, when you… When you…"

"When I what?"

"When you stopped taking me to your functions and started canceling our dates."

"What did you think I was telling you?"

"What you said when you didn't come ho…here the past three nights. What you just said very clearly. That this time around it took much less than six months for you to get tired of me."

Her lips, her chin, shook on the last words. The tethers of his heart shook, almost tearing themselves out.

"But then I expected that from the beginning," she choked out. "And now that I realize what you think happened in the past, I'm even wondering why you wanted me again at all. This is why I brought you the prenup, since I thought you must have been regretting not taking it, must be worried about repercussions with no provisions in place when you ended it with me again. But it's a good thing I didn't let my condo go as you told me to. I'll move back there tonight."

"Glory…"

She spoke over his plea, as if hearing his voice hurt her. "I will pretend we're still together so no one will know anything before you're ready to announce our split when the year is over. Until then, whenever you need me to make appearances with you, y-you have my number. If I'm not traveling, I'll play the part I agreed to."

And he was on his feet, then at hers, his hands going around her beloved head, making her raise her wounded gaze to his. "Every single thing you thought has no basis in fact. I didn't get tired of you. I would sooner get tired of breathing."

Redness surged in her eyes, her whole face shaking. "D-don't say that…don't say what you don't mean. Not again."

"The only time I said what I didn't mean to you was that day I kicked you out of my life. I did… I *do* love you, I never loved anyone but you, never had anyone since you."

Her eyes seemed to melt, her cheeks flooding with tears. "Oh, God, Vincenzo…I can't… I don't…"

"You have to believe me." He aborted her headshake, pulling her into a fierce kiss, before drawing away to probe her stunned face. "But you said you now realized what I thought in the past. You mean you now know why I left you?"

Her nod was difficult. "You knew about my family's crimes—thought me their accomplice?"

"It was much worse than that."

Her eyes flew wider. "What *could* be worse?"

And he finally confessed. Everything. Everything but the latest blow Brandon had dealt him.

By the time he'd fallen silent, she was frozen. Even her tears had stopped midway down her cheeks. She wasn't breathing.

It felt like an hour later when she finally choked out, "Your research *was* stolen and my…*mother* told you…told you…"

The rest backlashed in her throat, seeming to go down as if it was broken glass. Anguish so fierce gripped her every feature, radiated from her, buffeting him.

"I now believe that they must have forced you…or something…I just know it wasn't your fault. Just like I believe this latest security breach can't be your doing."

Her wounded eyes widened. "What latest security breach?"

Feeling as if he was spitting razors, he said, "Top secret data in my current negotiations have been leaked. According to this security report I got today, the leak came from your phone and computer."

She jerked as if he'd shot her.

He grabbed her shoulders, begging. "I can't think anymore, Glory, and I won't. I want you to tell me what to think. Trust me, please, tell me everything and I will solve it all. I'm on your side this time, and only on your side, and will always be, no matter what…."

She started shaking her head, her hands gripping it as if to keep it from bursting.

"*Amore, per favore,* please, believe me, let me help…."

Her incoherent cry cut him off as she exploded to her feet. Before another nerve fired, she'd hurtled out of the bedroom and slammed out of the penthouse.

By the time he ran after her, she was gone.

Glory stared at the woman she thought loved her beyond life itself. The woman whose betrayal had wrecked her life.

Her mother's silent tears poured down her cheeks, her eyes pleading.

For what? Glory's understanding? Her forgiveness? How could she give either when there was nothing left inside her? Everything had been destroyed. Nothing was left but shock and disillusionment. They expanded from her gut, threatening to burst her arteries, her heart. They crashed through her in torrents of decimating agony.

"You have to know the rest, darling," her mother choked out.

There was more? She couldn't hear any more. She had to get out of here, hide, disappear.

She escaped her mother's imploring hands as she ran again. She never wanted to stop running.

She spilled out into the street, ran and ran.

But there was no outrunning the realizations.

Everything was far worse than her worst projections. But one thing was worse than anything else. One realization.

Vincenzo's cruelty to her perceived betrayal hadn't been cruel at all. Cruel would have been to have her arrested. Even that would have only been his right, what he should have done. But he hadn't. That meant one thing.

He *had* loved her.

He'd loved her so much that even getting incontrovertible proof of her betrayal hadn't made him retaliate. He'd only tried to protect himself, cutting her off. Then, when she wouldn't let him, he'd pushed her away in a way he'd thought wouldn't harm her, since he'd believed she'd felt nothing for him, had been manipulating him from day one.

And she'd always thought getting answers would resolve the misery that had consumed six years of her life. In truth, it had dealt her a fatal blow.

Despair and exertion hacked through her lungs as more details and realizations sank their shards into her heart…

"Glory."

Vincenzo. His booming desperation shattered everything inside her into shrapnel of grief, of panic. It all burst out into a surge of manic speed.

She couldn't stop. Couldn't let him catch her.

Not now that she knew he'd always loved her. Now that she knew it could never be.

* * *

Vincenzo arrived at the Monaghans' house just as Glory exited it. It was clear the confrontation with her mother had devastated her.

A man in his right mind would have caught up with her without alerting her. But the mass of desperation that he'd turned into had just bellowed her name the moment he'd seen her, sending her zooming faster, screeching for a cab.

But he could have overtaken a speeding car right now. A woman running in high heels looked stationary compared to his speed. He intercepted her as she opened the cab's door.

His arms went around her, filling them with his every reason for living. "Glory, *amore,* please, let's talk."

She pushed weakly at him. "There's nothing more to talk about, Vincenzo. Just forget I ever existed. In fact, when your situation allows, just prosecute me and my family."

Before he could utter another word, she surprised him by ducking out of the circle of his arms and into the cab.

His first instinct was to haul her out, carry her back to their home and tell her he'd never let her go again.

The one thing that stopped him was knowing it would be pointless without performing another imperative step first. Another confrontation with her mother. He had to break whatever hold she had on Glory, once and for all.

After Glory's cab disappeared, with his every cell rioting, he turned and walked back to the Monaghans' house.

The woman who opened the door exhibited Glory's same devastation. He wanted to blast her off the face of the earth for what she'd cost him and Glory, but he couldn't. She looked so fragile, so desolate, so much like an older version of Glory, that he couldn't hate her. He even felt a tug of unreasoning affection.

She grabbed at him with weak, shaking hands. "Glory wouldn't listen to me, but please, Vincenzo, you have to."

Suddenly, looking into those eyes that could be Glory's, everything fell into place.

It had never been Glory. It had always been Glenda.

He staggered under the blow of realization. How had he never considered this?

"It was you. In the past, and again now."

The woman's tears ran thicker, her whole face working. "I—I did it to save Dermot and Daniel!"

Her sob tore through him, with its agony, its authenticity. So he'd been right, just about the wrong person. Glenda Monaghan had been the one who'd been forced to spy on him.

She was now weeping so hard he feared she might tear something vital inside her.

His arm went around her as she swayed, helping her to the nearest couch. He sat beside her, rubbing her shaking hands soothingly. "Mrs. Monaghan, please, calm down. I'm not angry this time, and I promise, I won't hurt you or them. Just tell me why you did it, let me help."

"No one can help," she wailed.

He forced a tight smile. "You clearly don't realize what kind of power your son-in-law has. I would turn the whole world upside down for Glory, and by extension for her family."

"You're a scientist and a prince. You can't possibly know how to handle those...those monsters."

"Who do you mean?"

"The mob!"

And he'd thought nothing could ever surprise him again.

He raised his hands as if to brace against more blows. "Just tell me everything from the beginning."

She nodded, causing her tears to splash on his hands. It made him hug her tighter, trying to absorb her upheaval.

Then haltingly, tearfully, she began. "Fifteen years ago, I was diagnosed with lymphoma. Dermot panicked because our insurance would pay only for a tiny percentage of my treatments, and we were already in debt. At the time, Dermot and I worked in a huge multinational corporation, him in accounting, me in IT. Our financial troubles were soon common knowledge and a guy from work approached Dermot with a way to make easy, serious money."

She paused to draw a long, shaky breath.

"Dermot told me and I refused. But I was soon in no condition to work and with only one income and the bills piling up, it was soon untenable. Dermot began to gamble then fix books and was soon so deep in debts and trouble that when the recruiter approached him again, he agreed.

"For a while, I was so tired and drained, I was just relieved we weren't scrabbling anymore. I bought his stories that he'd entered a partnership in a thriving import/export operation. Then things started getting uglier with his mob bosses asking terrible things of him. And the worst part was they'd also dragged Daniel, who was only nineteen, into their dirty business.

"Unable to go on, Dermot had us pack everything and move across the country. We kept hopping from one place to another in his efforts to escape the mob. During remissions, I worked from home, but my relapses kept draining us. Dermot and Daniel kept trying everything to keep us afloat. But at least the mob was off our back. After seven years, I thought we were home free.

"Then six years ago, I got a call. The man said that they'd always wanted *me*, the real expert in the family, and that they had some jobs for me, if I valued my husband's and son's lives. They owned us. Not only with the debts but with what they had on them. They'd send them to prison if I didn't cooperate." Shame twisted in his gut, that he'd once employed the same method with Glory. "But it wouldn't end with prison if I said no. Accidents happened on the inside, even easier than on the outside. The job was you. They'd found out about your relationship with Glory and thought it put me in a perfect position to spy on you."

He stared at her, six years worth of agony being rewritten, the realization of the needless loss of his life with Glory choking him up.

Glenda sobbed harder now. "As a taste of what they'd do if I refused, they beat Daniel up—we told Glory it was a bar fight—and he was hospitalized for a month. I was ready to do anything after that. And I did. I used Glory's total trust in me, and your total trust in her, to hack her computer, and yours. Then you discovered everything.

"I was so scared Dermot and Daniel would be the ones who'd be dragged into this when everything they'd done came to light during the investigation. I found only one way out. To tell you it was Glory."

And he groaned with six years of heartache. "*Per Dio,* why? Didn't you think what you'd be doing to her, to me? Didn't you realize how much I loved her?"

"It was because I knew exactly how much you loved her that I did this. I knew you loved her so much you might forgive her, or at least wouldn't be able to bring yourself to punish her, would let her get away with it—let us—let *me*—get away with it. And I was right. You did."

He shook his head in disbelief. "You don't consider breaking her heart a punishment?"

"It was her heart or my husband's and son's lives."

Silence crushed down as he gazed into the woman's drowned eyes, the pieces falling into place like hammers.

Then he said, "Then it happened again."

Her tears ran continuously now. "They gave me the new assignment as soon as your wedding was announced. I begged them to let me go, tried to tell them that there was no way you wouldn't be prepared this time, that you wouldn't find out. They only said that with Glory as your wife now, it would be impossible to guard yourself, and that even if you found out, you wouldn't be able to expose her—or rather me. They didn't care what happened as long as they got their info. I owed them for giving them what had turned out to be useless info before. And they still owned my men. So I did it again. But I was only waiting until you caught me at it."

"But you still left tracks leading to Glory, to take refuge in my love for her again."

Her face crumbled. "And I was right again. Even when you thought she'd betrayed you twice, you wouldn't have ever hurt her."

His groan was agonized. "I already hurt her beyond what you can imagine. I'm only now beginning to realize the magnitude of the pain and damage I caused her."

She clung to his arm, her feeble grip barely registering. "I beg you, don't blame yourself. It was all my doing."

He covered her hand with his. "I do and will blame myself. I loved her, should have given her the benefit of the doubt. I didn't. And I hurt her so much she no longer wants to have anything to do with me."

"No, Vincenzo. You're her heart. She must only be running away to lick her wounds. She's shocked and anguished at what I did. Don't give up on her, I beg you."

He hugged her gently, defusing her panic. "I would give up on life before I gave up on Glory." He withdrew to wipe the tears of the woman he now hoped would live to see his and Glory's children and be their grandmother for long years to come.

"Now give me names. I'll get those people who've turned your lives into a living hell off your backs once and for all."

Keeping his promise to Glenda had taken far longer than he could stand. Two full, unending days.

But at least it was over. He'd terminated the hold those mob bosses had over the Monaghans' lives.

Contrary to Glenda's belief, he wasn't so refined that he couldn't handle criminal scum. He'd negotiated a perfect deal with them. He'd paid more than handsomely for the lost revenue ensuing from losing some of their efficient operatives. And he'd let them know how much they'd lose, in every way, if they came after his and Glory's family, or his work, ever again.

Now one thing remained. The only thing that mattered to him anymore in the world. Glory.

"We'll get to her in time, *Principe*."

Vincenzo gritted his teeth at Alonzo's assurance. He didn't know if they would. The flight taking her away to Darfur was in less than an hour. She must already be at the gate. Not that he'd let that stop him. Even if she flew away, he'd follow her. To the ends of the earth.

In minutes that passed like torturous hours, Alonzo pulled up at the airport's departure zone. He lowered the window as Vincenzo exploded from the car, yelling after him, "Just ring when you get your princess back, *Principe*. I'll be waiting to drive you back home."

Vincenzo ran, Alonzo's last words skewering his heart.

If he didn't get her back, he'd never go home. He had no home to go to without her.

But then, not getting her back wasn't an option.

He tore across the airport, only stopping to ask about Glory's flight. It was boarding in twenty minutes.

He bought a ticket, produced his diplomatic passport and begged for security checks to be rushed so he could catch up with his runaway bride. Then he was streaking across the airport, bumping into people left and right. He'd run out of sorrys by the time he'd reached her gate.

She was standing in line, holding her boarding pass and

one of those nondescript handbags of hers, looking terrible. And the most wonderful sight he'd ever seen. The only one he wanted to live his life seeing.

His heart kicked his ribs so hard it had him stumbling into another run, pushing through the line to reach her. She was so deep in her misery she only noticed the commotion he'd caused when someone bumped into her. Her eyes, his own pieces of heaven, looked up at him with a world of pain and desperation.

The drain of anxiety and the surge of relief shook his arms as he enfolded her and his voice as he groaned against her cheek, her neck, her lips, "Come home with me, *amore, I beg you.*"

She only went inert in his embrace.

Deadness crept up Glory's body like fast-growing vines.

She welcomed its suffocation, its stability, which allowed her to stand in the circle of his arms, feeling his beloved body seeking her and enfolding her, without collapsing in a mass of misery.

It also gave her the strength to push away, even though she felt she pushed away from her life source.

She staggered a step, barely aware of the hundreds of people around, watching them. She had eyes and senses only for Vincenzo, for noticing how his hair and face were captured by the atrocious lighting of the airport, enhancing every gleam, emphasizing every jut and hollow.

A blaze of love and longing shriveled her heart. She'd been too optimistic thinking there had been a chance she'd survive this. There wasn't.

He reached for her again, hands urgent, coaxing, moving over her back, her arms, her face, leaving each feeling forever scarred with the memory of what she'd never have again.

"Come with me, *amore,*" he urged again.

"I can't." Her voice sounded as dead as she felt.

"You can't do anything else, *amore*. You belong with me. To me. You're the only one for me."

"That's not true, never was, never will be."

His arms fell away, and he looked at her as if she'd just emptied a gun in his gut.

"You—you don't…" His bit his lower lip then his voice plunged to a hoarse rasp that sounded like pain and dread made audible. "You don't love me?"

She should say she didn't. He'd stop blaming himself for his role in her devastation, stop trying to make amends. This was what he was here doing, after all. And she no longer blamed him for anything. She only wanted to set him free.

She still couldn't bring herself to lie. Not about this.

She escaped answering. "I am not the one for you, Vincenzo. *Anyone* else would be better for you. Anyone who doesn't have a family with a criminal history."

His devastated expression fell apart with the snap of tension, morphed into the very sight of relief. "This is what you meant? What you're thinking?"

"It's not what I'm thinking. It's the truth."

"According to whom?"

"To the world."

"Does it look like I care what the world does or doesn't think?"

He spread his arms, encompassing the scene around them. Everyone was staring openly at them, the buzz of recognition, curiosity and amusement rising. Some were even taking photos and recording videos.

Embarrassment crept up her face. "You do care or you wouldn't have married me as a social facade. And when the truth comes out…"

"It never will."

"…it will cost you and Castaldini too much. That's why

it's a fact that any woman who doesn't have a family with a criminal history and connections would be better for you."

"No one is better for me. No one is better, period." She started to shake her head, her heart ricocheting inside her rib cage at his intensity and the unwilling rise of hope. He caught her face, his hands gentleness and persuasion itself. "And pretending to care about that social facade was just so I could have you without admitting the truth. All those years I've been looking for a way to have you again. Because I haven't been truly alive since I walked away from you. And now I can't live without you. I only cared about your family's crimes when I thought you'd been involved in them, but lately, not even then. And now none of that is an issue. I've managed to wipe your family's slate clean."

"Y-you did…? How?"

He told her, quickly, urgently, as if needing to get this out of the way, to move on to what he considered relevant.

And she felt her world disintegrating around her again.

"I never suspected… I always thought… God!" Tears gushed, then burned down her cheeks. "The years I spent being angry at Dad and Daniel, thinking they were irresponsible, criminal, when they…they…"

He dragged her to him, protecting her from her anguish, all the missing parts of her fitting back. "You can now have your family back, forgive them for everything that has been beyond them and be happy loving them again."

She raised her eyes to his, unable to grasp the enormity of it all. "How can you be so…so forgiving, so generous, after all they've done to you?"

"Conceiving you is an achievement that would make up for any past or future crime. And then they were under threat. A threat I ended, so they can now go on with their lives without the shadow of fear."

She started to protest and he scooped her up in his arms,

clamping his lips over hers. As the power of his kiss dragged her down into a well of craving, she thought she heard hoots of approval and clapping.

He pulled away, groaning, "*Gloria mia, ti voglio, ti amo—* I'm going crazy wanting you, loving you."

She felt he was letting her look deep into his soul, letting her see what she'd always thought would remain an impossible fantasy. Vincenzo didn't only love her, his love was as fierce and total as hers.

But this was why she'd had to walk away. So she wouldn't disrupt his life and destiny.

She had to protect him, especially since he clearly wasn't willing to protect himself. "You can't only consider your heart…you have duties, a status, and I'm…"

He clamped his lips on hers again, aborting her panting protest. "My first duty is to you. My status depends on honoring you first."

She shook her head. "My family…if the truth comes out… God, Vincenzo, you can't have them for your in-laws…."

His expression was resoluteness itself. "I already have them as my in-laws, and they'll always be my in-laws, and I will be proud to have them as the family of our children."

"Our ch-childr…" With those two magical words, a fierce yearning sheared through her, draining every spark of tension holding her together. She swooned in his hold.

His arms tightened until she felt he was trying to merge them. "Yes, our children, as many and as soon as you want."

The magnitude of what he was offering, the future he was painting, stunned her into silence as her mind's eye tremblingly tried to imagine it all. A future, a whole life, filled with love and alliance and trust, with him. Children with him. Even her family back, because of him.

Vincenzo took advantage of her silence and strode away with her still in his arms, talking to many people, then on the phone. She watched everything from the security of his embrace, as if from the depths of a dream. Somewhere it registered that he was arranging their exit after they'd been checked in as far as the boarding gate and arranging for her luggage to be sent back.

Then a sound penetrated the fog of her bliss. A horn.

Her dazed gaze panned around, found Vincenzo's car with Alonzo at the wheel, waving to them urgently as he stopped in an unloading-only zone.

In seconds, Vincenzo had her inside the cool, dim seclusion of the limo. As Alonzo maneuvered smoothly into the traffic, Vincenzo bundled her onto his lap.

After a kiss that left her breathless, he drew away, his faced gripped in the passion she couldn't wait to have him expend all over her.

"I have to get this out of the way once and forever, *gloriosa mia,* then we'll never speak or think of it again. You had nothing to do with your family's mistakes. You are the one woman I could ever love, the soul mate I would be forever proud to call mine, and to call myself yours. I truly care nothing about what the world will bring me as long as you're mine forever."

Her head rolled over his shoulder, her lids and insides heavy with need. Every nerve alight with delight at his declarations, she caressed the wonder of his hard cheek. "As long as you understand it will probably take the rest of my life to get used to all those unbelievable facts."

He pressed another urgent, devouring kiss on her lips as if compelled to do it. "I don't think there is any such thing as 'getting used' to this—" he hugged her tighter "—what we share. Just to always marvel at it, be humbled by it and thankful for it."

Then his smile suddenly dissolved, leaving his face a mask of gravity. Her heart quivered with a tremor of uncertainty.

Then, with all the solemnity of a pledge, he said, "Will you marry me again, Glory? This time with our love declared, because we are each other's destiny?"

Joy exploded inside her, making her erupt in his arms and rain tears and kisses all over his beloved face and hands. "Yes, Vincenzo. Yes, yes, *yes,* to everything, forever."

Smiling elatedly, as choked with emotion as she, his own eyes filling with tears, Vincenzo took her lips, drowning her in the miracle of his love.

Deep from the security of his love and embrace she heard Alonzo exclaiming, "*Eccellente.* I not only get my princess back, I get to arrange another wedding. But now with true love declared and the catastrophe of separation averted, this calls for a much more elaborate ceremony."

Glory gaped up at Vincenzo. "There could be anything more elaborate?"

Vincenzo poured indulgence over her, pinching her buttock playfully. "Have you even met Alonzo?"

Carefree giggles burst out of her for the first time in… She didn't even remember when she'd laughed so freely.

But she still had to make a stand. "While I loved the first ceremony, Alonzo, I really would rather we used all the expenses in something… uh…"

Alonzo smirked at her in the rearview mirror. "Is *worthwhile* the word you're looking for?" At her apologetic nod, he sighed. "I can see it's not going to be as much fun as I thought having a philanthropist for a princess."

At her chuckling sigh, Vincenzo smoothed the hair he'd mussed off her face lovingly. "How about we have everything? The figure you name for your worthwhile endeavors, the all-out-expenses wedding—" He turned to meet Alonzo's eyes in the mirror. "Preferably a double wedding this time."

She looked between both men then exclaimed, "Gio proposed?"

A smile of pure happiness spread Alonzo's lips, even as his green eyes misted. "Ah, *si*…and how he did."

She waited until he stopped at a traffic light, then exploded from Vincenzo's arms and jumped on Alonzo, hugging him and soundly kissing him on his widely smiling cheek.

After she milked him for details and whooped and exclaimed with excitement over being his matron of honor, he resumed driving.

She returned to the place she never wanted to leave, burrowed deep in Vincenzo's embrace, letting the last of her tension escape in a long sigh.

Stroking her hair gently, Vincenzo echoed her sigh, the sound of contentment. "Take us home, Alonzo."

Many, many hours later, a delightfully sore and thoroughly sated Glory turned luxuriantly in her lover, prince and husband's arms, filling her eyes with his beauty. "Is it possible? Could everything be so perfect?"

He shifted to accommodate her closer, sweeping caresses down her back and buttocks, as if imprinting his love into her, coating her with satisfaction. "If you need some imperfections to settle your mind, I have plenty for you. Like having to start my negotiations from scratch and roping you in as my top consultant. Like trying to create a method so I can get hands-on, steady involvements in your missions."

Her eyes widened with each word. "God, Vincenzo…you mean it?" At his smiling nod, she tackled him on his back and attacked him with kisses and tickles. He was guffawing by the time she pulled back, frowning. "But wait—that's only more perfection." She threw herself beside him on her back, covered her eyes and cried out, "Argh, I can't stand it."

He rose above her, letting her fill her soul with his unbridled love. Then he suddenly cupped her breast, lazily flicked her nipple, a look of mischief replacing the passion. "You can't? Shall I leave you to rest then?"

She pulled him on top of her. "Don't you *dare*."

As she took him inside her again, as he joined them into one flesh, one future, she thanked the fates that nothing, not betrayal nor pain, not desperation nor separation, had dimmed this miracle they had between them.

And now she knew. Nothing ever would.

* * * *

MILLS & BOON

THE HEART OF ROMANCE

A ROMANCE FOR EVERY READER

MODERN

Prepare to be swept off your feet by sophisticated, sexy and seductive heroes, in some of the world's most glamourous and romantic locations, where power and passion collide.

HISTORICAL

Escape with historical heroes from time gone by. Whether your passion for wicked Regency Rakes, muscled Vikings or rugged Highlanders, aw the romance of the past.

MEDICAL

Set your pulse racing with dedicated, delectable doctors in the high-pressure world of medicine, where emotions run high and passion, comfort love are the best medicine.

True Love

Celebrate true love with tender stories of heartfelt romance, from the rush of falling in love to the joy a new baby can bring, and a focus on t emotional heart of a relationship.

Desire

Indulge in secrets and scandal, intense drama and plenty of sizzling ho action with powerful and passionate heroes who have it all: wealth, stat good looks…everything but the right woman.

HEROES

Experience all the excitement of a gripping thriller, with an intense romance at its heart. Resourceful, true-to-life women and strong, fearless face danger and desire - a killer combination!

To see which titles are coming soon, please visit

millsandboon.co.uk/nextmonth

LET'S TALK
Romance

For exclusive extracts, competitions
and special offers, find us online:

JOIN US ON SOCIAL MEDIA!

Stay up to date with our latest releases, author news and gossip, special offers and discounts, and all the behind-the-scenes action from Mills & Boon...

 @millsandboon

 @millsandboonuk

 facebook.com/millsandboon

 @millsandboonuk

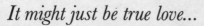

It might just be true love...

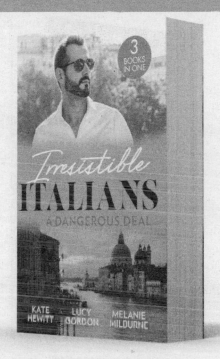

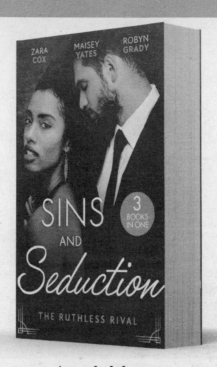

GET YOUR ROMANCE FIX!

Get the latest romance news, exclusive author interviews, story extracts and much more!

blog.millsandboon.co.uk

About the Authors

Rebecca Winters lives in Salt Lake City, Utah. With canyons and high alpine meadows full of wildflowers, she never runs out of places to explore. They, plus her favourite holiday spots in Europe, often end up as backgrounds for her romance novels because writing is her passion, along with her family and church. Rebecca loves to hear from readers. If you wish to e-mail her, please visit her website at: cleanromances.net

Susanna Carr is an award-winning author known for her contemporary romances. Readers throughout the world find Susanna's stories a delightful escape that has often helped them through difficult times. Reviewers frequently describe her work as 'fun', 'sexy' and a 'must-read'. When she isn't writing, or spending time with her family in the Pacific Northwest, Susanna enjoys reading romance and connecting with readers online. Visit her website at susannacarr.com

USA TODAY bestselling author **Olivia Gates** has published over thirty books in contemporary, action/adventure and paranormal romance. And whether in today's world or the others she creates, she writes larger than life heroes and heroines worthy of them, the only ones who'll bring those sheikhs, princes, billionaires or gods to their knees. She loves to hear from readers at oliviagates@gmail.com or on facebook.com/oliviagatesauthor, Twitter @Oliviagates. For her latest news visit oliviagates.com

Royal Temptation